TERRA NOVA

THE WARS OF LIBERATION

BAEN BOOKS
by TOM KRATMAN

A State of Disobedience

A Desert Called Peace
Carnifex
The Lotus Eaters
The Amazon Legion
Come and Take Them
The Rods and the Axe
A Pillar of Fire by Night

Caliphate

Countdown: The Liberators
Countdown: M Day
Countdown: H Hour

with John Ringo
Watch on the Rhine
Yellow Eyes
The Tuloriad

Edited by Tom Kratman
Terra Nova

TERRA NOVA

THE WARS OF LIBERATION

Edited By
TOM KRATMAN

TERRA NOVA

This is a work of fiction. All the characters and events portrayed in this book are fictional, and any resemblance to real people or incidents is purely coincidental.

A Baen Books Original

Baen Publishing Enterprises
P.O. Box 1403
Riverdale, NY 10471
www.baen.com

ISBN: 978-1-4814-8416-9

Cover art by Kurt Miller

First Baen printing August, 2019

Distributed by Simon & Schuster
1230 Avenue of the Americas
New York, NY 10020

Library of Congress Cataloging-in-Publication Data
Names: Kratman, Tom, editor.
Title: Terra Nova : the wars of liberation / edited by Tom Kratman.
Description: Riverdale, NY : Baen Books, [2019]
Identifiers: LCCN 2019021555 | ISBN 9781481484169 (paperback)
Subjects: LCSH: Science fiction, American. | BISAC: FICTION / Science Fiction
/ Military. | FICTION / Science Fiction / Adventure. | FICTION / Science
Fiction / Short Stories.
Classification: LCC PS648.S3 T428 2019 | DDC 813/.0876208--dc23 LC record
available at https://lccn.loc.gov/2019021555

Printed in the United States of America

10 9 8 7 6 5 4 3 2 1

TABLE OF CONTENTS

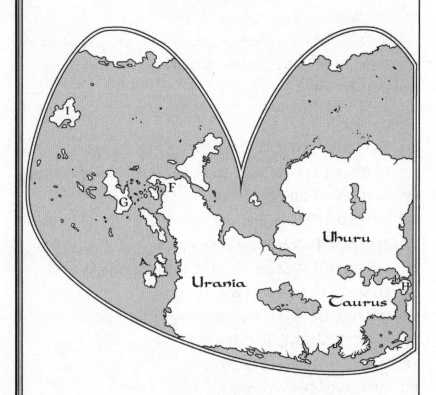

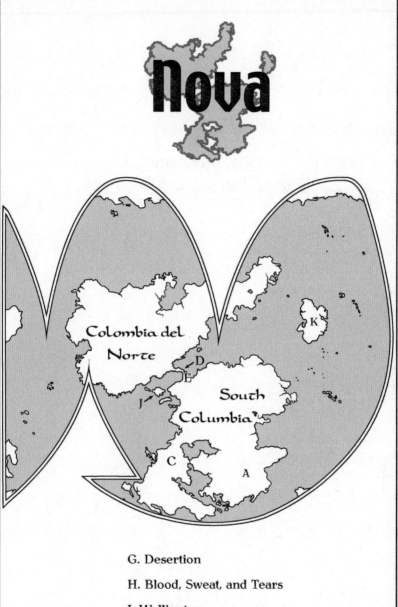

To:
Julia, Inez, Sarah,
Juliana, Patrick, and Cossima

PROLOGUE:

From Jimenez's *History of the Wars of Liberation*

There is an old saying, originating, we believe, on the mother world, to the effect that "you are what you were back when." We, here, on the new world, a world of war, the world we call "Terra Nova" or something that means just that in some other language, know this better than most.

The whole planet knows the story of the first colonization effort for Terra Nova, under the aegis of what was then Earth's United Nations, via the Colonization Ship *Cheng Ho*, how order broke down and then morphed into a shipboard civil war.

We have two well-known versions of the story, of course. One is the story given us by the Earthwoman, Marjorie Billings-Rajamana, who was among the few survivors and whose tale of events—an escalating ethnic and religious breakdown, centered on Islamic intolerance and belligerence, which was smuggled out from Earth through what must have been a maze of censorship. The other, maintained to this day by the more progressive elements of this planet and all of the United Earth Peace Fleet, lays all blame on mechanical and technological problems, exacerbated by Christian opposition to science, with prominent place given to those same Moslems as self-sacrificing saviors of those who managed to survive.

What actually happened we are unlikely ever to know . . .

1.
THE LONG, DARK GOODNIGHT

Vivienne Raper[1]

I saw a lot of death as a copper. Accidental suicides, drug over-doses . . . I once saw a bloke with the back of his head blown off and his face flopped over his neck like a mask. Most of them didn't get to me—I could block it out somehow.

But the dead kids got to me. Still get to me, even here, in this spinning can, billions of miles from Mother Earth.

The girl lying in the mortuary drawer had thick, long dark hair and smooth caramel skin. Her slim hands were folded in the lap of her hospital gown. There wasn't a mark on her. When they look like that, you half expect them to climb off the tray.

"What happened?" I asked.

Angel, the senior doctor, pulled open a second drawer. "Besma came in with her boyfriend. They both had headache and dizziness. She was worried about the baby."

I nodded. Last time I'd seen this girl, she was waiting for a checkup. Sixteen years old. Twenty-three weeks pregnant. Now she was dead. Angel rolled back the sheet on the second corpse: thick

---

1 Vivienne Raper is a freelance science writer whose Ph.D. is in satellite engineering but somehow ended up writing about biomedical science for a living. Her major fiction project is trying to finish *A Murder at Perihelion*, an epic SF crime-thriller combining her interests in space travel, synthetic biology and Sicilian organised crime. She lives in a crumbling Victorian house in London with her medium-sized husband, huge poodle, and small son. Her hobbies include trying to repair the house, reading Warhammer 40K tie-in novels, and collecting over 300 board games (which she occasionally finds time to play in between writing sessions). Her nonfiction work has been published in the *Wall Street Journal*'s European edition, *Spiked*, *How It Works* magazine, and numerous other venues. (PS: Vee's too shy to mention this, but I'm not. She's Oxford, and I don't mean Oxford, Mississippi, too. —Tom)

blond hair, acne scars on both cheeks, long rectangular jaw—the boyfriend. Seventeen last month. Both of them, still just kids.

I smoothed the sheet back over his face. "Any idea on cause of death?"

Angel shook her head.

You get a hunch sometimes, when you've been working as a cop. I joke that it's my spidey sense, yes, after the superhero. It's this niggling itch that you're not getting the full story.

I looked at Angel closely. She was a small, slim woman with freshly-ironed scrubs, her hair in a neat black bob. Not chatty like the nurses in MedLab, she'd worked in a private hospital in Manila and had one of the bigger cabins on A Deck. Her lips were pressed into a tight line.

"What about cause of illness?" I asked.

Her lips twitched. "We had an equipment failure. We've been monitoring patients, but . . ." She shrugged, unhappily.

"What caused that?" I asked.

"Local computer issues. We've called out an engineer."

She folded her arms. I took a couple of deep breaths. I pride myself on acting professional but, as I say, dead kids get to me. "It's my job to ask these questions," I said in a softer voice.

"Tony . . . I know." She lowered her head.

Asked her some easy questions. The kids came in two days before. They were okay until they weren't. MedLab treated their symptoms but—with the equipment gremlins, the cramped and crowded clinic—there wasn't much they could do. She rolled the corpses back into the cabinet and I couldn't help looking at the soft swell of the girl's belly.

"What happened to the baby?" I asked.

"Emergency caesarean," she said.

Didn't want to ask. "Alive?"

She made a seesaw motion with her hands. "Touch and go."

I went to see the baby. She was squirming about in a clear plastic bag, hanging on a rail, with black tubing emerging from her navel. I watched her for a while—the first baby born in space. She was red, with veins on her knees. Her little hands were clenching and unclenching. I could have held her in the palm of my hand.

They'd told the crew and colonists not to have kids. We had a talk on precautions in basic training. Not to get political about it, but we needed it—half the colonists on the *Cheng Ho* are teens. A physicist from NASA flew over to present on cosmic rays and brain damage. "Forget life insurance," he'd said; "you can't afford the premium."

Not that I needed life insurance.

My daughter died six years ago; killed by a drunken scrote in an uninsured car, crossing the road on her walk home from school. He got community service and a disqualification. I kept calm watching him laugh his way out of court. My wife never got over it. Our marriage didn't survive it either. I was a sergeant in the Met serving London south of the river. I knew I'd either get cynical about road traffic or I'd get fanatical. I didn't want to get either.

When they advertised for a security officer with European policing experience for a UN mission to the new world, Terra Nova, I had nothing to lose. I'd always been a bit of a science fiction geek. Asimov, Heinlein, the old stuff—reading it under the covers until midnight as a kid.

Lizzie, the Scottish nurse, handed me a mug of tea. "She's doing well for a wee one, given what a hard time she's had," she said, nodding at the baby.

I cupped the warm mug in my hands. Lizzie was a Brit, like me— or close enough, anyway—and I liked her for it. The familiarity of home.

"You were monitoring the girl, weren't you?" I asked.

Lizzie rubbed her eyes. "Yes, sweet lass she was. Excited about the bairn. A bit scared too, to tell you the truth, but the wee one was developing well enough."

"No sign of suicide?"

"No. Not a hint of it." She grimaced and rubbed her eyes again. A tear rolled down her cheek. "Forgive me, I'm blubbering like a bairn myself."

Waiting for her to get it together, I prised the 'low-pressure' lid off the mug. The tea was lukewarm. You can't boil water properly with the air pressures you get aboard ship. I sipped the tea: it tasted of powdered milk. Motorway service station tea on the highway to the stars.

I handed the mug back to Lizzie. "Anything physically wrong with Besma?"

She looked straight into my eyes.

"Ach, if you ask me, the only thing wrong with Besma was her father, the sexist Arab bastard. If you're looking for who killed her, you should talk to him."

I inwardly groaned at that. I'd arrested Dr. Akbar al Damer, Besma's father, a month back. My mate Jamal and I responded to a call of a male shouting and being disruptive in what had become the 'European quarter' on B Deck.

No sign of a weapon, but it was 23:00, and the people in the nearby cabins were wanting to get some sleep. The Portuguese woman who called OpSec (the nick) thought he was shouting in Arabic—so, before I could attend the disturbance, I had to get Jamal out of bed.

Jamal was the UN Africa Group liaison. He was pretty cheesed off at me for getting him up, but—as I said to him—he was the only member of our team who spoke Arabic.

The way policing works on the *Cheng Ho* is a bit like policing in international waters—the 120 nationalities onboard are subject to their own laws. What this means in practice is 120 different bodies of law, policed by six security officers who need to be on call 24/7 in case—for example—an Indian and a South African get hammered and into a fight.

I'd like to say that drunks on the *Cheng Ho* were rare, but we get about two calls a week dealing with people lying in the corridors. The week before, I'd arrested a bootleg brewer who'd been cooking up moonshine in the botany lab. Space makes people go mental. It's the isolation, seeing the Earth receding behind you, being on a one-way mission . . . some find God. Some go berserk. The rest get drunk.

They've even got a name for it—the Lunar Effect.

As it was, Dr. al Damer was an observant Muslim who frowned upon alcohol, and especially his teenage daughter getting pregnant after drinking it with her German boyfriend. Not that I blamed him, really. When we arrived, he was trying to have it out with the boyfriend by hammering on his cabin door and threatening to murder him (in heavily-accented German, as it turned out).

The minute he saw us, he left off banging on the door and planted himself in front of Jamal. "قارتخالاب كبلاطا! اتفطخ ميتنبا !طباض اهفطاخ لاقتعاو كانه!"[2] he said, indignantly.

---

2 Officer! My daughter has been kidnapped! I demand you break in there and arrest the kidnapper!

(I didn't need a translation. He was demanding Jamal "do something"—like every bloke with an exaggerated sense of his own importance I'd ever met on the job.)

"What's going on here?" I asked.

"Officer, my daughter has been kidnapped! By a German boy," he said, gesturing. "She is in this boy's cabin."

I advised al Damer to vacate the area as security were now in attendance (or, at least, that's what I put in my report). He started ranting that this was about his daughter and a private matter—somewhat surprising as five minutes before Jamal told me he'd wanted us to break into the cabin.

Jamal warned him under Section 5 of the Public Order Act (or the Saudi equivalent, at least) and took a firm grip of his arm to pull him away from the door. Whereupon, he resisted, so I assisted by pulling his arms behind his back and cuffing him. Then Jamal dragged him, shouting and kicking, away from the cabin and I knocked on the door.

It turned out that Besma had run away to her boyfriend's cabin earlier that evening—after finally telling her dad she was twenty weeks pregnant.

"I knew he'd go crazy," she said. "I was scared of him. When I told him, he told me he wouldn't let me leave."

Back at OpSec, al Damer was ranting on about how he was an eminent Saudi chemist and was going to make a complaint to the authorities back on Earth. Part of my job, as it's turned out, has been top-level diplomat. When any jumped-up scrote can claim that the reason they were restrained, drunk and in a fight, is because of geopolitics back on Earth, it makes security harder for everyone.

Luckily, as the mission's gone on, it's become clearer; if we were a bunch of nationalist thugs, Terran bureaucrats couldn't do a thing about it.

I explained this to al Damer. Then I explained the onboard contract where he agreed to keep away from his daughter, and I didn't throw him into the brig.

"But she's my daughter," he protested. "She's my responsibility."

"She's the responsibility of the ship," I said.

I left him in the brig while we called an emergency shipboard summit. This was the first pregnancy aboard ship. The girl was risking her life—and that of the baby. We needed the medical team to look her over.

As we waited, Jamal told me a story about two Saudi girls who wanted to go on "adventures," aka dates. The strict dad drowned his daughter in their swimming pool, in full view of the family, to put off any other girls. The tolerant father locked his daughter in an attic and fed her through a slit in the door. She died a few years later.

"That book was banned in Saudi, but people read it in secret," said Jamal, who'd lived there a few years.

"Al Damer is a tolerant father?" I asked.

Jamal shrugged. "Something like that. Although killing your daughter is not, in truth, the Saudi way . . . "

At 8am ship's time sharp, I presented myself to the shipboard summit. It's a room full of senior crew and colony council bureaucrats—the bigwigs chosen to rule over us, God forgive us, when we get to the other end. I put forward my view that dad couldn't stay living with his daughter and we don't have the brig space to lock him up until we reach Terra Nova.

We spent hours and hours discussing this. The geopolitical, philosophical and legal ramifications of a baby aboard ship and granddad being out of the picture, blah blah. Almost everyone on this ship, except yours truly, has a Ph.D. in something or other. The medical team report that the baby is developing normally. Eventually housing agrees with me that Besma and her boyfriend need to move to their own large cabin in the European quarter. To make room for the poor sod currently in the cabin, housing will convert a storage container on C Deck.

In the meantime, dad will sign a contract to keep out the European quarter. Daughter and dad will talk to the ship's counselor—the 'go to' option for every fight aboard ship.

I let out al Damer. He was as meek as a baby. He went back to his cabin, his daughter moved out, and I started to believe I'd hear no more about it.

Shows you can never be too cynical as a cop.

I'd like to say the next thing I did was investigate the suspicious deaths, but the truth is that OpSec doesn't work that way. As per usual, there were only two of us on duty—myself and Larry, the USA Group Liaison.

On the way back to OpSec, I was diverted to the botany labs. A Dutch botanist had called to report that the bootleg brewer was up to his old tricks again. The complainant was European and Larry had to hold the fort.

I spent the next half hour talking to an American botanist who was adamant that, *no siree*, he was *nothing* to do with the French bloke I'd nicked (arrested) for brewing booze the previous week, and—yeah—the fermenting potatoes were one hundred percent for research purposes.

We took him down to OpSec where, because it was busy, Ryan and I (we were on first-name terms by this point) spent an hour talking about American spelling and mutual friends. Turned out that he was Angel's boyfriend.

His fingerprints matched up with the ones on the vodka we'd confiscated the previous week. I persuaded him to sign a waiver and left him in the waiting area while Larry got a warrant to search his cabin.

Later that day, Larry told me there'd been a drunken fight on the American side of A Deck. Two people taken to MedLab with minor cuts and bruises. A third bloke arrested. An hour later Larry found five litres of vodka stashed in the bootlegger's cabin.

I'd love to say that we banged him up until we hit Terra Nova, but the captain told Larry that "prohibition didn't work." So, later that evening, I let the bootlegger go. He and his mate'll get to carry on brewing booze, but under close supervision . . . apparently.

Yes. Babysitting bootleggers. This is why I joined a mission to the stars.

Death knocks were the worst part of being a copper. You're telling a loved one that they're never going to see their mother, wife, husband, son, or daughter ever again. Even when it's an accidental death, and you weren't on the scene, it doesn't make it any easier. That said, I've had a few weird ones where I had to call HQ to check that it wasn't suspicious and the family member had an alibi.

Al Damer, I expected to be a weird one. We picked him up after Larry got a report from MedLab "Male arguing with staff. Wants to see his daughter." I was still babysitting the bootlegger, so he woke up Simon Zhang, the Singaporean Asia-Pacific Group liaison.

By the time I arrived, al Damer was sitting in the MedLab waiting room. He'd been handcuffed and his head was down. I'd be lying if I said I'd expected him to be upset, but his whole body was shaking with grief, poor bloke. Someone, possibly Simon, had made him a cup of tea—although, with the cuffs on, he couldn't drink it.

Now, I wasn't a detective. I'd never wanted to be, and I certainly wasn't trained in interview techniques like you see on TV. The closest I'd got to criminological profiling was talking a drunk guy down off a roof in Brixton. I had no idea how to interrogate a Saudi chemist who may—or may not—have murdered his kid.

So I did my usual routine for death knocks. Introducing myself. Expressing sympathies. Looking sympathetic.

Al Damer looked up at me. He was a well-turned out bloke; neatly-trimmed goatee beard, black-rimmed designer specs, but right then his eyes were red rimmed and bloodshot. Either he was the world's greatest actor or he was genuinely gutted by the death of his daughter.

"You know I've got to ask you some questions?" I said gently.

He nodded stiffly.

"Do you want to speak to anyone? A lawyer, maybe?"

A slow dark flush spread across his cheeks. "You believe I killed my daughter. But it is you who is responsible . . . "

"Okay." This was news to me.

". . . You took her away to be with the German boy."

"Okay."

"You let her continue drinking . . . whoring . . . when she is just a girl and it is haram."

"Okay."

"Our people are not like you. We don't do this. That boy changed her. She was a good girl. Because of this, Besma, the flower of my life, she is dead."

I reflected on this for a moment. This was the bloke who'd locked his daughter in his cabin, and then gone crazy, threatening to kill her boyfriend. I gently pointed this out. Then I asked him when he last saw his daughter.

He shook his head, "I have not seen my daughter. How could I see her? You stopped me. I promised my wife, Allah have mercy, I would keep my children safe."

He sounded honest. We hadn't heard a dicky bird about him. He began to pray, "Allah, have mercy on my daughter. Have mercy on me. Guide me. Guide me." Looking into his tear-streaked face, I could have been looking at myself, six years ago. Grieving dad. Trying to make sense of a new world.

"Look, I need your help, Akbar," I said. "We think your daughter's death could have been suspicious . . . "

"Your colleague says that you have no idea how my daughter died."

"Investigations are ongoing," I said, ". . . But if it is suspicious, I want to catch the bugger who did it. You're her father. You might know."

He thought about this. "Tony," he said, shaking his head slowly with each syllable, "know that I did not kill my daughter."

"You allegedly locked her in your cabin. At least ten people heard you threatening to kill her boyfriend. You can see how that might look?"

"It was in the heat of anger. There is no reason for me to kill my daughter. She is my blood. We are going to a new world. We have no other family. We are blood. How can you think I would kill my own blood?"

"She shamed you?"

"Honor killing is not part of my culture."

"Then why lock her up?"

He met my eyes. "My daughter had gone wild aboard this ship. It is full of temptations . . . I wished to protect her. I have a good friend, a good Muslim. He lost his wife to cancer and, awash of grief, he came on this mission. I wished him to marry my daughter—I thought he would be a calming influence upon her."

"And you locked her up?"

"I needed her to be without child. I knew she would not agree."

I was interrupted by a pat on the shoulder. Simon, the Asia-Pacific liaison, said, "Sorry . . . Lizzie wants to talk to you outside."

I stepped into the corridor and Lizzie handed me a tablet PC. "The doc's got a preliminary COD [cause of death]."

"Which is?"

"Probably methanol poisoning, poor bairns. He's trying to firm it up right now."

I looked down at the pad. It was all numbers and percentages. "Any idea where the methanol came from?"

She shook her head.

I thought about al Damer. "How about the chemistry labs?"

"Ach, I suppose so."

I thanked her and walked back into the waiting room. Al Damer was exactly where I left him.

"You're a chemist, aren't you?" I asked.

He nodded, warily.

"How often do you use methanol?"

He put his head into his handcuffed hands. "That is how she died, isn't it? This is all your fault—she drank, which is haram, and she died—" I heard him choke up, and then he howled like a wounded animal.

I left him with his grief. And maybe I took a little of it with me, too.

Food. It brings people together across cultural barriers—or, at least, that's what the cultural diversity people at UN Headquarters insisted, during our training. Now, don't get me wrong, I don't object to the idea of cultural awareness. The reality, though, was some of us—Jamal and I included—privately questioned why we were spending so much time on stuff that seemed unnecessary.

I don't think we were interested in a sociology professor from Geneva discussing "diversity of cultural expression"—and other jargon—while we watched Japanese puppet theatre. Us security officers fondly imagined our job was stopping a Japanese linguist getting into fisticuffs with his Malaysian counterpart over something that happened in World War II (which only happened *sometimes*).

Yet, twenty days in, we still hadn't covered basic questions like: "Why do cultures differ?" "How does this lead to misunderstandings?" "What tips, tricks or advice are there for social mediation, i.e. helping people from different cultures get along?"

Maybe even, "How do you deal with a Saudi bloke who may have killed his own daughter?"

Luckily, like all good coppers, Jamal and I aren't averse to a great dinner or two. So I met him at the Ban Kai Moon saloon for a freshly-made curry. It wasn't a good curry, let alone great, made even less tasty by the thin air interfering with the smell, but it was the best you're likely to get 50AU from Earth.

I showed him the audio-visual recording of my conversation with al Damer. Jamal used an earpiece to keep anyone else from listening in.

"You think he did it?" I asked.

He shook his head. "I don't think so." He prodded his curry with a spoon, thinking. "He's not a psychopath. The pre-mission tests weeded them out. He is correct that honor killing is rare in Saudi Arabia. It's more common in rural Pakistan."

Jamal had family in Saudi Arabia. He loved them. Talked about them all the time. He'd lived in Saudi for twelve years and New York for five. That made him either an unbiased expert or a lying patriot— although, to be honest, it didn't matter either way.

"So what does happen if a girl shames her family?"

"By getting pregnant? She has a secret abortion. If word gets out, she is quickly married off to an older man. If not, Saudi women are smart. My relatives tell me girls use goat's blood capsules to fake virginity."

"What al Damer said, then."

"Do you believe him?" asked Jamal.

"He's a grief-stricken dad," I said.

So, yes, I believed him. I had first-hand experience. Thing is, what I believed was entirely irrelevant to whether he would end up being spaced as a murderer. The way the law works, even in space, is that you can only get convicted of a crime if there's evidence—beyond reasonable doubt—that you committed the crime.

And, right then, neither Jamal or I had any evidence.

We squeezed into al Damer's cabin on A Deck and found nothing but kids' clothes and a well-thumbed Koran. I picked it up and looked at it. I knew there was not a word in the book that sanctioned honor killings. Negative evidence counts, too. We took the lift down to B Deck and chatted to the scientists working overnight shifts. They didn't use methanol and had no reason to suspect al Damer. We rode another floor down to the maintenance area on C Deck where we found a stash of ganja in the head technician's office. I told him to bag it up and OpSec would give him a ration card.

Jamal and I went back to the canteen to search the shipboard surveillance systems for footage of al Damer in MedLab or outside his daughter's cabin. He'd never been in either place.

At 01:00 ship's time, I finally made a call to Earth to report the murders. It would be fourteen hours—more than half a day—before I got a reply, even an acknowledgement. With no excuse to hold him, and two drunks asleep in the waiting room, Jamal and I told Dr. al Damer to keep out of trouble and released him to his cabin. By Sod's law, I shouldn't have.

An hour later, I rode the lift back to my cramped cabin.

I'd only been in bed ten minutes—or that's how it felt anyway—when OpSec put out a general call for assistance:

"All officers to attend B Deck, Section 2. Reports of youths fighting in the Middle Eastern quarter. Weapons seen."

It was 04:00. My cabin was in the aft of the ship. Section 2 was towards the bow. I couldn't hear anything. At that stage, I didn't know how bad things were going to get. I thought it was the usual. Drunks . . . lover's tiff . . . I didn't make the connection.

I started shrugging my uniform back on. I was about to clip on my communicator when I felt the floor shake beneath my feet. Then the lights flickered and went out briefly. I heard the shipboard PA crackle into life: "Warning. Air system failure. Air system failure on B Deck," and I thought *shit, that's bad.*

For the first time since we'd blasted into space, I felt my life was in danger. It was an odd feeling in a cabin with no sign of a problem, on a space mission that was dangerous by definition.

I was the frontline of security on the ship. The ship was designed to automatically close off corridors and cabins to maintain oxygen and Co2 levels. I didn't want to go outside the safety of my cabin, but I sort of had to. I raided my closet for my emergency spacesuit— chunky helmet, thick padded chest plate, protective boots—and opened the door onto the B Deck corridor.

The first thing I noticed was . . . well, nothing. The corridor's usually busy 24/7, all the time, with the ship having no true night or day. But it was empty and silent. I guess people were staying in their cabins, for safety.

My protective boots made a heavy thudding sound, but I soon heard shouts and chants above my footsteps. An insistent amber light popped up on my heads-up display to report that oxygen concentrations were twenty-six percent and rising. I turned a corner and heard Jamal shout "No sparks," and was in the thick of twenty lads fighting . . . just like a pub fight.

Except that it wasn't.

Our officers, some crew, and a couple of big Turkish colonists, were trying to break them up. In the low light of the ship's corridor, claret [blood] was splattered across faces. The youths, all mid-teens I'd guess, were coded like a football team, but without the strips—Arab-looking lads on one side, and a smattering of black teenagers and various white Europeans on the other.

I've dealt with a fair few ruckuses as a cop, but my instinct was to stop and gawk . . . We were in a narrow, rotating tunnel with broken ventilation pipes lining the walls and the metal gangway splattered with blood. A few of the Arab lads had makeshift weapons you'd never find in a pub brawl . . . a spacesuit tether line, a zoologist's tranquilizer gun, and nail scissors.

I felt my hands sweating in my spacesuit gloves. The total Twilight Zone-ness of the situation was unnerving. The low gravity, half that of Earth, gave the rioters' movements a clumsy, unworldly grace.

"Tony," someone shouted. "Over here."

I rushed over to help a group of crew members who were holding two youths apart. They were trying to get them into handcuffs, but the Polish youth was spitting and shouting. "Calm down. You're under arrest," I said, and locked handcuffs onto his wrists while he cursed me—for "protecting a murderer."

The fight, I realized, was close to Dr. al Damer's quarters.

Some of the maintenance crew had arrived from C Deck. They dragged the shouting youth off towards the brig while I ran back. I had sweat pouring down my back—completely terrified and trying not to show it—and my skin was prickling with fear. The oxygen percentage was up to thirty-one percent, but the teenagers were still in full punch up mode—either too angry or too drunk to care.

Jamal was grappling with an Arab-looking teenager armed with a short rod with a spike at the end (a soil penetrometer he'd nicked from storage). He was quite tall and lanky, and brandishing it overhead like a short spear. I rammed into him like a rugby prop forward, which sounds brutal, but there's no good way of subduing a crazy drunk. "Police, police," I shouted, and the rod went skidding across the deck. The youth swore and yelled, "Get the fuck off me," and we rolled about on the metal gangway, until Jamal and a guy I didn't know managed to grab both his arms.

By the time we got him into handcuffs, the others had got control of the fight and the various combatants were being dragged towards nearby cabins for questioning. I was about to send our youth off with the rest of them when I noticed his narrow face, thick wavy hair and slightly angular eyebrows. They had a family resemblance to the girl on the mortuary slab.

"Al Damer?" I asked.

"Fuck you," he replied, which was all I needed to put two and two together.

Taking that as a "yes," we wrestled Besma's brother, Rashid, into a nearby cabin. Jamal gave him a cup of coffee while the rest of us spent what seemed like days interviewing a motley collection of Arabs and Westerners—many of whom turned out to be Rashid's ex-drinking buddies. Unsurprisingly, they all blamed each other.

It was all "Rashid drunk himself stupid." "Then his Muslim friends attacked us" and "this mob of Westerners set upon us—for no reason. They're all Islamophobic, man."

From what I could tell, Rashid and a bunch of other teenage wasters of various nationalities had taken to hanging around the hydroponics bays on C Deck. Mostly boozing and having sex behind the dwarf wheat—just like every bored yobbo back on Earth, but with a decent excuse for having nothing to do and a better class of parent.

At some point, earlier that evening, Rashid had started getting lairy (or, rowdy, as I put in my report), accusing everyone of discriminating against his dad. One of the French kids said it was Dr. al Damer who killed Besma, and Rashid started attacking him. The Muslim teenagers sided with Rashid and, when he started losing, everyone fled to B Deck.

At least, that's the story according to Jan-Frederick Muller, a friend of Besma's dead boyfriend. Rashid's mates, of course, had a different story. But to be honest, I didn't care whose fault it was.

You don't fight on a spaceship.

It's not Star Wars.

And most of them were underage.

Anyway, by the time I'd finished, Rashid had sobered up. He sat in the cabin with a coffee, looking faintly sheepish, while I asked him questions. He was a lot more Westernized than his sister, clean shaven with gelled hair, and a UNCS *Cheng Ho* T-shirt and jeans underneath his regulation canvas trousers.

"They're just fucking Islamophobic," he said, in a strong American accent. "My dad's a liberal guy. I'm a liberal guy. How can they believe crazy stuff like he killed my sister?"

His side of the story was that his so-called European friends started accusing his dad of murdering his sister. When he defended him, they rounded up an angry mob and tried to storm al Damer's cabin. "I was just trying to protect my dad," he said.

"I'm going to need to talk to your dad," I said.

His face turned faintly gray. "Please don't tell him I'd been drinking. Please . . . He'll kill me. I mean . . . not literally, he'll kill me, I mean, he wouldn't . . . actually kill me, you know . . . but . . . he'll get mad."

I didn't get to tell him: *you should have thought of that before you and your mates went Rebel Alliance and cracked an oxygen pipe.* My communicator buzzed. It was Lizzie.

I went outside.

"We've got more from forensics," she said.

"Go ahead."

"Nothing much of interest . . . "

It was my spidey sense going again. "Except?"

"She'd got alcohol in her bloodstream. Both of them had." Lizzie sighed and paused for a moment. "Don't want to speak ill of the dead. But she shouldn't have been drinking with a wee bairn on the way."

"Baby is doing well?" I asked.

"Squirming away . . . she's a real little fighter."

"How long did they drink before they died?"

"Same time as the methanol."

"Doped booze?"

"Ach, maybe. I'm not a doctor . . . or a detective."

"Lizzie. Neither am I."

I went back into the cabin. Now I had something to ask Rashid. I sat directly in front of him, leaning forward, with my elbows on my knees—a look that meant business.

"Tell me about your sister." I said.

Rashid put his head into his hands, and began to sob. "It's my fault. It's all my fault."

"Your fault?" I asked.

"I was her brother. She was all I had . . . my family, my blood. I should have protected her better."

"Do you know what happened to her?"

He shook his head.

"The autopsy says that she died of methanol poisoning. She'd been drinking before her death."

"NOOOOOOO . . ." He began rocking backwards and forwards, without looking up. I had a niggling feeling that he knew something, and it was causing him unimaginable guilt. I gave him a moment to compose himself. Then I asked, softly, "Your friends say that you often went drinking in the hydroponics bay."

"Fuck, don't tell my dad that."

I sighed. "Rashid, you're how old? fifteen, sixteen?"

"Seventeen."

"That's still underage in most jurisdictions; even if you weren't supposed to have a religious objection to booze. Look, how about I'll be vague with your dad—provided that you tell me what you know about your sister."

He finally looked at me, nodding.

"Okay. When did you last see your sister?" I asked.

He swallowed and knotted his fingers together. "Last Friday, three . . . no four days ago." He paused. "She was with her boyfriend, you know, Hans, who died. We were hanging out in the hydroponics bay . . . "

"Drinking?"

He shuffled uncomfortably. "Yeah."

"Where did you get the booze?"

He swallowed again. "Ryan. He's an American botanist."

"I know him."

"He brews it in the botany labs. Seriously, though, he wouldn't have murdered Besma, he's got no reason to kill her. He really liked her. And he's not the type."

"We had psychometric testing to get aboard this boat. No one should be the type."

He gave me a wide-eyed look of terror. I couldn't blame him. I wasn't exactly happy with the idea of sharing a three-hundred-meter-long flying can with a double murderer myself. "Is there anyone among your mates who might have wanted Besma dead?"

He shook his head again and put his hands across his face. I patted him on the arm and stood up. "Look, I've got to slap on a curfew for rioting, underage drinking, and damaging the ship, but—I swear—I'll find who killed your sister and make sure they're held responsible."

He glanced up with a hopeful look.

I'd remember that look as long as I lived.

We just got lucky on casualties—it could have been a lot worse. Two of the kids needed to go to MedLab—one with a broken nose and the other with a stab wound in his chest. One of the Turkish guys had a mild concussion from being hit on the head with a pipe. I was bruised all over—hips, thighs, elbows—from rolling on the floor with Rashid. Nothing serious, but not how I'd have wanted to spend my evening.

Contrary to what you hear, cops like me don't like fighting. We do the job for the pay and to catch criminals. If you get into a fight, you risk getting injured. It's rarely worth the pain.

Larry insisted I go to MedLab to get checked out, but there wasn't any point really. Bruises are bruises and I just wanted to go to bed.

I limped back to my cabin, stripped off my clothes and went out like a light. I dreamed of my daughter. She was running down a smoke-filled corridor, her arms outstretched towards me. Her body was engulfed in flames.

I woke to find my pillow damp with tears.

I'd never cried before my daughter died. There was a time after she did when I dreamed about her every night and woke every morning with a damp pillow. But since I'd applied for the *Cheng Ho* mission, I'd never cried at night. Not even when they quizzed me about her death.

Maybe it was the sudden anger of the kids that had got to me. I was used to people who hated cops and were out of control—it comes with the job. I was a dab hand at dealing with criminal scrotes who used any excuse for a fight and a bit of looting. And I'd seen my fair share of pub scraps where the combatants were drunk, lairy [aggressive], and mates again the next morning. But those kids . . . They'd been buddies for months and, the next minute, they were breaking noses and cracking oxygen pipes.

Riots weren't supposed to happen aboard the *Cheng Ho*. The crew and colonists had been chosen to be tolerant and law-abiding people. Well, that's according to the powers-that-be, anyway. So the reality was that we weren't equipped for mass disorder. We were six security officers for a couple of thousand crew and colonists, no backup, no tear gas, water cannons or rubber bullets, and no riot gear. There was nowhere to lock up rioters. If anyone did anything wrong, we were expected to talk them out of it.

We'd been lucky this time to have a bunch of colonists willing to muck in and make up numbers. Even luckier that there weren't any fatalities. I reckoned we wouldn't be so lucky if—*and it was an if*—there was a next time. And, on a ship in deep space, that wasn't a good thought.

My morning shift began with me walking to the cabin of Ryan, our friendly American bootlegger, so that I could arrest him.

Ryan, as I'd learned last time, was a former university botanist who signed up for *Cheng Ho* because he had "nothing better to do." He gave off the strong impression of a surfer bum, but minus any passion for surfing. He was also Angel's boyfriend although, when he opened the door of his cabin, she was nowhere in evidence. His blond hair was mussed from sleep, and he had on stripy boxer shorts and a pair of Birkenstocks.

The smile dropped right off his face when he saw me.

"Fuck, I didn't do anything," he said.

"What do you think you did?" I said.

"B Deck last night," he said. "I swear . . . I only supplied the booze. I wasn't even there."

I informed him that he needed to be arrested so that I could interview him. Afterwards, he was free to go. Then I read him the Miranda Warning off a card—a relief because, since the 2023 Criminal Justice and Public Order Act, the British right to silence goes on for pages. I always joke that it works as a form of torture; the perp will confess just to get me to stop.

After that, I waited outside his cabin while he threw on a crumpled lab coat and boardshorts. He acted the same as our first meeting—not especially bothered about the situation. If anything, he was even less concerned than last time—possibly because he knew I wasn't about to nick him for bootlegging. I fetched him a coffee and we walked back to the OpSec interview room.

"Ryan," I said. "We have evidence to suggest that Besma al Damer and Hans Schwerz died from consuming methanol—administered deliberately, or by accident—in an alcoholic drink. We have reason to believe that the alcohol they consumed before their death came from your brewing operation."

That took a minute to sink in. He began to drum his fingers on the table. "Shit. Shit. Shit," he said. "Shit, man. I check all my booze. No way . . . "

"They couldn't have drunk the methanol accidentally?"

"No way! I taste everything before it goes out . . ." His voice tailed off, and he looked at me for reassurance, which I didn't give him. Eventually, he stammered, "Seriously, dude. I loved Besma, she was the sweetest; I wouldn't do a thing to harm her."

"Apart from giving her booze in pregnancy?" I said.

He shrugged. "Well, I told her. But it's her choice." That was the kind of public-spirited comment usually reserved for the better class of drug dealer I'd arrested: the ones with an IQ greater than their shoe size.

I pulled up the transcript from his interview a few days before, and went through the details of his bootlegging operation. "Who else has access to your booze when it's in storage?"

He shrugged. "Me and my mate. Well, actually just me and . . ." His voice trailed off.

"You and who?" I asked.

He shrugged.

"Do you know of anyone who might have reason to harm Besma?"

He shrugged again.

"Look. I know you know something."

He thought about it. "It's nothing." I waited. "It was just . . . I talk to, you know, my girlfriend."

Now that was a surprise. "Angel?"

"And, a month ago, she got moved from A to C Deck . . . "

I realized where he was going. Space was a premium on the *Cheng Ho*. The senior staff, medics and navigators, were allocated the larger cabins on A Deck. The smaller cabins on B Deck, like mine, you couldn't swing a rat in. They simply weren't big enough for a pregnant teen and her boyfriend. Someone—Angel—had been moved to a converted storage container on C Deck.

". . . She was really mad about it," Ryan was saying. "I mean, man, she's not me. She's kinda uptight."

And that was the shape of it: Angel was angry about being moved to C Deck to make room for an irresponsible teenager.

It wasn't much to go on.

I nodded to Larry to check out this story. Then I wracked my brains for questions to ask Ryan. I was sure he was involved. I had a niggling suspicion that he knew something, and was blaming his girlfriend to keep us off the trail. So I went through the details of his bootlegging operation yet again. Then I went through his movements in the twenty-four hours after the couple were admitted to MedLab and the events leading up to his arrest.

"The five litres of vodka in your cabin . . ." I said.

Silence.

"Was that the same batch you gave to Besma and Hans?"

He shrugged. "Yeah . . . no . . . I mean, maybe, man."

I pride myself on remaining calm and professional, but I felt myself losing it. There was a dead girl and Ryan was covering his arse.

"You know, I'd taken that vodka to my cabin . . . "

The color drained out of his face. "Man, you're not drinking it?"

I leaned forward. "There's something wrong with it?"

"Man, seriously . . . it's not . . . "

I gestured to Larry, who was outside the interview room. "Look, I'm switching off the AV recording now." I stood up. "Then I'm going to go to our evidence room, take your vodka and test every last bottle . . . "

His back slumped in the chair. "You're not?"

"Drinking it? No."

At the door, I turned back to him. "If I find meths, mate, you are straight out the fucking airlock and floating your way home."

★★★

Next stop . . . the five litres of vodka stacked in the evidence room. Larry and I carted it down to the chemistry labs for testing with firm instructions that it was evidence in a poisoning. You'd think that no one would nick bootleg vodka, but there isn't much use for cash on the *Cheng Ho*. Booze, movie memorabilia, food rations—you name it, it gets swapped for just about anything. Social prestige, future favors, time off the work rota . . . yeah, we've nicked a few Toms-in-training [prostitutes] too.

No one's obvious about it, of course. After all, we're supposed to be building humanity's home for the future here. But it still happens—the people with the most 'stuff' (what they called "social capital" in training)—get the best perks.

At 10:00hrs, Simon came on shift and I sent him off to arrest Angel. Then I went down to the botany labs and nicked the French bootlegger. He hadn't seen Besma or Hans for a fortnight and claimed Ryan's booze was nothing to do with him. Can't say I believed him, but he didn't act dodgy either.

I walked down B Deck to MedLab where Lizzie was on duty to ask if they'd finished on the forensics. She shrugged at me. I asked what had taken so long.

"Ach, it's the equipment," she said.

"Which equipment?" I saw the pain and confusion in her face, and added, "Sorry for asking."

"Well, all the analyzers . . . "

". . . For blood tests?" I asked.

She nodded.

"For methanol poisoning?" I asked.

Her eyes widened. "No . . ." Her hands flew to her mouth. ". . . It couldn't have been deliberate." Lizzie was a sweet soul—she needed to catch up to reality. Eventually, she said, quietly. "The poor wee lass."

I left Jamal to go through the MedLab audio-visual records and went back to my cabin to look up methanol poisoning. Now I'm no chemist—it was my worst subject—and half an hour on the ship's intranet wasn't going to change that.

So excuse me if this account isn't the best. I'm not on this boat to be smart.

When you hear of old guys going blind on moonshine, that's no joke. If you fancy amateur distilling, you should do your homework. Throw away your first runs; make sure you're not producing methanol. Thing is, methanol is a lot like booze, but it breaks down in your body to formaldehyde. If formaldehyde sounds familiar, you'd be right. It's the stuff they use for pickling the animals you see in museums. If you drink methanol, the formaldehyde hits your eyes and your gonads first.

So, if you drink the stuff and you're a bloke, you're pickling your balls.

[This also explained how the baby survived—premie infants can't make formaldehyde].

Now, I'm not a detective, and methanol poisoning isn't your usual brand of southeast London murder (that's usually teenagers stabbing each other). But, going by the symptoms, if you suspect it, you can confirm your suspicions with a gas chromatograph—if you can find one. You might be able to save the poor sod's life by giving them alcohol, which competes with methanol for "binding sites"— whatever that means. As I say, I'm not a chemist.

Either way, you can't get anywhere without a suite of blood tests. And, if your analyzers aren't working, you're flying blind.

At 13:00hrs, Jamal came around to show me the audio-visual records. They showed what I'd expected; Angel acting suspicious near the MedLab equipment. Looking behind her, entering the room, and messing with the equipment. Angel—a doctor—tinkering with analyzers in MedLab: that wasn't evidence of anything. So I sent him to talk to the IT guys.

An hour later, I went back to OpSec. Angel was seated in the interview room. I looked at her through the glass. She wasn't my usual brand of criminal scrote . . . the sort I caught running away with a blood-covered shiv. Her back was straight and her hands were folded primly in her lap . . . a proper little Miss Perfect.

"I want a lawyer," she said, as I walked in, in her strong American accent. "I'm permitted competent and independent counsel under Filipino law."

I folded my arms. "You can have the ship's lawyer if you want," I said. "But he's been a bit busy; you'll need to wait until he gets back on shift."

"Fine," she said. "I'll wait."

I asked her some questions anyway. She'd been moved cabins. Was she angry about it?

She shook her head.

"Your boyfriend said you were angry," I persisted.

Her lips formed an angry line. "Then my boyfriend is a fool. The cabin on C Deck is larger than my old one."

"Did you blame Besma for that?"

"That little whore. No, I did not. Or, at least, not enough to murder her." She frowned at me. "I'm not insane, Tony."

Larry came into the room. I went outside to speak to him. He'd sped up the lab tests on the vodka. They'd found methanol in one of the bottles. Per unit of booze, it was a lethal dose. I walked back into the room and sat, quietly, facing Angel. She stared back at me.

"Did you tamper with the equipment in MedLab?" I asked.

"The equipment failed. I told you. We asked local IT to assist."

"There's footage of you near the equipment."

"Yes, I'm a doctor."

"We're asking local IT to investigate."

She blinked at me. It was the first sign that I'd fazed her.

"Did you tamper with the equipment?"

"I may have been near the equipment. I did not kill Besma al Damer. Certainly not over a cabin."

I stared into her face. She stared back without blinking. I try to keep it professional with people . . . we meet a lot of very nasty people on the job, but I couldn't deal with someone like her. Someone acting so cold.

"You know that . . . you must know, being a doctor, that young couple could have been saved with the right tests."

She stared at me. "I said I wasn't talking to you without counsel."

"Isn't that against your Hippocratic Oath?"

"I said I wasn't talking to you . . . "

I turned off the audio-visual feed and went outside. I got the lukewarm powdery water that passes for coffee in these parts, and stood for a time in the B Deck corridor . . . thinking. This was outside my years of experience as a cop in southeast London. A bit more like Agatha Christie's *Murder at the Vicarage* than Peckham Gone Bad on a Saturday night. And, as I thought it, I wasn't sure if there was a murder. There are the usual tragic cock ups that define us humans. Not what you'd think of as the best story, but—at the same time— they happen.

I finished my coffee and went back into the interview room. Angel stared at me, defiantly.

"You knew all about your boyfriend's bootlegging operation, didn't you?"

Silence.

"Let me run something past you."

"If you insist."

"Maybe your boyfriend made a mistake. He's not a legal distiller. Maybe some methanol got into the mix. Maybe a pregnant lass and her boyfriend got ill, and ended up in MedLab. You suspected what was going on . . . "

Her left eyelid twitched.

"Maybe you thought he'd get spaced . . . so you tried covering up for him?"

"No, certainly not. Now, if you will leave me to await counsel," she said, in the same stiff voice. And then she put her hands across her face and began to sob.

I left her. There was nothing else I could say.

The last thing I went to do before I got off-shift was see the baby. Bigger than I remembered her, although I might have been imagining things. She was squirming around in her bag. While I watched, she opened and closed one little fist.

Lizzie put her hand on my shoulder.

"How's she doing?" I asked.

"She's doing really well. She's just a bit small," she said proudly. "We definitely think she's going to make it."

"She's got a name yet?"

Lizzie smiled. "Oh yes, we've named her . . . We've named her Hope."

The most frustrating part of being a copper back in London was probably the Crown Prosecution Service (CPS).

Or, as we liked to call them, the "Couldn't Prosecute for Shit."

What you've got to realize is that the British police only do arrests and interviews. It's up to the CPS, a government department, to decide whether to bring a case to court. The experience of cops like me is that they're risk averse in the extreme and disorganized to boot. Even if they decide to prosecute, they're going to have lost the (paper) file by the time you get to court.

It's very frustrating. You get a watertight case, or so you think . . . and then, oh sorry, we can't prosecute. Or their solicitor doesn't have the file, the case gets postponed to another court date, and your criminal (who's got no fixed abode) goes AWOL. Then you've got to tell the victim who blames you and hates your guts.

Same pattern, as it turns out, on the *Cheng Ho*.

The next morning, I had the pleasure of going down to the shipboard summit to present my evidence. I was trying to get them to understand that this was outer space. We weren't equipped for murders. There were no experienced detectives aboard and it took sixteen hours to get advice from Earth—which was, broadly speaking, "do whatever you're doing and don't scare the horses."

We had the methanol test results, the audio-visual footage from MedLab, and all the forensics and interviews. It all pointed to my theory—Ryan had accidentally poisoned Besma and Hans, and his girlfriend had tried to cover it up.

"On balance," I said. "Given you're not likely to space them, I'd lock them both up. It's not like they've got anywhere to run."

There was a bit of oohing and ahhing about that. Then the Chief Liaison for the European Colony Council raised his hand. He was in his mid-fifties, plumpish, with a drinker's nose and gray hair. A bureaucrat from Liechtenstein who had an annoying habit of talking down to me and using my "Mr." title to rub in his two Ph.D.s.

"Do you actually have any evidence beyond the circumstantial, Mr. Martin?" he asked me.

"Look, we've . . ." I began.

"It seems to me," he added. "That the unfortunate deaths of this couple could be due to anyone or—indeed—almost anything onboard the ship. Have you fully investigated the possibility that they drank methanol deliberately, in a suicide pact?"

"Yes, we have. And no, that's not the way to bet . . ." I said.

We spent another hour going back through the evidence. They didn't want to "incarcerate anyone needlessly," but they did want "a speedy arrest to improve morale." They thought we could fingerprint everyone. Or use trackers. Or some high-tech forensics they'd seen once on an American cop show.

Crazy.

An hour later, Marjorie Billings-Rajamana, another European Colony Council bureaucrat and—to my shame—a fellow Brit said, "I think you should carry on questioning Dr. al Damer. Maybe he will crack under pressure."

They all agreed to that. So no one got charged. That afternoon, Simon and I went back to Dr. al Damer's quarters to arrest him again. Rashid was there, hanging about in the corridor with a couple of mates. He responded about as you'd expect.

"You promised me you'd find who'd killed my sister," he said.

And then he told me to fuck off.

We were four and a half billion miles from Earth.

And I may as well have been back in southeast London . . .

A few years back, a mate of mine was investigated for police brutality. He and a colleague attended a reported break-in at a warehouse. A well-known crook called Liam was handing canisters of freeze-dried coffee to his mate Wayne through a broken window.

As my mate tells it, his colleague nicked Wayne while my mate wriggled in through the window to chase Liam, who tried to leg it. I say, tried, because—as my mate puts it—Liam was a lard-arse. Big gut hanging out of his T-shirt, flabby pockmarked face, and prematurely bald on top of it.

Not one for the ladies, our Liam.

My mate called for backup, and then jumped on him, and they started rolling around on the floor together. Liam was going mad, thrashing and shouting, and throwing his weight around. By the time he got outside, he was huffing and wheezing. They called an ambulance for him.

As my mate said, he was a heart attack waiting to happen.

A week later, someone leaked the CCTV footage from the warehouse. It was trial by media. A grandfather of five with a dodgy heart and lung cancer, brutalized by the police. No mention that he was a career criminal, or that he was resisting arrest.

The complaint was dismissed in the end. But the way he was

treated . . . no smoke without fire. He never got promoted beyond sergeant, despite twelve years in the force with an exemplary record.

It's no joke that a handful of complaints can end your career.

And that's why I came out in a cold sweat when, a couple of weeks after the shipboard summit, Jamal and I got called into the office of Dominic-Rubin Frick. Neither Jamal nor I had any idea what the complaint was about. So we compared notes while we sat outside the office like naughty school kids.

"Sadly, I think it is the case of Besma again," said Jamal.

That put a dampener on things.

As it turned out, it was the case of Besma again. One of Rashid's mates, a British bloke called Mohammed Khan, had taken the trouble to film the riot on B Deck on his mobile phone . . . (yes, you're probably asking the same questions I am). He sent the footage back to Earth with a voiceover about Islamophobic cops.

Unbeknownst to us, our UN-approved arrests had caused riots in countries worldwide—Muslim kids burning flags, cursing the UN and America's space policy.

"This is a major interplanetary incident," Rubin-Frick said, glaring at us. "I have spent this entire cycle discussing with Earth, at the highest levels, how this incident could have been . . . "

"With due respect, sir, the crew and colonists were in danger," I said.

"Nevertheless, this situation required sensitive handling, which you and your team failed to display . . . "

"They were textbook arrests, sir," I said.

He snorted. "Textbook, indeed."

"We used UN-approved techniques for riot control and restraint. We reviewed the AV footage with the Master at Arms, as part of the post-incident briefing."

He leaned forward. "Regardless, you gave these young men cause to believe you were hostile towards them, thereby eroding racial and religious relations aboard ship."

I said nothing. If you've arrested an angry drunk, you know it's hard enough to get them to comply without either injuring them, or getting injured—without having to acting 'non-hostile' as well.

Rubin-Frick flicked off the AV. "I'm extremely disappointed with the performance of the security team throughout this investigation."

He pressed a button and the door opened behind us. "With this in mind, I have authorization from Earth to take over the handling of this case."

And, with that, the bureaucrats took over.

You can imagine how well that went.

15 months later . . .

Britain's biggest export is bureaucracy. That's what I say to Jamal, anyway. That, and our national sport is queuing. So, if you're a British copper, you're well-versed in being subject to petty bureaucrats who see government initiatives as the practical alternative to catching real crooks.

So I had every confidence in Dominic-Rubin Frick . . . Every confidence he'd achieve nothing.

I was wrong.

He achieved worse than nothing . . .

The man lying in the mortuary drawer was wearing frayed jeans and a pair of Birkenstocks. His head was covered with a white sheet.

"Do you recognize him?" asked Lizzie, pulling back the cloth over his face.

"Yeah, it's Ryan . . . the bootlegger," I said.

Lizzie bit her lip, nodding.

"Methanol poisoning?"

Lizzie nodded.

"Who brought him in?"

"A friend . . . a French botanist," she swallowed. Tears glistened in her eyes. Can't say I was too upset myself. To be brutally honest, he probably deserved everything he'd got.

I covered his face again. "What about the others?"

Lizzie led me into the adjoining ward in silence. The six beds were occupied by naked bodies swarming with wires and breathing masks. I recognized some of them by sight—they were kids who I'd caught boozing in the hydroponics bay. The only sound was the steady beep-beep of machinery.

"Are they going to make it?" I asked.

She nodded slowly. "Ach, I'm crossing myself for them."

"Any of them spoken to you?"

She shook her head. "Only with symptoms."

I followed her through the ward into the duty doctor's office. A nurse came into the office, picked up a mediscanner, and walked out onto the ward.

"Angel off duty?" I asked.

Lizzie shook her head quickly. "She's never been on duty." She quickly corrected herself. "Not since they came in, anyway."

I stared off down the ward. The nurse was bending over the beds, checking vital signs with the mediscanner. Angel had carried on working as a doctor after I arrested her for being an accessory to manslaughter.

Rubin Frick said there wasn't enough evidence to arrest anyone. He'd dropped the whole case after six months of questioning.

Now Angel's ex was dead. And six kids were fighting for their lives.

I felt my stomach constrict with righteous fury.

I tried not to let it show.

Angel wasn't in her cabin on C Deck. I called her communicator, but it was off. I rode the lift back up to A Deck and dropped into OpSec, where I found Simon and Jamal booking a big Polish cook who'd gone for his co-worker with a meat cleaver. I asked Simon to find Angel on the shipboard surveillance system, and talked Jamal into helping me catch the French bootlegger.

At 9:00hrs, I took the lift back to MedLab and spoke to the nurse on the ward. The kids had brought themselves in. They were dizzy, sick with blurred vision—same as Besma and Hans. The duty doctor was treating with alcohol, which still sounded crazy to me (but I'm no clinician).

She hadn't seen Angel since the previous cycle.

I went back to OpSec where, in the brig, the big Polish guy was headbanging the wall and shouting. Jamal had tracked the French bootlegger down to C Deck so we took the lift down to the labs to interview him. He denied everything. We found six litres of vodka stashed in a storage compartment and nicked him anyway.

At 11:50hrs, I left Jamal with the bootlegger and walked to the Annan canteen in what had become the 'European Catholic' quarter, and an altogether pleasanter task. I was providing security for Hope's first birthday party. You wouldn't think a baby's birthday would need a bouncer, but both granddads—and their family—wanted custody. The dispute had got so vicious, the shipboard summit had given her to Lizzie.

Not sure what to make of that—all things considered—but my job, such as it was, was to stand outside the canteen door to make sure Hans' dad, Immanuel Schwerz, didn't gatecrash.

After an initial rush of guests, mostly pregnant ladies from Lizzie's antenatal class, nothing happened . . . which was bliss.

At around 12:30hrs, a petite Kuwaiti lady brought me a cup of tea, and a slice of freeze-dried lemon cake with "Welcome to Terra Nova!" iced into the top.

I washed the dry cake down with the tea and wandered up and down the corridor.

On my third trip, I noticed a dripping symbol of green paint on the dirty bulkhead. It was smeared into the shape of a tree with arrows at the top.

Underneath, they'd written *Protect. Defend. Phalange.*

Typical . . . Graffiti.

I hoped someone else would do the door-to-door. Catching kids vandalizing walls is the kind of policing you don't want to do. It's like catching swans on the M25: there's a lot of running and spitting, but it's all a bit pointless, and you've got better things to do.

I knocked on a couple of doors, anyhow.

Then I left a message for the colonists on clean-up duty.

No one had seen anything.

They never do.

At around 14:30hrs, I walked back to the canteen. The party was breaking up. Lizzie had Hope clinging to her hip. She was talking with a Spanish colonist with a baby swaddled in a torn-up blanket. As I arrived, the colonist excused herself and hurried away.

Hope watched me with her mother's large dark eyes.

"What's Phalange?" I asked.

Lizzie shrugged. "Never heard of it."

We spoke for a while—or, rather, she spoke and I nodded along. Hope was starting to walk, but Lizzie was worried about her muscle mass. Terra Nova had gravity similar to Earth, but Hope had been born in low-G.

And it wasn't just Hope.

The ship now had six children to worry about, and there were ten more babies on the way.

After she'd left, I walked back through B Deck. Every door I passed had the official name plaque crossed out. With couples marrying and children being born, the colonists were playing musical cabins, and housing was struggling to cope.

People marrying people like them—who thought like them, shared their culture and values.

Business as usual for humanity, I guess.

We had a few suicides on the job. Back on Earth I'd one guy put a hosepipe through the window of a vintage Prius. Must have taken him an age to die. I felt sorry for him, to be honest. He'd lost his job a week before and his wife had gone to her mother's. She found him a week later, slumped in the front seat.

The wife told me he'd felt guilty.

At 17:00hrs, I got a call from OpSec. "Can you attend an unauthorized opening of E Deck Escape Hatch 2?"

I sighed at that. The escape hatches were standard airlocks. Two doors—one into the depressurization chamber. Another out into space. We'd had a few suicidal people opening the escape hatch on A Deck. It was usually a cry for help. Thankfully, someone usually spotted them. That's why they chose the residential decks.

E Deck was a new one on me.

"Can you see who it is?" I asked.

Simon's voice cut onto the call. "It's Angel."

I ran, or—rather—I bounced through the low grav. Two elevators down to the lowest gravity deck and then I kicked my way through engineering like a big hairy frog. Can't say I didn't want her to space herself, but we needed to chat under oath about her dead boyfriend.

I knew as soon as I floated to the outer door. The airlock was a round metal disc, like a big manhole cover, with a thick glass window in the top. Angel was tumbling around in the compartment behind, her limbs blue and horribly swollen. But the thing that stuck in my mind most was the red light flashing on the airlock controls. She'd climbed in and manually depressurized the compartment.

No cry for help there.

I repressurized the compartment and went in to retrieve the body.

Protocol was we documented the death, even if it was suicide. For the scientists back on Earth. I had to check over the body to confirm she was dead. I knew she was dead. I'd watched the demos. She'd watched the demos. They said it was a nasty way to go.

I called MedLab and waited for a doctor to take her away.

Before I finished my shift, I had to interview the Polish cook, Przemys. He was a stereotype of an eastern European bloke. In his early twenties, square jaw, short brown hair, a short brown beard, and a nonregulation black sweatshirt with a load of "Cs" and "Zs" in bold white font.

As I walked into the brig, he was sitting quietly on the bed.

"You shouldn't arrest me, Mr. Martin," he said, looking up. "I did you favor."

We agreed I'd call him Dennis. I read him his rights. He looked like he couldn't care less. "Your victim is in MedLab with a shoulder injury," I said.

He blinked at me. "He is criminal, Mr. Martin."

"What did he do?"

"He is dirty. He cleans plates badly. I have told him for six months . . . "

"Is that why you attacked him?"

He shook his head. "He tried to bring his brother to volunteer in the canteen. After our shift, I told him no, in the early hours, while we were drinking, and he argued. My girlfriend is expecting baby and eats in the Cafe Internationale, Mr. Martin. I do not want her to die."

"Because he's dirty?"

"Because he is *ciapak*," he said. I looked blank. He leaned forward, intently. "I was there when they trashed ship, Mr. Martin. They tried to kill you. They would have killed us if they'd had chance." Now I realized he meant Rashid. "Now two more people are dead, and others are in hospital."

"That's nothing to do with it, mate," I said.

"Then why have you arrested no one?" he replied.

I didn't think the truth would help. So I told him that investigations were ongoing and he should leave the job of vigilante to security. Then I did the usual procedure—handed him a contract that he'd stay off the booze and keep away from sharp objects. Fat lot of use if he didn't, but my job's what keeps me sane.

As he took the pen, I noticed a green tattoo on his wrist, a tree with arrows at the top. Underneath was written *Protect. Defend. Phalange.*

Dennis told me nothing about the Phalange. I didn't have grounds to hold him, so I let him go. Then I walked to MedLab to check on his victim. He was asleep. Lizzie told me he was a Turkish teenager who'd got into the riot. He'd sided with Rashid and got a mild concussion. I finished my shift and walked to the Annan canteen. The graffiti was still on the wall. *Protect. Defend. Phalange.* I called the cleaning team before I went into the canteen. I had to hope the graffiti was Dennis' handiwork.

It wouldn't be, knowing my luck.

I asked the canteen manager about the graffiti. He said, "Fucking kids." I told him we'd arrested Dennis. An Irish bloke asked, "The kid defending Rashid's lot?" I named the victim. "Rashid's fucking crazy," said another guy at the bar. The Irish bloke nodded sadly. "He's like every stereotype of a Muzzie I never wanted to believe."

Both guys knew about the Phalange. "It's some security thing Schwerz set up," said the Irish bloke. "He doesn't think we'll get off this ship alive."

I thanked them for their time. I thought about nicking them for hate speech, as well, but what would be the point?

I finished my curry and sleepwalked to Dr. Schwerz's cabin. It was one block from the canteen and shipboard surveillance told me he was in. I wasn't looking forward to seeing him again. He was outraged when Liz got Hope. Can't say I blame him, really. He'd lost his son—no fault of his own—and then we take his granddaughter away.

He opened the door and frowned at me. He was in his late fifties, with precisely trimmed salt-and-pepper hair and a tidy gray beard. His gray suit had creases down the legs. He was soft-spoken, polite . . . just like you'd imagine a middle-aged academic. He wasn't how I remembered myself even a few months after I lost my daughter.

And graffiti-wise, he didn't look the type.

He invited me in. "I am sorry to hear about Przemys," he said.

"How do you know him?"

He raised his eyebrows. "We are on the same spacecraft . . ." He paused. "Ah, I see what you mean now. We worship together. I am a Bavarian Catholic."

I squeezed onto his narrow sofa.

"Did you suspect he might attack someone?"

He shook his head vigorously. "No, no, of course not."

I couldn't tell if he was lying. Sometimes you can't. "So what's the Phalange?" I asked.

He sat on his fold-down bed "It is what it appears, Tony. My son is dead. The security team has not found the killer. We are very frightened here in the European section of the ship. We think a murderer is free and more people will die."

"D.I.Y. policing doesn't end well." I was thinking of a case where a vocabulary-challenged mob went after a pediatrician. We cops may not have Ph.D.s, but at least we can spell.

He leaned forward. "I do not encourage violence, Tony. We just patrol corridors in this quarter. We only defend ourselves if attacked. And our thought is we do attack if there are more murders that security fails to solve."

"I've solved your son's death," I said.

He waved his hand, dismissively. "So I have heard. And they are dead, *jah*. Very convenient for you, I think."

I ignored him. I'd heard this before. It's not like it didn't bother me. Ask any cop. You get accused of all sorts by the public when you're just trying to do your job.

"How many people are in this Phalange?"

"We are few, but our numbers are growing."

"Why 'Phalange'?"

He frowned and his voice went cold. "Why are you here, Mr. Martin?"

"I'm investigating graffiti. Put up by your Phalange."

He laughed. "Graffiti, hah!" He stood up, opening the door. "It was not me."

"Do you know who it was?" I asked, standing up.

He shook his head. "I am not responsible for all the people here, Tony."

I walked back to my cabin. I couldn't blame him. Rubin Frick messed him about for months. No one took responsibility. It shouldn't surprise anyone the colonists lost their trust in the crew and security. Over those long months, I'd thought about security taking over the ship; we'd make a better job. Thing is, if anything was likely to set off a riot, it was that.

Later that sleep, I dreamt of my daughter. She was running towards me with a fireball roaring along the corridor behind her, Little Hope holding tightly to her hand.

Two months later . . .

I got a call. "The recycling crew have found a dead body. Can you check it out?"

It was 2:00hrs ship's time. I remember crawling out of bed in my emergency spacesuit, staring at a patch of mold on my sink unit. I was thinking of the worst possible option, which was Besma and the bootleggers over again.

"Not one of mine, is it?" I asked.

The guy on the other end sounded apologetic. "I think it's one of yours."

I got dressed in the storage locker adjoining my cabin. Not in my cabin, you understand, as the temperature controls in the sleeping section had been on the blink for a fortnight. I'd taken to sleeping in my spacesuit, calling the repair crew regularly, and praying for the end of the mission. Terra Nova was three weeks away, by this point, and the old boat was falling apart.

So I call OpSec on the way down in the elevator. The recycling crew had found the body in a distiller in the urine recycling system on D Deck. Not knowing what a distiller was, I was disappointed that it was a big silver drum like a beer keg. The recycling manager told me it spun to create artificial gravity, while boiling off clean water.

He opened the lid of the drum. I remember feeling relieved the crew had drained the urine—we were in low-G. The body was curled up in a tight ball, didn't smell too bad, so we decide to get it out to do an ID. So we don protective gloves and ease out of the barrel what turns out to be the naked body of a non-Caucasian guy. His skin is a bruised fleshy mass. His legs have been tied together with cables. His hands are trussed behind his back.

There's one thing I'm sure about. He hasn't crawled in there on his own.

Once he's out to head level, I realize it's my worst nightmare. Al Damer, blindfolded, urine drifting around his face. I remember thinking about the distiller. Al Damer's been stuffed into a machine for cleaning up piss. There must be a message in there somewhere.

I ask the recycling manager a few basic questions. No, he doesn't know when al Damer went into the drum, but it was probably between 23:00 and 2:00hrs ship's time. He hadn't seen anything unusual. "I did see some graffiti though," he volunteers. "It's just behind the recycling system."

I knew what I was going to see before I saw it, and—to tell you the truth—that's when my hands got sticky with fear. Directly behind the drum, a green symbol had been splattered on the bulkhead wall. *Protect. Defend. Phalange.*

I call back OpSec. "It's al Damer. Get everyone up and ready." Then I call Jamal and tell him to meet me on B Deck. Right then, my plan was to nick Dennis and Schwerz, go and nick Rashid, and, hey presto, nothing kicks off.

Back on B Deck, the corridor is vibrating with a low thudding sound. As I start wondering about that, my comms buzzes.

". . . all security officers. We have reports of a woman being assaulted by youths. Local comms are down. Please attend Cabin 624 B."

That was a few doors down from Dr. Schwerz's cabin, so I thought I'd kill two birds with one stone. I remember the thudding getting louder as I ran into the European quarter, and then, as I pass through the first set of bulkhead doors, I see two bodies facedown in the corridor ahead.

Dead? By this point in the mission, I don't assume anyone's blind drunk anymore. Then, I recognize the short brown hair. Blood is trickling over his ear. I bend down and check his pulse. Dennis is alive. His chest is rising and falling. I check the guy next to him—no pulse.

Shit. Another dead body—this is really turning into Agatha Christie. Or maybe another golden oldie, *300*, because tonight I'm likely to dine in hell.

I hear footsteps pattering down the corridor. I turn around, adrenaline pulsing, my hands sweating cobs, but it's only Jamal and Larry. I stand with them, while Jamal calls MedLab and tells them to send a doctor for Dennis and the dead bloke.

Then Jamal and Larry fall in with me, and we thunder into the Catholic section. First thing we see, is a cabin door hanging off its hinges. I can hear sobbing in the cabin beyond. I hold up my hand to Jamal and Larry. There's a blond woman tied up and gagged on the bed. She's clothed in a labsuit and soil-covered boots, probably a botanist just come off shift. Her huge, tear-filled blue eyes give me a beseeching look.

I rip off the tape on her mouth. "Thank God you're here," she says, in a strong American accent. "They've kidnapped Wanny."

The name rings a bell. The petite pregnant lady who gave me a cake a few months before.

"Who kidnapped her?"

The woman starts sobbing. "The . . . Arabs . . . fucking Arabs."

"Where are they now?" I ask gently, trying not to scare her. I start to untie her hands.

Suddenly, there's a metallic crash, not far away. A door? Someone breaking a door down. Then I hear a woman scream.

"I'll be back," I tell the woman, and rush out into the corridor. The scream comes again, and I'm trying to follow it with my head. Then Larry says, "down that way," and points through a maintenance corridor, and we go that way, following the crashes and screams.

We come out in the main corridor, right in front of a group of Arab-looking lads gathered around a cabin door. Two of them have a huge oxygen cylinder balanced on their shoulders, which they're ramming into a cabin door. Thud . . . Thud . . .

"Stop! Security!" I shout.

A couple of them turn around. The scrotes with the battering ram ignore me. Thud . . . There's a loud creak, a woman screams inside the cabin, and the door crashes down. Jamal and I rugby tackle the rearmost lad to the ground, pulling his arms behind his back. I'm calling for backup from the crew, while we cuff him and get out the homemade pepper spray. He's screaming and yelling—he can't be more than fifteen.

Two of the lads drag the woman past us, unconscious. Her head lolls forwards, long dark hair tumbling across her slack face. There's no sign this is a drunken brawl—I don't know what's happening.

Larry's pepper sprays another lad. Jamal and I go past him, after the two with the woman. They're heading back down the corridor towards the Middle Eastern section. They stop and look around as we approach.

"Stop! Security!" I shout again.

"Fuck you," says one of the lads. I remember arresting him during the riot.

I realize I can still hear thudding. The lad taps his ear and says something in Arabic, and I realize he's wearing some kind of makeshift communicator. Jamal and I go for him, wrestling him down, cuffing him, and sitting on him, and hoping the other lad will run (he does).

Suddenly, I hear running footsteps in the maintenance tunnel. Abruptly, we've got twenty lads crowding us, armed with steel rods, cables and oxygen canisters. I'm trying to run back down the corridor, knowing they've killed someone already, and thinking that's not how I thought I'd die.

Something hits me on the head.

I feel myself falling, with blows raining down on my head and shoulders. The last thing I remember is heavy footsteps and fresh shouting.

There are coppers you meet on the force who like a good fight—gives them an adrenaline rush. We had one guy, six foot five, ex-army, big guy, played rugby, used to rush headlong into pub fights like a cartoon character. He'd come out with blood pouring down his face, high fiving everyone. He was always getting hospitalized, broken nose, cracked ribs. . . . I used to feel a right wimp in comparison, until the poor sod died in a charity parachute jump. Then I was glad I had healthy sense of self-preservation.

That's not to say I've never had the occasional broken bone on the job, but it's nothing I couldn't handle. I've been concussed a couple of times too, which I'm less keen on, because you see these blokes on the TV, getting hit on the head all the time, and they're drooling vegetables by the time they're forty-two.

I said that to Lizzie when I came around . . . and had my senses back . . . and she just laughed at me. We might be on a moldy tin can, but the UN had spared no expense on a top flight brain scanner, so apparently I was going to be fine.

I wasn't so sure about the UNCS *Cheng Ho*. We'd lost control of the ship. Jamal and Larry had brought me in. They'd been fighting their way out, like I had, when twenty or thirty Phalange rushed in. The guys had risked their lives hauling me out, to MedLab, past twenty, fifty, eighty colonists scrapping in the corridors.

The camaraderie, the feeling of us against the world, that's the one thing I'll take to my grave.

I called Jamal, after a while, for an update. I felt dizzy, queasy, couldn't focus on a book right in front of me, but I felt powerless sitting on my arse (or lying on it, at least).

He was down on the reactor deck with the guys and gals from the recycling, engineering and maintenance crews. They'd had a few colonists trying their luck at taking control of the ship (fucking idiots), but they'd managed to chase them off. I asked him if he had a plan, but he didn't, and I felt sick to my stomach that colonists were smashing up the ship, kidnapping and murdering innocent people, and we were just standing about watching.

You get mood swings with concussion, or—at least—I do. So I got pretty depressed just thinking about it. What sort of security team were we? I imagined myself as Rambo in the old movies, single-handedly taking them down with machine guns, but—realistically—I'd be dead in a minute.

We didn't have the numbers . . .

(*Nor the machine guns, unfortunately*).

I just couldn't help blaming the UN and NASA. Why didn't they think this might happen? We didn't get any training for it (unlike Japanese puppet theatre). Surely astronauts going nuts was a fictional trope.

I started crying.

Lizzie asked, "Is it the concussion?"

And I said, "No, it's the crooks."

We had civilians arriving by this time—injured or just frightened—and she felt sorry for me.

So she was like, "Ach, I'm off shift. Can you look after Hope for me?"

And I knew she was giving me something to do, to stop me dwelling on it. So I said, "Yes," and she bought over a box of toys they'd made in the postnatal group—hand-drawn books on cardboard, cardboard tubes and boxes.

Next minute, she walked Hope onto the ward, and I had a toddler on my hands for the first time in a decade. I remember holding her on my knee, the warm weight of her, looking at the little brown pigtails, feeling her chubby little hands clasping mine, with the memories of my daughter flooding back like a tide.

I sat there, watching the colonists come in wrapped in blood-stained bandages, listening to them talking, telling Lizzie that the Phalange and Rashid's lot had barricaded themselves into their respective sections, and they were scared to go back.

I looked back at the little girl, grinning with a gap-tooth smile, and I thought poor little sweetheart. You don't know what a tough life you've had.

She'd escaped death, as her name suggested, and I thought: you're the reason I became a cop. I'm not going to let you down.

Later that afternoon I met Rashid again.

I was reading to Hope a hand-drawn book about space ships. I wasn't a great reader, with having slightly blurred vision, and the story wasn't great either, but she was an appreciative audience. Toddlers generally are, in my experience. She snuggled down in my lap, and pointed at the wobbly stars and comets, going "Spa . . . Spa . . . "

What a beauty salon had to do with space travel escapes me (ha!), but you've got to make your entertainment somewhere—especially when you're seventeen months old.

Suddenly, I hear voices shouting in the reception area, not clearly, but I recognize Rashid and Lizzie's voices. He's telling her to give him bandages and the triage nurse, a petite lady, to check up his injured cronies and the pregnant women. Lizzie is telling him, she'll treat anyone, but he'll have to bring his injured cronies to MedLab.

By the time I get out the ward, Hope tucked under my arm like a rugby ball (it's an ex-dad thing), Rashid and his five goons are menacing the nurses with sharpened metal bars. They've backed them into the corner of the reception area. Lizzie has her head up, defiant, and her body blocking the doorway to the nurses' office. The other nurse is still behind her corner desk, looking uncertain, but not terrified.

I can't help but admire their guts.

"What's going on here?" I ask.

Lizzie gives me a look of relief. "He wants bandages, and for Maryam to come with him," she says, nodding at the triage nurse, a petite, Eritrean lady with a shy smile and large, wide eyes.

Rashid waves his metal rod at me. "What's he doing here?"

"Ach, he was concussed . . . by your lot," says Lizzie.

Rashid blinks at me. "You've got to get them to help me. I've got people dying," he says, gesturing with the rod.

"You shouldn't have kidnapped those girls then," I said.

He frowns. "I was trying to protect them, Mr. Martin." His voice is that shrill you hear when you attend a domestic. His eyes are red-rimmed and bloodshot, and he's got blood trickling from a wound on his forehead. "My sister was with a European boy, Mr. Martin. Now she is dead. My father is dead." He spat on the floor. "I was taking them away for their own safety."

Shame they didn't agree with you, I thought.

"You've been out there, Mr. Martin. You know I can't bring the injured here. The Europeans would kill them. They want us dead."

I couldn't exactly disagree with him. They all looked like the typical patrons of accident and emergency in the early hours of a Saturday morning . . . or, maybe, as they were sober, the walking wounded in a World War I documentary. They were covered in cuts and bruises. One guy had a makeshift bandage wrapped around his forehead. Another had the blooded sleeve of his sweatshirt pinned to his chest.

Not that I could talk. I had more bruises than an unsuccessful parachute jumper and, right then, Hope was kicking me in the back. I put her down. She ran to Lizzie with her arms outstretched, saying, "Mamma." Rashid looked at her, silently, and I had to feel for him. Hope was his dead sister's kid.

"I'll go," said the triage nurse, Maryam, quietly.

"Ach, you don't need to," said Lizzie, picking up Hope.

Maryam got up from her desk. "They trust me. I became a nurse to save lives. It's my job."

"Just come back, okay?" Lizzie said.

She nodded. "I'll come back." Then she glanced at me and added. "I'd feel safer with Tony along."

And that's how I came to walk across B Deck in the company of five Arab thugs and a small nurse. The only sign of fighting was the occasional dented pipe where someone had got carried away with a blunt weapon. They could've hacked straight through the life support systems. This was among the sane reasons security weren't issued with firearms on the *Cheng Ho*.

Halfway down the corridor to the Middle Eastern section, we came to a makeshift barricade made out of cabin doors and broken chairs. A couple of youths crouched behind it with spears made out of sharpened pipes. Rashid acknowledged them in Arabic, and we climbed over a chair and went on into a cabin with a youth with a leg wound and a broken arm. Maryam set the broken bone, put some stitches into the leg wound, and gave out some painkillers.

In the next cabin was a youth with a head injury sat with a woman who said she was his mother. Maryam checked him over, but said she couldn't do more without the brain scanner. The mother nodded slowly and looked upset.

The third cabin had two older guys sitting with the woman I'd seen being kidnapped. Maryam checked her over, asked if she was pregnant, and reassured her the baby was okay. I asked if she was happy where she was. She said "yes," but kept looking to the older guys for reassurance, and I didn't believe a word of it.

At the fourth cabin, Maryam told me that she wanted to stay with the son with the head injury. She was worried he might slip into a coma. She assured me that she'd return to MedLab once her work was over. I wasn't happy, but I let it go.

I was shit-scared walking the long, empty corridors back to MedLab. The slowly spinning tubes with their bright white lighting at cross-junctions reminded me of every SF horror movie I've ever seen . . . aliens loping down corridors, and all that.

It was a bit stupid of me, to be honest. All the cabins on the corridor were occupied, and I could hear people talking, but you do worry about aliens on a mission like this. Terra Nova is a planet the scientists are pretty sure was seeded by ETs. We all gossiped about it, back on Earth, even when the boffins at HQ assured us there was no sign of them. Seems a bit crazy, thinking back, that I was worried about aliens, and not rioters and crooks.

Turns out I'm too idealistic for a cop.

Anyway, as I gets to MedLab, I see my favorite Polish cleaverman,

Dennis, standing guard outside the door. He's got a kitchen knife and is a crazy nutter when pissed, so I'm not keen on wading in, but then I hear a crashing sound and a woman screaming. So it turns out I've got two choices—stand there like a wet towel or let the Phalange terrorize a bunch of mostly-female nurses, none of whom are over five foot five inches.

My heart's pounding, but I walk straight up past him, like I'm going into MedLab.

"What you doing?" he asks. Luckily, he sounds sober.

"I could ask you the same question," I say.

He glares at me. "Fuck off. It not your business."

I know he's not a trained killer, so I go for the knife, and he's not prepared at all. There's a fight lasting a couple of minutes, in which he yells like a maniac, before I manage to knock him out (not standard procedure) and cuff him on the floor. I'm sure, if I'd been back on Earth, I'd have been kicked off the force for excessive violence, no questions—but I was billions of miles from the Big Smoke, so who cares.

No one's heard Dennis go down.

So I'm on my own.

Looking back, I couldn't have forgiven myself if I'd walked away. So I picked up Dennis' kitchen knife, and pushed open the double doors to MedLab. I was humming the music from an old western. I really felt like I was pushing open the saloon doors, and taking on the bad guys.

The reception area of MedLab looked like a bomb had gone off . . . smashed chairs, broken AV screen, the works. There's a nurse sobbing behind the triage desk, but I don't have time to check she's okay, because I can hear crashing and tinkling glass from inside the main medical suite. I burst through the doors, and run straight into a group of three European guys, all shouting in Spanish as they smash the equipment with heavy piping.

"Security! Drop the pipes!" I shout, and they completely ignore me. By then, I'm looking right and left like a maniac. I can't see the nurses, and don't know whether to save them or the life-saving kit that we need on Terra Nova.

I go for the nurses.

I'm sure I can hear voices on the ward, so I fling open the door, and it's like a hostage movie in there. Lizzie cuddling Hope tight against her chest, about twenty women either pregnant or with babies, a handful of walking wounded, and several nurses, are huddled into the corner of the ward. They're guarded by five European guys, armed with makeshift weapons, a couple of whom I remember from the riot, and Dr. Schwerz in his clean, pressed suit.

Several babies are crying. I'm guessing the Phalange arrived at the same time as Lizzie's weekly post/antenatal class.

Schwerz turns around and stares at Dennis' knife.

"Are you crazy? Stop smashing up MedLab," I shout at him.

"You're not in charge here," he shouts back.

"I don't care who's in charge. Are you bloody nuts?" I say.

I'd have taken on all five of them, but I'm not James Bond—even with a knife. My training didn't stretch that far.

So I walk up to them, and they point weapons at me. My heart's thudding with terror, at this point, and my mouth's like parchment, and I'm certain I'm going to die. I'm literally counting on my natural authority to stay alive, and my belief the Phalange were sorted enough to know that one bloke with a knife, even a cop, wasn't a threat.

"You had Rashid visit you this morning," Dr. Schwerz says to me. "You accompanied Rashid and a nurse, to his sector."

"He threatened us. Tony offered to protect us," shouts Lizzie. "We provide medical services to everyone."

Hope starts to cry.

"You provide medical services to the Arabs so they can carry on killing us and we'll never get to Terra Nova alive." He shouts at her, "You're a traitor to your people."

"She's a nurse," I say, quietly.

"Be quiet," he says. "You've been sympathetic to the Arabs all along. You've favored Dr. al Damer, believed him, when it was obvious he was responsible for my son's death. My only child, Mr. Martin, I have no other."

I can feel the adrenaline pounding. "So you murdered him?"

He raises his eyebrows. "No, sadly, I did not."

I don't dwell on that. Instead, I say, quietly, "You should let these people go. They're just medical staff, pregnant women and babies, and wounded people on your own side."

He stares at me. "My side?"

"I'm on the side of the law," I say.

He stares at me again, and I can feel him weighing up whether to shiv me, and I'm wondering if I'm done for. After what feels like forever, he says, "Very well, you're right. Take these women and children, and go."

Lizzie looks up at me, hopefully. I realized she'd expected to die too. So I think for a second, knowing that I can't take these ladies back to the European quarter, back to anywhere on B Deck, in fact.

Where to go?

We did training on "hostile action" back at HQ (aka aliens—they didn't admit to that). In the case of hostiles, there was a secure corridor between MedLab and the bridge. Reinforced sides, own oxygen supply. Inaccessible from anywhere else on the ship, and protected in the event of a hull breach.

"We're going to the bridge," I say.

I start helping up the injured people, trying to get them moving before this loony and his friends change their mind. Lizzie and I get the women and babies to their feet, and we guide them through the medical suite, to the secure lift. I can't help looking at the broken screens and scattered syringes and medicines—we've got two weeks to Terra Nova and I know people are going to die.

As we get into the lift, my legs start quivering and I'm freezing cold. Maybe we're all going to die. After all, you've got to be pretty crazy to destroy the only hospital for a billion miles.

Crazy . . . or desperate.

I start thinking of my dreams. My daughter running through flames. And I wish I could cry like a babe.

How do you imagine the bridge of a spaceship? I'd bet you're thinking an open space with a wide view into space, glossy screens, holograms and a big leather captain's chair . . . like in Star Trek.

I certainly did. Or I did until I went onto the bridge of the *Cheng Ho*.

Spaceship bridges that aren't on TV are more like aircraft cockpits, or the bridge of a cargo ship. Loads of consoles packed in, bundles of hanging wires, and a low ceiling, with a couple of bolted-down chairs for the first mate and captain, and four doors leading to crew cabins, auxiliary offices, wardroom and officers' kitchen.

With twenty-eight pregnant women, wounded colonists, nurses and kids camped on the bridge and in the crew cabins, the air felt hot and stagnant. Hope and the babies were in makeshift nappies and, within a couple of hours, the wardroom area began to smell of poo. The captain got me to promise to take the women off the bridge once B Deck was secured, but—as the afternoon wore on—I realized it wouldn't be. About 15:00hrs ship's time, we finally got hold of Jamal and Larry. They were still trapped on the reactor deck. The Phalange and Rashid's lot were fighting to take control of the lifts on C Deck, and several dead bodies had traveled down to the decks below.

The master at arms and I went to the captain's cabin for an urgent meeting. Aarav was a tall, stocky bloke, joined the mission from the Indian Army, and didn't scare easily. I'd never seen him look terrified before. The colonists were in full-scale mutiny, he told me. Every ethnic or religious group was holed up in their own sector, and neither A or B Deck was safe.

"How many crew do we have left?" I asked.

"Not as many as the captain would like," he said, looking despondent. "We've got one hundred crew members unaccounted for across all the decks, and half the crew upon the bridge have joined with the colonists."

"Jamal and Larry are with the maintenance and engineering crews," I said. "There can't be more than a hundred mutineers. It's possible we could make a coordinated attack, kettle the troublemakers and space them. It would help if we had the guns."

Aarav gave a throaty laugh. "Dominic-Rubin Frick will not sign off on the guns, even if he had not joined the Phalange for his own self-protection."

My eyes widened at that.

"Luckily, he'd need the captain to give them the guns." Then he added, "You will need to speak to Jamal and Larry. I was in OpSec when the Arabs attacked it. Now Jamal thinks I deserted my post."

I called Jamal who went off to speak to the maintenance and engineering crews. Then I went back to the bridge to stare out of the square windows with their thick, bottletop glass. It felt like being at the bottom of an aquarium. We were within Terra Nova's star system now, and—off to the left of the bridge—I could see the yellow ball of another sun. A bright star was straight ahead and the captain told me that was Terra Nova.

A shiver went down my spine. I remember thinking this was an alien world, and I would be one of the first people to step onto it, not a bad achievement for an ordinary London copper . . . if we made it out alive.

Jamal buzzed me back. My heart sunk the moment I heard his voice. "I've spoken to the crew downstairs," he said. "Sorry, Tony, but they are all in agreement that it's too risky. They have already lost crew to the mutiny and none of them have military training. They tell me they are loyal to the ship, not the colonists, and have enough food stores for a fortnight. They intend to barricade off the reactor deck and life support systems, reach Terra Nova, and let the mutineers disappear into the jungle and kill themselves there."

I told Aarav and we both did a walk around the bridge and cabins. There were thirty people squeezed into quarters made for ten. We went to stand back at the windows. Terra Nova looked a long way away.

Two weeks later . . .

I've never thought about dying on the job. You hear cases of coppers getting killed and, when you're in a sticky situation, that's closest to your mind. But, ultimately, I'd always imagined myself dying in bed, with a cupper in my hands, and my wife and kids weeping by my bedside. Or, at least, that's how I'd imagined it early in my career. Then my daughter died and my wife left, and all bets were off.

We did do the whole death spiel during training. Medical disclaimers, next of kin, video statements that'll get released on your death. So, yeah, you think about it, your nieces reading how you crashed into the sun, or spent your last moments sucking in vacuum.

But you never believe it, not really. And you certainly don't think you're going to die in a scene from a movie—fighting your way off a ship.

A fortnight after the Phalange smashed up MedLab, we arrived at Terra Nova. We had thirty people bunked in the cabin area, squeezed four to a room, with babies crying 24/7. Aarav and I kipped on the bridge, rolled up in spare blankets.

We did eight-hour shifts for twelve days. Riding in the secure lift, keeping an eye on MedLab and the C and D Deck corridors. Before the lift doors opened, I'd patch into shipboard security, but you never knew if you were going to get jumped. The time I did get jumped, I'd got complacent. I think I'd slept three hours that day. I got the lift doors shut, and the colonists couldn't call the lift back down. I took a knife and a padded jacket after that—didn't want to risk the colonists getting past me.

We'd cordoned off part of B Deck with the blast doors, but, from shipboard security, I knew the colonists were still fighting for control of the upper decks. We could see dead bodies in the Ban Kai Moon canteen and I'd started smelling decay when I opened the blast doors. That's a smell you never forget, as a cop, and you can't describe it either. . . . Maybe the stench of garbage left in the sun for a week. You're dry heaving with it and, even when the doors close, you can't get it out your nose and throat.

The day we entered orbit around Terra Nova, I was on shift on the bridge. I remember seeing the planet below us and thinking it was Earth, except—when you looked closely—the continents were different. Otherwise, you could almost think the UN/NASA were playing a cruel joke on us, and the *Cheng Ho* been going around in circles for years.

I told the captain not to say anything until we'd got a plan for getting off this old boat, but—even then—he was an optimist. He believed the colonists would pull together to get everyone down to the surface. Within an hour, the ship was in uproar, colonists fighting on B Deck, trying to get to the shuttles. The Phalange attacked the long-term storage area on D Deck where they stowed the food and weapons.

Jamal's crew, camped on the reactor deck, fought them off with a chainsaw. An hour later, I went to the bridge to catch some kip.

Within an hour, I was woken by a siren howling. So I roll out my blanket and look around the bridge. We're still in orbit around Terra Nova. When I get up, Aarav comes onto the bridge with me, and yells, "It's a gas alarm. There's a gas leak somewhere! The sensors are picking it up."

Anyway, we check over the sensors, and it looks like D Deck/the reactor deck. Call Jamal, who's down there, but I can't raise him on comms. Typical, thinks I, that we get a gas leak in engineering at the eleventh hour.

Hopefully, someone's fixing it, but Aarav and I decide to go down to D Deck, with gas masks and knives, just in case. We check the corridor near the lifts, looks okay, so we go down there, doors open, looks clear . . .

We get out, and suddenly we've got ten European guys hurtling towards us, armed with metal spikes, knives, the works . . . Aarav is hammering on the lift controls, I'm in a floating crouch with the knife, defending the doorway.

The lift doors start closing, two guys try barging into the lift with me. They're both early thirties, both got razor blades. Aarav pushes one of them into the closing door, getting a bloody wrist for his trouble. The door starts opening again. I start fighting with the other one, getting razor cuts all over my arms, trying to twist his arms around his back to subdue him.

After about ten seconds or so, I get him to drop the razor, and—as he's thrashing around—the lift jerks upwards and clouts his head on the handrail. Then I hear a piercing scream, and I realize the other guy is trapped in the lift door. He's half-in, half-out the lift, the lift is going up, and his torso is trapped in the metal doors. He's screaming and screaming—the noise is like nothing I've heard. I look around, and see Aarav has opened the cover to the manual override.

The shit I was fighting hunches over, vomiting on the lift floor. I cuff his hands and turn him around. He's got a bandana across his face with a green tree symbol drawn onto it with felt-tip pen.

"Where's the gas leak?" I shout at him. "Where's the gas leak? Where's Jamal?" He's looking past me, at his mate trapped in the lift doors. I can't see him, but I assume he's dead—he's not screaming anymore, and it's not a pretty sight. I wrestle off the bandana—I'm getting this cold sick feeling that it's a makeshift gas mask.

"Do you know anything about the gas leak?" I shout.

He looks straight into my eyes and starts laughing. "We're gassing the rats," he hisses, coughing. "They're all traitors—we're gassing the rats."

His eyes are bloodshot . . . he's completely doolally. He's totally lost it—either before he got into the lift, or after seeing his mate cut in half. I'm not doing much better. Every time I've woken up, the last fortnight, I've felt this creeping sense of dread. It reminds me of when my daughter died, and I'd wake up every morning thinking *what am I missing?*

I'm not certain I'm going to get off the ship alive.

I grab him by the collar. "Let me get this straight, you and your mates have caused a gas leak?"

"No," he said, staring into my eyes. "We've taken the labs. We're going to get off this ship. We're the chosen ones. We're going to survive."

I remember feeling this red rage overtake me, thinking this psycho was laughing about killing Jamal . . . people I'd served with for three years. I wanted to run the knife right through him, but I just couldn't in the end. Stabbing a guy in cold blood, just pushing the knife into him as he stood there, didn't sit right with me.

I've never been to a war zone. I'm just a cop.

Anyway, back on the bridge, I leave him tied up and gagged in a kit locker. I still have a vision we'll regain law and order, once the colonists are down on Terra Nova, and the colony councils will decide what to do with him, but if he gets left aboard in the chaos, no skin off my nose.

His mate had made a right mess of the lift. So we take the body up to MedLab, and leave it in the mortuary to stop it stinking the bridge up. The saddest bit about that trip is, opening the mortuary drawers, I realize Besma and Hans were never dealt with. They're still there, on ice, waiting for a proper burial.

In the absence of sleep, I spent the rest of the morning trying to raise Jamal on comms. I knew he was probably on D Deck. I knew there was a fight going on down there. I knew the Phalange were trying to gas him.

To be honest, I just wanted to know he wasn't dead.

About 13:00hrs, he finally calls me. "Tony," he starts off, in a resigned voice. "I am calling you to say goodbye to you, and to tell you to get off the ship."

My mouth goes dry. I realize Jamal's dying, or he thinks he's going to die, and this is the end.

"What's going on?" I ask, calmly, trying to not to let it show. "Tony, please make sure that my family hear my goodbye tape. Tell my family that I sacrificed my life to save us here on Terra Nova," he says.

"Okay. What's going on?"

"We are all trapped on the reactor deck, Tony. We cannot get out. The storage area has been filled with gas; we have lost twenty defending it."

My heart pounds in my ears. I barely hear what he says next.

"We think we have minutes before the gas enters the reactor deck. We have no gas masks or space suits. The ventilation is not working. We think the colonists hope to get a shuttle to Terra Nova. It is not my decision, but the maintenance crew have decided to irradiate the reactor deck. I have called you to warn you to get off the ship in case this does not work."

My palms are sweating. "How long do I have?"

A second siren began to howl around the deck, and the lights went dark bloody red. "Engine unstable. Engine unstable."

He was silent for a moment. "Tell my family that I loved them."

"Okay," I say, and then I realize Aarav and the captain are on the bridge looking at me, and Lizzie and Hope are coming out onto the bridge, with a couple of other women behind them. I look at the little girl, and I realize this is like the *Titanic*.

Pregnant women and children first.

"They're going to nuke the reactor deck," I shout to Aarav and the captain. I'm drenched in freezing sweat, cold shivers passing down my spine. I jerk my head to Lizzie and Hope. "We need to get the women and kids onto the shuttles."

Lizzie is crying, big sobs that shake her body. I remember then; after our little girl was killed, my wife couldn't cry. She just held it all in, cold and distant, until she exploded.

I sweep up Hope, put her into a fireman's lift, start chivvying women and babies down towards the secure lift. In my mind's eye, I'm plotting a route to the shuttle bay, to the aft of the ship. I wasn't thinking about dying right then, I was just thinking about getting out, getting the women and kids out.

And that's how I ended up taking the lift down to E Deck, with Aarav and me leading thirty women, babies and injured civvies kicking and floating down the hundred meters or so of maintenance tunnels running down to the shuttle bay.

The main thing that struck me, crawling along, was much how the old boat looked like the closing scenes in a horror movie. The emergency lighting drenched everything in a blood-red gloom and the sirens howled constantly. The air stank of damp and rotten meat, and the walls of the tunnels were covered in mold—I guessed the Phalange or Rashid's lot had wrecked the hydroponics bay. At an intersection with the main corridor, I saw two crumpled shapes— dead bodies, by the smell of them.

We didn't go fast, with multiple pregnant ladies and babies, and I kept having this fear that we'd be irradiated before we got there. As we floated along, the gravity got lower and lower, and I started hearing yells and shouts over the sirens.

When we get to the docking port, I could hear yelling and screaming, so I stick my head out of the maintenance tunnel, and see fifty people scrapping in the tunnel to my right, and the hatch door onto the shuttle bay off to my left. No one looks to have got onto a shuttle, but there are pasta shells and spaghetti floating around, so I'm guessing the fight is over supplies. They must have heard the sirens and the shrill robot voice repeating, "Engine unstable. Engine unstable." So I don't know why they haven't got onto the shuttles. *Twats.*

I duck back into the maintenance tunnel, and tell the people behind me we're going to have to make a break for it.

"We're going to die. We're going to die," someone whimpers behind me.

I'm breathing heavily. I'm not certain I'm going to make it myself. I pull myself out the tunnel, and just float around, waiting for the women to kick past me. They've got babies strapped to their chests, one pregnant lady is bobbing uncontrollably between floor and ceiling.

There's limited heating in this part of the ship, but I'm sweating cobs under my padded sweatshirt—I can feel it trickling down my back. I've got my hand on my knife and I keep looking at the fight. It's a surreal scene—fifty blokes, mostly youths, grappling with each other, droplets of blood floating around them.

After three or four minutes, we've got twenty-five people out of the tunnel. "Cycle the hatch doorway," Aarav yells. "We'll cover you."

As the doors start opening, we start floating backwards towards the shuttle bay, and I start believing we're going to make it. I've only been there a couple of times—on the pre-mission tour and on the job—but I know it's basically a long corridor sticking out the back of the ship with airlocks at regular intervals. If we can get into there, and lock the hatch behind us, we're basically safe from the colonists.

Suddenly, I realize there are three guys in the shuttle bay already—Dennis and two guys in Phalange bandanas. They're clinging to the guide rail beside the nearest airlock and, as we arrive, they start yelling. "Fuck off. Fuck off. Fuck off and die." Five seconds later, they're kicking towards me, weapons outstretched, trying to stick me with them.

I grab the first guy around the neck, pull him towards me, trying to twist the weapon out his hands. I can hear one of them yelling, "I kill you. I kill you properly," and realize it's them or me—there's no good way out of this one. I thrust the knife into his stomach, and he flails away screaming, droplets of blood bubbling into the air.

The other guy pauses, taken aback, and I slash at his shoulder with the knife. My adrenaline is thumping. Something hits me on the shoulder and I twist around to see the second guy spinning off towards the hatch door. He yells, suddenly, and I realize Aarav is slamming his body into the airlock.

Then, I don't have time to take breath, because I'm in a knife fight to the death with Dennis. He stabs me in the shoulder, forearm, and slashes me across the jaw. Then he stabs at my chest, but luckily I'm wearing a padded jacket. I finally get my arm around his neck, choking him out, wrestling the knife off him. I relax my arm, and he drifts away, unconscious, the knife clattering against the walls of the shuttle bay.

A blizzard of blood droplets is drifting off my face and arms, towards the ceiling of the shuttle bay, and I start worrying I'm bleeding to death. Below me, I can hear shouts and yelling, and I notice that about fifteen women with babies are clinging to the guard rails around the airlock. Marjorie Billings-Rajamana is messing with the controls. Her bodysuit is torn and she has a huge open cut across her forehead. No idea where she came from; some of the colonists must have been making for the shuttles.

Two of the women start gesturing at me. As I float down to them, one yells, "Lizzie's still out there." The hatch doors are still open, so I kick my way out there. One of the heavily pregnant ladies is vomiting, next to the guard rails near the maintenance tunnel. Lizzie and another lady are trying to hold onto her . . . and Hope.

"Get into the shuttle bay," I yell, and take hold of the woman's arm. She's gasping and moaning.

Suddenly, the whole ship shudders and the sirens rise to a screech. There's a small explosion somewhere.

"Get into the shuttle bay," I yell, leading the woman by the arm.

Then I hear someone yell, "Kill them," and realize that the Phalange and Rashid's crew have finally spotted us. A second later, there's a ragged cheer over the sirens. Billings-Rajamana has finally got the airlock open and the first group of women are filing onto the shuttle.

I push the vomiting woman forward and two people grab her hands. A few seconds later, she's been pushed towards the airlock.

"Ach, Tony, come on," yells Lizzie.

Hope is crying, her face screwed up, tears pouring from her mother's big, dark eyes. I glance out of the shuttle bay, towards the yelling colonists who are hurtling towards her. I realize there is no time to cycle the airlock shut and launch the shuttle before they reach them.

In my mind's eye, I see my daughter running down the corridor, a fireball rushing behind her. She's holding Hope's hand.

"Lizzie, get Hope onto the shuttle," I shout.

"But . . . but . . . "

"They've seen us. I'll hold them off."

Lizzie heads for the airlock.

The ship shudders again. I turn back around, facing the colonists who are heading towards me.

Tears brim in my eyes.

I've heard about officers dying in the line of duty. But it's not something I ever thought I'd see.

I tighten my grip on my knife, set my ear-mounted comms device to record.

"This is Tony Martin, Security Officer and European Liaison aboard the UNCS *Cheng Ho*," I say. "Whoever finds this, give my love to the ex-wife—I'll always love you. I'll see you, in Heaven, with my daughter one day."

"Now I'm finishing my report here and switching off my personal record."

"Thank you. And good night."

INTERLUDE:
From Jimenez's *History of the Wars of Liberation*

Of course, the result of the *Cheng Ho* Incident was that the ethnically and nationally mixed colonization program was dead literally on arrival. Instead of continuing that approach, Old Earth parceled our world up amongst most of its own nations.

There were a number of interesting effects of this. One was that almost all the nations of Old Earth were recreated here, complete with their old animosities. Another was that, with widely scattered planetary authority, some under their own government, some under the old United Nations, a great deal more creative accounting was possible than might have been under a single colonial office.

Very quickly, in other words, Terra Nova became a highly desirable posting for bureaucrats, nominal peacekeepers, corrupt do-gooders, venal executives, aspirant royalty, and the like, because whatever could be found and sequestered could be kept.

A great deal in the way of illegal drugs, slave-extracted gemstones, and presumptively magic animal parts made their way off planet and back to Old Earth in the holds of the various ships that came and went, supplying, reinforcing, or replacing the Earth's orbiting fleet. It is said, too, that a certain number of slaves, generally female or, if male, very young indeed, were carted from Terra Nova back to Earth where there was no record of them to incite inquisitive police or journalists.

Gold was a big draw. Gemstones were too valuable for simple everyday trading for the necessities and luxuries of life. Slaves were too noisy and obvious, as a general rule. Drugs had an important place in Earth's back market, but also some risks, as did the trade in rare animal parts. But gold? Gold could be coined, measured out by weight as dust, carried without inciting comment. Gold was very nearly the ideal reward for a UN flunky eager to pad his or her nest. And so gold . . .

2.
THE RAIDERS

Mike Massa[3]

Champlain shuffled into the debriefing room at the Neuf Quebecois forward operating base.

Stripped of visible weapons, he still carried the battlefield stink of cordite, aviation fuel exhaust and sweat. Blood, dried to a dark brown, stained his neck and the collar of his combat blouse.

His remaining equipment clanked as he sank into the straight-backed chair.

Across the square table he could make out the gray uniform of his interviewer. Although the carefully placed light prevented him from making out the man's features, Champlain easily read the four gold stripes and blue collar facings of a major of dragoons.

What a dragoon was doing in the Security Police, or SecPol, wasn't as clear.

"Lieutenant, ah, Champlain," the major began, consulting a file that lay open before him. "My name is DeGrasse. You will pardon my insistence that we meet without affording you a moment to rest."

"Get on with it Major!" a second officer entered the puddle of

3 Mike Massa has lived an adventurous life, including stints as Navy SEAL officer, an investment banker and a technologist. He lived outside the U.S. for several years, plus the usual deployments. Newly published in several Baen S/F anthologies, Mike is collaborating with *NYT* best seller John Ringo on two Black Tide Rising novels. Mike is married with three sons, who check daily to see if today is the day they can pull down the old lion. Not yet . . .

urine-colored light cast by the locally manufactured incandescent bulb. "We don't have time for your gentle niceties."

The newcomer wore a spotless khaki uniform. He remained standing so that, like the major, his face remained shadowed. He continued to speak.

"'Acting Lieutenant' Champlain has managed to be one of the few survivors of a critical mission," he spat. "Again. The last time you ran, Champlain, you were awarded a suspended death sentence. If I can prove your cowardice a second time . . ."

"Thank you Colonel Bin Ra'ad," DeGrasse interrupted. "If you would be so kind, allow me to get the lieutenant started."

He turned his eyes to Champlain.

"Simply commence at the beginning of the mission, Champlain," he asked, not unkindly.

Champlain looked down at the table. The fatigue poisons of combat ran thick in his blood. He roused himself and sat a little straighter.

The job wasn't over.

"Sir, the insert started out routine," he began, his words ringing loudly in the small room. "Or as routine as they ever do . . ."

The shakes had worn off as soon as he boarded the transport, hours before. Now, despite the overwhelming pressures of his first operation as company commander, he was composed, focused.

And impatient.

"One minute!"

Senior Lieutenant (acting) Wilsyn Champlain, Second Revanchiste Quebecois Commando, didn't bother to look back at the sound of the rope master's voice. It was pitch black inside their aircraft anyway, preventing any last minute checks. Either their rope and personal gear were rigged correctly, or shortly he was going to be the first man-shaped blood stain outside the personal vacation chateau of the Secordian Army Chief of Staff. Landing normally was contraindicated, since they were about to visit entirely unannounced.

And, you know, there was a sort-of-war on.

In the months since their unit had been formed from barracks dregs and all-purpose fuck ups he had learned that Senior Sergeant "Razor" Bowie didn't need baby sitting. And although he rode the second aircraft with Chalk Two and their Earther advisor, Bowie had trained the rope master on Champlain's bird. That man, Senior Corporal Tremblay, would sooner depart the aircraft without a rope than face Bowie after a fuck up.

Of course, that's exactly what Bowie would make Tremblay do anyway, should he or any "his" noncoms screw up the lieutenant's op.

Approaching the LZ, their aircraft banked hard, and the combined weight of his armor and equipment made Champlain's knees sag despite his iron grip on the chicken rail that ran the length of the troop bay.

Even though the operation was a supposed to be a quick in and out, Champlain carried more than just his allotment of ammunition and demolitions. He also bore several liters of water, enough to make his equipment webbing and pack straps cut brutally into his shoulders under the increased pull of the aircraft's deceleration. Between the long-range patrols that their advisor *cum* instructor had required of them, and the inbred pessimism of a junior noncom breveted to officer, Champlain understood that carrying so much water might slow him down. It still beat the desperation of a parched mouth and swollen tongue while the sun overhead baked you dry, even as enemy rounds pinned you in place and your squadmate moaned uselessly for water from under the bandages that covered his face.

Injuries from Champlain's own fuck up.

"Thirty seconds!"

As the turbine driven propeller nacelles began to pivot upwards into helicopter mode, the previously smooth if overwhelming humming shifted into a syncopated beating of rotors that would have been instantly recognizable to any pre-space flight aircav soldier.

Suddenly the starboard machine gun began to chug. Inside the fuselage, Champlain couldn't tell if there were actual targets, or if the gunner was just spraying the buildings surrounding their LZ in order to discourage nosy spectators.

He approved of outgoing fire, just on general principles.

The priceless tilt-rotor slowed and pivoted, orienting the ramp towards the briefed LZ.

"GO!" Tremblay screamed as he kicked the fast-rope off the ramp. The selected method of insertion had been new to the men, since the helicopters and tilt-rotors it required were not commonplace on Terra Nova.

Suddenly the interior of their ride was lit by shockingly brilliant white light. In the moment of insertion, some local, likely inspired by the rotor noise to figure out what jackass was hovering over their quarters, decided to turn on the court lights. The loss of night vision was instantaneous. Without hesitation, Champlain threw himself off the aircraft ramp towards the thick sisal rope, gripping it firmly in his gloved fists. Despite the thick leather, his palms immediately registered the friction heat which was an unavoidable byproduct of the barely controlled descent. The world spun bright-dark-bright as he dropped thirty meters toward the now fully illuminated emerald green tennis court outside the local officer's mess.

And of course, it left the attacking Rangers pinned to the bright yard like specimens awaiting the collector's kill jar.

At the last moment, Champlain squeezed the rope as tightly as he could, camming his wrists together. The staggering impact of the cement was only partially absorbed by the composite soles of his boots, but he unlimbered his personal weapon and scrambled sideways in order to avoid the descending size thirteen feet of his radio operator, Royce. He squinted into the brilliance, looking for the nearest concealment.

From somewhere off to his right, the familiar sound of another Quebecois-built thirty caliber machine gun coincided with dozens of sparkling impacts across the rows of court lights, which crashed down faster than a strong man could yank a drapery off a wall.

Trust Bowie to get the job done.

The fire rate on the guns was slow, but the relative simplicity of the two-hundred-year-old design brought them within reach of on-planet industry, unlike the aircraft still vomiting out his platoon of thirty.

More importantly, their maintenance was simple enough that even a backwoods Quebecois Commando could do it.

His night vision was still gone, stolen by the short lived but intense electric lights. However, the voice at his shoulder was as familiar to him as the bolt action carbine that Champlain bore.

"Chalk Three is down," Major Hermann Kuhlman said conversationally. "Time to send your breach teams in."

★★★

"Why, exactly, was Monsieur le Major Kuhlman actually on the ground with your company?" asked Bin Ra'ad from outside the circle of light that defined the table. "As a United Nations observer, he was specifically enjoined to avoid direct combat. The Charter of Assistance limits the role of our advisors to training!"

The outburst had the flavor of rehearsed outrage.

"The Major led from the front." Champlain eyed the colonel. The silver globe and wreath of the UN winked conspicuously from the taller man's light blue collar points. "He trained with us for months, set the example after the original company commander was removed. I was in charge, but he taught us, well, everything. Which I think you know."

"Where were your Quebecois instructors?" asked DeGrasse. "Why was Kuhlman so deeply involved in your training?"

Champlain considered his answer carefully.

"We still don't have as much experience in larger formations." he said. "And our unit wasn't used to working together, at first. The major's been to every hotspot on Earth during the last decade. He had five times the combat experience of the most seasoned commando. And he understood us."

"Understood you?" sneered Bid Ra'ad. "What did he have in common with the rabble that he was supposed to whip into shape?"

"We hated him at first," admitted Champlain. "But everything we did, he did. Every forced march, each night obstacle course, every live fire training problem—he was soaked by the same rain and ate the same shit food that you allotted us. Can't do that and not understand the company."

"Quite," said DeGrasse. "And he was your mission briefer as well, Lieutenant?"

"Negative," replied Champlain. "Kuhlman and I planned the actual operation. But Colonel Gagnon supplied our mission parameters."

"And what did you understand to be the primary operational goal for this mission, Champlain?"

"Gagnon briefed us, lectured us really, about the hostage." replied the weary yet on edge officer.

He was tired and still reeked with both the mental and physical residue of battle. Champlain needed a drink, a shower and another drink—in that order. This interrogation could not end fast enough. Still, he had to finish the op.

"Everyone knows that Jacques Hebert, son of the foreign minister, was arrested a few months ago on false espionage charges. They let his school friends go but the Secordians had Hebert in a secure location. We were supposed to get in, grab him and such intel as we could, then extract and bring him home. In exchange, we get our convictions reversed."

Bin Ra'ad snorted derisively.

"That was the deal," said Champlain, leaning forward. "That's why you picked us!"

"You and the rest of the men were chosen because we could afford to lose you," retorted the tall, khaki clad colonel. "You were an expendable forlorn hope. Brig rats. Prison toughs."

Champlain blinked, shocked at the unexpected honesty of his interviewer. He leaned further, meeting Bin Ra'ad's sneer.

"My boys were hard enough and aggressive enough, sure." he answered. "If Command had a better option then they would have taken it. But they needed us and they offered the promise that Quebecois Command would reverse their criminal convictions!"

"And they will, just as soon as we sort out all the questions," DeGrasse said, smoothing over the sudden electric tension. "The legal arrangement is entirely legitimate." He stared meaningfully at Bin Ra'ad, who stepped back half a pace and turned indifferently to examine a wall map.

"Now, please continue."

"Everyone, even our friend from headquarters, made it down in one piece and the tilt-rotors are clearing the area," Kuhlman reminded him. "They're too easy to shoot down and we need them for the ride out."

The company was already spread out, well away from the beaten zone of the LZ, but they remained vulnerable to the inevitable reaction force, which was supposed to be at least thirty minutes away. Third platoon, under Bowie, was detailed to set up a blocking force on the main access road to the compound. Champlain sent Second to screen against the adjoining cluster of military buildings while he personally led First against the officers' quarters and main residence, keeping Weapons platoon in reserve.

"Right, sir," Champlain replied. He turned to his faithful

radioman Royce, "Pass to all teams, take positions briefed." Much more loudly he yelled, "Breachers up!"

Two pairs of men ran pell-mell for the main doors just as a spattering of ground fire began.

The building's stout outer doors were built fortress style for looks rather than to hold off an attacking army, but they still overmatched simple crowbars or hammers.

Plus Champlain was in a tearing hurry.

The breach teams each worked one door, carefully placing the meticulously proportioned charges, just as they had done on the mock-up back home. The pre-made explosives rode flimsy wooden frames whose dimensions were hastily adjusted to each door before the charges were joined with heavily waxed detonation cord.

"Fire in the hole!"

The assaulters and the command group huddled together in the lee of the courtyard, hands over their ears and mouths open to relieve some of the overpressure. The charges went off simultaneously for once and the doors flew apart with a sharp blast and a pattering of wood and stone.

"Attaque!" yelled Champlain even as the first squad rushed the door. He followed immediately upon their heels.

Inside the anteroom there were two men in shirtsleeves, one clutching a pistol, already crumpling. A few more weapons banged as Champlain's men fired into the hallways on either side. He motioned second squad towards one side and dove towards the other, following the team that had already jumped ahead, yelling like banshees.

The hallway was dimly lit and lined with alternating doors, clearly quarters. Groups of three prepared to tackle each room in turn. Two rooms down a Secordian spun into the hallway, leveling a shotgun. Time slowed suddenly as the bore yawned wider than the mouth of hell. Champlain's gut tightened futilely against the expected buckshot before the gun boomed. The shot was answered instantly by several carbine rounds, tumbling the figure back into his room, but not before one of Champlain's men coughed a sheet of blood across his belly and folded onto the floor.

The thick burgundy carpet soaked up Champlain's footfalls as well as the blood draining from the fresh corpses in the hallway. Ignoring the sharp iron scent of blood, he stepped over the casualties and brought his own bolt action carbine to present as the team cleared the next room. More yelling resulted and was met with the muted thudding of clubbed rifle stocks. Moments later that pair of men stepped out of the now quiet room into the hallway, and the next team kicked their door open.

This time feminine screams met their sally.

There wasn't time to collect prisoners, so the prostitutes were left in place, once the room was swept for weapons or combatants.

"We need to hurry, Lieutenant!" Champlain was surprised to hear Colonel Gagnon at his elbow. "We need to check both his quarters and the communications building!"

The short, dour-faced colonel was an unusual addition to the ground team. Supposedly only he could confirm Hebert's identity. In the absolutely regrettable event that the political officer met with an accident, Champlain carried the hostage's recognition picture as a backup. There couldn't be too many soft-faced teenagers in a Secordian brigade commander's headquarters area.

Outside the building more rifle fire rattled as the security element engaged the Secordians who were slowly, but forcefully, reacting. Weapons platoon had been the last on the ground, but judging from the distinctive sound, at least two of their tripod-mounted medium machine guns were now in action. Nothing the Secordians would have immediately on hand could match that.

Or so the intelligence section had assured them.

Champlain could hear more doors splintering as the Rangers cleared the last hallway and entered the target room with a clatter of equipment and the sound of splintering wood.

"Clear left, clear right, one civilian! Wait, he's not here," exclaimed one of his troops. "It's just a girl!"

Champlain shouldered his way into the nicely furnished room. In their haste the searchers had overturned the walnut desk set, and the closet door hung askew from one surviving hinge. The lieutenant saw an obviously terrified young woman in her bedclothes. Sleep tousled bangs framed pale blue eyes and an exquisite heart shaped face whose porcelain skin was the province of only the very young. One of his men watched her at gunpoint.

Champlain stepped closer to the woman, who clutched the deep blue bedspread to her chest.

"Pardon, mademoiselle," Champlain said. "We are here to find Jacques Hebert, to save him. Quickly, where is he?"

"I . . . I don't know," She shook her blonde curls, wide eyed. "I . . . mustn't say."

One of his troopers growled and advanced a step; each additional minute that they tarried invited disaster and every commando knew it.

She shrank backwards even as Champlain raised his hand to motion the trooper to the wall. There was so little artifice in her terrified regard that he instinctively chose a softer approach.

"We are friends and we aren't here to hurt him," he said. "Or to harm you. Please, help me get Jacques home."

Gagnon bravely shouldered his way into the cleared room and produced a small, flat automatic pistol. He aimed it menacingly at the shivering young woman.

"Where is Jacques Hebert, slut?" he demanded. "Answer, or your life is forfeit!"

Behind the political officer, one of Champlain's door kickers visibly rolled his eyes.

"Colonel, I am happy to interrogate . . ." began Champlain but the shorter man waved backwards, irritated.

"I am quite capable, Lieutenant." Gagnon stepped closer to the woman, moving the pistol closely enough that her eyes crossed as she watched the muzzle approach.

"I don't know for certain . . ." she stammered. "He was restless, he . . . sometimes he takes his notebooks and writes in the library, I think. Please, please don't hurt me!"

Champlain fished around in his blouse and withdrew the target map. Scanning for the club area he noted the position of the library and club across the tennis courts, adjacent to a building labeled "Communications." Behind him he heard Gagnon continue.

"And how many guards will he have?"

"Just the night guard sir, please, please don't hurt me!" the woman pleaded.

Before Champlain could issue the orders to clear the room and organize movement to where he hoped they would find the target, the report of a pistol filled the small space.

He snapped his head about in time to see Gagnon holstering his weapon. The stout colonel stepped into the hallway, jostled by Kuhlman, who shouldered his way into scene at the sound of the shot.

He looked at the bed and then exchanged a glance with Champlain. After a pause, both of them turned and followed the political officer.

The teenager lay across the bed, one perfect blue eye staring at the ceiling, and the other a bloody ruin.

"You sound mildly disapproving of the colonel's interrogation technique, Lieutenant," stated Bin Ra'ad smugly.

"I was entirely comfortable with his questioning," retorted Champlain. "I rather object to the murder of noncombatants. Sir."

His last syllable rhymed perfectly with "curr."

"You little jumped-up nobo—" Bin Ra'ad began to sputter. This time the other interviewer pushed Bin Ra'ad back lightly before scooting his chair all the way into the illuminated center of the table.

"Now Wilsyn, you don't mind if I am familiar, do you?" asked DeGrasse.

Champlain raised one hand palm upwards, indicating that he didn't really care.

"Wilsyn, let's back up just a little," He flourished a pack of Earth brand cigarettes.

"Smoke?"

Receiving a nod in reply, DeGrasse tapped out a cigarette and offered it to the lieutenant who accepted both the tobacco and a light.

The little ceremony complete, DeGrasse took a drag on his own cigarette.

"Wilsyn, I want to just briefly touch on your comment about murder," he said. "Did you actually see Colonel Gagnon shoot the, eh, female?"

"No," replied Champlain. "But there's no question that he did it."

"Yes, certainly. But, isn't it possible that at the last moment the woman made some motion or reached for a weapon, compelling the colonel to defend himself, and of course the other . . ." Degrasse paused significantly, ". . . loyal Quebecois in the room?"

"It's absolutely possible, *Monsieur le Capitaine,*" Champlain replied. The friendly smile beginning to spread across DeGrasse's smooth countenance froze as the lieutenant finished. ". . . that the terrified teenage prostitute accessed a hidden weapon in an already cleared room, attempted to murder us all and then somehow disposed of it after Gagnon gallantly defended us from her perfidy."

"It's clear, DeGrasse," Bin Ra'ad spoke into the long pause that followed. "This one is not reliable. We should return him to rot in your gaol, with the rest of the survivors."

DeGrasse watched Champlain patiently.

"I'm not a hasty man, Colonel," he said. "I will complete this interview first and offer Lieutenant Champlain every opportunity to complete his mission."

"Sir, Weapons platoon reports heavy resistance past the original LZ and Bowie at the roadblock wants you!" panted Royce. Following at Champlain's heels as the men moved towards the next cluster of buildings, his message was delivered with the rhythm of his trotting.

"Who wants me?" Champlain yelled back even as he accepted the proffered corded handset.

"Sir, Sergeant Bowie," the radioman replied, shouting to be heard over the now ceaseless background crackle of small arms.

"Go for Charlie Six," Champlain said, keying the handset.

"Blocking force here, Lieutenant," Bowie replied, eschewing radio protocol. "We got vehicles approaching—wheeled APCs. Looks like they got mounted machine guns. We used a few rockets t' make 'em dismount and push on foot, but we can hold ten minutes, mebbee twice that. Then they work around ma' flanks and I've got t'withdraw."

"Casualties?" the assault leader asked.

"Light," the noncom shouted over the sounds of combat. The Crack-Boom! that signaled the launch and nearly simultaneous impact of an outbound rocket testified to the short range of Bowie's firefight. "One deader an' one injured so far."

"The package has shifted." Champlain informed him. "We're searching, but the timeline holds. Even if you can hold longer, withdraw in time to get your casualties to the LZ."

"Copy." Bowie said unceremoniously.

Champlain passed the handset back and felt a heavy slap on his shoulder.

Major Kuhlman wanted his attention.

The broad-shouldered veteran moved lightly in his equipment and the friendly blow was only a reminder, but Champlain had seen him handle two of the worst Commando discipline cases by the simple expedient of picking them up at arm's length until they quieted.

Even Bowie approved of the Earther, and the senior noncom hated officers as a simple matter of principle.

"We've got to hoof it," Kuhlman not quite ordered. "Doesn't matter if the kid's at the club or library. His guards will know that there's an attack underway, but they won't know what we're after."

"So we take this bunch," Champlain said, gesturing at First platoon. "And bust the resistance that is pushing on Weapons platoon. From there we split First and Second and we each take a building. First person to find the boy calls the op and we move Weapons to back Third at the roadblock."

A bullet whirred overhead, the buzzing sound suggesting a ricochet instead of a sniper. Of course, a ricochet in the right place was still lethal.

Standing next to Royce, Gagnon ducked. The other officers declined to notice.

"I like it," Kuhlman gave him a tight grin. "It's a plan, Wil. Prevent the good colonel from exposing himself overmuch but keep him close, he's a caution."

The faintest wink accompanied the last statement.

On the run, the platoon shook itself out into a blunt wedge as Champlain directed the squad leaders towards the two-story complex. Ahead, they see could the irregular lines of muzzle flashes that demarcated the defensive lines of Weapon's platoon, which was now pressed on two sides. The intersecting web of red Secordian and green Quebecois tracers dominated the exchange of fully automatic fire from both sides.

The formation broke into an outright run as they passed a corral of horses that supplemented the base motor pool. The whinnies, snorts and overall movement covered the sound of assaulters as they approached.

Champlain could see that his force had remained unnoticed. The Secordians were wholly absorbed by the action to their front as they gained fire superiority over the beleaguered Commandos' Weapons platoon. Champlain caught Tremblay's eye and gestured sharply toward one end of the line of Secordian skirmishers which was pouring fire into the exposed flank of raiders.

Sucks to be you, boys, he thought.

Tremblay pulled his men into a ragged halt, laying down a base of fire and *carefully* shooting past the remainder of the still running platoon. Their targets included almost a score of gaudily dressed Secordian Marines and one half-dressed officer. The brightness of their palace-ready uniforms didn't reduce the effectiveness of their rapidly firing lever action rifles, which could maintain a much higher rate of fire than the bolt actions carried by Champlain's men.

As the first Quebecois rounds reached their targets, killing and maiming several Marines, Champlain could see the blank O's of surprised faces as the Secordians turned to look behind them. Midway up the defenders' line, one Marine horsed around a large gun. The disk-shaped magazine on top marked it as another example of an ancient design brought back to life on Terra Nova.

The stuttering orange muzzle flash strobed, dropping several Rangers in moments.

"Grenades!" yelled Champlain as he dove into cover face first. Too quickly for them to have been in response to his order, several explosions crumped along the line of Marines, the last centered perfectly on the machine gun. Unfortunately, the detonations were also uncomfortably close to the company commander. Nearest the enemy, Champlain felt the sting of gritty dirt and sand on his exposed neck, but he appeared to have dodged the shrapnel.

His ears rang deafeningly. He must've lost a few moments, because Champlain suddenly registered that the Secordian machine guns had stopped firing. In fact, the entire enemy line was being mopped up. When he rubbed his neck, his hand came away with a smear of blood, underscoring two important lessons: he hadn't dodged perfectly and grenades don't have friends, after all.

"You hit?" Kuhlman asked as he pulled Champlain up to his knees with one hand. The other held a very short, sleek looking gun while the American observer's Quebecois MAS carbine dangled muzzle down from its leather sling. What Champlain had assumed was a binocular case swung open under Kuhlman's left arm.

The major noted Champlain's look.

"I decided to bring along Vera," he explained. "Collapsible over and under pistol caliber carbine. Integrated microgrenade launcher, autoranging multiband laser-optics. Totally proscribed for use here, so don't mention it in your report, all right?"

Champlain shook his head again, and yawned, uselessly trying to reduce the overwhelming tinnitus.

"Didn't see nothing," he answered muzzily. Over the other officer's shoulder he could see desperate attempts at first aid.

"Medic!" Tremblay called. *"A moi! A moi!"*

His platoon had at least a dozen wounded and killed. As Champlain scanned his surrounding, some of the supine figures resolved into men clutching their wounds. Others lay with a limp finality.

"There's no time!" Champlain shouted, shocked by the losses. Despite the residual impact of the explosions, he continued on. "We have to take that building now! Royce! Royce!"

"Sir!" Royce yelled into Champlain's ear.

"Pass to Weapons platoon that we are going to leapfrog into those building," he gestured at the nearby structures. "They're to hold security while we clear."

"Sir!"

Champlain turned to Kuhlman as the latter fitted a matte black block of polymer into the action of his Earth manufactured weapon.

"Where can I get one of those?" he asked.

"Can I get another cigarette, Major DeGrasse?"

Wordlessly, the Secordian intelligence office slid the pack and a lighter over to Champlain. He looked up at Bin Ra'ad.

"Were you aware that Major Kuhlman had imported advanced weaponry, Colonel?" he asked.

"It doesn't matter," replied Bin Ra'ad, folding his arms. "What matters is the mission. We can presume that any evidence of Kuhlman and his weapon were both totally destroyed when the damaged tilt-rotor, imported at great cost by the UN and intended exclusively for medical evacuations *I might add*, crashed. And since the crash site lies in Quebecois territory, there won't be any forensic evidence for Secordia to recover."

Champlain paused for a moment. Bin Ra'ad was clearly rehearsing the lines which he would use to finger the Rangers for an independent and unauthorized mission, should Bin Ra'ad's scheme risk exposure.

"Apart from the bullets," the Commando lieutenant said, hoping to point out the obvious. "The major did a lot of shooting afterwards. By that point everyone had seen him use the thing and it was better than anything else we have. If we had one or two of those per squad, I would've gotten almost everyone out!"

"Your job was to execute the mission with the weapons on hand, Lieutenant," DeGrasse said, sharpening his tone. "That was the whole point."

"Well, you have Hebert back, don't you?" Champlain answered, his voice strained. "So, the next order of business is for Secordian High Command to honor the deal."

"Not quite Champlain," said Bin Ra'ad. "As I suspect you know. You see, we've already interviewed young Hebert."

It cost Champlain the rest of another squad before they reached the final room, having reduced the Communication building to a smoking ruin along the way. In front of Champlain, the lead commando staggered back, his arm riddled with pellets from a defender's shotgun. The last two Secordians fought back tenaciously from behind the shelter of the thick steel radio room door which was jammed slightly open by the commando's last breeching tool.

Champlain decided to donate them a grenade in recognition of their vicious defense. If the kid was inside, tough. They'd retrieve his body, but Champlain was sick of losing men, his men.

His remaining team huddled away from the door for a moment. Champlain straightened and withdrew the safety pin from a fragmentation grenade. He let the spoon fly and then *very* carefully underhanded the fist-sized metal egg through the partially open steel door. The crack of the grenade sounded different, contained by the heavy masonry and metal construction. The overpressure banged the door shut, springing the frame. Thin gray smoke drifted out from behind the security door, now hanging slightly askew. Despite the protection of the reinforced wall, the attackers were still rocked by the blast.

Champlain took the lead position this time and pushed the door open, riding it closely all the way into the room, keeping his carbine up. Quickly, his number two and three men slid through behind him.

There was no more resistance.

He surveyed the room. No hostage. Just wrecked equipment, smoldering paper and death. Radios and maps were decorated with the blood spatter of the last two Secordians whose faces exhibited the gruesome injuries caused by the intense overpressure of the explosion.

"We got him!" in the hallway Royce yelled triumphantly. He waved the handset at Champlain again. "Kuhlman says he's got him!"

Champlain's heart lifted even as his minder sounded off in the hallway outside.

"Where?" demanded Gagnon. "Where's the boy?"

Gagnon had elected to shadow Champlain's detachment. The company commander didn't dwell on the significance of Gagnon's choice, but it did leave Kuhlman alone as he took another group into the adjoining recreation area.

"The major says to come to him," said the radioman, ignoring the Quebecois politico. "Says it's easier than dragging the package directly to us."

"Right," answered Champlain. "We'll head that way. Colonel, stay closer to me this time and keep up. We have to move quickly."

He ignored the glare from the bandy-legged man.

The real problem was the Secordian shelling. One of the armored personnel carriers pushing on Bowie's defenders mounted a mortar. At the roadblock, the Rangers were pinned by the ever increasing small arms fire from the Secordians. Bowie had reported by radio that without overhead protection, they were steadily absorbing casualties from the high angle of attack weapons. The lethal HE shells were relatively inaccurate, but the Secordian design was fed by clips of three shells. The overlapping detonations of each stonk covered enough ground to offset the lack of pinpoint accuracy.

One lucky hit could kill or maim his whole group, so Champlain kept them under as much cover as possible as they ran towards Kuhlman's position.

"*Alors!*" A voice rang out from a doorway ahead. They slowed clumsily, Gagnon rebounding from Champlain's equipment harness before the group filed in, chased inside by a brilliant starshell.

"Here's our man!" Kuhlman brought their target over, effortlessly towing him despite Hebert's seemingly reluctance. The burning magnesium shone through the windows to reveal the rapidly blinking eyes of a pale college age youth. Shadows tilted across his face as the Secordian para-flare scudded ahead of the breeze.

Gagnon muscled through the press of troopers.

"Do you have it?" he asked, his eyes greedily taking in the schoolboy pack that Herbert clutched to his chest. "Do you?"

"Uncle Gagnon!" exclaimed the boy, clearly surprised. "I mean, yes, of course!"

Champlain met Kuhlman's eyes but the Earther only gave him a miniscule head shake in return.

Hebert flipped open the pack, which was decorated with a Quebecois fleur-de-lis patch. The starshell died, so Champlain helpfully used his expensive, civilian pocket torch to illuminate the interior. Hebert's shaking hands lifted a plastic sleeve. Four golden compact discs gleamed, each slotted individually into the transparent plastic.

There was a brief murmur from the ranks. Most of the men had never seen in person what passed for advanced Earth technology.

"CDs?" Champlain asked. "What do we care a—?"

"Close that!" In a single motion, Gagnon slapped the pack closed and yanked the bag away from Hebert. "Classified!"

"Master Hebert explained about the discs already, Colonel," drawled Kuhlman. "He insisted on bringing them with him, you see. Took a bit since he hadn't finished copying the last one over from the entertainment unit in the corner."

He nodded his head at a rare, but clearly damaged Earth made computer. It was plugged into the wreckage of a large televisor unit, and its housing and screen were cracked and starred from heavy impacts—marks about the right size to have come from the buttstock of a Quebecois carbine. A commando stood nearby, carefully holding one of their few demolition packs.

"Also cost us another two dead and one more wounded," he added, "Since the Secordians appeared to object to us fiddling with their video equipment."

"What gives, Colonel?" asked Champlain, turning towards Gagnon, anger tinging his words. "We have the hostage. What's was the point of the discs?"

Advanced technology was sharply limited outside the UN enclave at Atlantis. The optical CDs could be read only by scarce Earth supplied computers. Outside instances where the extremely wealthy could use them on smuggled entertainment units or inside the laboratories of very well funded universities, the number of reliably functioning CD readers and computers was infinitesimally small.

"Although we tried to disable the equipment manually, it needs a little extra effort," Kuhlman said, not quite answering Champlain's question. "Master Hebert also explained the importance of destroying local copies and hiding his activities. Therefore, as soon as we move out, Private Cote will ignite the charge."

"Yes, well, fine," harrumphed Gagnon, grudging approval apparent. "We have what we came for then!"

Champlain looked the question to Kuhlman, who nodded.

"All right, Craveaux," Champlain said to the surviving corporal from First Platoon. "Do a quick head and ammo count, cross load what we have left. Royce!"

"Right here, sir," the tall radioman piped up behind him.

"Get me the Senior Sergeant Bowie. Tell him to withdraw towards the LZ. We'll meet him there after we collect Weapons Platoon outside. Tremblay!"

"Sir?" The assistant rigger was also one of the squad leaders in Second.

"Your job is to stay with Monsieur Hebert," ordered Champlain. "His physical safety is your personal responsibility, which isn't over until his feet touch Quebecois soil. You aren't relieved till I relieve you. Understood?"

"Sir!"

Despite the casualties and his sense of confusion at the byplay between Gagnon, the hostage and Major Kuhlman, Champlain felt a growing sense of elation.

By God we're gonna pull it off!

Then the windows blew in, ahead of a sleet of shrapnel.

★★★

"The data! You have it!" exclaimed Bin Ra'ad. "Where is it!"

"Not with me," replied Champlain.

"Lieutenant, or may I amend, *Captaine* Champlain, you are to be congratulated," DeGrasse said, ignoring the outburst from his partner. "Not only did you extract the boy, but you have preserved the valuable information that young Monsieur Hebert happened to chance upon, as he informed us when we spoke with him."

"Yeah," answered Champlain wryly. "We have the discs that young Jacques made."

"So give them over, now!" ordered the tall UN colonel, stalking over to Champlain's side of the table. "They contain critical, potentially priceless military intelligence!"

"Well, sir," Champlain said, drawing out the last syllable again. "I have to agree that they might be priceless, but I'm not certain about the *military* part. And that bit about 'chanced upon' is what my old tactics instructor would call a polite fiction."

"Happenstance or not," DeGrasse said politely, "The crux of the matter is that you have them and will deliver them to us now."

"And our pardons will be granted?"

"*Certainement*," replied the Quebecois major. Still standing over the tired commando, Colonel Bin Ra'ad partially clenched his hands, like talons.

"I'm betting that our deal is unlikely to be honored once those discs are in your hands," replied Champlain, totally ignoring the Earther. "Unless our signed pardons are in my hands first."

DeGrasse lit himself another cigarette and exhaled luxuriously.

"Exactly what position do you think that you are in, that you can dictate terms, *Capitaine?*" asked DeGrasse. The urbane major presented a small pistol and laid it on the table. "While it pains me to make so obvious a statement, I must insist that you produce the discs now, if you please."

Champlain noted in passing that it was the same model as the gun that Gagnon carried. He looked back up and briefly imagined a bloody red crater where DeGrasse's perfect left eye was. Fatigue slipped away and Champlain chuckled. The smile cracked the blood that had dried on his neck.

"Sure, you can shoot me," he said. "Shooting is easy. But that doesn't get you the discs because they aren't with me."

He leaned backwards, stretching his legs straight out under the table.

"If I don't walk out of here, those discs will remain beyond your reach forever," he said, casually crossing one ankle over the other. "I'm betting that since no one else has checked on us so far, you two are the only ones on this base who really know about the discs. And the UN survey mining assay data on them. Data that is supposed to be locked away in a UN vault in Atlantis and that somehow ended up in the personal cache of a Secordian general."

"What nonsense is this?" Bin Ra'ad said angrily. "How do you know this? Those data are UN property, to be returned immediately!"

"Oh, maybe there are some other conspirators who know about the gold deposits documented in the assays," Champlain continued, ignoring the indignant UN officer. "But Quebecois high command? The High Admiral in orbit? I rather doubt it. And after this mission and the loss of UN aircraft, you won't get a second chance to retrieve the data from anywhere else, if it even exists."

"That damned Quebecois whelp talks too much." Bin Ra'ad ground his teeth. "If he were back on Earth I would teach him, and his father, a very long lesson at the end of a very short stake."

DeGrasse looked at the automatic and then back up, meeting Champlain's eyes.

"We appear to be at an impasse," he said, tapping one manicured fingernail on the table top, a few inches from his gun. "What do you propose? For if as you suppose, we are the only ones who are aware of the mining assay data, then surely we are desperate men. Without the discs, I can't imagine a reason why you should depart this room with that knowledge."

"So we exchange one for the other, sir," replied Champlain. "You prepare the signed pardon for the entire unit, even the dead. You then loan me a phone and I reach a party that will bring the discs to us here."

"You dare . . ." repeated Colonel Bin Ra'ad. "You dare to dictate terms to me! Do you know what I can do to you, to everyone that you care about?"

"I can guess, Colonel," said Champlain. "And that's why we're going to do it my way, or not at all."

★★★

"Sir, sir! Wake up!"

Champlain blinked, his eyes gummy. Cool liquid splashed on his face and he raised a hand to try to wipe it away. It came away red with clotted blood.

"It ain't yours, sir. C'mon, you with me?"

He rapidly came all the way back. Bowie was kneeling next to him in the wreckage of the library courtyard. Champlain drank a little water from the canteen at his lips.

That's twice in one night I've been blown the fuck up, he thought.

In the background, a heavy machine gun stitched the compound. The faster rate of fire identified it as a Secordian weapon. The high-pitched cracks overhead meant that the rounds were still supersonic and the enemy was uncomfortably close.

"Sitrep, Senior Sergeant," Champlain said, slightly slurring the words.

"Tha' Secordians pushed those APCs all the way up and your team got hit by a stonk from the mortar. Gagnon's dead. You're wearing bits of him across your face. Tremblay dove on top of the hostage and caught a bunch of shrap in the neck, he's down hard. Tha' kid, he's shook but okay, hell—Kuhlman even gave him his schoolbag back. Tha' major took what's left of Second to push back on the Secordian react squad. As soon as he left, a pair of sappers tried to blow the courtyard but I potted them before they could arm the charges."

"Weapons Platoon?"

"Sir, there ain't no more Weapons Platoon." answered Bowie. "Major said that you, me and First are gonna head for the LZ. And we have less than fifteen minutes to get there before those fancy tilt-rotors leave without us."

"How we set for the heavy stuff?"

"We're just about out of ammo for the belt feds," the noncom replied. "I used tha' last of tha' rockets to break contact in order to get here, just to have that crazy Earther go right back out t'tha' road. If youse tired of living, we got those sappers' demo charges and that's it."

"Right, help me up," the lieutenant ordered, after a very brief pause. He and Bowie clasped forearms and Champlain stood all the way up, barely swaying.

"Everybody's getting out, Razor," he said. "Even the wounded. You organize movement to the LZ. Protect the package at all costs. I'm going for Kuhlman and Second and we'll fight our way back to the LZ. If we're not there in twelve minutes, you get the fuck out. Got it?"

"Sir, you're a crazy fucker," replied Bowie. "But it's your call."

"Royce, on me!" ordered Champlain. "We're heading to the sound of guns."

When radioman and his officer left the courtyard, Champlain was barely weaving at all.

The fighting was a lot closer than when Champlain had entered the building. Red tracers spurted overhead. Periodically they ducked when they heard the faint whistle of a mortar round descending on final trajectory.

Overshooting their objective, they nearly surprised the crew of a Secordian APC that was gathered on the open ramp of their vehicle, arguing on their radio. Hastily backtracking around a low brick wall, they crawled as fast as they could heedless of the skin on their knees and palms. Two hundred yards further on they came to an abrupt halt.

"*Sans Peur!*" came a harsh whisper from ahead.

"*Coeur robust!*" replied Champlain, completing the challenge and password. "Where is Major Kuhlman?"

"Over here, sir."

They followed a Second platoon runner to the UN major who was peering through the sights of his high tech weapon, which projected a faint green glow on his brow. To either side, the remains of Second were strung out in hasty firing positions that blocked the road leading further into the Secordian base. Less than fifty yards away, an APC was stopped in the middle of the road, pale flames licking up from the open driver's hatch.

A few still bodies lay beside it, illuminated by dull orange flames that dripped from the undercarriage.

"I thought I saw a couple friendlies scuttling about out there," Kuhlman said conversationally, scanning the near distance. "Figured it was Bowie, not you."

Intermittently, commando carbines answered the much larger, but diffuse, incoming Secordian firepower.

"Major, we got to get the fuck out, now!" said Champlain. "Birds are gonna leave in less than ten minutes."

He glanced at his luminous wristwatch.

"Make that nine minutes!"

"Thing is, Wilsyn," Hermann began to answer. He paused, and his weapon coughed once. "That's eleven."

"Thing is," he repeated. "The moment we pull out, the Secordians are going to roll 'hey diddle-diddle' right up this here road all the way to the LZ."

He turned to look directly at Champlain, carefully keeping his modern weapon pointed down range.

"If they get line of sight to the extract birds then no one goes home," he said exasperatedly. "My way, at least you were going to get out with kid and have a shot at freedom for your men. But without you, whoever Gagnon was working with will just roll over top of the survivors. No pardons for any of you, get it?"

"So we use these," answered Champlain, shrugging out of his pack in order to reveal a linked pair of scratch built Secordian demo charges. "My radioman has two more."

He tumbled out the crudely taped and fabric wrapped bundles. A coil of yellow prima cord and metered pull ring fuses flopped to once side, making Kuhlman wince.

"Well, ordinarily, given the choice between chancing a demo charge improvised by what passes for a demo expert on this planet and wrestling a bear," Kuhlman said, more closely examining Champlain's payload. "I'd say, bring on the b'ar. But . . ."

His fingers gently plucked at the connections, checking the integrity of the explosives while Champlain spoke aloud.

"We give them a final defensive fire, set the charges to stagger every minute and haul ass," the Quebecois lieutenant urged. "By the time that the last one goes, we're all the way to the birds. So fuck your b'ar, sir. Everyone goes home."

It worked.

The first of the charges appeared to stun the Secordians and covered the withdrawal of the remains of the Second. After the first burst of speed, the dozen or so Rangers slowed from their initial headlong sprint into a more sustainable running pace. The slow motion ripple of subsequent explosions along the road must have done the trick.

Or near enough that Second just passed the crest of the rise that shielded the LZ before the first Secordian APC poked its snout through the wreckage of the Secordian base, emerging into view.

A dozen meters behind the survivors, Champlain brought up the rear, trotting alongside Kuhlman, Royce faithfully dogging his heels. The feeling of elation was stronger now. The rotors of the aircraft were plainly audible over the sound of small arms and the faster Second platoon Rangers were already descending towards the LZ.

Champlain flashed a wide grin at Major Kuhlman, who just shook his head, returning a more restrained smile.

The merest whisper overhead was all the warning that they had, before the faithful radioman tackled his officer to the ground, even as the triple hammerfist of mortars bracketed the road.

Three times. That's three fucking times I've been blown up tonight. Fucking mortars. thought Champlain. He struggled to roll a soft, heavy weight off his back.

"Royce, hey Royce!" the commando officer said. "Hey, man, you all right? Get up, Royce!"

He felt warm wetness soaking his shirt.

Though the radioman didn't answer, some slight movement suggested that Royce was alive. But when Champlain finished sliding out from under his man and carefully sat up, the gush of lifeblood spilling from the radioman's gaping head wound was already slowing to a trickle.

Kuhlman was alive, however.

"Hey Wilsyn," he said. "Now you got to beat it."

"Let's go, sir!" Champlain crawled the short distance between them. "We got to go!"

"Can't feel my legs." The UN officer coughed, and a light pink froth speckled his lip. "Can't see too good; look there's something you need to know."

Champlain let him talk, but ditched his own equipment. It was the work of a minute to sling the Earth made gun across his chest, and then roll Kuhlman to a sitting position without hurting him too much. Despite Champlain's best efforts to be gentle, a grunt of pain interrupted the major's message, which he hadn't stopped muttering.

With a muscle-tearing effort, Champlain got Kuhlman's weight across his shoulders and then straightened.

A few more shots whined overhead but the extract aircraft beckoned just down the slope. A spill of light shone like hope, and his Rangers were waving him on.

Bowie entered the room, Hebert's backpack hanging negligently from one scarred hand. In the other an olive drab steel egg was partially visible. The grenade was tightly enfolded in the big man's fist and no one missed the glaring detail of the safety pin missing from the striker device.

"Over here, Razor," said Champlain, beckoning him closer. "Keep a hand on the bag, but let Major DeGrasse here have a look on the table."

Cigarette dangling, the intelligence major flipped the bag open, the fleur-de-lis winking like quicksilver in the dull light. If the grenade bothered DeGrasse, it wasn't evident. He looked inside where the CDs gleamed, easily visible. DeGrasse nodded to Bin Ra'ad.

"Here, you rotting extortionist!" the UN colonel said, angrily shoving a sheaf of paper over the table. "Take your pardon and pray that we never meet again."

Champlain nodded as he read the top page, examining the signatures, the great seal of the Terran Novan nation of Quebec and the counter stamped endorsement of Atlantis Command.

"Colonel, that's my earnest desire," he said. "And given what Senior Sergeant Bowie is capable of, you might want to make that a mutual wish. In fact, the sergeant has had a particularly trying night. We all benefit from him not suddenly deciding to frag the officers that cost us three quarters of our team."

He nodded to Bowie, who slowly relinquished his hold on the pack. He kept the grenade visible.

"Thank you *Capitaine* Champlain," DeGrasse said, replacing the flap on his pistol holster. "You have my word that it ends here."

"I know what you word is worth, Major," Champlain said, folding the pardons and tucking them inside his blouse.

A sudden bitterness invaded his tone for the first time.

"And I know why you arranged this entire mission. In fact, I'd wager these pardons that the only ones who were supposed to know about the existence of the UN assays were Gagnon, the kid's father and you two. You dare not tell anyone else or you would get in trouble. Not for raiding Terran Novan gold from under our noses but because you didn't invite anyone else in. The High Admiral would certainly take exception to missing his cut, no?"

"As you say," replied DeGrasse. "But this business is complete. Take your pardons and your men and enjoy your life. *Bon soir.*"

Champlain rose and walked to the end of the hut, the papers crinkling audibly under his chin. He held the door for Bowie, who continued to look at each of the two officers.

The fingers on his grenade hand whitened for a moment.

Bin Ra'ad sneered but otherwise remained silent as the tall commando slowly backed to the door.

Outside, they quickly exited the checkpoint manned by a pair of Security Police.

"You mind sliding the pin back in that bombe, Razor?" asked Champlain.

"Naw, sir, I don't mind," said Bowie, fishing in his pants pocket for the cotter key that would secure the grenade's bail. "I just wish that I'd tossed this into the hooch as we walked out. Really chaps my ass that those spooks are gonna make money off our dead. Doesn't feel right."

"Here's your pardon Top," said Champlain, tapping his blouse. "That should feel pretty right. Besides, they've got the CDs. I didn't say shit about promising them the data."

"Huh?"

"Before I got Kuhlman out," Champlain remarked. "He told me what was what. During the confusion when we got mortared the first time, he used the ranging laser on his fancy gun to light up the discs."

"So what, sir?" replied Bowie.

"Kuhlman was an Earther, trained on high tech," said the officer. "The UV range finder was in the same wavelength as the lasers used to record the data. He scrambled the CDs so that the data was trashed without leaving any marks. It'll just look like they didn't get copied properly. That's on the kid."

"The kid that we thought was the whole point of the op?" Razor started laughing. "The kid that already pissed off that tall UN asshole?"

"Yeah, the kid that I risked my life, your life, all of our lives for," Champlain shared a final, feral grin. "I'll risk it all, *risk us all*, for *la belle patrie*, or to save a hostage. But, I'll be damned if I'll do it so some UN Earther or SecPol can make a fortune. And Kuhlman? He felt the same way."

INTERLUDE:

From Jimenez's *History of the Wars of Liberation*

It is altogether too easy for us, from the vantage point of almost five centuries, to look back on the old UN, the predecessor of Old Earth's Consensus, as being nothing but a hive of corruption and villainy. Certainly there was a good deal of that, but also there were good men on the other side, as the wars began to unfold, fighting well in a bad cause. Sometimes, they even fought well in a *good* cause. . . .

With control of space, and no genuinely heavy manufacture anywhere on the planet in the early years—small engines, flintlocks, wooden ships, and a little surface collection of petroleum were the height of industrialization on Terra Nova for at least seventy years, and even then rare—the UN was in an excellent position to create of the planet its bureaucrats' wildest fantasies by withholding arms from Faction X and giving them to Faction Y.

One reason it never quite worked that way appears to have been the nature of the UN, itself, being both factious and fractious. There were high ranking Muslim bureaucrats, who favored their co-religionists on planet, just as there were Catholics, Jews, Atheists, and Communists. And that was only one fault line in the UN's colonization regime. There were also ethnic splits, with Han favoring Han, English speakers favoring "the cousins," Spanish speakers doing no less for their co-culturalists.

3.
SACRIFICE

Peter Grant[4]

Father Francisco shivered, pulling his ankle-length cloak closer around him as he walked down the hill in the half-light of dawn. He watched the boats pull into Pescara's little harbor, the rumble of their engines echoing off the stone quay and the walls of the processing sheds. Clouds of dirty smoke drifted up from their exhausts, and the slowly undulating water was churned to white froth as they jockeyed for position. Those who'd had good catches headed for the processing sheds. Those who'd been less fortunate pulled their vessels into berths further away or tied them up to a row of buoys on one side of the small harbor.

He stopped at the corner of a shed, watching as the burly skipper of a big, blue-painted fishing boat argued prices with a buyer. Their gesticulations and loud, histrionic discussion eventually subsided, and they shook hands as the bargain was concluded. The buyer gestured to his clerk, who dug out a form and began writing on it as a quayside crane hoisted the big fish boxes out of the hold and stacked them at the entrance to the shed. Teams of women wearing

---

4 Peter Grant was born and raised in Cape Town, South Africa. Between military service, the IT industry and humanitarian involvement, he traveled throughout sub-Saharan Africa before being ordained as a pastor. He later immigrated to the USA, where he worked as a pastor and prison chaplain until an injury forced his retirement. He is now a full-time writer, and married to a pilot from Alaska. They currently live in Texas. See all of Peter's books at his *Amazon.com* author page, or visit him at his blog, Bayou Renaissance Man.

heavy rubber boots, long waterproof coats and protective gloves emptied them onto the sorting tables, cleaning the fish before tossing them onto conveyor belts that whisked them into the freezer plant. Gulls circled eagerly overhead, screeching their anticipation of the fish guts that would soon be their breakfast. The most daring among them hovered just above the sorting tables, pecking at the offal as the women swept it into the water-flushed gutters that would carry it into waste tanks, and thence into the harbor, where seals and other scavengers waited their turn.

The skipper accepted the form from the buyer's clerk, scanned it swiftly, and nodded his satisfaction as he folded it and slipped it into his pocket. He half-turned away, then caught sight of the priest waiting at the corner of the shed. He stared at him for a moment, then nodded, very deliberately, and held up one finger. Father Francisco nodded in reply, then turned on his heel and headed for the café at the head of the dock. He walked through the rapidly filling dining area to the counter, ordered a coffee, then sat down at an empty table at the rear of the room.

The boat's captain came in about twenty minutes later. His *basso profundo* voice rumbled as he ordered coffee and a mammoth fisherman's breakfast, then sat down at the same table.

"You are well, Father?"

"I am, Ramon. The fishing was good?"

"It was very good—one of the best nights of the season so far, thanks be to God and Saint Peter." The big man grinned as he sipped his steaming coffee. "That makes me laugh. You answer to the See of Peter, and we sail the sea of Peter, patron saint of fishermen."

The priest couldn't restrain a chuckle. "Yes, but at least my see won't drown me if I make a mistake. Yours will!"

"I suppose that's why we both need Saint Peter's intercession, eh, Father?" The man looked around casually, to make sure he was not being watched, then drew a small envelope from an inside pocket of his dungarees. "Abdullah made rendezvous, Father. Here is his message. He also gave me some more information for you—new things, very bad things."

"Oh?"

A heavy sigh. "He says that yesterday morning, ten members of the *Ikhwan* arrived at Alsamak. They brought with them weapons, and are going to teach the villagers how to use them. They say anyone who doesn't report for training is a traitor to Allah and unfit for jihad. They'll be treated as infidels and apostates, to set an example to the rest. They've already killed three men who protested, including the Imam. They say it's the duty of all true believers to drive out the 'crusaders,' as they call us. They've claimed this island for Allah."

"The whole of Pescara, not just their village?"

"That's what Abdullah said."

"What is he going to do?"

"He said he can't abandon his family to the Brotherhood. He asks your forgiveness for what will probably happen now. He says he won't be able to make rendezvous again."

The priest's face twisted in sympathy. "God help him, then. Abdullah's a good man, but he's no match for fanatics. The *Ikhwan* have been spreading their poisonous tentacles throughout his people for years. Now they're in his village. He'll have no choice but to fall into line with them, or die."

"But . . . what can we do, Father? We have no way to resist armed fanatics! Even if we had enough money to buy guns, no one would sell them to us. We're just a poor village of itinerant fishermen at one end of a rocky, worthless island. We're not important to anybody. We can't ask the UEPF for help, even though we sell much of our catch to them on Atlantis, because they won't get involved in local disputes. They even search our transport, coming and going, to make sure we aren't smuggling contraband."

A harried waitress slammed down a huge, heavily laden plate in front of the fisherman. "Eat it while it's hot!" she admonished as she hurried away, avoiding the seaman's attempted pinch with a practiced twist of her ample posterior and a playful swat of her hand.

The priest thought, while his companion took a big mouthful of food and chewed mightily. "Did Abdullah say where the Brotherhood were staying in Alsamak?" he asked.

The skipper swallowed. "He said they'd commandeered one of the processing sheds in the harbor to store their extra gear. After they killed the Imam, they took over his house next to the mosque for themselves. One of them will do the preaching from now on."

"That gives me an idea. Go home, get some sleep, then pass the word to Dimas and Guillermo. I want the three of you to meet with me at the rectory after Mass this evening. Don't be late, and don't mention this to anyone else, get it?"

"Is this about the Brotherhood?"

Father Francisco shook his head. "Don't ask me questions yet. I'll tell you more tonight."

The fisherman nodded slowly. "Very well, Father. We'll be there."

Rain was falling softly as the congregation assembled for Mass that evening. There were more worshippers than usual. Despite the priest's injunction, word had spread of the clandestine encounter the night before. The arrival of *Ikhwan* fanatics on the island had set everyone's teeth on edge. There were many tales of what had happened to other communities they'd targeted . . . none of them good.

After the service, Father Francisco took off his vestments, then opened the door of his small rectory next to the chapel to let in his visitors. The fishermen were surprised to find three more people waiting inside.

"I think you all know Zacharias, Nicolau and Esteban," he began as they sat down. "They served in the army, as I did. I rose to troop sergeant. Esteban was a sergeant, Zacharias was a corporal, and Nicolau a lance-corporal."

"I didn't know you were a soldier, Padre," Guillermo said, his eyebrows rising in surprise.

Francisco shrugged. "It was a long time ago, but we all remember our training. If we're going to face Brotherhood fanatics, the four of us will have to teach the rest of you how to defend yourselves."

"With what?" Dimas demanded. "We have no guns!"

"Not yet."

A sudden silence fell around the table as they looked at him. At last, Ramon said cautiously, "Father, you're a priest now, not a soldier. Priests aren't supposed to be men of violence."

"In normal times, you'd be right, my son; but these aren't normal times. Besides, violence isn't always ungodly. Didn't our Lord say to his apostles, 'When a strong man, fully armed, guards his own palace, his goods are in peace'; and again, just before His crucifixion, 'He who has no sword, let him sell his cloak, and buy one'? That was to his *apostles,* mind you: the future founding bishops of the Church. If it was in order for them to be armed, it must also have been in order for them to use their weapons. The one implies the other."

"I . . . I suppose so. What is it you have in mind, Father?"

Three nights later, two of Pescara's larger fishing boats put out to sea after full dark had fallen, to prevent prying eyes from seeing what they were about. At the northern tip of the island, three hours later, farewells were shouted across the gap between them. Guillermo turned his boat to the west. Her holds were filled with barrels of extra fuel, and her crew quarters stuffed with food and other supplies for an extended voyage.

"Do you think the authorities in Castilla will listen to him, or the bishop to your message?" Ramon asked softly as they watched his vessel fade into the night.

Father Francisco heaved a sigh. "I truly don't know. That's why I gave him the second message, to a friend in Balboa. If the authorities won't listen, he will."

"Let's hope someone will help, not just listen!"

"From your lips to God's ears, my son. How long to Alsamak harbor?"

"About two hours, Father."

The priest took his pipe and tobacco-pouch from a pocket, tamped down a bowlful of tobacco, lit it, and puffed contentedly as he thought about what was to happen tonight. With luck, nothing would go wrong . . . but he'd learned the hard way, and far too often, that military operations seldom went according to plan. At least he and the other three wouldn't be coming at this cold. They would need every bit of their prior training and experience if they were to succeed tonight.

He ran his eyes over the rugged terrain of the island as they chugged along, a few hundred yards offshore. It was almost barren, growing nothing but scrubby, tangled thorn bushes between its rocks, and had no other resources, which is why no major nation had ever bothered to claim it. It rose steeply from the coast to a jagged, uneven ridgeline, forming a spine running the length of the island. Pescara was at the southern end, Alsamak at the northern. Both had been founded to serve fishermen during the summer, and were almost deserted at other times.

As they drew nearer to Alsamak, Esteban joined him in the stern. "Ready, Padre?" he asked softly, taking a sharp bayonet from its sheath at his belt and testing its edge against his thumb.

"I am. Be careful with that thing. Remember, we want no casualties tonight if at all possible, on their side or ours."

"I hear you, but the enemy gets a say, too."

"Too true!"

"Did you bring your little souvenir along?"

Francisco patted the left chest of his bulky jacket. "It's in my shoulder holster now."

"What made you bring a pistol with you to a fishing village?"

"I suppose it's the same thing that made you bring that bayonet. I'd have felt lost without it."

"You know the planetary authorities have declared guns contraband out here, so close to their observation post at Jebel Musa?"

"What gun? You said it yourself. It's just a souvenir of past times and good company."

"Sometimes not so good, as I recall, but who am I to argue with a priest?" They laughed softly together as he handed over a heavy, tubular object. "Here. Wet sand in a sock. It makes a handy cosh. We all have one."

"If we need any weapon at all tonight, let's try to use these rather than something more lethal."

"If you say so, Padre, but those *Ikhwan* bastards won't be so kind-hearted if they see us coming."

"If they see us coming, we're beaten before we start. Pray they're fast asleep."

"They should be by the time we get there, unless they've left a sentry at the harbor."

"We would, if we were in their shoes. Don't assume that just because they're extremists, they're also stupid."

Ramon throttled back the engine when they were a mile out, and they coasted slowly towards the small fishing harbor. The skipper and Father Francisco scanned the port carefully through night glasses as they approached, the big binoculars gathering every scrap of moonlight and concentrating it in the optics. No movement was visible, and only two boats swung at the buoy line.

"The rest are out on the fishing grounds," Ramon murmured, "taking advantage of the full moon. It'll bring the fish to the surface."

"When do they return?"

"The last moon sets at zero-four-thirty or thereabouts, so they'll start back soon after that. They should begin trickling in at about zero-seven-thirty. We'll be long gone by then. I'll go back round the other side of the island, so they don't notice us."

"Very well. I'm worried that the Brotherhood may have left a sentry to guard their gear. Esteban and I will row ashore in your dinghy, and make sure there's no one to sound the alarm. Wait offshore until we signal you to come in, then make as little noise as possible."

"Do you know how to row?" the skipper asked, surprised.

"We both trained with paddles and inflatable boats, once upon a time. We'll each take an oar, and paddle your dinghy the same way."

The fisherman shook his head. "Sounds daft to me, but I've never rowed like that. Good luck to you."

They hauled in the dinghy, towed astern of the fishing boat, and climbed over the side, settling themselves on the thwarts and picking up the short oars, holding them like paddles. The boat towed them to within half a mile of the harbor entrance, then released them to cover the rest of the distance under their own steam. They began plying their paddles, moving slowly and carefully so as to avoid splashing and making a noise.

By the time they were halfway to the entrance, both men were breathing heavily. "Damn, I'd forgotten how much hard work this is!" Esteban whispered.

"I hadn't realized how out of shape I've become," Father Francisco admitted *sotto voce*. "Our assault training instructors would fail both of us on the spot, if they could see us now."

Chuckling softly, they plied their paddles with renewed vigor.

As they drew near the entrance, the priest whispered, "Let's land on that patch of sand outside the breakwater and walk up round the back of the processing sheds. That way, if anyone's patrolling, they won't see us enter the harbor."

They pulled the dinghy up onto the sand, stowed the oars carefully, then took a moment to recover their breath before walking up the rocky slope to the edge of the breakwater where it joined the land. They looked around carefully, but saw no one. However, the biggest and most distant of the processing sheds showed a light inside, visible through a small side window.

"That must be it, Padre."

"Don't speak too soon. There are five sheds. Let's check each one in turn, very carefully."

Slowly, moving with agonizing care so as not to make any sound, they checked the nearer sheds. All were empty. By the time they came to the largest shed, the clock had ticked past zero-one-hundred.

"We've not got much time," the priest whispered. "We've got to be out of sight of the port before their fishing boats come back."

"Do you see any movement?"

"Not through the side window. We'll have to go in. Let's use the back door."

They crept around the shed to a rough-hewn wood door, looking as if it had been knocked together from the planks of derelict fishing boats. Esteban grasped the handle and turned it carefully, then pulled the door open. They both winced as the hinges squeaked and squealed an urgent protest at being disturbed.

A voice came from inside. Both men could understand the gist of it, having studied Arabic during their military service, it being the language of their most likely opponents. "Is that you, Akbar? Couldn't you sleep, or something? You're only supposed to relieve me at four."

The priest thought fast, and mumbled aloud, "Yes, it's me," as he stepped inside, trying to disguise his voice as he drew the pistol from its concealed holster. Behind him, Esteban slipped through the door and to one side, moving behind the cover of a row of crates.

"What are you chewing?" the other demanded, drawing nearer. His footsteps sounded from beyond the crates. "Did you bring some for me?"

The priest lined his pistol as a man appeared around the crates. He was young, his long black hair and unruly beard making his face look shaggy and unkempt. An automatic rifle was slung across his chest. His eyes widened for a brief, incredulous instant, then he drew in a sharp breath as his hands snatched at his weapon—only to slump as Esteban stepped out behind him and swung his cosh viciously against the back of his head. Francisco jumped to catch him before he could hit the ground, lowering his body silently so that his rifle didn't clatter on the concrete floor.

"Nicely done, *compañero!*" he praised.

"*De nada.* He was careless. He should have been more alert."

"I'm glad he wasn't. Watch him. I'm going to make sure there are no others."

The priest paced slowly and carefully through the big shed, finding no one else present. A dozen big wooden crates were piled just inside the open loading dock, facing onto the quay. His eyes gleamed as he saw them.

He hurried back to Esteban. "The weapons are there. We must hurry if we're to load them and get away before his relief gets here. I'll signal the boat."

Esteban nodded as he took the sentry's rifle and slung it over his shoulder. "What should we do with this *cabron*?"

"We daren't leave him here to tell the others what happened. He has to disappear, to add to their confusion. We'll take him with us."

"Where are we going to keep him? We have no cells."

"We'll cross that bridge when we come to it. Drag him over to the crates."

The priest hurried out of the loading dock, looking seaward to the faint bulk of the fishing boat, half a mile offshore, but visible in the moonlight. Taking a small flashlight from his pocket, he aimed it at the boat and pressed the button three times. He sighed with relief as a single flash came back. The boat's bow swung towards the harbor as it began its approach.

Francisco spun around as the noise of a scuffle came from within the packing shed. He ran back inside, to find Esteban standing over the sentry, puffing and panting. His left hand was locked tightly around the man's neck, and his right held a bloody bayonet.

"What happened?"

"This bastard tried to jump me. Luckily, I got my fingers around his windpipe, to stop him shouting. I was able to get my bayonet out while he struggled to pull my hand off his neck. It was him or me, Padre." As he spoke, the figure at his feet gave a final shudder, and went limp.

Francisco felt a chill run up and down his spine. The Brotherhood would never forgive or forget the death of one of their own. He knelt, laid his hand on the dead man's forehead, and prayed silently for a moment. Even though the sentry had been of another faith, and probably guilty of many crimes, he would not willingly see any man in Hell, to be punished for all eternity. *If it is possible, Lord, let his sins be forgiven him,* he prayed mentally. *May he be washed in the blood of the Lamb, and find mercy—and may we, too, be forgiven for what we have done this night. I don't think we could have done anything else . . . but forgive us, too.*

He rose to his feet. "Make an act of contrition, Esteban."

The other bowed his head. "Lord Jesus Christ, son of the living God, have mercy on me, a sinner."

Father Francisco spoke the formal words of the absolution, making the sign of the Cross over his comrade as he did so. "This is to take care of things if we should meet more trouble tonight. See me for confession as soon as you can when we get back, and we'll do it properly."

"Thank you, Padre. What about him?" He indicated the body on the floor.

"Wrap him up in that tarpaulin. Tie it securely with plenty of turns of rope, up and down its length. Make sure there's no blood left on the floor, or any sign of a struggle. Get his ammunition and empty his pockets before you wrap him up. We'll take it all with us, and bury him at sea. Find something heavy to tie to his feet, to make sure he sinks and doesn't come back up."

While Esteban went about his grisly task, Francisco lifted the lids of a couple of crates that had already been opened. He nodded in satisfaction as he saw the rifles and ammunition inside. As soon as the fishing boat tied up alongside the quay, he hurried aboard and told Ramon what had happened.

"I want every crate loaded, quick as you can. The guard's relief will arrive in two hours, and we've got to be out of sight before that happens."

Ramon nodded, clearly shaken by the news. "They're really serious about this? They brought so many weapons to attack us?"

"Yes, but they'll have to get more before they can continue with their plan. Meanwhile, I and the others will train our people to use these in our own defense. Oh—load those cases of soap, too." He pointed to two big cardboard boxes containing cartons of powdered laundry detergent, stacked next to a washing machine.

"But we have enough of our own."

"We'll need that for washing our clothes. We'll use this for something else."

Willing hands loaded the crates and boxes onto carts and dollies, wheeled them out to the fishing boat, lifted them over the side, and lowered them into the empty hold. They had to use the hoist on the boat's mast to handle three of the heavier crates, cursing as the wood creaked under the strain; but no lights appeared in the houses farther up the hill, to suggest that anyone had heard the noise. Esteban slung the guard's corpse over his shoulder and deposited it at the stern of the boat, along with a heavy steel mincing machine that would make a good sinker.

It was after three by the time they finished, the setting moons providing light for their efforts. "Hurry up!" Ramon hissed at his crew as the last crate was swung aboard. "We've got to get out of here!"

As soon as the lines were cast off, he put the engine slow astern, backed away from the quayside, swung the boat around and headed for the harbor entrance. Despite their urgent need to get out of sight, he held the speed down to what seemed like an agonizingly slow crawl until they were half a mile clear of the harbor entrance, so as to minimize the noise of the engine. Only when he was sure it wouldn't be noticed did he advance the throttle, first to half speed, then, when they were a mile away, to full speed ahead.

As the vessel approached the headland, where the sea deepened as the bottom fell away steeply, Father Francisco tied the mincing machine to the corpse's feet. Esteban helped him drag the body over to the rail. He intoned a short prayer, commending the dead man to God once more, then they rolled the weighted body over the side. It entered the water with a splash, and sank swiftly out of sight.

By zero-three-forty-five, the boat had disappeared around the corner of the headland. Alsamak slept on beneath the fading moonlight.

They reached Pescara at dawn. The other fishing boats were on their way back, and the women were preparing the processing sheds to deal with their catch. They ignored the blue vessel as it tied up near the uneven road leading up the hill to their houses.

"We'll use Urbano's shed," Francisco decided. "It's not in the harbor, so if they try to steal back their weapons, they'll have to carry them further; and we'll lock up the carts and trolleys when they're not being used, to make the job harder for them. Esteban, run and ask Urbano for the key while we move the crates up to the door."

When everything was inside, the priest thanked the fishermen for their help, and dismissed them to get some sleep. Esteban had woken Nicolau and Zacharias, and they helped lever the tops off the crates to examine their loot.

Zacharias whistled softly. "They were really loaded out! There's enough weapons and explosives here to support a platoon in the field for a month!"

"Not so much ammunition, though," Nicolau pointed out. "I don't know how they expected to teach their villagers to shoot. They only brought about two hundred rounds per rifle. That's nowhere near enough for training, let alone a fight."

"No," Francisco agreed, "but they probably weren't going to teach them to be marksmen; only how to work the trigger. A group of people charging forward, shooting as they come—even inaccurately—will draw attention away from trained people moving in behind them. The villagers would have been no more than cannon-fodder. The *Ikhwan* have done that elsewhere."

"So what do we do next, Father?" Esteban asked.

The priest heaved a sigh. "Will you all take my orders—not as a priest, but as a troop sergeant?"

The three nodded in unison. "I will." "Yes, Father." "Of course."

"Very well. Esteban, take a few of the young men. Teach them how to use these." He pointed to one of the crates, which contained a dozen two-way short-range radios. "I don't know this particular model, but I'm sure you'll figure it out. I want two people on watch on the ridge above the village at all times, day and night, to warn us if anyone approaches. They must watch the sea approaches as well as the path. Tell them to use their radios on the lowest power setting. It'll be enough for short-range line-of-sight communication, and it won't carry the length of the island to where the *Ikhwan* might overhear it. We'll also teach them how to use a rifle, and arm them as soon as they're safe with a gun, so they can protect themselves if necessary.

"Nicolau, I'll assign a couple of men to help you. Cut the tops off some of the old fuel barrels stacked behind the processing sheds, and clean them out properly; then dig them into the ground at the base of the defile leading down from the ridge, to cover the path. Make wooden covers for them, loose-fitting, but secure against wind and weather."

Nicolau began to smile. "I think I know where you're going with this."

"I daresay you do. That'll take you two or three days before the next step. Zacharias, while he's doing that, you and I will clean all these rifles, load all the magazines, and check out the rest of the crates. I want us to draw up training plans for every able-bodied person in the village. We'll pick a dozen of the best shots for more advanced training."

"Got it. Mind if I make a suggestion? You've seen the young men with their slings, right?"

"Yes." The youngsters competed with each other to hit impudent seagulls with pebbles as they tried to steal fish from the sorting tables. The stones were too small to hurt them badly, but stung enough to make them back off.

"Why not teach a few of the older, stronger ones to sling heavier rocks, the same size and weight as a grenade? If they get that right, we can give them some of these. They'll reach out further with them than we can by arm strength alone. We can hold on the spoons with loops of twine or cloth, so they'll only fly off when the slingers release the grenade."

"That's a really good idea! Well done, my friend. Yes, do that."

Esteban grinned. "I wonder what those extremists are doing and saying right now?"

"I imagine they're furious with us, and blaming each other. Let's hope so, anyway. They're sure to send a boat to the mainland to get more weapons. I reckon we've got no more than a few weeks to prepare."

"If I were in their shoes, I'd want to hit back at us. If they still have their personal weapons, some of them might try something—maybe even to steal back their weapons."

"I think you're right. That's why I want sentries on the high ridge."

Problems soon emerged. The priest was summoned to an urgent meeting of the village council.

"How are we supposed to earn enough money to carry us through the winter if you insist on taking everyone off the boats for training?" Pablo, the council chairman, demanded.

"How much of a living can you earn if you're dead?" Francisco riposted. "You've all seen the weapons those fanatics brought to Alsamak, and you heard what Abdullah said they were going to do with them."

"What if he was wrong? What if they're just here to set up a base, and not bother us?"

"Why would they need a base so far from any major center? That makes no sense. Wherever they've gone, they've made trouble. They're sure to be getting more weapons, even as we speak; and when they arrive, they'll be coming for us. Our fishing boats can't carry all of us, plus enough food and fuel to get us to safety. We're stuck here until the freighter arrives at the end of summer. We can submit to death or slavery, or fight back. If we fight, we need to know how to fight and how to use weapons, which is what I and the others with military experience are teaching you—but we can't do that if you're all busy fishing. Make up your minds."

After much debate, a compromise was reached. The council would allow a dozen men to join the four military veterans and receive training. The remaining three dozen or so able-bodied men would continue fishing, and share their catch with those learning to defend them.

"However, that's only for the next four, maybe five weeks," Pablo warned. "If there's been no attack by then, I don't think there'll be one at all; so I'll want them back on the boats. We can't afford this distraction."

"The man's a fool!" Esteban fumed when the priest reported back on the discussion.

"No," Francisco replied with a heavy sigh. "He's just faced with a situation he's completely unequipped to handle. He's denying it, rather than dealing with it. There are many like him. He'll learn soon enough—that is, if he isn't killed in the process."

"So who are they giving us?"

"I got them to agree we could have the younger men, those who weren't as experienced on the boats, and who won't be missed as much."

"That's good for us," Zacharias observed. "They're fitter, and more willing to learn than the old farts. Also, by the time they're trained, Guillermo should be back. Hopefully he'll bring us some more help."

"Yes. We'll divide them into six teams of two for the time being. Each morning, I want one team on the ridge as lookouts; one or two helping Nicolau prepare our defenses; one or two on the shooting range, training with their rifles or throwing rocks with their slings; and two teams sleeping after sentry duty the previous night. During the afternoon, we'll rotate them among those duties, and the sleepers can join in. Every night, two teams will mount guard on the ridge, with their rifles, some grenades, and a radio to warn us if they see anything. We four will continue to divide our time among the teams; check out all the weapons, cleaning and preparing them; and work out the next training sessions."

A few days later, the priest accompanied Esteban and the two guard teams for that night on the arduous climb up the ridge. Panting and puffing, they arrived at the lean-to shelter they'd constructed for the guards against the back of a large boulder. The team coming off-duty had built a fire to make coffee. Francisco frowned as he noted the thin wisp of smoke.

"Didn't I tell you not to do anything that might give away your position?" he demanded.

"Yes, Father, but there's no one here to see it. We've been looking all afternoon, and seen nobody."

"Just because you haven't seen them doesn't mean they're not out there."

The two shuffled, rebellion plain on their faces. "But it's cold up here! How can we stay alert without coffee?"

Esteban tugged at Francisco's sleeve, and muttered, "There's no point in yelling at them. They're not soldiers. They don't understand military discipline."

"I suppose you're right." The priest heaved a frustrated sigh. "On the other hand, there's no reason we can't take advantage of their mistake. I reckon those *Ikhwan* fighters will have been sneaking around, to find out what we're doing. They must have seen that smoke, which means they know where our sentry post is. What if we stay up here with the teams tonight, and prepare a warm welcome for them if they try something?"

Esteban began to smile. "Why not?"

They spent half an hour examining the terrain in front of and around their position, selecting new locations from which to fight. "I think anyone wanting to creep up on the lean-to from the front would have to use that shallow draw," Esteban said, indicating it with a pointing finger.

"I think you're right. There's also that clump of thorn bushes—they can get between it and the rocks behind it, masking their movements."

"Yes. I'm glad there's no moon tonight. They won't see a tripwire until they hit it."

Staying low to avoid detection, they strung two lengths of fisherman's twine across the approaches at ankle height and attached them to fragmentation grenades. Francisco carefully pulled the grenades' pins, then wedged them between rocks to prevent the spoon flying off and arming them until they were needed. They then sited the two teams of watchers in new locations overlooking the lean-to shack, warning them to stay awake and alert, and took up their own position covering the booby-traps. They took it in turns to keep watch while the other slept.

The priest was dozing when an explosion jolted him awake. He seized his rifle and shuffled up alongside Esteban as the other peered out into the night. "That was the grenade behind the bushes," he said tersely. "They didn't take the easy way in, down the draw."

A moaning cry in Arabic came from the darkness. "Fawzi! Help me!" There was no reply, and the voice switched to English. "Hey! You up there! Help me!"

One of the youngsters half-stood in his concealed position, turning to look at the two senior men. He called, "I'll go and—"

Before they could yell a warning or tell him to get down, a burst of full-auto fire came from the darkness. The young man screamed in agony, spun around, and fell across a rock. His rifle clattered as it struck the stone. Even as he fell, Francisco and Esteban instinctively lined their rifles. They could tell from the enemy's muzzle flash that he was too far away to reach with a grenade. Each triggered five rounds rapid fire towards and around the position from which the shots had come. A muffled cry indicated a possible hit, but they didn't move towards it. Instead, they crawled sideways, vacating the position they'd just revealed by their own muzzle flashes, trying to move silently, straining their ears to hear any sound that might indicate the enemy's movements.

The radio at Francisco's side vibrated silently, warning of an incoming transmission from the others in the village, but he made no move to listen or respond. He'd already turned off the speaker and the display, so that no untoward sound or light would betray them.

After a few moments of silence, the injured fisherman moaned, and his partner called in a panicky voice, "Rodrigo's hurt! We must help him!"

Esteban whispered a vitriolic curse next to Francisco, but didn't reply or make any movement. The priest squeezed his forearm briefly, then returned his attention to the darkness. He knew the youngster was giving away his position. If there was another enemy out there . . .

The other man called again, louder, "We have to help Rodrigo!" His last word was punctuated with a flash of light and a blast of sound. He screamed, a short, sharp, agonized sound, and fell silent. Both men knew a grenade had found him. Almost instantly, they heard the scuffle of rapidly retreating feet, followed almost instantly by another explosion from the draw and a cry of pain.

"The bastard hit Emilio, then ran for it and hit our other booby-trap," Esteban whispered.

"Sounds like it. We'll wait right here until dawn. No sound, no movement."

"Got it."

Francisco used the radio's keypad to send a text message to those below. "Stay there until we call you."

The night drifted by almost interminably. They dared not smoke or talk. They listened to two sets of faint moans and gasps from out in front of them, and one from the position occupied by their team, which died away after a couple of hours.

As the faint half-light of dawn began to suffuse the sky, the priest signaled those below to begin ascending the slope. By the time it was light enough to see through the gloom, Nicolau and Zacharias joined them, along with four more of the young men under training. They waited until they could see far enough to cover each other, then Francisco and Esteban moved out to check on the sounds they'd heard overnight.

The two young men who'd so unwisely called out from their place of concealment were both dead, one from three bullets in his chest, the other from blood loss caused by grenade fragments that had sliced through his neck and opened the blood vessels there. Esteban spat grimly to one side. "We told them what to do, and they wouldn't bloody well listen. We'd better make sure the others see this. They need to learn what happens if they don't obey."

"I agree. It'll be hard on them, and on the families, but we have to do it."

"What about the enemy?"

"We heard three of them, but there may have been more. We got at least one with the first grenade, and I think we hit a second with our rifle fire. The third hit the second grenade. I don't know how badly they were hurt, so we'd better check very carefully."

"All right. You're our leader, and we need you alive, so let me go first. Cover me."

Before Francisco could object, his partner moved out from the rocks, crouched low, rifle ready, scanning the rocks and scrub as he moved slowly forward from cover to cover. Francisco followed him, moving cautiously. Both men kept their eyes open for anything that might provide cover or concealment from incoming fire if necessary.

The first victim they reached lay in the draw. The grenade had blown off most of his left leg, and his blood had soaked into the ground around it. He'd tried to tie it off using his belt, but clearly hadn't been able to stop the bleeding, which had eventually killed him. They secured his weapons, then moved towards the clump of thorn bushes.

The second man was still alive; they could see his chest rising and falling as he breathed. They took cover, and Francisco called out in Arabic, "Don't move! You can't escape. Raise your hands and surrender!"

The man slowly, painfully, turned his head towards the rocks from which the priest was speaking. "Who says this? Show yourself!"

"I'm not that stupid. Come on, show me your hands—and there'd better not be a weapon in them!"

The man half-smiled, half-gasped, "We thought you were all fishermen down there. We didn't know you had soldiers among you. I—"

He suddenly hurled a grenade, but he'd lost so much blood that his throw was weak. It bounced off the rocks and rolled back as Esteban fired three rapid shots into his torso. The man cried out, then the grenade went off with a deafening bang. Pieces of shrapnel whined in all directions. Francisco and Esteban ducked, then peered over and around the rocks.

"Did you get him?" the priest asked.

"I think so. Let me make sure."

Esteban lined his rifle again, this time more deliberately, and put a round through the man's head. Francisco nodded grimly. He could only approve of the precaution, given the extremist's last act. You couldn't afford to give such an enemy an even break.

They checked the man's body, then tried to find the third fanatic, the one at whose position they had fired. There was no body, but a rock had traces of blood on it.

"Looks like he wasn't hurt too badly," Esteban said unnecessarily. "He got away."

"Yes. If he isn't already back at Alsamak, he soon will be, and he'll tell them we're armed and alert. They'll be more careful next time, and better prepared." Francisco stretched wearily.

"Funerals this afternoon?"

"Yes, before the boats go out. I want the whole village to see this, and understand what just happened. If any of them doubted what those fanatics were up to, they'd better think again!"

Over the next two weeks, the four veterans trained their remaining young assistants, and strengthened the defenses of the village as best they could. The rugged terrain provided only limited approaches from landward for attackers. The draw leading down from the ridge, being the most likely attack route, received special attention. Zacharias supervised as a mixture of marine fuel, fish oil and vegetable oil was poured into the open-topped barrels that had been dug into the dirt at its sides and base, concealed by rocks and thorn bushes. When each had received its ration, boxes of laundry detergent were stirred into them, creating a sticky, sludgy mixture. Meanwhile, Esteban dismantled several satchel charges, separating the blocks of explosive each contained. He fused each block, waterproofed it, dropped it into a drum, and led a firing cable to a switch in a central fighting position at the base of the draw. When all was ready, the loose-fitting wood covers were replaced over the drums, to protect the fuel inside from rain and dust. The edges were sealed with grease to prevent leaking.

There was no shortage of rocks for ammunition, so the slingers were able to practice every day. Before long they could drop a grenade-sized projectile within a couple of yards of their aiming point, inside a radius of up to eighty yards, depending on the individual's strength. When each had demonstrated proficiency, Francisco allowed them to throw one live grenade as a reward. Their feral grins as the blast rang out, and the training targets were riddled with shrapnel, boded ill for would-be attackers.

They were ready only just in time. Early one morning, Francisco was roused from his sleep by an urgent shout. "*Padre!* The sentries report a crowd of people advancing along the ridgeline! They're still a couple of miles away, but coming towards us."

Cursing to himself, splashing cold water on his face to wash the sleep from his eyes, the priest grabbed his rifle and a satchel containing spare magazines and grenades, and set off on the climb up to the ridge. He had to admit, it was much easier now, after several weeks of daily trips up and down. All of them had become a lot fitter and stronger.

He arrived, puffing and panting, to be met by Esteban. "It looks like the villagers and fishermen from Alsamak," he reported. "I recognized some of them through the binoculars. They're carrying rifles, so I guess the Brotherhood must have sent replacement weapons. There are several men in uniform moving behind them. I think they're the Brotherhood people, using the villagers as cover."

"That's what they've done elsewhere," Francisco commented as he lifted Esteban's binoculars to his eyes. "Yes, I see Abdullah in the front rank. He's carrying a rifle. He'd never be there like that unless he'd been forced."

"You trust him that much?"

"As much as I trust anyone who isn't one of us. Don't forget, he warned us about the arrival of those *Ikhwan* fanatics. Without that, they'd have taken us completely by surprise. We'd have been defenseless."

"The fact that we aren't is to your credit, Padre—*hey!* What the hell is that?" He pointed over Francisco's shoulder, out to sea.

Francisco spun around. A small freighter was on the horizon, steering straight for the small harbor. She was moving at a brisk pace, to judge by the white water kicked up around her stem. He focused the binoculars, peered, and frowned. "She's wearing the Balboan flag!"

"What would she be doing here?"

"I gave Guillermo a message to a friend there, in case he couldn't get any help for us from the authorities. He owns several ships. This may be one of them." There was new hope in the priest's voice.

"Let's hope so! They're still an hour out. We'll have to hold off this lot until they get here."

"Yes. Take command up here, Esteban. You've got the four sentries from last night, plus the two who came up to relieve them. The seven of you should spread out into fighting positions. Don't shoot until they get inside five hundred yards, and even then, shoot only if they don't stop. Aim high at first, to give the villagers a chance to take cover. I expect they'll duck out of the line of fire, and expose the extremists behind them. If they do, nail them."

"Got it. Two of the boys are slingers, too, and we have a dozen grenades here. I'll use them if they push closer."

"All right. I'm going down to the village, to alert everyone and tell them to head for the fishing boats. If these bastards push down the ridge, we may have to hold them off while the rest get away as best they can. Perhaps that freighter can take some of them."

Esteban sucked in his breath. "If we do that, we may not be able to get away ourselves."

Francisco looked at him. "Yes, but I don't see any other way. If you can't accept that—if any of you can't—you need to get down to the village at once."

Esteban's face stiffened with resolve. "If you can face that risk, I can too. Don't worry about me, Padre, or any of us. We'll stand firm."

The priest embraced him. "I know you will, brother." He looked around at the others. "All of you, make an act of contrition." As they did so, he gave them the general absolution for those in danger of death. "God be with you. Remember, you're defending your families and loved ones down there. Be strong in your faith, and have courage."

They were already spreading out as he headed back down the

slope. He blinked back the incipient moisture in his eyes. He knew that, if worse came to worst, few of those on the ridge would live long enough to retreat to the village.

He found Pablo and the council waiting for him at the uppermost houses on the steep slope. "What's going on?" the chairman demanded.

He explained briefly. "Esteban and the others will hold the ridge as long as they can. I'm going to marshal the others to delay them on the slopes, if they come down. You see that ship coming in?"

"Yes. We don't know who she is or what she's doing."

"She's a Balboan freighter, and she's headed towards us. Send out a fishing boat to meet her, and ask whether she can take our people on board. Send a radio, too, so the captain can talk to me. Start putting the rest of our people aboard fishing boats, and get them out to sea."

"But we don't know if we need to evacuate! You may be able to hold them off!"

Francisco cursed openly, causing the councilors to look at him in bewildered amazement. They weren't used to their priest using such language. "You're a damned fool, Pablo! If we wait until they break through our defenses, we won't have *time* to get the families out! Get them aboard *right now!* Tell them to leave everything behind except food, water and medicines. Nothing else! No furniture, no pets, no prized possessions. The boats will be overloaded as it is. It'll take you an hour or two to get that done, and we'll be fighting long before you're finished. If it turns out okay, we can come back when it's safe. Now *move, damn you!"*

The councilors scattered like chickens being chased by foxes, yelling at the tops of their lungs. "Everyone to the harbor! Take food, water and medicines—nothing else! Move! *Now!"*

As the other armed men hurried to their preassigned positions, Francisco ducked into the small church for a moment. He knelt before the tabernacle, looking up at the gold vessel that held the consecrated Sacrament, and tried to remember an old warrior's prayer. "Lord, you know how busy I will be today. If I forget you, please don't forget me! I . . . I'm sorry if this is wrong, Lord. I've done my best to be a good priest; but sometimes a shepherd has to protect his flock from the wolves. I don't know any other way to do that, here and now. Please help us!—and if today should be our last, receive our souls into Your mercy. Holy Mary, mother of God, pray for us sinners, now and at the hour of our death."

He crossed himself, rose to his feet, and opened the tabernacle. He hurriedly consumed the consecrated hosts in the chalice. There was no point in leaving the Sacrament to be desecrated by the fanatics, if they won here today. Closing and locking the tabernacle, he headed for his position at the base of the draw.

He'd only just settled into it when his radio crackled. "Padre, this is Ramon. I've talked to the skipper of that freighter. Guillermo is aboard her. He says he asked for help, but they had no men or weapons to spare. However, your friend sent this ship to collect us all and take us to safety. She's not very big, but she'll do. The captain says he'll load us aboard, but we have to hurry. His radar shows boats heading this way from the other side of the island. I reckon some of those *Ikhwan* bastards have commandeered fishing boats, and are planning to attack the harbor while their friends come down the mountainside."

Francisco cursed again, and keyed the microphone. "Does the captain have any weapons to hold them off?"

"No, he doesn't. He asks if you can spare some of your men. They can take cover with their rifles behind the gunwale, and use slings to toss grenades at the Alsamak boats."

The priest hesitated, then made up his mind. It was critical to get the families away. If some of the defenders had to protect the evacuation, so be it. He looked around.

"Zacharias! Take these four trainees, a case of grenades, and extra rifle ammunition. Get aboard a fishing boat and head for that ship. You must defend it against boats from Alsamak while our people get aboard. Aim for the helmsmen in their wheelhouses, so they can't safely steer. That should keep them at a distance. If they get closer, use slings to throw grenades at them."

"But what about you, Padre? How will you get away?"

"Never mind me! The ship must be kept safe! Go! Go *now!*"

Zacharias hesitated, then snapped to attention and peeled off a salute that would have gladdened the heart of a drill instructor. "I hear and obey, Padre. God be with you!"

Francisco looked around. Only he and Nicolau were left now, to defend the upper slopes of the village. "I guess it's up to us now, my friend," he said heavily.

"Oh, well. I always used to enjoy a good fight. Looks like I've got one of the best coming my way!"

They smiled shakily at each other, and set about preparing their fighting positions. Francisco laid out grenades and magazines where he could reach them easily, and checked the detonator switches for the napalm barrels dug into the sides of the draw. Nicolau moved to the other side of the draw, and settled down behind some rocks.

Scattered shots sounded from the ridgeline above them, a few at first, then more and more, until the sound of firing became a constant rattle. As the advancing enemy drew closer, a few grenades began to explode. The radio next to the priest crackled. "Francisco, are you there?"

He snatched up the microphone. "Yes, Esteban, I'm here."

"The Alsamak villagers tried to duck as soon as the shooting started, just as you thought they would; but the extremists began to shoot at them, forcing them to stand and run forward. I'm sorry to tell you that Abdullah was one of the first they shot." The priest closed his eyes, murmuring a soundless prayer for his friend's soul as Esteban continued, "They've kept coming. We've hit two or three dozen of them, including three of the uniformed men, but they won't stop. Two of my men are down. The enemy is only a hundred yards away. What should we do?"

"Come down! Send your people down in twos, and cover each other's retreat."

"I'm on my way. Carlos, Elias, down the hill! Move! Ignacio, Cornelio, you're—*aaaah!*"

Francisco's heart froze at his friend's agonized cry. "Esteban! *Esteban!* Are you all right?"

A barrage of shots and the sound of multiple grenade explosions came from the ridge. Two figures showed themselves, leaping down the slope as fast as they could. There had been seven villagers up there . . . but no more appeared. Instead, half a dozen brown-uniformed men appeared and began chasing the two survivors, shooting as they came.

Francisco steeled himself. "It looks like that's all there are left, Nicolau. Let them get through the draw, then we'll take on those chasing them."

"I hear you, Padre."

He cast a glance behind him. The crowd of people that had thronged the jetty and quayside in the harbor had grown much smaller. Fishing boats were heading for the freighter, figures crowded on their decks, while others that had already unloaded their human cargoes were on the way back for more. Faintly he heard the sound of shots as Zacharias and his men fired at three Alsamak fishing boats. They appeared to be circling aimlessly, a few hundred yards from the freighter. He nodded approvingly. Rifle fire from the steadier platform of the larger freighter should render their wheelhouses untenable, making it impossible for them to get closer. Now, if they could just get the last of the villagers to safety . . .

He felt cold inside as he reached for the microphone. "Zacharias, do you hear me?"

A brief pause, then, "Yes, I hear you, Padre. We're holding them off."

"Good. Listen, Zacharias. When the last people are aboard, tell the freighter to get out of here. Don't wait for us. We won't be able to break contact long enough to get aboard a boat and reach you. Save the villagers at all costs. Don't try to rescue us."

"But, *Padre!* We can't just abandon you!"

"*Do as I say!* God bless you, my son. I'm switching off now."

He heard Zacharias' voice squawking from the speaker as he laid down his microphone, reached for the power switch, and flicked it off.

The freighter's skipper listened as Zacharias reported the priest's instructions. He nodded slowly. "You've got one hell of a pastor there, brother. I wish we could get him out, but he's right. If we tried, we'd simply make ourselves targets for those *Ikhwan* bastards, and we'd probably lose everyone who tried to reach him."

There were tears in Zacharias' eyes. "I don't reckon the Church will recognize him as a martyr, but in my book, a sacrifice like his is right up there with the greatest of them."

"I'll not argue with you." The captain picked up his binoculars, and scanned the harbor. "The last fishing boat's coming out now. That's everyone who's coming, I guess."

He trained his binoculars on the slope above the town, watching as the two survivors bounded down the draw and ducked into prepared fighting positions. A man in black—he presumed it was the priest—half-rose from a central fighting position, peering up the draw, then pressed something beside him. Gouts of flame and fire spurted out from both sides of the draw, immolating three of the brown-uniformed attackers. The three behind them screamed their anger and frustration, charging forward, throwing grenades and firing. The captain cursed as smoke from the burning napalm, and the dust thrown up by exploding grenades, drifted across the scene, hiding it from view.

As the last of the villagers came aboard, the smoke and dust began to clear. He could see no movement at all on the slope. The black-clad man had fallen forward over the rocks that had protected him, almost touching the last of the attackers, who had collapsed with his head down the slope.

He laid down his binoculars with a sigh, and called down to the deck. "All right, that's it. Cast off that fishing boat. We can't take it with us. Everyone get below!" He turned to the helmsman. "Full ahead, hard a-starboard. Let's go home."

As the freighter began to turn away, he cast a last, long look at the slope, and the bodies that lay there. Quietly he murmured, "God rest your soul, Padre. You surely were a shepherd to your flock this day. I hope they appreciate it, and remember you. You deserve that much at least."

INTERLUDE:
From Jimenez's *History of the Wars of Liberation*

Indeed, in the wars on the borders of Terra Novan Islam, it was very often the Spanish-speakers who proved just why their mother country, *España*, had once been called, "The nation with the bloody footprint." It was there, where Spanish culture was strongest, too, that the more fanatical branch of Catholicism arose, rather, re-emerged, in answer to Islamic jihadism. This was especially so once the New Pope canonized Father Francisco *Matamoros*.

Not only were there UN personnel of admirable ability and even honor fighting against us, we would be remiss, indeed, if we neglected to give due regard to those UN personnel who, looking at our people, seeing out plight, changed sides or helped us until, driven by the threat of prosecution, actively changed sides.

In the early days, in particular, before open war even broke out, while the UN was jockeying for position and our soon to be rebellious ancestors were, as well, it was often the good offices of someone in the UN who spelt the difference between defense and massacre, who stood by the people he'd been sent to govern or help, even unto the last extremity . . .

Secordia is said to resemble very deeply its antecedent nation on Old Earth, Canada. How far this goes back is impossible to say. Certainly, there were several centuries when Secordia was culturally almost indistinguishable from the Federates States of (Southern) Columbia. We can also surmise that very early on in the colonization program, Secordia was nothing like what became the Federated States. For one thing, the early settlers were essentially disarmed, where the Federates came to the planet armed to take on dinosaurs, should any have been found. For another, the area that was to become the Federated States was at no time under UN governance, where Secordia seems to have insisted on it. For a third, while the original Secordians were someone conservative, the people to their north were extremely so.

It should not have been a shock to anyone, however, that certain essentially tribal entities came to Terra Nova with their hearts firmly in the more distant past, and a determination to recreate that past life and culture anew . . .

4.
DOING WELL
BY DOING GOOD

Chris Nuttall[5]

[The following letter was recovered from the archives in UN FOB #34, after it was overrun and occupied by coalition troops during the later stages of the war and subsequently buried in the files until it was recovered and verified during the post-war assessment of UN operations within the region. As far as can be determined, the letter is actually genuine—it is unclear if it actually reached its destination. Accordingly, it has been annotated by a team of experienced historians and published for public consumption.]

My Lady Marchioness of Amnesty,

I do not write this letter to beg for mercy. I have no doubt that my death warrant has already been written and—one hopes regretfully—signed. Given the nature of my conduct, which you will no doubt consider treason, I have no reason to expect anything beyond a quick march in front of a firing squad. Instead, I write this letter to explain precisely what happened and why. It is my hope that many of my former comrades will learn from my experience and come to realize, perhaps, that our system is broken. It needs to be fixed.

---

5 Christopher Nuttall was born in Edinburgh and spent most of his life reading science-fiction and fantasy novels. It was perhaps inevitable that he would eventually try to become a writer himself, crafting the best-selling *The Empire's Corps, Ark Royal* and *Schooled in Magic* series. Chris lives in the UK with his wife Aisha and his two sons, Eric and John.

My appointment as Political Commissioner (New Manitoba) came as the culmination of my career, of thirty years of working my way up the ranks through good service and the occasional piece of favor-trading. I have no doubt that you have already started to cover your ass by claiming that you knew I was a weak candidate all along, but you—and many others—were quite happy to support my promotion at the time. And I myself was enthusiastic. Five years spent wrestling with the bureaucracy in the Terra Nova Settlement Commission had dulled my enthusiasm for political infighting. It was extremely difficult to get anything done. I boarded the flight to New Manitoba with a certain amount of relief, mixed with concern. It didn't give me any pleasure to hear that my predecessor had become one of the richest men on Terra Nova. UN bureaucrats exploiting the people they are meant to help is a major cause of social disharmony.

New Manitoba was settled twenty-two years prior to my arrival. Like many other such settlements on the mainland, the population was primarily drawn from groups that resented UN hegemony on Earth. In this case, the vast majority of the original settlers and their successors were North American farmers, specifically Canadians, men and women who had resisted our encroachments back home until finally agreeing to be transported to Terra Nova and resettled there. They hadn't received anything like the level of support they had been promised—a major cause of resentment—but they successfully broke the ground and tamed the land. By the time I arrived in 'forty-two, New Manitoba was a thriving community spread out over three hundred square miles. It was genuinely important. A good third of its produce was shipped out to the rest of the world.

It was also nothing like Earth. Instead of concentrated population centers, the settlers were spread out over the entire region, which was dotted with small towns, villages and farms. The sole city within my area of responsibility—officially called Ingalls, but unofficially referred to as New Manitoba City—was tiny. It would have vanished without a trace in any major conurbation on Earth. Indeed, despite UN regulations insisting on population registration and centralised schooling, it was difficult to say for sure just how many people were under my jurisdiction. A significant number of births were never recorded.

[The UN used the birth registry as a way of determining a settlement's obligations (tax and suchlike) to the planetary government. It wasn't uncommon for settlers in the more self-sufficient communities to deliberately hide births to escape increasingly resented demands.]

The settlers—the Manitobans, as they called themselves—were tough, hardy stock. They were *very* self-reliant, often reluctant to spend money on importing goods and services from the remainder of the planet, let alone Earth itself. The debts many of them had incurred were greatly resented by the Manitobans, particularly as they believed (rightly) that the debts were manipulated in an attempt to keep them under control. They certainly didn't seem too interested in the offers I extended to provide UN services to help the settlement. I think, by the time I arrived, they had come to think of such offers as poisoned chalices.

[All such debts were formally renounced in the aftermath of the war of independence.]

I came to love them. I admit that freely. There was something about their "can-do" attitude that I admired. They never waited for government assistance to get the job done. Nor did they waste time pushing the decision further and further up the chain until it reached Earth itself. It was an attitude I found refreshing, after spending so long in the bureaucracy. And I like to think they responded well to my lack of corruption. I certainly had no intention of copying my predecessor and trying to turn the settlement into a money farm. That man put UN-Manitoban relationships back *decades*.

[Unsurprisingly, Commissioner Rawls went on to a long and successful career in the UN bureaucracy and retired a very wealthy man. His children (through seven different women) form part of the UN's aristocracy, save for a lone illegitimate child who ended up joining the resistance in Balboa.]

It started seven months after I took up my post.

There had been reports, vague reports, of people vanishing along the edge of the district, near the Badlands. I didn't take them too seriously at the time. It wasn't uncommon for indebted farmers to disappear, trusting in the bureaucracy's incompetence to save them from having to sell their children to pay their debts. After discovering that my predecessor *had* tried to run such a racket, I had taken to quietly ignoring all such reports. (Indeed, I purchased the

contract of an enslaved daughter so she could live near her family.)
Perhaps I should have paid more attention. But I didn't, right up until
the moment the Alstead Homestead was attacked.

[Mr. Lamprey is being surprisingly blunt here. Slavery existed
within UN-controlled territories for decades, both on Earth and
Terra Nova, but it was rarely *called* slavery. It was far more common
for the slaves to be called "indentured servants," providing both a
fig-leaf of political justification and the possibility, however remote,
for eventually earning one's way out of servitude. It is likely that
Lamprey was influenced by Sarah, as he clearly had strong feelings
for her. He would eventually marry her.]

The homestead was seventy miles, as the crow flies, from Ingalls.
The report reached me within a day—radio transmitters were rare
outside the towns—and I flew there at once, accompanied by Sarah
Olson (my secretary) and Jasper Olson (her father). I recall
shuddering in horror as I saw the smoke, rising up from the remains
of the homestead. There was no sign of any attackers, so we landed
and started to look around.

I cannot tell you, my lady, of the horrors I saw that day. Mr.
Alstead and his sons had been tortured, scalped and killed; his wife
and older daughters had been systematically raped and then killed.
His younger children—he had a boy and two girls under ten—were
missing. The farm had been looted and the animals had been taken
into the Badlands. We searched the entire homestead, once more
settlers had arrived, but we found no trace of the missing children.
It was clear that the attackers had carried out a brutal raid and then
escaped without punishment.

We had no doubt who was responsible. It was the Apaches.

Officially, the Apaches are descendants of the *real* Apaches, a
Native American tribe that was almost completely destroyed during
the colonization of North America. In reality, they were a pastiche of
half-remembered traditions that had been transported to Terra Nova
along with a substantial quantity of supplies and settled on the far
side of the Badlands. (The fact that the Apaches had received more
assistance from the UN than the Manitobans was yet another source
of resentment in New Manitoba.) Unfortunately for the myth of the
noble savage in touch with the land, Terra Nova's generally hostile
environment made it hard for them to establish themselves. By the

time they came to my attention, they had scattered into the Badlands and were eking out an existence there. The Manitoban homesteads—on one hand, crammed with food and women; on the other, utterly undefended—were a *very* tempting target. They couldn't resist the urge to start raiding the settlements.

[Precisely why the Apaches, who had few *official* ties to Canada, were established so close to a Canadian-ethnic settlement has never been satisfactorily explained. Sarah Olson's best-selling book about the war, for example, asserted that it was a deliberate attempt to limit the Manitoban expansion out of the original settlement. A more likely explanation, however, is that the UN simply didn't care. Their attempts to get Terra Nova to mirror Earth were often half-hearted.]

And raid they did. Three more raids followed in quick succession, destroying farms, raping and killing adults, kidnapping children . . . the entire western border seemed to be catching fire. Something had to be done. But what?

"We need weapons," Jasper told me, after the second homestead went up in flames. "We have to fight."

I believed him. Jasper was the only farmer who was more than minimally polite to me. I'd bought out his daughter's contract and given her gainful employment and he was, I think, silently grateful. And he was right. I'd contacted my superiors and requested military support, but none was forthcoming. The war was heating up in other parts of Terra Nova and our resources were being pushed to the limit. Even if troops had been available, the Manitobans might not have been thankful. UN troops had a nasty reputation for brutalizing the settlers they were meant to protect.

[This was unfortunately true. It was often said, correctly, that a hundred rebels within one territory would become a thousand after the troops arrived. If anything, this was an understatement.]

But I couldn't get them weapons. The laws against private ownership of weapons—even simple pistols—were unbreakable. I was sure there were some illegal weapons in the district, but nothing I could afford to acknowledge. I fretted backwards and forwards for days, trying to find a way to protect my people. And yes, they had become *my* people. I was more attached to them, perhaps, than my superiors would have preferred. How could I help them?

[Although weapons were *technically* forbidden within the

Manitoban region, it wasn't uncommon for the settlers to have *some* access to primitive weapons. Mr. Lamprey might well have been unaware of any privately-owned weapons, as their owners would have gone to some trouble to make sure they were concealed from UN inspections. They would have believed, not without reason, that even something as primitive as a black-powder musket would have been confiscated.]

The situation got further and further out of hand. Hundreds of farms were being abandoned as the Apaches grew bolder. Countless refugees were making their way towards Ingalls, hoping to find a safe place . . . they were disappointed, of course. My heart broke as I watched them, pretending not to hear the angry mutterings. We—the UN—were being blamed for the disaster. And you know what, my lady? They were right. It *was* our fault. We had dumped the Apaches on Terra Nova.

[This marks the one and only admission of any UN operative that the UN bore some responsibility for the social unrest that eventually led to the war of independence.]

And then I had my brilliant idea.

You will know, of course, that a Political Commissioner has wide authority. Indeed, the regulations are suspiciously vague on just how *much* authority a commissioner actually has, particularly in a state of emergency. A commissioner could, for example, draft settlers to assist with . . . well, anything. If I wanted a mansion, I could force the locals to stop working and build one for me. And if I needed a posse of fighting men, I could raise one. Maybe I couldn't arrange for weapons to be sent to the farmers—that was strictly forbidden— but I *could* raise a small militia of my own. There was even *precedent*. The policing units deployed in Anglia and Jagelonia were largely composed of settlers.

Jasper was happy to help, once he got the idea. I spent the next two weeks battling paperwork and requisitioning weapons—and tactical manuals—while he raised an army of fit young men. Once we had the weapons, we started training. The farm boys—all raised in a disciplined household—responded *very* well. Indeed, man for man, I believe they were vastly superior to UN-trained forces. It helped, I suspect, that we had less to unlearn.

[Sarah Olson's book makes it clear that Jasper actually served in the Canadian military until he was dishonorably discharged for refusing to kowtow to the latest set of politically-correct requirements. It seems Lamprey was unaware of his service.]

We were the blind leading the blind. None of us had any real military experience. The tactical manuals hindered as often as they helped. We didn't need advice on watching the environmental impact of our footsteps, let alone treating POWs honorably. The manuals were long on detailed lectures and short on practical advice. I'll spare you a blow-by-blow description of the training process, of the problems caused by shooting off thousands of rounds of ammunition just to make sure our troops knew which end of the gun fired the bullets. Suffice it to say that I received a number of sharply worded questions about our ammunition expenditure, even *before* we had engaged the enemy. It turned out that we had fired more bullets, during training, than the average UN battalion fired in a year on active service.

But Jasper was insistent that we had to train and train and train until we knew what we were doing. And he was right.

My farmers, once they realized that they *were* being backed, came up with dozens of ideas for making our army more lethal. We obtained radio transmitters as we moved small forces out to the border, as well as makeshift drones and other surprises. The Apaches didn't seem to be aware that the frontier was becoming more dangerous. They kept pushing towards Ingalls, darting in to raid and then darting back before we could organize a counterattack. It was a constant frustration, all the more so as we *were* establishing garrisons. But the next time, we told ourselves, was going to be different.

[The UN did not encourage its troops to show initiative. Indeed, part of the reason they lost the war of independence was because troops would often continue with a plan even after it was blindingly obvious that the plan had gone off the rails. The troops on the ground, even the officers in command, might know what had happened, but they didn't have the authority to alter their tactics.]

And it was. The Apaches moved out of the Badlands—again—and headed west, directly towards the Ramirez Homestead. It wasn't really a surprise. The Ramirez family had taken in a number of refugees over the last couple of months, helping them to rebuild their lives. But it also made their homestead a very tempting target for the Apaches. We watched them coming through a drone and quietly moved troops into position to intercept them. Jasper commanded on the ground while I watched from a helicopter. It was hard, so hard, to keep track of what was actually going on.

But, in the end, it didn't matter. The Apaches suspected nothing. They came on, fat and happy, right into our gunsights. Jasper held his fire until the last possible moment, then barked a command. The militia opened fire . . . and slaughtered them. I saw dozens of bodies falling from horses and hitting the ground, crushed like bugs. Jasper's men advanced, striking down the handful of survivors. Only a couple of men were spared. We wanted—we needed to find their camps.

Jasper took charge of the interrogations. I don't care to know what he did to make them talk.

[Given the UN's later willingness to order the use of drugs, torture and even direct brain stimulation to compel prisoners to talk, this line seems rather odd. But there is no evidence that Lamprey was ever part of the UN's intelligence service.]

I landed and we conferred. The tactical manuals stated that we should wait to see if the enemy was interested in negotiating, but Jasper insisted—firmly—that we should take the offensive. We'd killed over seventy Apaches. There was no way to *know* how many were left, but it was clear that we had an opportunity to end the war in one fell swoop. Jasper pushed—and I agreed. We rallied the troops, stripped the dead bodies of anything useful and then marched on, into the Badlands.

The Apaches saw us coming. They tried to stop us. The Badlands were practically *designed* to frustrate an army. A strange mixture of mountains and swamps, rivers and ravines . . . it was a hellish engagement. They sniped at us constantly. We lost thirty men pushing through the trees towards their camp. Thankfully, they didn't have time to establish a few more booby traps or it might have gone differently. They honestly hadn't expected us to launch an actual counterattack. (They probably read the same manuals too.) In the end, we broke through their defenses and stormed their camp.

And Jasper gave the order to kill them. *All* of them.

I was shocked, utterly horrified. Forces under *my* command had carried out what was, unquestionably, a war crime. The death of nearly two hundred men, women and children was unforgivable. And yet, I knew there could be no peace. I had learnt that the hard way. The Apaches weren't interested in anything, but looting, raping and burning. Jasper pointed out, coolly, that nits bred lice. And— God help me—he was right. The Apaches had committed hundreds of little atrocities. They had long since forfeited any claim to legal protection.

[There are actually several different versions of what happened here. One version insists that the only people killed were Apaches, born and bred; another insists that the dead included Manitobans (and others) who'd been kidnapped when they were very young and brought up as Apaches. A third even insists that some of the former prisoners were rescued, only to discover that they no longer fitted into Manitoban society.]

But I knew my superiors wouldn't see it that way.

We burned the camp to the ground, then returned to Ingalls. The soldiers were warmly greeted—of course. I don't think a single one of them escaped getting laid that night. But I had another duty. I went back to the UN building and composed a message for my superiors, explaining what had happened. I hoped—perhaps naively—that the UN High Commission would turn a blind eye. The farmers of New Manitoba were *important*. The food they produced fed thousands of UN troops, spacers and bureaucrats. But it was not to be. The orders I received, two days later, stated that I was to assemble the former militiamen for deportation. UN troops would take them into custody. Jasper and the other leaders would be executed; the ordinary soldiers would be banished somewhere far from New Manitoba . . .

[The Manitobans believed, at the time, that the UN was punishing them, either for daring to defend themselves or for turning against the UN-backed Apaches. However, post-war research suggests that the UN was simply too detached from the situation on the ground to have any real understanding of what was going on. A war crime deserved punishment, they thought; they didn't bother to consider that it might be justified, necessary or both.]

It wasn't fair. They hadn't taken up arms against the UN. They deserved so much better.

I don't know how long I sat there, staring at the instructions. I'd believed in the system. I'd believed the UN meant well, even though it was often clumsy. And yet, the UN was prepared to betray men who'd fought to defend themselves. It was prepared to betray men who had secured the food supply for an entire continent. It was prepared to betray its loyal servants . . .

The UN had gone mad. And my faith in the system snapped.

And I, reluctantly, came to a decision. I called for Sarah and issued orders.

Two days later, three helicopters flew over Ingalls from the north and descended towards the landing strip. As per orders, I had lined up the militiamen to greet the UN troops—informing the newcomers that the militiamen were unarmed. I waited, beside Jasper and the others, as the helicopters touched down . . .

. . . And then we opened fire.

The helicopters and their passengers never stood a chance. They were torn to shreds before they could disembark, let alone take cover. Two of the helicopters exploded, knocking the third over. We watched long enough to make sure that everyone was dead, then hurried to leave the city. The majority of the population had already left. The irony of setting up camps of our own, in the Badlands, did not escape me. I was sure that retaliation would be on the way soon enough.

[Ingalls was fire-bombed two weeks after the brief engagement. The town would later be rebuilt after the war of independence.]

I write these words, my lady, as we prepare to leave Ingalls for the final time. I make no apologies for my actions, either for arming the locals or opening a new front in the ever-expanding war. Like I said, I do not expect mercy. But I ask you to understand why I chose to betray you. The system is broken.

We should have offered protection to the Manitobans. Instead, we preyed on them. We taxed them, claiming half their produce . . . and we expected them to be grateful that we hadn't taken everything. And when they were attacked—by tribesmen *we* imported from Earth—we refused to defend them. Why should they be loyal to us, my lady, when we show no loyalty to them? Their reward for serving us was more demands for service. I can no longer, in good conscience, serve the UN.

[This *cri de coeur* is perhaps the most honest statement ever issued by a UN bureaucrat.]

You will say, perhaps, that I grew too close to my subjects. Perhaps I did. But I believe that I understood what was actually going on, while my superiors—thousands of miles away—did not.

We are fighting to control a world. And yet, our tactics are merely turning the population against us.

I do not expect to see you—or Earth—again.

Farewell.

Roger Lamprey, UN Political Commissioner New Manitoba (Retired).

[Roger Lamprey vanishes from the history records at this point. Research carried out after the war of independence makes it clear that he married Sarah Olson and had four children, all of whom took their mother's name. (They apparently believed that the UN would hunt Lamprey and anyone who appeared to be related to him, although it seems fairly clear that the UN didn't bother to do more than put a small reward on his head.)

[Jasper Olson would go on to become the first leader of the Combined Canadian Militia, but was unfortunately killed in action during the Battle of Berger's Bluff. His name was later immortalized in both a regiment (Olson's Offenders) and his daughter's account of the Manitoban-Apache Conflict.

[Sarah Olson remained a farmwife and mother until she started to write late in life, but her first work—an account of the Manitoban-Apache Conflict—was very well received and put the family finances on a secure footing. Her later works, ranging from a biography of her father to a call for more local independence for Manitoba, remain popular today (and banned on Earth.) Despite that, a number of revisionist historians have attempted to pick holes in her work, including suggestions that she wrote subjective history or suffered from Stockholm Syndrome. Professor Dandridge's *Manitoban Girl*—her first true biography—goes to some lengths to disprove such claims.]

INTERLUDE:
From Jimenez's *History of the Wars of Liberation*

Twenty-seven different modern countries claim the honor of having fired "the shots heard across two worlds." Record keeping of the day being what it was, and propaganda being what it has always been, no one really knows. It's not entirely clear that anyone at the time, to include the Earthers, knew, either.

For Balboans, at least, the first shots were fired by poorly armed and untrained villagers under the command of Belisario Carrera, in the course of ambushing a slave raiding party led by the UN's High Admiral, Kotek Annan.

If we cannot say for certain exactly who began the wars of liberation on our planet, it is much easier to track the progress, or lack of progress, of the various independent liberation movements, from Northern Uhuru to Wellington to Secordia to Balboa . . .

From *Primer Grito: The Memoirs of the Liberator,* Belisario Carrera

What did I know of soldiering? No more than might be gleaned from one of the war films emanating from Hollywood, in the United States, back on old Earth. And if there was any correct guidance in those, it must have been inadvertent.

No, I knew farming, raising cattle, horsemanship, all the things I'd learned as a boy at my father's, uncles', and grandfathers' knees back in our home in Panama before it was stolen from us. Those, and I knew how to shoot, too. I learned back home before the UN came and took our guns away, along with our land and liberty.

Still, there were things that came with having been a farmer. I understood the lay of the land and how, not wanting to tire out men and horses, to use it to conserve strength. I understood something of camouflage from the animals I'd hunted, especially when we first arrived on Terra Nova, before we got our first harvest in.

It was from hunting animals, actually, that I recognized that the new high admiral, Kotek Annan, was leading a hunting party, hunting *us*. I never did know if it was mere sport the high admiral was after, or if he'd gone back into his family's old business of hunting slaves. I didn't know but, then again, it really didn't matter, either.

I did know that, before the damned pirates would get at my wife and children, or those of the others, it would be only over the dead bodies of myself and my men.

The helicopter that brought the hunters dropped them in two groups, one south, one north of the village. Which were the beaters and which the net? It wasn't clear to me until I heard the shots; those to the north were many and moving toward us. The ones from the south were stationary and relatively few.

The people of our little town clustered around me. We'd never had an election but I'd been fairly well-to-do back on Earth and the mannerisms, and the habit of command; they stuck.

"What's wrong, *Patron?*" asked Pedro, called "*el Cholo.*" Pedro held one of the flintlocks I'd brought from Earth. His son, Little Pedro, stood beside him, clutching a bow in one hand and a quiver with a dozen or so arrows in the other.

I thought I knew why the UN had come.

Pedro asked the question but I spoke up to answer the several hundred people in what passed for our town square. I sensed that with the support of the women we had a chance; without it we were just rabbits.

"We have nothing material for them," I said. Then I looked from one woman or girl to another. "They're here for other rewards."

That got me a collective gasp. I'd been exiled here specifically for defending my daughter, but any decent Latin man defends his women and girls. And our men and boys were all decent.

Little Pedro's hand whitened around the grip of his bow. "We must fight them," he said, in a high voice. He was just turned twelve.

Again, I looked around, but this time at the men. Yes, I saw; they agreed. Fight them we must. The boys would follow their fathers.

There was a river close by the town, between us and where I thought the net was. It ran from the west to the east. I pointed to my dear wife and said, "*Queridisima*, that way. Lead the rest of our people to the river, then descend to the water and follow it to the caves. Move quickly. Keep your heads down below the river's banks. Head for the caves. If we win here I will send someone for you. If we lose . . . run. Run deep into the jungle and wait until you know the helicopter has gone away." She had her shotgun in her hands. With a nod, she began to move off, women, girls, and younger boys following her.

I'd always thought my wife was braver and tougher, both, than I was. Nor did she disappoint that day. She bit her lip, nodded, and led the rest of the crowd away with only a gesture and a few steps to take the lead.

For the rest I had seventy-three men and older boys, having among them a dozen bows and the rest old fashioned flintlocks. It was easy to count the bows with a glance; less so the ammunition, little of which would fit any rifle but its owner's.

"Show of fingers; how many shots?" I asked. None of the men held up more than ten digits. Most were several fewer. One made what used to be called, on Old Earth, the "peace sign."

I thought, *Shit. And I've only a dozen, myself.*

Still, we had the numbers; we had a chance.

I divided the men—yes, some were boys but they did a man's job that day, so you will pardon me my generalizations, yes?—into three groups. The oldest and youngest dozen and a half—less Pedro's boy who stuck with his father—I left at the village, with orders to, in the first place, engage the raiders as they showed themselves, and, in the second, buy us a little time in case it turned out I was wrong and the southern group were the more dangerous. Another dozen and a half I sent to the river, but in the opposite direction from my wife's, to a ford we all knew well. The rest, about three dozen, received the benefit of the one decent bit of advice I'd ever seen in all those *gringo* movies; I told them, "Follow me."

There was an open field—mostly open, anyway; it did have a few scattered palms and a couple of mangos—between our little settlement and the direction in which I could still hear their helicopter whining. Keeping low and out of sight behind the thick brush and reeds growing at the edge of the treeline, I led them and placed them more or less evenly spaced out.

When I finished that I went back to the center of the line, where they'd be better able to hear me, got on my belly and crawled forward. When I looked up I found Little Pedro grinning down at me from a tree, bow in hand, arrow knocked, and the quiver slung. I grinned back.

It was a game for a boy, but I don't mind saying I was scared shitless.

Then I saw them on the ground, nine men wearing body armor, on line, ahead of one brightly dressed dandy behind. They began firing at the village, without having too much effect initially. The men I'd left there returned fire, but with each shot announcing the position of the shooter and inviting a hail of fire in return, our shots were not too effective.

It didn't matter, I figured, since I didn't want them to be effective so much as enticing.

Oh, it was hard, HARD, waiting for them to advance on our little town. I waited . . . waited . . . waited. Each moment seemed longer than any hour. I thought my heart was going to pound its way right out of my chest. And then, finally, their line of skirmishers was parallel to the center of my line of ambushers. I lifted my own rifle to my shoulder.

"READY . . . Fire!"

5.
No Hypocritical Oath

Robert E. Hampson[6]

It wasn't bad enough that medical school was harder than any other class or schooling that Anthony Nuné had attended, but he had to put up with the *putito* "elites" like Lucas Carvalho. The United Nations/Duke Medical School should have been a respite from the constant struggle for "status" and power that Anthony had endured in the Panama schools—after all, the United States was supposed to be the "Land of the Free and the Home of the Brave" where a poor but smart student could succeed no matter his family ties. It had even once been true—just not so much anymore.

UN/Duke had its roots in the "Duke Brazil Initiative" to promote research partnerships between Duke University and several universities (and medical schools) in Brazil at the beginning of the twenty-first century. As the partnership grew and started a medical student exchange program, the UN had taken over and directed

---

6 Robert E. Hampson, Ph.D., turns Science Fiction into Science in his day job, and puts the Science into Science Fiction in his spare time. He has consulted for more than a dozen SF writers, assisting in the (fictional) creation of future medicine, brain computer interfaces, unusual diseases, alien intelligence, novel brain diseases (and the medical nanites to cure them), exotic toxins, and brain effects of a zombie virus. His science and SF writing (as both Robert E. Hampson and under the pseudonym, Tedd Roberts) ranges from the mysteries of the brain to surviving the Apocalypse, from prosthetics to TV & movie diseases, and from fictional depiction of real science to living in space.

Dr. Hampson is a Professor of Physiology / Pharmacology and Neurology with over 35 years' experience in animal neuroscience and human neurology. His professional work includes more than 100 peer-reviewed research articles ranging from the pharmacology of memory to the effects of radiation on the brain—and most recently, the first report of a "neural prosthetic" to restore human memory using the brain's own neural codes.

Duke Medical School to exclusively provide American-style medical education to top university graduates through Central and South America. Unfortunately, "top graduate" didn't always mean grades, thus Lucas S. Carvalho the Third terrorized his tutors (like Anthony, despite being two years ahead of him) who were necessary to his continued presence in the school, all while lording his status over them. The fact that Carvalho's father was a doctor with the World Health Organization, his uncle was the Brazilian ambassador to the UN, and his great-grandfather was the neuroscience professor who first established the Duke Brazil Initiative, gave Lucas leverage over faculty and staff of the university that his fellow students could never hope to achieve.

Thus Anthony found himself struggling to complete not only his own Infectious Diseases case study for Friday's Grand Rounds, but also Carvalho's. The tutoring job paid real money, and The Sainted Hammarskjold knew that Anthony needed it; his scholarship paid tuition and board, but little else. He just had to hang on another month until the Licensing Board exams and Graduation. Unlike Carvalho, with his new Porsche-Benz, tailored white doctor coats, and uptown apartment, Anthony had to suffice with public transportation, used academic supplies with thrift-store clothing and sharing a flat with five other students who were just as poor as he was.

Lucas had told Anthony to forget "tutoring" and just write up the presentation for the Grand Rounds; it was worth an extra fifty UD's or university-dollars that Anthony could use at the hospital cafeteria or any campus shop. As long as Anthony handed over the presentation before it was due, Lucas could read it for the first time and still give a masterful performance. In fact, he usually did—to the commendations of the faculty supervisors. It just proved that you didn't have to be *smart* as long as you could follow a script and had the right family connections.

Anthony was struggling with the case. The patient history and physical had been taken by another of Carvalho's "tutors," and were nearly illegible. Technically, the notes were supposed to be recorded in the computer systems, as part of the patient digital record, but most physicians only put what the insurance companies demanded in the patient file. Grand Rounds insisted on *real* details, which were often excluded from official records to ensure that the patient met the WHO treatment quotas. Fortunately, the unlucky scribe was one of Anthony's roommates.

"Julio, what does this say?" Anthony asked when he'd finally managed to get his roommate's attention away from the girlfriend he'd been spending a lot of time with that semester. "You know I can't read the notes you write for case studies!"

"You mean the ones for 'His Honor'?" Julio Cisneros spoke the honorific with a sarcastic tone of voice—as most of the other students did when referring to Carvalho out of hearing distance. "Why don't you just make it up? That's what the rest of us do."

"You know I can't do that, this is Grand Rounds, and I have to present, too, so I need to finish this and work on mine, too. I'll be up all night as it is."

"Speaking of 'up all night,' you *have* noticed Annalise, right? She paid her way through nursing school as a *dancer!*" Julio waggled his eyebrows to convey just what sort of dancing the young lady had done.

"Enough, Casanova. I need help, here."

"Yes, you do, and Annalise shares a flat with three other nurses, all single, and all looking to score a freshly licensed doctor. Besides, didn't you hear that Casanova's grandson studied right here at Duke?" Julio waggled his eyebrows again. "So I have to keep up the tradition; besides, the patient had duck fever."

"Huh? What?" Anthony was too tired to follow Julio's line of thought.

"Sure, Mike Casanova, back in the 2000's, he worked with Saint Nicolelis."

"Not that. What is it you always call me? *Tonto?* Idiot? No, I'm asking what you mean by 'Duck Fever.'" Keeping up with Julio's train of thought was like trying to catch kittens.

"Oh yeah. Avian Influenza, H9N6, traces back to a virus in ducks in Hong Kong over a century ago. The first known human cases were seen just last year. This poor guy just happened to have an allergic reaction to the vaccine, so his throat swelled up and he literally '*quacked*' when he tried to talk. Anyway, here are my *real* notes, not the scribbling I handed 'Lord Lucas.'" Julio pulled out his *Phablet* and sent Anthony a digital file containing the case notes.

"Thanks, Julio. I might be able to get a couple hours' sleep tonight!"

"I keep telling you, Tonio, you don't need sleep, you need one of Annalise's roommates!" Anthony just threw the wadded up paper with the scribe notes at him.

"Very good, Mr. Nuné. Excellent summation. The treatment plan is sound and the patient seems to be recovering just fine." Dr. Pegram had led the questioning during Anthony's presentation. The attending physicians always sat in the front row of the lecture hall, and most of the time their questions were polite and professional. They didn't necessarily wait until the end of the presentation, though; attendings frequently interrupted to ask questions meant to clarify descriptions or test a student's thought processes in coming up with a diagnosis. It could be unnerving, even if all went well, as Anthony's presentation had.

Carvalho was up next. Anthony had handed him the case study several hours ago, but Lucas had barely glanced at it. With a smirk, he stepped up in front of the room, immaculate in grooming, tailored white coat, and a highly expensive—and anachronistic—stethoscope draped around his neck. He began his presentation in a smooth cultured voice. Several of the female students, plus a few males and even one of the faculty had a look of sheer infatuation on their faces. Except for the attendings. Dr. Pegram's looked like he had turned to stone. Strangely, there were no questions, and Lucas finished without interruption.

"Mr. Carvalho, is this supposed to be a joke?" Dr. Pegram's voice was as icy as his expression.

Lucas stopped and stared, confused, as he thought back over his presentation to determine how he had angered the attending physician. The patient had presented with muscle spasms which caused spinal contracture inhibiting posture and gait, tightening the cheek muscles causing pursing of the lips, and of course, the spasm of the hyoid region coupled with swelling to cause the odd vocalization. As he recognized the implications, he began to flush, and a quick, angry glance at Anthony indicated that he'd already decided on someone to blame.

When Lucas didn't answer, Dr. Pegram continued: "Mr. Carvalho, we are professionals. Our patients do not have 'fits,' they have 'seizures.' They don't 'bleed like a Mother F—' . . . whatever . . . they have 'profuse hemorrhage.' Under no circumstances will we accept 'if it looks like a duck, walks like a duck and quacks like a duck, it's Duck Fever' as a diagnosis." As one, he and the rest of the Attendings stood and exited the room. "Dismissed," he called over his shoulder.

"You've made a powerful enemy, Mr. Nuné." Dean Thompson rose from his desk as Anthony entered the office. He gestured to indicate that the two would sit at a pair of chairs to the side of the office. The dean of students indicated Anthony's bruised and swollen face and continued, "but I suspect you've already learned that."

"I fell in the stairway," Anthony muttered.

"Of course you did, and the ER report does not indicate injuries consistent with a beating." Anthony did not respond, so the dean resumed. "Mr. Carvalho comes from a very powerful family. Not only is his father deputy director of WHO, his uncle is being talked about for secretary general. There's also talk of investing them with noble titles. I shudder to think of the possibility of 'Viscount WHO,' but there's even talk of making the titles inheritable. There's nowhere on Earth that you can go to escape them, and believe me, they intend to ruin you."

A small sound escaped from Anthony's throat. It was as near a sob as he could manage through the swelling. All he had ever wanted to be was a doctor, and now that was permanently out of reach. He couldn't even really blame Julio for setting him up, the symptoms were exactly as described, it was only the interpretation—and delivery, he had to admit—that were at fault. Of course, if Lucas had actually read the presentation ahead of time, he could have changed it enough to avoid embarrassment, but Lucas would never take the blame for his own actions. He was already circulating a story that Anthony had pranked him out of spite and had replaced Lucas's *own* scholarly work with the fake diagnosis.

The dean was still speaking, but Anthony had missed something. "—accept transshipment to Terra Nova and we can ensure that you are licensed and certified. Balboa needs doctors, and you may even have family there."

"Excuse me, Sir, but . . . what was that?"

"Some of our more 'indigent' students agree to serve on Terra Nova to pay their loans. You were on scholarship, but it's still an option. The United Nations Interplanetary Settlement and Boundary Committee, or UNISBC, is in charge, but it will be a bit easier to get a clean start, since it's handled at a much lower level than the WHO. Your friend Cisneros is one of several upcoming graduates due to head there, but even so, you're unlikely to run into people who would know you."

"Terra Nova? The colony planet? What would I do there?"

"The same thing you would do here. Your grades are excellent, and you've passed all of the exams. You'll have to complete a residency in Hamilton and then you'll be assigned to a clinic, probably in Balboa City since you are Panamanian. It's a twenty-year commitment, or else you will have to pay back the transshipment costs; but it pays better than you could expect here. Besides, it's your only real option."

Terra Nova? It was too much all at once. He was supposed to go to Panama City next month to start a residency at the "Hospital del Niño"—the children's hospital—with the statue of Vasco Nuñez de Balboa in the park across the street. Now the dean was talking about going to the *country* of Balboa on the only other planet that humans had ever discovered. Not to mention, it was a planet filled with plants and animals that were deadly to humans.

On the other hand, it was a chance to escape the attentions of Carvalho. He'd be needed. Just *maybe* he could make a new start . . . but at the cost of leaving friends, family . . .

He felt a cold lump in his stomach. His shoulders slumped and he felt as if a heavy weight had fallen on him. "Yes, sir. I'll go," he said in a quiet, defeated voice.

"*Has sido una buena chiquita,* Janina. You've been a good girl." George Noonan taped a small bandage over the site of the vaccination, then lifted her off of the examining table and handed her to the mother. "She probably won't be hungry tonight, but make sure she has plenty to drink. No *cacao, por favor.* She needs water or juice. Watch for fever, and come back if she is not feeling better in three days. *Tres días, señora.*"

The mother nodded and muttered her thanks in heavily accented

English. George thought it highly ironic that the patients and family considered him the *"gringo doctor"* since he had come to Balboa from his residency in the largely Anglo areas of Hamilton. The relocation deal had included a legal name change. The beating he'd received at the hands of Carvalho's thugs had carried an unexpected benefit— reconstructive surgery that had changed the profile of his face just enough to fool facial recognition, although close friends, if he'd had any, might have been able to recognize him as once going through school as Anthony Nuné.

Residency had been totally different from anything he'd experienced on Earth, and he truly felt that he'd gained a fresh start, so much so that he'd extended the residency in Pediatrics to include Obstetrics and Gynecology as well as Emergency Medicine. He knew he'd certainly need it for some of the UNISBC's hospitals and clinics. He'd hoped that residency would count toward his twenty-year obligation, after all, he worked seventy-two-hour shifts at county hospitals and ERs throughout, but the UN was adamant. Twenty years in service as a fully qualified doctor, residency most definitely *not* included.

Here he was, six years of residency and eight of practice, he should have been at least two thirds of the way through his commitment, but instead was less than halfway. He *really* should have read the fine print on his transportation contract. He couldn't really complain, though; he was alive, wasn't he? He'd intended to spend quite a few years at the Children's Hospital in Panama City before moving on to private practice, so it wasn't as if he had something urgent to do other than treating children and their mothers. The UNISBC Women's and Children's Hospital in *Ciudad* Balboa was both challenging and rewarding. It was a small hospital, only a dozen beds, a family clinic that doubled as an emergency room, and a small laboratory filled with outdated equipment. He rented a room in the building next to the hospital, and spent most of his time at those two locations. He was paid well despite his "indenture" and the families he'd treated had spread the word that the *"gringo doctor"* was a good man. There was at least one restaurant in town that would not allow him to pay, and the butcher at the market near his apartment always ensured that he received choice cuts of meat.

The only thing he didn't have was a family of his own. He'd dated a few times, but residency, like medical school, was time consuming and he was reluctant to get involved with a girl he would have to leave behind when the UN reassigned him. He'd officially been at W&C for eight years, now, but he spent weeks at a time working rural clinics, and even a month per year on-call for emergency services at the forts along the Rio Gamboa. The river provided a navigable waterway from the continental divide to the Shimmering Sea—more than halfway across the narrow Balboan Isthmus—and there was a *lot* of cargo on the river and roads crossing Balboa. The UN Marines built several forts to protect official commerce, and naturally, needed medical services for their troops; who better than someone that already owed the UN their service? Despite the primitive conditions at some of the sites he worked, they were still a damn sight better than his boyhood home in Chorillo.

The mothers of some of his patients, not to mention some of his older female patients, had started to hint about finding him a *"muy buena señorita."* While he feigned disinterest, he had to admit that he'd been thinking about it; the butcher's daughter was rather cute. Then there was the girl with the construction company building the pediatric wing. He'd seen her several times when he'd had to go to the company office to discuss the new patient rooms. Now *there* was a girl who could stop traffic! What was her name?

Yelena! That was it. Yelena . . . Guerrero, or Carrera, or Callejo, or something like that. Maybe he should ask her out. After all, he *was* the Gringo Doctor; that had to be worth something! His work habits didn't leave much time for dating, though—or, at least they hadn't until lately. The out-of-town duties had reduced as word of a new insurgency had arisen. Yes, he could ask her out, although it seemed strange that back-country terrorists would provide him an excuse for a normal love-life.

After six months of seeing Yelena Guerrero, George had to admit that he'd made the right decision. Finding time to spend with her and her family had gotten easier once he decided to *make* the time, rather than simply *find* the time. He'd met most of the family by now since many of their "dates" were chaperoned; Balboa had a *very* traditional culture, and it was getting time to have The Meeting with her father . . .

It would have to wait, though; he'd been called out to Fort

Cristóbal on an emergency. It was nearly time for his annual trip to the fort overlooking the mouth of the *Rio* Gamboa, so he'd been told to simply report early and plan to stay the extra time. He'd hurriedly packed, arranged for one of the other doctors to cover his hospital duties, and stopped briefly at the construction office to say good-bye to Yelena. He promised to meet with her father once he got back, and received a *very* enthusiastic kiss in return!

This had been a strange tour of duty, though. The patient had been shot with a bullet that had somehow become coated with progressivine sap—more than could be accounted for by shooting from within heavy foliage. There had long been rumors of groups of insurgents in the undeveloped areas between cities, but that was supposed to be mainly concentrated in Northern and Southern Columbia, the continents connected by the isthmus of Balboa. If the terrorists were this close to civilization, and coating weapons with poisonous sap, then it might be time to agree to having a guard when he traveled between clinics.

The local flora and fauna had been a problem for as long as humans had been on Terra Nova. For a planet that seemed perfect for terrestrial life, it seemed to have a particular animosity to *intelligent* terrestrial life. The planet had plenty of plants and animals that appeared to be directly equivalent to those on Earth, leading many to wonder if it wasn't *too* convenient and wonder what or who had arranged the coincidence. However, there were a few native plants such as the progressivines and bolshiberries with toxins selectively inimical to intelligent life, and animals such as the *antaniae* with obvious alien genes and bad attitude.

George had studied the literature on the uniquely Terra Nova species during his residency. The prevailing theory was that the Novan equivalent of DNA was a hybrid of the four known nucleotides of terrestrial DNA, plus four unique nucleotide bases. The DNA "code" produced by the sequence of nucleotides determined the structure and function of proteins in all organisms; thus the Novan species produced proteins that were *similar* to terrestrial proteins, but had subtle differences due to the presence of extra codes. It was hypothesized that those proteins acted similar to prions—basically a fragments of protein made from normal terrestrial genes, but with abnormal structure—that mainly affected animals with complex brains. The scientific theories didn't really matter—bolshiberry juice and progressivine sap could lead to a very painful death. Deliberate use of the toxins on other humans was attempted murder, and George had a responsibility to report it as such.

The rising insurgency was not the strange part, even though George always felt as if someone was watching. No, Novan technology was . . . schizophrenic . . . to put it mildly. At Duke, he'd had access to the best medicines and medical technology that the twenty-second century had to offer. His residency in Hamilton had mostly modern facilities, at least up to the best of the twenty-first century, although that slipped to twentieth century in the rural areas. In *Ciudad* Balboa, he had some modern medications and facilities, but most of the country seemed to be struggling to keep up with Earth's seventeenth century. Fort Cristóbal was a perfect example, a large brick and adobe walled fortress overlooking a river that served strictly human and animal-drawn barges.

In contrast, soon after George had treated the soldier with the contaminated wound, he received several ultra-modern diagnostic devices and a shipment of a new vaccine with instructions to vaccinate all of the personnel at the fort. The devices consisted of a new blood analyzer, diagnostic scanner, biometric recorder and a rapid DNA sequencer. Every person receiving vaccine was to be scanned to confirm the infection (or lack thereof), provide a blood and tissue sample for analysis, and have their biometrics recorded. The instructions were from the Terra Nova Health Organization— the UNISBC's version of WHO.

George shuddered with the memories that thinking of TNHO or WHO brought up. This was highly unusual; most of his patients didn't *need* ultramodern medicine, even if it would have saved more lives. Life on Terra Nova, and in Balboa in particular, was hard and rather primitive. The people were strong, and they were survivors. They made do with what they had, as did most of the doctors, hospitals and clinics. Even twentieth-century medicine was good enough for most needs, so to be issued materials that literally screamed "most modern" was unheard of.

There was more to it, and the instructions he'd been given upon returning to *Ciudad* Balboa were the most confusing of all. There was a new influenza, and the TNHO had decided to stop its spread with the vaccine he'd been given. However, before he could administer the vaccine to any non-military or non-UNISBC personnel—even children—he had to take the biometric and genetic samples and wait for approval. It was supposedly for epidemiological research purposes, but why would he have to wait for approval if the data was simply being used to track which patients contracted the disease?

Normally George enjoyed performing his duties at the forts and outposts; after all, treating pregnant women and sick children was rewarding, but not particularly exciting. His trips out of the city presented many different challenges, but also allowed him a measure of autonomy that was absent at the hospital. This time, however, he couldn't wait to get back. Perhaps it was his unease about the new vaccine, or maybe it was the constant sense that someone was watching him every time he was outside at the fort. Then again, maybe he was just looking forward to getting back to Yelena. No matter the cause, George was ready for the tour to be over so that he could get back to the city.

The pounding on his door woke him at three a.m. He'd been asleep only for a couple of hours, and would have to be awake again in an hour in order to be at the hospital to complete his rounds before six a.m. He was training two young students to act as medical technicians. There was no let-up in patient load, so he had to do all of the training in the early morning and late evening. George threw on a long coat in a nod to decency and to ward off the chill as he rushed to the door. His head was beginning to throb in time with the pounding at the door.

It was Yelena, and one of her older brothers. "*Jorge, mi Corazon,* it is my younger brother Rodrigo. He is badly injured and very sick. We need you to come quickly and help!" Yelena looked worried, while her brother—George struggled for the name, ah, Emilio—just looked impatient.

Pleased as he was to see Yelena at any time, George was not at his best, with only two hours sleep and no caffeine. "You can take him to the hospital. Dr. Espinoza is on call and can help him. I'm in no shape to help him right now."

Emilio grunted, and looked as if he was ready to pick George up and carry him out the door, but Yelena put up a hand to stop him. "No. No hospital, this is . . . this is *muy importante* that you come."

George sighed. If it had been anyone but Yelena, he would have refused, but it was her brother—soon to be his brother-in-law—so he relented and told them to wait in the small living room of his apartment while he went back to the bedroom and dressed.

When he came back out, he went to the tiny kitchen to heat water. "I'll need some coffee, first. I'm sorry, but I am just not awake enough." He was surprised to find Yelena already at his side; she laid one hand on his arm to stop him from reaching for the kettle, while the other held up a ceramic mug already filled with steaming liquid. He took a sniff, then breathed deeply of the rich aroma, already beginning to wake up at the smell alone. *Ah, her grandmother's coffee.* This thoughtfulness was one of the things he truly loved about her, not to mention that the Guerrero women were all excellent cooks!

Despite his continued protestations that Rodrigo should be seen at the hospital, George grabbed both his emergency bag and the military kit that he had yet to unpack from the recent tour of duty. Yelena and Emilio had brought an additional mount for George to ride, and they quickly traveled to the family home just outside the city. It was far enough that they could no longer see light from the taller buildings, but still close enough to smell the smoke left over from the previous night's cooking fires.

The family had decided to keep Rodrigo out of sight of the younger children, so he was lying on a table in the building Yelena's father and brothers used as a workshop. The room was filled with adult family members; the usual smell of sawdust and wood shaving tinged now with blood, sweat and human waste. The boy—at seventeen, a man by Balboan standards—did not live with the family, but spent most of his time in the back country. George had never been told what he did, and had never asked. It was a large family, after all, with parents, children, grandparents, and grandchildren living under one roof.

There was a blood-soaked bandage on Rodrigo's leg, but it was dark and dry. An old wound, and not necessarily an immediate problem. He was pale, though, sweating and shivering at the same time, with occasional muscle contractions that caused him to grimace, to flail his arms and legs, or even to curl his spine to the point where he lifted most of his body off of the table.

After a particularly severe contraction, Yelena let out a whimper and clutched at her mother, who'd been tending to Rodrigo before they arrived. The two began to speak in whispers. George couldn't quite follow the words, but he recognized the inquisitive tone and worry on the part of the older woman, but Yelena began to look very nervous. She saw his look, and forced a smile. "She asked what was wrong with him and wondered if we should call for the priest?"

George was silent for a moment as he examined his patient, then looked back at the women. "The fever and chills could be infection, but not the spasms. This looks like a toxin of some sort: his face is swollen, as well as his neck, fingers and toes. His skin is hot to the touch—that could be allergic reaction or infection, but it looks like . . ." He paused. *No, that doesn't make sense.* Every once in a while a parent would bring in a child that had eaten bolshiberries and suffered a reaction to the deadly plants. *This looks very similar . . . but an adult wouldn't eat bolshiberries.*

George jerked upright as he remembered the wounded soldier at Fort Cristóbal. *An adult wouldn't eat bolshiberries!*

He spoke decisively. "Okay, first things first, he needs an antihistamine to stop the swelling. I can't do much about the convulsions until I know what this is, but we need to cool him down. Get some cloths and soak in *cold* water from the well. Place them on his forehead and throat, then wrap his arms and legs." When they nodded, he continued, "I need to look at this wound."

Yelena turned to go, but her mother placed a hand on her arm. At a nod, two of her older sisters departed for the house, and a brother was sent to the well. Yelena seemed even more nervous, and her mother's restraining touch did not seem to be helping.

A suspicion began to form in the back of his mind, but George pushed the thought away as he unwrapped the bandage, cutting away the part where the dried blood had stiffened and stuck to the wound. He retrieved a bottle of sterile saline from his emergency bag to wash the blood and dirt away and reveal the wound. It wasn't bad, entry wound on the front of the thigh, exit wound on the back. It appeared to have been cleaned and bandaged soon after it happened, by someone who knew what they were doing. there was no sign of infection despite it obviously being days old, just a bit of redness around the wound itself. "How did this happen?"

Yelena's brother's looked at each other, but didn't speak until her father nodded.

"Hunting boar. It was an arrow." Emilio said.

"No, I don't think so." George's rebuke provoked an angry glare from the father and restless stirring from the others present. "This is a small caliber rifle wound, entered from the front, slightly bigger wound on the exit in back. An arrow doesn't do that. Besides, you hunt boar with large caliber rounds that would have left a gaping hole on exit!" George looked up at Emilio, then turned to glare at their father. "Care to tell me exactly what happened? You know I have to report this."

Yelena sobbed. "No!" and ran out of the shed.

George stared at Señor Guerrero until the older man finally looked down. "He is with the resistance."

Hmm. "Resistance," not "insurgency," thought George. "And just what was he resisting?"

"Agents from *Los Grillos* were attacking a farm." Guerrero spit on the pressed sawdust floor. "Men from 'Penal Interstellar Servitude' were hunting a fugitive slave. They are monsters. The child was not a slave; she was born free, here in Balboa. A child should not be held accountable for crimes of her parents, especially when they were political prisoners that Earth wanted to be rid of!"

George had heard of *Los Grillos*. Named for the Grillo Building in *Ciudad* Balboa that held many of the UNISBC offices, P.I.S. (or Pen.I.S. as it was called by the young men with muffled laughs and hidden grins) was notorious for using any excuse to prolong a transported prisoner's term of indenture. It was slavery in every sense, including inventing reasons for indenturing children of prisoners as well.

"So you say, but that doesn't change the fact that this was a small caliber wound, probably from a military rifle, not a boar hunting rifle or even *Los Grillos*' stun sticks. How do I know he was defending an innocent and isn't a terrorist shot by the military for plotting to bomb civilians?"

"Because he was with me." George turned as the new voice spoke. Yelena had returned leading a cloaked man who removed his hood as he spoke. "He was with me, Tonio. He was doing exactly as they said; he stopped one of *Los Grillos'* men from beating a child, fought back, and was shot by one of the *mercenarios* they bought from the UN. I dressed his wound; I brought him here when he fell ill. I told *Don* Guerrero that you could be trusted."

George stared, speechless, not even protesting at the use of a name he'd abandoned over fifteen years before. The cloaked man accompanying Yelena looked like . . . sounded like . . . "Julio?" he managed. "You're one of the t—"

"The word you want is *'resistencia,'* The Resistance, *tonto*," Julio corrected before George could finish the word. "We are not terrorists; the only terror we strike is to the heart of the UN. No civilian targets, only military." He gestured toward Rodrigo, ". . . and *Los Grillos.*"

"*Tonto*, indeed. You must think I'm an idiot as you always have. First you set me up to be almost killed on Earth, now you hunt me down on Terra Nova, reveal my past and what, you set all of this up? Played me the fool with Yelena?"

At mention of her name, Yelena stepped forward and laid a hand on George's arm. "No, George, it was not like that."

He shook off her hand and continued. "You set me up. Are you planning to blackmail me so that I'll treat your terrorists?" He practically spat the word, but was rocked backward by the sudden slap from Yelena.

"No!" The shout and slap silenced George and he worked his jaw but remained silent while Yelena yelled at the rest of the men in the room in rapid-fire Spanish. Everyone except for Yelena and Julio left the room—and Rodrigo, who was lying on the table, occasionally shivering, but neither convulsing nor conscious.

"No. You *are tonto*. I love you, but you are *estupido*." Yelena faced him, eyes blazing. "People are being enslaved, their farms robbed or taken, girls raped, boys killed. Now people are getting sick. You see only a part of it because you are in the city. When you go to the towns, you work at the TNHO stations and you treat the *soldados*. People trust you to care for the *niños* or *bebés* but do not know if they can trust you not to report to the UN." She paused, briefly. "Rodrigo is not *terrorista*." She stopped and breathed heavily, anger evident in her body language as if she were preparing to strike him again.

Julio reached out an arm and placed it between the two. He

pushed Yelena back slightly, and she relented, still glaring, but less angry. "Rodrigo is a good boy who was protecting a child that had committed the 'unpardonable sin' of being in the way of *Los Grillos*. Several of his friends had gotten sick, though, that was why they came to me. I have been helping to treat the outcasts and resistance fighters. After a few years of practice in Aztlan, the TNHO decided I wasn't worth their attention. I work in the city a few months per year, but mostly in the countryside. I can move around and I don't have the '*sombra*' that you have when you go out to the farms and forts."

George was confused. It wasn't just the head-rattling slap, or the shock of seeing his old roommate, or even the growing sense that he was missing many things that were happening around him. "Wait, you're saying I have a 'tail'? A shadow?"

"In the countryside, yes; in the city, no. When you were at Fort Cristóbal, there were *mercenarios* following you. Not UN Marines, these were 'security contractors.'"

"Umm," George stalled while he formed his question. "You know this how? You were following me?"

"Following, no. Observing, *si*. Several of Rodrigo's friends were getting sick. Influenza, they thought, but many of them ended up looking like he does now." Julio gestured at the boy. "They contacted me, and I met up with them. They also reported that Rodrigo's sister was seeing a *gringo* doctor, but they didn't know if they could trust him." He snorted. "*Mierda*, they barely trust me. So we followed you. There was supposed to be an attack on the fort, but I was watching through a pair of binoculars I liberated from some UN *puta* who tried to bust up one of my clinics. I saw their *gringo* doctor and told them to call off the raid. Carvalho may have had his men rearrange your face, but they didn't change your eyes, *mi amigo*! With your light skin, pale eyes and horrible accent, it's no wonder they think you are *blanco*!"

George started to retort, but was interrupted by a word from Yelena. "Look."

Rodrigo had started to convulse again and George had to turn his attention to his patient. Yelena and Julio held the boy's arms and legs while he quickly completed his examination. A quick glance around showed that the shed served not only for woodworking, but also leatherwork to maintain tack for the farm animals. "Grab some of the straps; we need to restrain him to keep him from hurting himself. Get the others back in here with the cold water and bandages!" He selected a wide, clean piece of leather and placed it between Rodrigo's teeth to give him something to bite on.

The convulsions were confusing. Julio had mentioned men in the Resistance getting sick with influenza, then showing more severe reactions. When they'd arrived, Rodrigo had presented the appearance of an allergic reaction, much as someone who ingested one of the toxic indigenous plants. Now, however, he had convulsions consistent with a high fever, yet was still cold and clammy to the touch. *The convulsions must be from a different toxin—but what?* He watched as the muscle twitches proceeded from arms and legs to the neck and face. Tendons stood out on the boy's neck, his jaw clenched and the mouth was drawn into a grimace resembling pursed lips. His breathing became heavy, then rasping, with a hacking or "quacking" sound as it passed through the constricted larynx.

"What?" George stood up and looked over at Julio. "Duck fever?" The memories that had so recently been painfully resurrected by his old friend's presence came flooding back.

"*Si, mi amigo.*" Julio nodded sadly. "You were always the best of us at infectious diseases. That is why I asked for you."

George reached for his emergency bag, then, as an afterthought, reached for the military kit. He'd try to avoid using the blood analyzer if he could; the DNA sequencer and biometric scanner almost certainly recorded all data and reported it to TNHO. He'd have to hope that the diagnostic scanner would be general enough to protect the identity of the patient. He took a blood sample anyway, just filled the tube and handed it to Yelena. "Put this someplace cool until I leave—perhaps one of the cloths soaked in well water. I will take it to the hospital and analyze it there." He pressed the diagnostic device to the side of Rodrigo's neck and waited.

"*Influenza A, H9N6/avian/Hong Kong/77*" was the result a few moments later. The diagnostic display continued with: "Gamma serotype, K-peptide conjugate, variant LSCIII2112." While the diagnosis and treatment display read: "K-fever. Administer vaccine LC12-TN." That was the new vaccine alright.

Julio looked over at the readout and grunted. "You have a vaccine.

How convenient." His voice was dripping with sarcasm. "How nice of the UN to have a vaccine ready for a disease they created."

"You think this is deliberate?"

"Duck Fever was always a joke we played on the First Years and *pendejos* like Carvalho. Somehow, they've made it real and they're using it against the Resistance."

"In that case . . ." He looked back at the scanner. He stared for a moment in disbelief as recognition dawned on him. "Oh hell. I know who did this." He turned the device so that Julio could read the display. "Look there. 'Ell-ess-cee-eye-eye-eye' Lucas S. Carvalho the Third. His name is all over it."

Yelena broke in. "You can give him the vaccine, then. You can cure my brother?" She looked hopeful until she looked in the eyes of the two doctors.

George shook his head. "I'm not sure it will work with symptoms this advanced. I can give him something for the convulsions and swelling, but he needs to be in a hospital."

"No." Both Julio and Yelena spoke at the same time. Julio continued, "If this is deliberate, and I agree that it sure fit's Carvalho's methods, then they've done it to flush the Resistance out. You have reporting instructions on the vaccine, don't you?"

"Yes." He turned to Yelena. "That is the *real* other reason I can't give him the vaccine. I have to report biometrics and DNA, then await an unlock code for the injector." He shook his head and turned back to his old roommate. "Very high tech—Earth tech, not Hamilton—that's just more evidence for your suspicion that this is all a UN plan."

The other family members had returned, so George conveyed instructions for treating the boy. He would need to stay unconscious to survive the night—well, morning. There was a local plant, similar to a very popular drug on Earth. Like that drug, it was often smoked for euphoric effects, but properly prepared it would keep Rodrigo sedated and reduce the convulsions. After providing the care instructions, he retrieved the vial of blood and returned to his lodging to prepare for the day's work.

Yelena had stayed with her brother. It had been a stressful encounter, and George hoped that their relationship would be able to survive it. Julio did not dare to be seen at the hospital or in George's company, so he, too, had left, with only the promise to be in touch. Fortified with *abuela* Guerrero's coffee and a mid-morning nap in an unused exam room, George finished his patient rounds and went to the small laboratory to work with the blood sample he'd taken from Rodrigo.

He'd just gotten started when one of the nurses entered to call him back to the Emergency clinic. A child had come in with convulsions and muscle spasms leading to contracture of the spine, neck and face muscles. He'd already treated three suspected influenza cases this morning. Fortunately, there was a vaccine that covered H9N6 freely available, but if this was K-fever, he would have to decide whether to report the case and give the vaccine, or withhold a potentially life-saving treatment to protect the patient's identity.

Fortunately, George did not have to choose. The patient was the eleven-year-old son of one of the other nurses and unlikely to be a threat. Under the supposition that all medical personnel would need to be protected, he took the biometric and DNA samples and waited for authorization. Within the hour, he'd also received instructions to vaccinate not only the child, but all personnel in the clinic, including himself. That was ominous. If the TNHO felt that all medical workers were at risk, then that meant K-fever was in the wild and spreading, not just targeting insurgents. Could the disease have been spread *specifically* to draw in the insurgents? To force them to come for the vaccine, only to be identified and hauled off by *Guardia* or UN Marines?

After administering the vaccines, George returned to the laboratory. He dared not use the portable DNA sequencer or blood analyzer. They were very likely to be monitored by satellite interface or by one of the UN Space Fleet ships in orbit. He'd have to use the frequently-broken sequencer in the lab. Fortunately, it was very similar to one he had used and often fixed as an undergraduate student in Panama. As long as he removed a side panel and kept it cool, it would work—eventually. After rigging a fan to blow air through a damp towel—both for evaporative cooling and to trap dust and dirt—he set the sequencer to its task and went home for the day.

Well, he almost went home, but decided to go out to the Guerrero farm to check on Yelena and Rodrigo. The boy was no better, but apparently his relationship with Yelena was. She greeted him warmly, in fact, rather hotly. She later mentioned that the very fact he returned to her—and Rodrigo—on his own, told her everything she needed to know about that man who was to be her husband.

After checking on his patient, and confirming instructions with the family members caring for him, George sat down with Yelena's father Enrique Guerrero. After asking, and receiving, the patriarch's blessing, they discussed Rodrigo's prognosis. Yes, the family understood that there was not much that anyone could do for him. No, they did not blame him. Life was hard in Balboa. They would mourn him, but life went on.

Determined to ensure that this life went on without drawing attention or suspicion from the unseen forces behind the spread of K-fever, George said his goodbyes. This time he was accompanied by Yelena, who would not let him return to the lab, but rather insisted that he be properly fed and rested for the next day. Mostly rested. It wasn't as if he was expecting results from the sequencer before morning, anyway.

The next morning he approached hospital rounds with more energy than he'd felt for the past few years. *Is it the challenge? Or the fact that* Don *Guerrero gave his blessing and Yelena said "yes"?* Nevertheless, he had clinical duties to complete before returning to the lab . . . or Yelena. Upon entering the small cluster of exam rooms that comprised the clinic, he was surprised to see a new nurse, freshly assigned by TNHO. He was immediately suspicious, particularly by her fair hair and complexion—clearly Scandinavian or other Caucasian derivation from Earth—although she covered it with a bit too much makeup. She looked familiar, though. For the rest of the day he tried to avoid her, suspecting her to be a UN or TNHO spy.

After his last patient, he sat at the desk he'd installed in a former closet at the back of one of the exam rooms. It was tiny, but it was an office where he could update records and store his years-out-of-date medical textbooks. A knock on the door surprised him. It was the new nurse, and she'd obviously just washed her face in one of the exam rooms—the excessive makeup was gone, and she held a wet cloth in one hand. "A mutual friend told me to tell you it's 'Duck Season,'" she said once she had entered and the door was closed.

As he peered at her it hit him why she'd looked familiar. The makeup had to have been a disguise, because she'd hardly changed in fifteen years. "Annalise." George greeted the girl—woman—who had been Julio's constant companion their final year at Duke. He looked at her some more. No, she'd changed, just not in the face. Still a dancer's physique, but a bit older, and quite a bit tougher. It showed in her body language.

"You look like hell, Doc, but I hear you're getting better." She smiled as she said it. The office was small, but it had a guest chair, and she sat in it. "I told Yelena to keep an eye on you and make sure you were rested last night."

"What, is everyone conspiring against me?" He paused. "Wait, how did you get here?" After a moment he hurriedly added ". . . not that I'm complaining."

"My family was never very compliant with the European Union. They were being punished because I moved to the United States for work and school, and of course they didn't approve of the work I did to put myself through school." She smiled, but it was sad and regretful. "Loss of their Basic Living Allowance unless they emigrated to Terra Nova. They came, so I came. Of course, I have a necessary skill set and was allowed to come voluntarily and choose my posting. It was about two years after Julio emigrated. I looked him up, he was a young idealistic doctor in Aztlan, but that was beginning to change."

"I managed to get my parents settled in Southern Columbia and married Julio, trying to keep him out of trouble since then. Well, actually, I've helped him get *into* trouble, too, but I've also managed to keep him out of the UN's notice."

George sat looking at the woman before him, remembering the nurse who was not quite the airhead that many of Julio's medical school crushes had been. She also had a Master's degree, if he remembered correctly.

"Yes, I do. Molecular Biology," she replied when he asked. The light finally dawned on George.

"Aha! So he sent you to spy on me?" he asked, half in jest.

"Not spy, no . . ." she smiled, this one friendly and reassuring. ". . . but he knew you would need help. I can be your contact and your assistant, both in the lab and clinic."

"In that case, we should get to work." George smiled back then stood, gesturing her to lead the way out of the cramped office and into the lab.

The DNA sequencer had completed its analysis. The output was still a bunch of numbers until compared to the nucleotide and peptide databases. The nucleotides would be used to determine the sequence of amino acids comprising specific protein products, and the proteins *should* identify the virus and any toxins present.

Since George was primarily interested in anything that looked like a virus, he assigned Annalise any sequences identified as normal human protein. She would check everything against known genetic diseases and medical disorders, while he looked for sequences that should not be there . . .

. . . and found it after almost seven hours of intensive scrutiny. He'd sent Annalise home at least an hour ago. It was already dark, but she'd promised to check with Yelena and send back supper if she could. George had identified the genes for H9N6 almost immediately. He'd then looked for the sequences defining the glycoprotein "coat" that formed the exterior shell, but kept coming up against gaps in the sequence that didn't make sense until he recognized that the nucleotides that were being identified were not terrestrial DNA!

He considered the implications. Deoxyribonucleic acid was a complex molecule made up of a long-chain of alternating sugar molecules—deoxyribose—and molecules known as nucleotides or "bases." DNA had four known nucleotides: Guanine, Thymine, Cytosine and Adenosine, which were typically identified by initials: G, T, C, A. The amino acid building blocks of proteins were encoded by sets of three bases, allowing sixty-four possible three base codes, such as A-T-G, G-A-C, C-T-A, etc. There were only twenty known amino acids, though, and George, along with many leading scientists, wondered what the other codes were for. In the early twenty-first century, scientists synthesized novel nucleotides "X" and "Y" and even managed to create single-celled organisms that could replicate DNA with the new components, but no novel naturally occurring amino acids or nucleotides were encountered until Terra Nova was discovered.

Despite decades of humans on Terra Nova, the genetics and

protein structure of Novan life was still largely unexplained. Scientists had identified four additional nucleotides—unimaginatively named simply "M," "N," "O," and "P." The additional bases allowed for up to 512 amino acids, and millions of novel proteins, yet only seven new amino acids had been identified, with about a hundred novel proteins. At least, that was all that was in the medical literature that George could access. Most of the unique proteins encountered on Terra Nova caused allergic reactions in humans, and some Earth life forms. Others seemed simply *inert* or useless except for the fact that they accumulated in the nervous systems of intelligent creatures and acted much like prions or the sludgelike amyloid protein responsible for brain diseases that had been eliminated over a century ago on Earth. Like those ancient diseases, accumulation of too much inert protein in humans ended in encephalitis, dementia and death.

The sequencer had identified the usual G, T, C, and A nucleotides, plus unusually high quantities of the U, uracil, nucleotide normally only found in RNA, plus trace amounts of M, N, O and P. The latter was not unexpected on Terra Nova, and presented no problem by itself. The danger lay in the proteins, not the DNA alone, which could easily be present on the skin. What was most unusual was that the sequencer had also identified two additional nucleotides: "R" and "Q" that George had never seen before. Even stranger was the fact that the nucleotide identities were in the sequencer database, even though the machine had to be at least twenty years old.

These nucleotides had to have been known on Earth when I was in medical school, thought George. On a hunch, he had the sequencer print out its nucleotide reference database; there might be a clue there. He also retreated briefly to his office to fetch a couple of his old textbooks. On the other hand, it would have to wait. He heard Yelena coming, and she was certain to make him stop for the evening, or at least pause for supper.

Yelena had indeed brought food, and news of her brother. He was no longer unconscious or convulsing, but was still in a lot of pain. It was still touch-and-go, and George was torn between getting immediately back to the lab versus heading out to the Guerrero farm to see his patient. She would not allow him to do either, however, claiming that he would not help her brother by being too tired to think straight. She made him lie down in an exam room and watched over him as he got at least two hours sleep.

Upon waking, George sent Yelena back the farm with some special instructions. He wouldn't need what he'd sent her for until tomorrow, but sending her back now would gain him several hours without her or Annalise nagging him to rest and keeping him from the lab. Now, he needed to read through the sequencer database . . .

Shortly after sun-up, George was running around the lab, talking to himself as he started to pull glassware out of cabinets and rummaged through the drawers in the lab looking for components. "It's a virus . . ." He took a long glass cylinder and clamped it to a stand. "Of course, we knew it was a virus . . ." He rotated the cylinder so that it stood upright and fitted a valve to the bottom so that it could be directed to drip into a row of test tubes in a rack below.

". . . but it's flu, not entirely . . . not entirely H9N6, that is . . ." He reached into a drawer and pulled out a packet of white crystalline powder. "There's an additional DNA strand in the viral shell . . ." He dug around for a funnel, placed it in the top of the cylinder, and started to pour the crystals into the cylinder. ". . . it codes a novel protein using synthetic nucleotides." Once the cylinder was nearly full, he tapped the sides of the cylinder to settle the powder.

Annalise walked in to find George frantically racing around the small lab opening drawers and cabinets and muttering hoarsely to himself. "Glass rod . . . glass rod . . . need a glass rod to tamp it all down." He was gasping for breath between words, there was a sheen of sweat on his face, and his eyes were wide and manic.

"DOCTOR!" She shouted, and it brought him up short. He turned and stared, not recognizing her for a moment. Of course she was back to wearing heavy makeup to disguise her face, but it shouldn't have taken quite so long for recognition to dawn on him. "George, sit!" She pulled a lab stool over, grabbed him by the upper arm and pulled him to the chair.

He sat for several minutes, breathing heavily, and slowly the frenzied expression faded. He eyes were still alight with discovery, though.

"You've found something, haven't you." It was a statement, not a question.

He nodded. She'd pressed a glass of water in his hands. Not coffee—the last thing he needed was coffee. He drank deeply, swallowed, then sat quietly for a bit more before calmly answering. "It's the nucleotides. Native Terra Nova life has additional DNA nucleotides."

"Right. That's the first thing we have to learn before getting licensed on Nova." She raised an eyebrow at him as he tried to rise from the chair. "Sit. Go on."

He took another drink and then continued. "We learned that the Earth has known about the Terra Nova nucleotides for decades and synthesized their own variants. They even named them in sequence with the Novan bases." He motioned to the separator column on the lab bench. "Have you seen the glass rods? I need to tamp that down before I run the separation?"

Glaring at him to keep him seated, Annalise opened a drawer and pulled out a glass rod no bigger than a pencil. She lit an alcohol burner, flame sterilized the glass rod, then used it to compress the white powder in the column. When George tried to rise again, she waved him back. "Stay seated; you're in no shape to load a column, you'll pour too fast and stir up the surface of the gel." Although manic, he'd maintained standard lab and clinical safety rules, so everything was clearly—well, within limits of his handwriting—labeled. She picked up a beaker covered with wax paper, looked at him with raised eyebrow, and he nodded.

While Annalise carefully added the clear liquid to the column of white powder, George continued. "Terra Novan life has M, N, O and P nucleotides. Earth synthesized Q and R . . . and they immediately found some unusual proteins."

Annalise tapped the side of the cylinder, dislodging bubbles. She poured more liquid in the top while gradually letting some out through the valve at the bottom, never allowing the level at the top to go below the top of the crystals. When she straightened up and looked back at George, she could see the signs of fatigue warring with the realization of discovery.

"So, that's what we're separating? One of those proteins?" She looked him up and down, then smiled sweetly. He knew that look. Yelena had one just like it. "And just how much coffee have you had this morning? Or should I ask how much since last night? Yelena said she was going to make you sleep where is she? Should I call her?"

He shook his head. "No, this can't wait. We need to do this for Rodrigo and we can't wait."

"I *know* that!" She responded hotly. "But I can do this for you! You have to see patients, and you're in no condition to do that right now. I should call for Yelena."

"No, no need." He shook off the hand she used to restrain him as he tried to stand. He went over to the tabletop centrifuge, removed the cover and took out a tube with a dark red solid on the bottom and amber liquid above. "Dr. Espinoza is in the clinic today, and he has the students helping him. I sent Yelena out to the farm. Told her to have the younger kids catch me four rabbits and a dozen frogs."

He went to place the tube from the centrifuge into the rack with the other tubes, but fumbled, and almost dropped the tube on the floor. Annalise gently took it from his hands, and not-so-gently pushed him back toward the chair. "I will do this. I am your hands, you're too jittery. You will drop it or break it. Now, what next?"

George conceded and dropped back onto the chair. "Electrophoresis. We use the electrical charge on the protein to separate it by size and weight. I found a control sample of green fluorescent protein close to the right size of the protein we're looking for. It will come out the bottom of the column right before the protein we're after. Then we drip some of it on frog's leg muscle to see if it causes convulsions."

"Wait. If we're doing electrophoresis, what's the separation column for?" She pointed to the powder and liquid filled glassware on the bench.

"Oh, I forgot!" George started to rise yet again, but stopped himself before Annalise would react. "Sorry. That's for after. Separate electrically, test on frog muscle, and if it works, we'll need the column."

"Okay. That's better. One thing at a time." Annalise found the components he'd prepared, then opened a packet containing a sterile pipette and carefully drew some of the amber liquid and placed it on the electrophoresis assembly. She opened another pipette and extracted some greenish liquid from a bottle and also placed it on the gel. She connected a battery, then set a timer and closed the drawer so that the room lights could not affect the process. "This is prehistoric medicine," she said as she pulled out some black fabric to drape over the separation column until they needed it.

"Mid-twentieth century," George replied. "But effective. If the extract causes the frog muscle to twitch, we'll inject it into rabbits to see if we can make an antibody. I also have some ideas about using P nucleotide from *antaniae* saliva to make an antitoxin."

There was the sound of the outside door, and a female voice called from the clinic. Yelena had returned with the frogs and rabbits. Annalise went to greet her, and George could hear the sounds of them talking. Probably deciding whether he needed to be forcibly restrained in order to force him to rest. He smiled at the thought—it meant they cared, and he couldn't argue with that. He sat back and closed his eyes. "For now, we wait."

It had been almost two weeks, but Rodrigo was still hanging on. He was pale and thin. The family forced him to drink rich broths when he was awake to maintain both nutrients and fluids. He spent most of his time unconscious, though, sedated by herbal extracts. George was concerned about the long-term effects of the drug, but the boy would have to survive for them to worry about that. It was doubtful that the antibody would work quickly enough to help, so, with the family's permission, he was about to try the antitoxin.

The boy's arms were so thin; George was unable to get the needle into a vein to deliver the injection. Julio had returned, and was about to try when Annalise pushed them both out of the way, manipulated the needle for just a moment, drew back the plunger to reveal a small amount of dark red blood, then deftly injected the antitoxin. She looked up and glared briefly at both men, then smiled sweetly.

"That's why I married her," Julio said. Annalise just snorted.

Rodrigo had been sleeping, mouth open, breathing heavily through his constricted larynx. The harsh snoring—so like the sound of a hunter's duck call—cut off. His body started to convulse and both doctors immediately reached to restrain the heaving body. Yelena gasped and started to cry, but after a moment, the convulsions eased and his breathing resumed with a gasp.

The snoring faded, and George could see the muscles in the face relax. He reached his hand to feel Rodrigo's throat. It too appeared to be relaxing.

This might just work.

The four watched Rodrigo for another hour before turning over the watch to Emilio and retreating to the farmhouse. It was late night, and Julio had men making sure that there had been no unwanted "guests" following any of them. George had been out to the farm many evenings, and it was now common knowledge that he was engaged to Yelena. No one from the UN or TNHO seemed to care too much about Balboa, given the reports that many insurgents were being caught elsewhere, having been discovered when UN and TNHO "humanitarian missions" were vaccinating locals against a virulent new strain of influenza.

"So we have a cure and a vaccine that the UN can't trace. Tell me, Tonio, operationally speaking, what's to keep them—to keep *Carvalho*—from doing this again?" Julio asked George while they sat in the kitchen drinking coffee with a healthy serving of Don Guerrero's whiskey.

"We know the gene sequence. We know what we're looking for. It will take them time to synthesize a novel nucleotide, and even then, they mostly don't work. R and Q only work because they just copied Novan nucleotides." There were dark circles under George's eyes, but with Yelena snuggled up under his arm, he looked at peace. "Besides, right now, I know more about Novan genetics and immunology than anyone on Earth."

"No, that's a technical answer," Julio corrected patiently. "I asked you an *operational* question. What is to *keep* them from doing this again?"

"Oh." George thought a moment. "Well, I *am* the person most knowledgeable about Novan genetics and how it interacts with human immune system. I suppose we could send them a message. 'Try this again, and we release a countervirus on Earth.' It could be a targeted direct-contact virus with secondary spread to anyone on Earth that's had contact with the Novan nucleotides. That would limit collateral spread to just Carvalho and the lab that made K-fever."

"Now *that* is an operational answer!"

George smiled as he wiped disinfectant on Julio's arm and gave him the second injection. "You're lucky you get to go back after only fifteen years."

Julio grinned back, "You should have read the fine print in the contract, *Jorge*. Standard loan repayment is ten years or fifteen including residency. Sabbaticals and fellowships kick after seven years. You got taken *amigo* . . ." He stopped as he saw the smile disappear from his friend's face. "I'm sorry, George, it wasn't supposed to happen that way."

"It's the past, Julio. I'm alive, and not in an unmarked grave in Durham or Chorillo. Besides, it wasn't your fault or mine; it was the fault of the WHO officials who promoted the bastard." George smiled again, "Besides, I met Yelena here. Her father said 'yes,' so we're getting married in the spring. I'd ask you to be Best Man, but well, you've got to go."

"Yes, *amigo*, I do . . . or well, that's supposed to be your line." Julio's grin was back as he pulled down his shirt sleeve and reached over to pull back the sleeve on the opposite arm.

"Nope, this one goes in the buttocks, drop 'em." George held up the third syringe as Julio winced, then complied. "Okay, that's vaccines for H9N6-gamma and K-fever, as well as the Payload." George put the empty syringe in a heavy red box and closed the lid. A light on the cover turned red and then blinked yellow, followed by a momentary flash of bright light around the edges of the lid, before turning green. "Okay, we're clean. Now, what are you going to do once you get to Earth?"

"The fellowship is with Pegram's old department. The *hombre gruñón* was forced out by WHO many years ago, but there will be people who remember what happened. They can extract the Payload from my blood and prepare the serum. The WHO annual inspection won't be for another four to six months after I arrive." Julio stood up and buckled his belt.

". . . and if Lord Lucas accompanies the inspection?"

"We have word that he's usually there at some point during the inspection. The new dean is his biggest fan, and Carvalho loves the adoration. We'll be ready. If I can't deliver the payload in person—or even if he doesn't come, we can get to someone in his office." Julio winced as he worked his arm. "*Maldito*, that stings."

"These sources of yours, you trust them?" George looked doubtful.

"We have a few friends in the new 'United Nations Peace Force' that is replacing the UN Space Fleet and at least one at WHO—but no, I don't trust them. That's why they all think the 'message' to Carvalho is a *computer* virus!"

"Hah," George responded mirthlessly as he disposed of the remaining syringes in the "sharps" receptacle and placed the used gauze and alcohol wipes in the 'cycler. "You'll need a source of either natural P or synthetic Q nucleotide to activate the payload. I don't think you'll find very much *antaniae* saliva on Earth."

"*Si, Madre.* I know, I know. The Genetics department should have it, or Biomedical Engineering. They were working on it during my previous sabbatical, and my sources tell me that they can get actual venom if I need it . . . just so long as I don't carry it myself." Julio reached out to clasp his friend's shoulder. "You know, *amigo*, you should have stayed in Infectious Diseases. You're very good at it."

George looked away. "I'm needed here."

Julio released his shoulder when George wouldn't look at him. "I know," he spoke quietly. "We could have lost a lot of good men. Besides, I need you to keep an eye on Annalise for me. This is probably a one-way trip." When George looked up, there were tears in his eyes. Julio continued, "I know, my friend. It shouldn't be this way. We took an oath: 'First, do no harm.'"

George's expression hardened. "Yes, but they broke it first—a long time ago." He put his hand to his face, remembering the contours of the face he'd been born with, and smiled a cold, bitter smile. "Sometimes, you have to be a surgeon and cut out the cancer before it spreads."

INTERLUDE:
From Jimenez's *History of the Wars of Liberation*

It's never been entirely clear whether or not Belisario Carrera knew, either at the time or for many years after, just who he had killed in defense of his village. His own memoirs smack a bit of revisionism, and of remembering with, as we say, "advantages."

What is clear, however, was that the death of High Admiral Kotek Annan spiraled very quickly into punitive expeditions, on the part of the UN, attempts at biological warfare by its medical branch, terrorism on the part of everyone, and a cycle of atrocity, reprisal, counter-atrocity, counter-reprisal, mayhem, massacre, not a little rape . . .

From *Primer Grito: The Memoirs of the Liberator,* Belisario Carrera

They can't have been very well trained, I thought. I wasn't either, of course; *I* wasn't trained at all. If I had been, I wouldn't have opened our ambush with the order, "READY . . . fire!" but with my own rifle.

Didn't make a bit of difference, as it turned out, since they couldn't hear me over the sounds of their own firing. Indeed, their first warning was when half of them went down in the course of a second or two. Since one of those had taken an arrow in the throat, that meant that our thirty-two shots had managed to inflict a grand total of four wounds, or about one in eight. At under one hundred and fifty meters. With no one actually shooting back. From a prone position.

Yes, we sucked at the time and for some time after.

On the other hand, since of the five beaters still standing, only two knew to take cover, we were not appreciably behind the learning curve of the UN Marines of the day, either. No, I had a hard time believing this, too, and I saw it with my own eyes.

"Reload," I called out, "reload!"

We weren't drilled for rapid reload, but some were faster than others. Over the next minute another thirty or forty shots rang out, irregularly. Sometimes it would be three of four shots within the second; sometimes there would be a gap of four or five seconds between shots. The last half of the minute was wasted, as the remaining standing Marines were bowled over. Me, I was too busy thinking to even attempt to reload.

There was a brief flurry of shots overhead. Out of the corner of one eye I saw Little Pedro fall limp and soundless to the ground. His father screamed.

I sent some more men up into the trees, shouting, "Cover us." Then I told the rest, once again, "Follow me," adding, "Kill them all, then we'll go after the other group."

I'd said, "Follow me," but the villagers weren't paying close attention. In other words, they rushed out on their own, rifles ready. I heard a lot of begging interspersed with the occasional shot . . . or the more frightful scream as someone bludgeoned a survivor to death. Myself, I followed them out but heading for the dandy who'd kept a bit behind.

As I advanced, I passed one of the UN Marines, laying flat on the ground with his arms stretched out above his head. A quick glance showed a lead splotch on his armor but I couldn't see where it had penetrated. Maybe he'd had a rib broken. Maybe he'd just lost his wind or been shocked.

He begged, but in a language I didn't recognize. Pedro el Cholo was standing over him pointing a rifle at his head, one handed. The Marine closed his eyes and began to pray; I don't know to who. The shot, mid-prayer, basically caused his head to explode, the top of his skull, skin and hair attached, flying away, spinning flecks of blood all around.

You'll get that when you use a fifty-seven caliber rifle firing a two ounce Minié ball at point blank range.

I continued on until I found my target, lying on his side, trying desperately to staunch the flow of blood from his shattered thigh.

His rifle, a very nice, expensive-looking rifle, lay by his side. By rights it belonged to me now. I kicked it out of his reach before he could try to take back *my* rifle.

For a joke, I cocked the rifle I carried and pointed it at his head, then pulled the trigger. I was rewarded with both a scream and the sudden aroma of voided bowels.

I told him, and this is exactly what I told him, though I don't know if he understood, "I should burn you alive. I should burn you alive, you bastard, but there isn't time. Still, you won't live to gain revenge for this."

I drew my machete and raised it. He put his arms up and squeaked like a little girl. I swung, lopping off one of his hands but then only digging maybe an inch into his neck.

His eyes widened bigger than I'd have thought possible. He reached with his remaining hand to try to stop the blood gushing from his neck. A coppery stink added itself to the stink of the UN bastard's shit. I hacked again, and then again. On my fourth slash, his head came free and began to roll . . .

I picked up my new rifle and looked around, seeing that my people were doing the same.

"Now let's go get the rest of them!"

6.
BELLONA'S GIFT

Monalisa Foster[7]

Mitzi stood on the lookout's cliff, right up against the ledge, sandaled feet solidly set atop the rock. Her boonie hat, with its broad, drooping brim and dark green, military mottling eased the late afternoon glare as she kept watch.

Hundreds of meters below, the crash of the waves wasn't quite right. Even after more than a decade, she could hear the difference of rhythm, like a song played on a piano with a missing key. Terra Nova's three moons rivaled Earth's only when they were properly aligned. Even then, the tides weren't as strong, and for some reason, it was the wrongness of those crashing waves that still stood out. Not the color. Not the smell. Her memories of those things had faded enough that *these* colors, *these* scents now had the familiarity of home.

Insidious progressivines had crept right up to the ledge. Like giant snakes or the tentacles of some vile monster, they would eventually choke out everything around them. An odd species, more parasite and man-trap than weed, the result was always the same: a slow blight of destruction in need of constant pruning. She stomped a vine into the soil. Within moments, her feet and ankles were stained with

---

7 Monalisa Foster won life's lottery when she escaped communism and became an unhyphenated American citizen. Her works tend to explore themes of freedom, liberty, and personal responsibility. Despite her degree in physics, she's worked in several fields including engineering and medicine, but she enjoys being a trophy wife and kept woman the most. She and her husband (who is a writer-once-removed via their marriage) are living their happily ever after in Texas, along with their children, both human and canine. Her publications can be found at www.monalisafoster.com/works.

an oozing, oily green-black. Taking a deep, cleansing breath she cast her gaze back out over the Shimmering Sea.

The breeze shifted with the clouds darkening the horizon. The line separating water and sky blurred. It hardly seemed worth making the climb, but there was something about all that unbroken water, that ever-changing sky, that beckoning vastness that made her volunteer to make the climb twice a day. She blinked the wind-sourced moisture from her lashes. Out there, a white speck separated the seam of water and sky.

She raised the binoculars to her eyes and adjusted one eyepiece and then the other. The speck was still a speck, albeit several times bigger. Shaped like a megalodon's fin, it rose peacefully from beneath the horizon rather than slicing through the water.

A mast and the hint of a sail. *Definitely not a meg.* Nevertheless, her stomach hardened, and the hairs on the back of her neck rose.

Calm down. *They* swoop in from the sky.

"They" being the enemy. The UN cowards. The thieves, murderers and rapists that had uprooted her family and sentenced them to "transportation."

Such an innocent word. Much better than exile or deportation or being forever torn from everything and everyone you've ever known, profound loss the only certainty in your life. Much better than being shoved into a coffin and frozen, not knowing if you'd ever wake up, your life now in the hands of the same people that took your lands, your home, and your innocence. Much better than being a troublesome piece of meat.

Even after all these years, memories of waking up on the *Amerigo Vespucci* colonization ship made an arctic chill seep into her soul. Despite the tropical heat, goosebumps rose on her body.

It had been years since anything good had come to Cochea. Uprooted once again, her people had fled the tiny settlement they'd come to call home: the women, children, and elderly to the caves; the men to the jungle. Mitzi's father, Belisario Carrera, and his men were now scattered across two hundred square kilometers on the other side of the isthmus, their numbers dwindling by the day, but not as fast as the ammo for their captured guns. For lack of ammunition to feed them, their best fighters had resorted to burying even their prized sniper rifles.

Her father had been known to say, "The war goes on until we are, all of us, free."

The dead are free, aren't they?

The binoculars quivered for a moment, then steadied. The main mast was joined by two others. At the bow, four-stacked sails swelled and billowed with the wind.

There was no flag, at least not that she could see.

She shoved the binoculars into her knapsack and carefully looked down. Nine-year-old Diego had climbed down onto a sliver of an outcropping about ten meters down the cliff-face. The boy was like a mountain goat, spry, sure-footed, and fearless, whereas it took all her will to just stand there. She called down, describing what she'd seen and told him to warn the others. He nodded and jumped to another ledge.

Mitzi took a step back, no longer able to bear the vertigo. She drank the last of her water from the battered canteen at her waist, and resumed her watch. It was nearly sundown when she left the cliff and headed down the trail. A cooling westerly breeze tugged the boonie hat off her head, sending her hair down in a tumble. She gathered and twisted it back into a sweat-soaked bun, reseated the hat and tightened the chin strap.

The muddy, well-worn footpath snaked into the perpetual twilight of the jungle's triple canopy. The vegetation intertwined so closely that by the time light reached the jungled floor, it lost to darkness.

Sandals sloshing, she raced past pools of fading light. She turned at a fork marked by the rusting, crumpled remains of an enemy vehicle. The cowards had abandoned it to the jungle.

Covered in slime and moss, it was slowly blending into its surroundings. The not-so-native trixies had claimed it as their own. One of the red-and-gold flying reptiles, its bony tail swishing back and forth, preened atop the barrel of the vehicle's roof-mounted mini-gun. The trixie screeched, revealing razor-sharp teeth.

"I know, I know."

Mitzi wasn't exactly small, or old, or weak, but she was alone, and the venom-less, septic-mouthed moonbats that came out at night could still take a bite out of her. Unarmed, she couldn't fight them off, and even one bite would debilitate her enough to allow the vile creatures to feed on her at their leisure.

They'd take their time too, the nasty things. They preferred the taste of still-living prey and, barring rescue by a flock of ravenous trixies—the moonbats' natural predators—well, it'd be a long, unpleasant death. She quickened her pace.

As much as she liked running, it hurt to keep up any sort of momentum for very long, even if she crossed her arms. And how well can anyone be expected to run with her arms across her chest?

Back on Earth there might have been a chance to do something about the stupid things that had sprouted from her chest, but here . . . Not that it was all bad here, or at least hadn't been until Kotek Annan and his thugs had decided that young Balboan women and boys made desirable slaves.

Maybe one day she'd look back and laugh at the irony of it all. Had one Robert Nyere, UN bureaucrat and *maricón*, not suggested that "something can be worked out" to her father—that something being Mitzi herself in lieu of taking their ancestral land for redistribution—they might have never been "transported" to Terra Nova in the first place. She wasn't supposed to know that it was Nyere's death—it wasn't murder to defend the life or freedom or safety or chastity of one's child—that had landed them here. Even at thirteen, men had found her sexy. Well, the assets on her chest at least. And those assets had only grown in the years since. Not that there'd been anyone to appreciate them. That was the downside to being *el jefe's* daughter.

By the time Mitzi made it to the beach, Hecate, the largest of Terra Nova's three moons, bathed the cove in silver light, giving everything a ghostly cast.

Even the jungle canopy—so green it had hurt her eyes when they'd first landed here—looked gray.

The ship—a caravel, she was sure now—had anchored in the cove, its sails stowed. A dinghy sat on the beach, rocking slowly with the paltry tide, almost in time with the sway of the black palms.

Two unarmed gringos—those light of skin, eyes, and, frequently, hair—knelt on the sand, their fingers laced behind their heads. Sweat stained the fine, if wrinkled, fabric of their shirts. Beads of moisture pooled to run down their faces, and tensing muscles strained with the rigid postures. They sported short hair darkened by perspiration.

Even in Hecate's light, one was still identifiable as blond. The other had dark hair like her own.

These weren't the big, strong men with red cloths around their heads that had come to Cochea with their curved knives, their tanks, and the reek of never-washed bodies. These men were little more than boys, clean-shaven and soft under their unusual clothes. She'd seen such well-made clothing before, in the big cities. The kind of stuff rich and leisurely UN personnel—or transportees who'd sold their souls—wore to be comfortable in the unforgiving heat and humidity of the Balboa Colony.

Mitzi's mother, Helen, had mounted her *escopeta*, and had it squarely aimed at the leader's head. Rather, it was aimed squarely at the young man who was at the front. Whether or not he was the leader appeared to be in question. They didn't seem to notice Mitzi as she trudged across the beach, kicking sand in her wake. Two *cholo* boys—Felix, aged ten, and Rafael, who had just turned eleven—both still too young to join the fighting men in the jungle, stood off to her right, bows drawn and arrows nocked. Their loincloth-clad grandfathers covered the kneeling men from the other side.

Would the gringos be so scared if they'd known that the muzzle loaders the old men had on them were probably loaded with too-wet powder? Or that her mother's shotgun likely held her last two shells? At least the boys were good with their arrows, as a number of wild turkeys and other tasty birds could attest.

"We're here to help," Golden Boy said.

"Sure you are," her mother said, leading with the *escopeta*. "We've heard that before."

Golden Boy stared into the double barrels. Whatever he was about to say caught in his throat.

"Mostly from those who say they come to do good," her mother continued, her voice full of menace. "Somehow they're the only ones who come out doing well, and it's by helping themselves."

For an overlong moment, only the sound of pounding surf, stirring wind, and the occasional hoot of a distant monkey could be heard.

"Ma'am," the tall, dark-haired gringo said. "We're from Desperation Bay. The Lansing Colony. Let me show you." His hand drifted from behind his head.

Her mother took a step back, placing herself out of Golden Boy's reach, and swung the *escopeta* toward Tall and Dark. His hand shot right back, lacing itself tight.

Without taking her gaze off him, her mother said, "Mitzi. Check the boat."

Mitzi circled wide, keeping her distance. She caught her mother's gaze as she crossed into the surf. *And I thought Mom was scary when she was pissed at me.*

Froth and a frond of Terra Novan seaweed tugged at Mitzi's feet as she pushed an oar aside and cautiously leaned over to get a better look. A single wooden crate rested within.

"The crate's not locked," Tall and Dark said. "I can—"

"Shut up, Juan," Golden Boy said.

Mitzi grabbed the hull and vaulted into the boat, landing with a thud that barely rocked it. Two metal latches held the crate's lid in place. She popped them both and lifted.

The scent of gun oil billowed upward, overpowering the saltiness of the sea, the stench of fear, the earthiness of the jungle. Six bolt action rifles—honest-to-God-as-far-as-she-could-tell modern arms—rested on carved wooden supports. With trembling hands she touched one. Small boxes lined the crate. She pulled one up and fumbled it open.

Ammunition. Thousands of rounds by the look of it.

A treasure trove. Life. Freedom. Liberty.

"We have more," Juan said. "Dozens of crates. A thousand rounds for each rifle." Eager blue eyes and the hint of a smile sent a wave of heat right into her face. She said a quick prayer, thanking God not just for the crate and its contents, but for masking her blush with Hecate's silver light.

"Mitzi, what is it?"

"Umm, Mom, you're going to want to see this for yourself."

"So, that's your mom," Juan said, stealing a sideways glance at the girl the Cocheans called Mitzi.

The answer was patently obvious. Tall and shapely, both women looked like they'd been cut from the same exquisite material by a master artist. That artist should've been around here somewhere, on his knees, playing Pygmalion driven insane, trying to decide which Galatea was the loveliest.

Joe Putnam elbowed him in the ribs and Juan almost lost his grip on the rope. They had lashed two crates together and were dragging them across the beach. One hundred and thirty eight steps away—he'd made the trip often enough to know the number very well—a cavern was tucked into the cliffs and the Cochean rebels had decided it was the best place to stow their treasure.

Joe, the oldest of their group, had set himself up as spokesman and his ill-chosen words had doomed their first contact with the rebels. They should've anticipated a less than friendly welcome given the rumors that had convinced Lansing Colony's leader, Elder Oliver Rogers, to send them here in the first place. If half the stories about the rape and dismemberment of pre-pubescent children were true, Juan wouldn't trust strangers either.

Even so, the rifles and ammunition hadn't gone to greasing the skids as much as he'd expected. These people didn't give their trust easily. That had to mean something. Maybe even something good.

Inside the cavern, Juan helped Joe lift one crate atop the stack already there, both of them straining under Mitzi's watchful gaze. She cradled one of the rifles they'd brought. Again, Juan silently questioned the decision to come ashore unarmed. He swiped his sweat-soaked brow and slapped Joe encouragingly on the back as they headed for the cave mouth.

They passed the other two members of their team, Carr and his half-brother Letham. Both were Elder Rogers' adopted kids, survivors of the wintery hell that had given their home the moniker of Starvation Bay. The Rogers had stayed aboard the *Carcharodon* to mind the cargo and make sure the hired crew didn't panic and turn tail. Joe had chosen the Rogers brothers because of their level-headedness. At least that decision had borne out.

Carr and Letham gripped the handle of a crate with both hands, their faces dark with exertion, arms and legs straining, moving with that awkward somewhat sideways shuffle while one of the Cochean kids covered them. The skinny, loin-clothed kid had some awful—and recent—scarring on his back. Juan averted his gaze and sought something nice to look at.

"Mitzi's a German nickname, you know," Juan said. "Is that short for Maria or something?"

She graced him with the barest hint of a smile. "How could it be *short* for Maria?"

"Oh, right. Five letters for five letters. Not short for something then?"

Mitzi stepped through a pool of light cast by a torch set in the sand to mark the makeshift path. She had taken her hat off, letting it hang down her back. A chin strap circled an elegant neck sparkling with a thin sheen of dewy girl-sweat.

Those cheekbones. Those eyes. Those . . . Wow. He cleared his throat. "Miriam? Marianne?"

"Alvarez!" Joe said, "shut it already."

Mitzi's smile widened, but just for an instant. A shout drew her attention towards the sea.

The old Indios had unloaded their oversized backpacks and piled them just outside the surf's reach. The dinghy was still beached, a few steps away. Set against the sea, the waiting crewman was in shadow, barely a silhouette, but obviously set to shove off as soon as he got the signal.

"You should go back home," Mitzi's mother said, her voice hard. At least she wasn't pointing that double-barreled monstrosity at them anymore.

"I'm sorry, but we can't do that," Joe said. "We swore an oath to deliver these arms to Belisario Carrera, and we won't be leaving until we've done that. Like I said, we're here to h—"

Juan stomped Joe's foot. It gave way in the soft sand, but it was enough to shut him up. Smart as a whip, Joe had no common sense. It was obvious to anyone with even a meager ounce of that precious substance that these people had been "helped" right off Earth and that they saw "help" as either thinly disguised meddling, at best, or as a prelude to ruin, at worst.

"Ma'am," Juan said, "if you don't stop the UN here in Balboa, it won't be long before they come to Lansing Colony, to Desperation Bay, to our homes. We'd rather help you stop them here and now. So, you see . . . "

Was that a tremor in her hands? If so, it was fleeting. As fleeting as the start of the smile he thought he saw.

One of the elders spoke to her in Spanish. Her slightly less suspicious gaze remained on Juan and his friends. The old man fell silent and took a step back. Not a woman prone to hasty decisions, she seemed to be considering his words.

She issued a series of commands, the word "gringos" the only one that Juan recognized. Despite his name, Juan spoke no Spanish. His family, like most of the Lansing Colony's transplants, hailed from English-speaking North America.

While missionary work had been the trademark of their faith since the early nineteenth century, the Gag Treaty had ended their proselytizing. Joe, the Rogers kids, and Juan had been chosen for this mission because they were young, strong, and single, not for their linguistic or diplomatic skills.

"Tell the ship to leave," she said.

Joe grabbed a handkerchief from his back pocket and waved it in a wide arc five times. The man by the dinghy shoved off like his life depended on it.

"You'll stay here for the night," Mitzi's mother said as Carr, Letham, and the boy guarding them returned. She issued a few terse orders in Spanish and headed for the jungle without so much as a backward glance, taking that double-barreled monstrosity with her.

"Grab your gear," Mitzi said, encouraging them with a nod of her all too pretty chin. A chin topped by the nicest set of lips.

Juan looked away. *Oh, look, sand. Lots and lots of sand.*

He followed Joe's lead. They grabbed their gear and with nothing but the most careful, slow motions of the cowed and non-threatening, built a fire inside the shelter of the cave mouth. Once the fire burned steadily, they laid out their bedrolls and broke out some of their supplies while the Cocheans watched. The old men were mere shadows outside the firelight's edge. The younger of the boys had disappeared.

Juan, sitting cross-legged atop his bedroll, held his canteen out toward the scarred boy. "Thirsty?"

The boy shook his head and blinked with the eyes of an old soul hardened by things too horrible to be spoken.

Juan took a careful sip and offered the canteen again. The boy retreated into shadow.

"Rafael doesn't like gringos," Mitzi said. She grabbed the canteen and took a long, hard swallow.

"His back. Gringos did that?" Juan asked.

She nodded and returned the canteen, flashing an ample bosom hiding inside a man's shirt. Not too well hidden, though. His mouth snapped shut. He prepared an apology, but Mitzi's attention was, thankfully, drawn by the flapping of wings overhead.

He followed her gaze, but couldn't make anything out. Desperate for something to do—lest he be tempted to gawk and reveal the baser side of his nature that seemed to rear its head whenever she was close—he reached for his backpack. She stepped back, one hand bracing the strap cutting diagonally across her chest like she was about to swing the rifle forward.

"Let me see what's in the bag," she said, her softness turning to steel. Her rifle remained behind her back. "All of you."

In unison, three sets of judging eyes were leveled at him. Carefully, they dumped their packs. Protein bars, extra socks and underwear, and compact versions of their sacred texts tumbled into piles, along with odds and ends. A harmonica. Folding pocket knives. A sparker for starting fires. Pens and fishing lures, bug repellent and never-used first-aid kits.

Mitzi picked up Joe's knife and flicked it open. She studied the blade and closed it with a snap. Staring, she apparently took his measure and then handed the knife back. He pocketed it and mumbled his thanks. She used her foot to nudge more of their things around, then nodded to each boy in turn. They took it as permission to repack.

Would Mitzi's mother have been so trusting? Or maybe he and his friends just didn't come across as a threat. Was that good or not?

By the time Mitzi got to Juan, she looked positively relaxed as she nudged his books aside. A family picture slipped out. She knelt and picked up the photograph by its scalloped edges.

"Your family?" Mitzi asked, casting him a long, puzzled look.

He nodded, pointing at the uniformed man standing in the center. "My father. He's our sheriff."

"Mother?" She pointed at one of his father's wives.

"No, my mother died some years before this was taken."

"And this one? Sister?" Again with that skeptical look.

"Kelly. Dad's number three wife." He proudly rattled off the names and ages of the bevy of siblings, introducing her to his family tree. As far as families went, his wasn't all that large, but her eyes kept going wider and wider, so he trailed off, pride fading to uneasiness.

"Three wives. Does that mean two men have to go without?"

He laughed at the innocent question. His friends chuckled, but a moment later returned to pretending not to overhear.

"No, not really. More of the women survived, that's all. It seemed . . . natural. The best way to handle things. Until things even out anyway." His gaze sought the ground again.

"Is that why you are here?" No longer innocent or curious, her voice had a hard edge to it. "For women?"

"No, no. We're not like the Earthers." He bit his lip. She'd probably been born on Earth. Elder Rogers and most of their colony had been too. "I mean those from Earth who'd set up *Ciudad* Balboa, the compound that Belisario Carrera attacked last year. The peacekeeping force the OAU and the UN sent—"

"I know what you mean." She pushed up from the ground and thrust the picture back at him. Her steps rang with vitriol as she walked off.

"Nice going, Romeo," Joe said.

Mitzi used a sharpened stick to stab the coals. Sparks flew skyward, caught in the updraft.

Felix had finally returned from a nearby river with a water skin almost as big as he was. She'd been worried about sending him anywhere near the jungle. Even armed with a rifle, his size made him a tempting target for the moonbats. What they really needed were more shotguns, like the one her mother had. Scatterguns made mincemeat out of the nocturnal predators, the two-foot-long moonbats also called *antaniae*.

When a campus of *antaniae* attacked, picking them off one at a time with rifle or arrow was a better way to go than not fighting back at all, but not by much. In the end you were still painfully, lingeringly, dead. And with only Hecate's miserly light to guide Felix and provide some protection, he'd been either lucky or careful or both. But they'd needed fresh water, and would need even more in the morning when Mother returned with a mule train and such women, children or elderly as could make the trip.

While Felix had been getting water, old Palala had netted several fish. They were now simmering inside giant eucalemon fronds, tied with string vines. She stabbed the coals again, almost dislodging the frond-wrapped morsels. Fish oil dripped and splattered onto the coals, sending up a hissing waft of lemon and eucalyptus.

The gringos were gathered together, praying to "Heavenly Father," thanking Him for blessing their voyage, their mission, and asking for His forgiveness. Whatever sins did these clean, soft-looking young men attribute to themselves?

Still, she'd never seen the *maricones* pray. At least not the ones giving the orders. *Some of their troops sometimes did. Mostly before Father shot or hanged them.*

There was a sincerity about these young men that bothered her. No one from a place called Desperation Bay should be so trusting. To come unarmed. To insist on staying.

There was a war on. Had they not heard? And they'd come to help the losing side. Even the "peacekeeping" *maricones* would shed their "enlightened" pacifist views for the crime of arms smuggling. These unfortunate young men would never make it to their tribunals. They were too old for the slave markets. If they didn't "suicide" they'd likely get shot while trying to "escape."

Stirring the coals unnecessarily again, she stole a glance at the one that didn't look at her chest, but held her gaze instead. And it was not in that don't-look-at-her-chest sort of way, but in an I-see-*you* sort of way. The Balboa Colony was not known for its tall men, which wouldn't matter much to anyone but a tall woman like herself. This Juan Alvarez was probably taller than Father, who remained the tallest Balboan she'd ever seen.

He was smart too, saying just the right thing to get her mother to give them a chance. Despite all that'd been done to their people, even her mother wasn't ready to kill the gringos for no reason, but she had been ready to force them back onto the boat. And she had been ready to wound one of them to make her point.

Well, Mother said "wound," but how do you wound with a shotgun?

Mitzi pulled the fish from the fire. She placed several bundles on a piece of flat driftwood and walked the offering to the gringos.

Juan's smile was spectacular; his thanks, profuse.

"It's just fish," she said more curtly than she'd intended and declined their invitation to partake in the packaged foods they'd brought.

She walked away, cheeks warming with guilt for her rudeness, resenting how this war had eroded her people's customs and culture. To think that once, her people had been known for their hospitality.

It had taken the better part of the morning for Juan and his friends to get the crates loaded onto the mules that Mitzi's mother had brought back. The rest of the day had been spent traveling under the jungle's soaring triple canopy, negotiating well-worn but twisting mud paths and traversing small streams.

Twice, the sky had released torrents of rain that stopped as suddenly as they'd started, as if the clouds had changed their mind. Juan went from being soaked in sweat to just being soaked, but mostly he didn't mind.

Mitzi walked ahead of him, distracting him from the way his backpack dug into his shoulders and strained his back, a reminder that he wasn't as well prepared as he'd believed. The way that belt hugged her hips as they swayed also softened the somber realization that they were, for the first time, truly on their own.

Did these Cocheans have the means to communicate with the outside world, or were they going to have to walk across the Balboan isthmus towards whatever passed for civilization?

How would Elder Rogers get word of their success?

Or their failure?

They emerged into a valley with forgiving slopes and a dozen or so huts with conical thatch roofs. Some of the huts were on stilts and had no walls. Others were walled with discarded sheets of metal. Some were made of adobe.

Monkeys called, their howls oddly welcoming. One of the mules made an odd sound in response, something that was neither bray nor whinny.

A dozen or so kids, some mere toddlers, hurried across cleared ground, swarming the returning women. A dozen conversations, some in English, others Spanish, raced around him.

"Wait there," Mitzi said, pointing to a central hut, much larger than the others.

At least a dozen handmade tables and benches sat under the oversized roof. She followed her mother up a slope and into one of the stilted huts set up against a hill.

Older boys took possession of the bell mare. The mules followed her without prompting, taking the guns and ammunition with them. They disappeared into the village, along curving paths.

Juan and his friends trudged to the shelter of the open-walled hut just in time to avoid another downpour. They dropped their packs and sank onto the benches with grateful huffs.

"Think we got the right people?" Carr asked.

"Gotta be," Joe answered.

"Why's that?" Letham asked.

"No men. Not fighting men, anyway," Joe explained. "Best way to make sure they don't bring the UN down on their families is to keep away from them."

"Best way not to get caught," Juan added.

"That too. Spread out. Stay out of sight." Joe took a long drink of water and then sprinkled the remainder over his downy head. "Juan, you think you can get some answers out of that girl?"

"Besides her name," Carr said.

"Actually, her family name would be useful," Joe said, scrubbing at the whiskers on his face.

With no time to shave this morning they all looked scruffy. The things itched like crazy in the moist heat. Going native had seemed like a grand adventure, but the pit stains and the fact that he could actually smell himself—

"Juan's only interested in her first name," Carr said, his shit-eating grin on full blast. "Plans on pinning his family name on her and wants to see how it fits."

"I thought it was only girls that tried on names," Letham said without cracking a smile. He was, by far, the more serious of the brothers.

"Not around here," Joe said. "They mix and match. Maybe Juan can try on her name, instead."

Juan tipped his head toward the old man standing at the edge of the clearing under a tree that provided no cover from the rain. He didn't seem to mind. Or even notice.

"How far do you think he'll let me get?" Juan asked.

An ancient looking gun, far older than anything Juan had ever seen, hung off the old man's shoulder. Come to think of it, that was the most ancient man he'd ever seen too.

"What's the plan, then?" Carr asked.

"Find out if they can point us to Belisario Carrera and his men or get us in touch with someone who can. Deliver the guns. See what else they need. Get word to Desperation Bay. Stay and fight if they'll let us."

"You think *she's* just going to pull out a map, give us the mules, and send us on our way?" Letham asked, giving the stilted hut a skeptical look. "What's to keep them from shooting us with our own guns?"

"Nothing. Which is why, if they wanted us dead, they'd have killed us already." Joe rocked forward, rested his elbows on his knees, and frowned. "Besides, if they want more guns, and they will, they can't kill us."

He stood as Mitzi emerged from the stilted hut and crossed the clearing. She ducked into the open hut and plucked the hat off her head. Her gaze swept each of them in turn.

"How many men have you killed?" she asked no one in particular.

Joe cleared his throat. "We haven't killed anyone."

She titled her head. "No one? Ever?"

They shook their heads.

"You're not trained soldiers either, I take it."

She grabbed Joe's hand and turned it over. She did the same to Carr and Letham, passing judgment with a heavy sigh and a drop of her shoulders.

A spark flew along Juan's fingers as she grabbed his hand and caressed its softness. Even the recent work they'd done on the caravel—it and its crew had sprinted away as fast as the winds could carry them—hadn't been enough to erase years of easy living. Easy at least in terms of what she probably knew as everyday life.

"You should've gone home," she whispered, thumb lingering in a sweep across his palm. Those beautiful dark eyes met his. "You can still go home."

"No." He wet his lips. "I—We can't."

She let go of his hand and turned to Joe. "Do you ride?"

The crank on the radio had broken months ago, but someone had "repaired" it by attaching a wooden spoon with a length of ribbon. Its color and pattern—yellow with a rainbow of happy polka dots— meant that it had probably once belonged to one of the younger girls, perhaps even to Mitzi's younger sister, Esmeralda.

With a surge of anger, Mitzi worked the crank, causing the radio to rev up just enough for a screech and something that could have been a human voice. The radio gave up in a burst of static and the ribbon slipped, releasing the wood.

She threw them both across the hut. They raced to the floor, the ribbon settling gently atop the rug, the spoon sliding under a table and out of sight. Static hissed back at her for a moment, then faded as the radio died.

From across the hut, Mitzi's mother cast her a sideways glance. Her mother was leaning over a large table littered with maps. They made a makeshift, layered tablecloth, some of them spilling halfway to the floor. Others curled around the broken remnants of their lives—a keepsake box, a picture frame, a wind-up clock that no longer worked.

Her mother had been studying the maps for answers, trying to guess the most likely place Father would be. She'd been doing this for days, waiting out the rain.

"Maybe it'll be sunny enough tomorrow to charge the battery," her mother said.

Maybe pigs will fly.

Mitzi crossed the dark, tiny room to stand on the other side of the table. She nudged one of the lamps aside to get a better view. The lamp oil sloshed, then settled in a swirl as the light flared, sending shadows dancing.

"The roads here"—she tapped the map—"and here will probably be washed out. I still think this is the best route." She traced the longer route with a dirty finger, smudging the recently inked markings for semi-permanent UN encampments. They'd been arguing about an unnecessarily long route that snaked through the jungle toward an uncertain destination, abandoning the idea only to reconsider it.

When the radio worked they could get reports about rebel attacks and UN deaths and get an idea of where Father was and what he was doing. But they'd heard nothing lately. Either Father was no longer engaging the enemy because he was out of things to fight with. Or he was dead.

The UN had reported defeating him on several occasions, even officially announced his death, only to be proven wrong. They could no longer count on UN braggadocio for news. Besides, her mother would never believe it.

And she'd never stop fighting. Never.

"I'd rather you avoided the Gurkhas and the Sikhs," her mother said, pointing out the areas for which those two groups were responsible.

While part of the UN contingent, both the Gurkhas and Sikhs showed little interest in coming to the OAU's aid. Attacking either the Gurkhas or the Sikhs, however, brought the other. Not that Mitzi planned on attacking anyone. Not with the soft, untried young men who insisted on coming along because they lacked good sense.

Mitzi nodded. "It'll take even longer. We'll need more supplies." The map lacked contour lines, but Mitzi didn't need them to know that the trails they'd have to take were steep. "The mules, donkey, and horses will tire fast. We'll lose some of them. Need reserves."

"Which means more supplies." Her mother rubbed her face and swept her hands through her hair.

"Cutting down on people will help," Mitzi suggested again. "You have no one else to spare anyway."

Which was the real reason the gringos had to come. Mitzi alone, or even with a few of the *cholo* boys, would make too tempting a target. The gringos mere presence should be a deterrent to most of the *maricones* looking for easy prey, at least as long as no one looked too close.

Her mother nodded. Unspoken between them was the knowledge that every day they waited pushed them toward taking the shorter, more obvious, and dangerous route. And every day they waited meant Father and his men had to fight with bows and arrows, flintlocks and muzzle-loaders.

Her mother grabbed her *escopeta* from its place against the wall and presented it to a wide-eyed Mitzi.

The *escopeta* was lighter than she remembered. She'd shot it before, under her mother's careful tutelage, but the antique twenty-gauge breech-loader with its faded engravings was her mother's constant companion and a very special piece—one that no one was allowed to touch, much less carry.

She checked the side-by-side chambers as she'd been taught and snapped the action shut. Her mother blinked like she had something in her eyes and pushed a drawstring satchel into Mitzi's hand.

"Don't spare the shells," her mother said. "If you don't get through this, it won't matter anyway."

Juan knelt on a pillow-shaped rock a mere step off the bank and thrust both hands into the waterfall-fed stream. The cooling water stung only for a second as it washed blood and grime off oozing blisters earned from handling the mules. Latham was indulging in similar relief just a few feet upstream. Their molly mules—called Baja and Seda—stood between them, dipping their soft, downy noses into the gentle current.

Downstream, the bell mare whinnied—a distinctively happy and grateful sound—as Mitzi led her to the stream.

Joe helped the two old Indios line up the rest of their animal train along the sandier part of the stream's southern bank. His rag-wrapped hands smoothed the mare's crest as Carr brought up the rear, dragging Terra Nova's most stubborn donkey behind him. Apparently you could lead a horse to water, but not a donkey. At least not this donkey—some sort of equine guard dog, his job was to stand and fight, and he took his role very seriously, fighting and standing up to everyone and everything, whether it made sense to or not.

"We'll make camp here," Mitzi, their very own bell mare, announced.

That image—of Mitzi leading her men, they instinctively following—had struck him somewhere along the endless, muddy road and he couldn't get it out of his head. Depending on his mood, the thought wandered into darkness—when had they become such mindless drones, operating on instinct? It's not as if she were *their* mother.

Not my call. And that grated. He wanted it to be his call.

And if it was, would it matter? Because Joe's decisions weren't based on feelings. He wasn't panting after her, stealing glances, wondering if . . . *Heavenly Father*.

Another type of darkness surfaced. The kind that wanted to show her that he was not some mindless drone operating on instinct. That he would never, ever, in a million years, see her as his mother. His instincts were of a different kind and he wanted to free them. Share them. Be appreciated for them.

He groaned.

"Put some antibiotic ointment on those hands," Latham said.

"Yeah, thanks."

An antiseptic for his thoughts would be better. Too bad no one had invented it yet. Hands dripping, Juan rose and reached for his own supplies. He fumbled with his saddlebag, favoring his fingers, as Seda drank, her steady, gentle breathing breaking the water's surface.

It took the remaining daylight to set up camp and relieve the mules of their burdens. Some of the rifles they'd brought had been partially disassembled, the parts sewn into scraps of cloth, and hidden inside all manner of chorley-seed sacks. False barrel bottoms filled with dry foodstuffs hid loose ammunition. They'd done all they could to give the impression of just simple villagers returning home with supplies from the seaports.

According to Helen-of-the-double-barrels, as long as they stuck to their route they'd avoid the UN patrols. Bribes had been set aside just in case—alcohol and tobacco and a few of the so-called luxury items he and his friends had bought along, everyday items in his world, like batteries and sharp, long-lasting razor blades. An itch reminded him that his beard was still very much a work in progress.

One of their Indio guides, a man called Miro, returned from the jungle with a wild turkey across his stooped shoulders. He dropped the bird by the fire and Felix set to plucking it clean and gutting it.

The meal passed with quiet conversation, the two groups sitting across the fire from each other, words only occasionally crossing between them, and even those focused on the order of the watch—one gringo and one Balboan per shift.

Somehow he ended up with first watch and Mitzi with the last, much to his disappointment. A mostly uninterrupted night of sleep was a blessing. He should think of it as such.

At least the heat made it easy to sleep in the open and he could enjoy the sight of Mitzi at rest, even if she turned her back as soon as her head hit the saddle *cum* pillow. What did that exquisite face look like in gentle slumber?

His curiosity did not go unnoticed. Miro, who had drawn the first shift as well, watched him with a wary eye. He put himself between Juan and Mitzi, warning vibes oozing off him like body odor mixed with blood.

It was an impressive intimidation given that Miro was armed only with a bow and knife while Juan hefted a fully loaded rifle. Not that he'd use it. Not in that way. The dark part of him smiled at the implication that at least one person didn't see him as a mindless drone. It didn't take long to figure out the distance he was expected to keep, or the direction in which he was expected to keep watch.

He gave Miro a cursory nod—message received.

The night settled, cloaking them in moonless sky, and an almost eerie, lulling silence. Occasionally logs hissed and cracked as the fading light drew in the darkness.

He caught himself nodding off and stood, shifting the rifle on his shoulder. It wouldn't do to fall asleep. He checked on the dozing animals and envied their ability to sleep while standing, then settled in, propped up and mostly upright, between a few boulders that let him keep an eye on his designated part of the camp and the surrounding jungle.

The hand that slapped him on the shoulder some time later startled the hell out of him. He jumped up and swallowed a yelp.

"Sorry I'm late," Joe said.

Heart still thumping, Juan curled sweaty, trembling hands around the rifle. "Don't do that."

Joe stifled a yawn. "I need to go water a tree."

He disappeared into the jungle, the beam of his flashlight slicing through the understory.

Juan checked his watch. It was almost a couple hours past midnight. No wonder he'd dozed off.

An ill wind swept past him, brushing his shoulder with an obsidian wingtip. The creature manifested merely as deeper, mottled darkness as it circled the clearing without sound. Juan knew the shape. Moonbat. A big one. Much bigger than any he'd seen at home.

They really got that big?

It avoided the center of camp, shirking the light, making the faintest sound—*mnnbt, mnnbt, mnnbt*—and turned away from the cone of light emerging from the trees.

The two-foot long, red-eyed, hissing nightmare drooled poison as it closed in, beating the air with its green-and-gray splotched wings.

The stock of the rifle was at his shoulder, cold against his cheek, and his universe shrank to framing the tiny dot at the front of the muzzle against the source of wings flapping just a few feet off the ground.

Recoil kicked at his shoulder. The front sight followed the moonbat all the way down to the ground.

He froze.

There should have been light. And sound. But the sulfur and copper scent reached him first, curling and caressing its way into his lungs.

Shouting voices chorused behind him, the words muffling through the ringing in his ears.

He thumbed the safety back on even though he didn't recall thumbing it off.

The moonbat lay in a sprawl, an intermittent fountain of blood gushing from its chest. It turned its head towards Juan and blinked its slitted saurian eyes as it foamed at the mouth. *Mnnbt—*

Felix drove a spear right through the moonbat's mouth. "Nice shot."

Juan blinked.

Everyone was up, if in various states of undress, some trailing tangled mosquito netting. All manner of arms were at the ready as they warily scanned the sky. But no wings beat above.

"Damn!" Mitzi swore, rushing past him in a blur.

Joe had returned. He'd dropped his flashlight, and looked like he'd been spun and landed on his ass. There was a sick, stricken look on his face. Even in the low light, his pallor went from ailing to ashen.

Mitzi and Felix reached Joe first. Juan moved forward as if gliding in a dream. A small voice chanted—*No, no, no*—in the back of his mind.

The rifle's—*his* rifle's—bullet had passed through the moonbat and hit Joe.

"Give me your shirt," Mitzi said, her voice steadier than she felt.

Joe paled as she and Felix lowered the fair-haired gringo to the ground. His left hand was covered in blood and firmly clasped over the wound on his right arm.

"Hey," she said, voice soft as she tried to pry his fingers away, "let go. I need to look."

Wide, desperate eyes met her gaze.

"It'll be all right. Now let me look."

He blinked at her, his breathing ragged.

"Tell me your name." She'd only heard one shot, and he didn't appear to have any other injuries, but . . . "Did you hear me?"

"Joe," he said. His grip relaxed and the pulse at his throat ebbed.

Satisfied, she spoke over her shoulder. "Juan, give me your shirt."

Juan had dropped the rifle and was as white as a sheet. *One thing at a time.*

"Juan, your shirt. Now."

She drew her knife and sliced through the fabric of Joe's sleeve. Blood flowed at a steady rate, rather than escaping in spurts. It looked like a through-and-through.

"It's okay, Juan," Joe was saying. "It wasn't your fault."

Mitzi held her hand out. Fabric dropped into her hand. She pressed the shirt against the wound and used the sleeves as ties. The jolt of the final tug made Joe grunt.

"Were you hit anywhere else?"

Joe shook his head. Sweat was beading on his forehead. She felt for a pulse at his wrist. It was weak and fast. She moved his forearm so it lay on his chest and confirmed that he had no other obvious injuries.

"Get him closer to the fire," she said.

She stood, grabbing Juan's shoulder with a bloody hand and pulling him out of the way so the others could lift Joe.

There was a pleading look on Juan's face and his mouth moved without making a sound.

"It'll be dawn in a couple of hours. I need more light, but I think"—hope was more like it—"he'll be all right."

Panic rose in his face again as if she'd said that Joe was going to die. He needed something to do or she was going to have two people down, and she couldn't—

"I . . ." he stammered.

"You're going to make sure he gets plenty of water and stays warm."

His mouth snapped shut.

"Understand?" she asked.

He took a deep breath, regaining some color and nodded.

She understood the fear, the guilt, even shared it in some measure. What had she been thinking, bringing these boys out here? She'd been thinking there were more lives at stake here than their own. Far more.

Felix had had the presence of mind to grab one of the first-aid kits the gringos had brought along. He passed it to her.

By the fire, Joe was wrapped in blankets, his eyes glassy with pain as she knelt at his side. Juan encouraged him to sip water from a canteen. The stricken, panicked look was gone, replaced by a frowning, grim determination. Good. Grim was better than panicked. Or useless.

Mitzi ripped through layers of packaging and found some pills meant for head and muscle aches, but no antibiotics. She set aside the emergency bandage. Sunrise was only a few hours away.

"Take these," she said, handing Joe the pills.

He swallowed them, his throat straining with effort. "It's really not that bad. I'll be fine."

She smiled. "You'll live."

There was nothing else to do. Not until dawn. Miro was watching the skies, musket in hand. Palala had calmed down the animals, and the gringos were focused on their friend. Felix could keep an eye on them for a few moments.

She didn't want to be here when the adrenaline hit. It always did, after, and turned her into a shaky mess. The last thing these gringos needed to see were her tears. She grabbed the nearest torch and headed for the river to wash off the blood from her hands.

It's not as if the loss of a stranger was the worst thing she'd faced. She'd thought it would get easier with time. It certainly seemed to have worked that way for her father.

Here I am, wishing I was like him.

She planted the torch in the soft sand of the riverbank, and let out a sound full of loathing as she dropped to her knees. Water wasn't enough though. She scooped up sand and worked it into her skin until it was raw.

She'd have continued scrubbing until it was too much to bear, but a shadow fell across the water.

"Go away. I'm almost done," she said.

The shadow remained. She stood and spun, ready to vent her

anger at the silhouette. All she needed was a few moments. Just a few.

Juan stood there as the torchlight played across his face. Anger swelled—the last thing she wanted was his whining apology. She could give him neither reassurance nor vindication. Her reserves for those kinds of things had been drained long ago.

She took a half step, determined to go around him, but he blocked her way. His shoulder was still stained with blood. And then his arms were around her, and her cheek was against his chest, and the blood no longer mattered.

She felt like a string that had been stretched to the breaking point. Something in her chest vibrated too. Something she'd buried long ago. Something that shouldn't be alive, because having it be dead was the only way to survive.

He never said a word. Not one. He simply held her as the salt of her tears mixed with the salt of his sweat, mixing to stain her lips and linger on her tongue as she breathed in his calming scent. His embrace became a welcome cloak of warmth and safety. For the first time since she'd set foot on Terra Nova, she felt . . . safe.

Foolish madness.

She pushed him away and instantly regretted the loss of contact. His mouth was set in a tight line as he held her gaze.

Her life had no room for such sentimentality, such weakness. He was a boy who could barely take care of himself and would be far better off—happier and safer—back home among his soft friends, his bevy of siblings, and his many mothers. He would be out of her life in a matter of weeks, months at most.

She swiped the wetness off her face and offered him nothing but a chin raised in defiance.

I don't need you. I don't need anyone.

As soon as Terra Nova's sun lit the clearing, Mitzi removed Joe's makeshift bandage. A trickle of dark blood had eased her worst fears. A pile of blood-soaked rags lay beside her as she cleaned Joe's wound. The *cholos* and gringos hurried through the morning routine as if they were planning on forging ahead in their mission.

It felt very much like some secret, testosterone-fueled meeting had taken place and the decision not to turn back had been made without her. She should resent it. But she didn't. The gringos may not be skilled, trained soldiers but they had spirit—even if it was misplaced.

If all went well, they'd have lost only a few hours of daylight.

She bound Joe's wound using the pressure dressing, weaving the fabric through the pressure bar. With steady fingers, she fastened the closure bar and felt for the pulse at his wrist. She grabbed his other wrist for comparison. The beats were strong and steady in both. Her sigh of relief was the most cleansing breath she'd taken since Juan had h—

"It's a good thing I'm left-handed," Joe said.

She sat back, eyeing him. "You are *not* left-handed."

"I'm ambidextrous," Joe said.

"Don't worry, I can't afford to send you back. Isn't there some sort of rule against lying that you should be more worried about?"

He gave her a rendition of an angelic smile as his face flushed red. She resisted the urge to roll her eyes.

A whoop went up by the tree line and Felix rushed into the clearing.

"Found the flashlight," he said, holding it up like a trophy.

Felix ran back and thrust it at Joe.

"Keep it," Joe said. "I have extra batteries in my pack."

Felix rushed off like a kid with a new toy, which, in a way, he was.

"That was nice. You didn't have to do that," she said.

"It's good to see him smile." He shifted forward.

She helped him up and tied the sling to hold his arm folded against his chest.

"Do me a favor," she said. "Shotguns for the next batch, all right?"

"Yes, ma'am. I think we can arrange that."

Juan noticed the slump in Joe's shoulders just after their mid-morning stop two days later. He nudged Baja closer, bringing her forward from their position at the rear of the train. He'd taken as much of Joe's workload as he'd been allowed, bristling needlessly whenever anyone took up the extra work that he saw as his penance. The fact that no one blamed him did nothing to assuage his guilt.

Even the small measure of comfort he'd been able to offer Mitzi had left him conflicted, frustrated, and angry.

He'd replayed the shooting in his mind over and over, wondering what he could've done differently. It always left him with a gnawing feeling in the pit of his stomach. Had jealousy contributed to his carelessness? Should Joe die, a court might call it manslaughter, not murder, but what if ill intent had guided his hand?

He'd reacted out of instinct, or so he'd been telling himself. He should've just let the moonbat get him and—

Juan caught Joe as he was about to slip off the saddle. The train came to a stop. Carr and Letham rushed to help ease Joe down. His forehead felt like he was on fire. He moaned and opened red-rimmed eyes.

"Hey, Juan," Joe mumbled. "How'd you get up there?"

Juan put his canteen to Joe's lips as his friend's eyes drifted shut.

Mitzi was at his side, taking Joe's pulse, her face hard and unreadable, her gaze meeting Juan's for the first time since she'd pushed him away. But instead of the accusing, angry look he'd expected, she wore that same vulnerability he'd seen in her when she'd run away to wash blood off her hands.

As she rose, she blinked something out of her eyes. With a few commands she set the Indios in motion. Machetes hacked young trees into poles. A tarp and ropes were set between them.

Joe was hoisted onto the hastily assembled litter attached to Seda's saddle, and they were in motion again, the litter's low end tracing grooves into the dirt.

That night, Juan tossed and turned as sleep eluded him. He'd taken first watch and had volunteered to take the mid-watch as well, but both Palala and Mitzi had insisted he get some rest. It was Carr's turn to tend to Joe, and Felix and Miro were keeping watch, while Leatham rested up for the pre-dawn shift.

Underneath a mosquito net, he turned his back to the center of camp. Maybe the swaying fronds and leaves around him would lull him into some semblance of sleep.

Motion caught his eye.

The light from Terra Nova's three moons silhouetted a hunched figure creeping along the camp's edge. It darted from shadow to shadow like it was trying to hide.

He stirred, slow and silent, like a man in slumber, tracking the figure.

One of the mules made a soft sound and shook its head, then fell silent. The thief eased a bundle off the top of the stacked supplies and scurried off into the jungle.

Juan rose, pushed the net aside, and followed the crouching form as it made its way through the trees.

It kept moving, weaving through the trees, straightening as its distance from camp increased. It turned to check over its shoulder and he hid behind a tree just in time to avoid giving himself away.

His breath caught—Mitzi. What was she doing?

She set off again, more confident now, tearing through the undergrowth until she reached the primitive road they'd been using, and slowed.

He lengthened his stride, easily closing the distance over the cleared ground, and grabbed her arm.

She pivoted, twisting out of his grip. Her hand went for the knife at her belt, but her face lit with relief and the knife whispered back into its sheath.

"Where are you going?" he asked.

"Going for antibiotics." Her voice was matter-of-fact as she readjusted the strap of her shotgun and kept walking.

"Alone?"

"Yes. Go back, Juan." She quickened her pace.

"Why the sneaking off?"

She took a deep breath. "Go back you stupid gringo."

"Yes, I'm a gringo, but you're the stupid one. Why else would you be sneaking off?"

She kept walking.

"Answer me." He spun her around, bringing them both to a halt.

She looked up at him, her face hard again.

"Because sneaking into the UN camp for antibiotics to save the man you shot is a stupid thing to do. But I'm going to do it anyway. I'm going to clean up your mess, gringo. Go back to camp. At least you can be of some use there."

She placed her hands against his chest. The shove was as harsh as her words. With a determined stride, she set off.

He regained his balance and followed. "You're right. It's my mess. My fault. That's why I'm coming with you."

She swung around. "You'll only slow me down. Go back."

"If I go back, it'll be to alert the others so they can stop you."

She paled, but didn't slow. "If they stop me, your friend will die."

"Better him than you."

She opened her mouth to speak. Her eyes went wide and distant and then her eyebrows drew together. Her gaze sought the road ahead of them.

"It's settled then," he said. "Give me the pack."

Before sneaking off, Mitzi had left a note with instructions: they were to continue along their planned route. On a map, she'd marked two possible sites for rendezvous, one in two days and another in three.

Joe was young, healthy. Three days of fever wouldn't kill him. A little luck was all they needed. Just a bit.

The lightly traveled road they'd been using intersected one where tracks from powered vehicles had left their mark. Until now, their little group had done everything to avoid such roads, but she and Juan no longer had a choice but to follow where it led—straight into the heart of the UN encampment.

As they neared the area, she led them upslope so she could get a better look at the changes that had no doubt taken place since she'd last passed through.

They climbed to a spot overlooking the once-quiet valley. She raised the binoculars to her eyes. The flatter area to the east had been cleared as a landing zone for helicopters, but the pad was empty. Several rows of octagonal tents were clustered west of the clearing, crowding out the few huts that had been the original Balboan village.

Hoisted above a group of interconnected Red Cross tents that resembled inflatable hangars, the enemy's baby-blue flag drooped in the still, moist air. Just outside the field hospital, in what looked like a staging area, crates had been stacked.

She zoomed in. Trixies—about a dozen of them. And nearby, in a giant cage, a smilodon paced, protesting its confinement. Specimens or trophies—they were valuable to someone high enough in the UN hierarchy to risk trapping rather than killing them.

She smiled.

Luck seemed to be on their side today. The sun would soon slip behind the mountains and cast the valley in early twilight. The scent from the mess hall announced that dinner preparations were under way. They had to hurry.

She grabbed Juan's hand and led him back down to the road.

There. A grove of tranzitrees, their pretty—but toxic—flowers forming a perfect visual marker. She drew her knife and carved a couple of parallel strips off the bark, just to be sure.

"What are you doing?" Juan asked.

"So we can find it later." She grabbed nearby bushes by their stalks, uprooting them. Juan did the same, adding to her pile.

She needed something to keep dirt out of the *escopeta*. "Give me your shirt."

He shot her a puzzled look.

"We need to look like a couple of poor peasants wandering through. The *escopeta* will give us away."

Reluctantly, he shrugged out of his shirt.

She wrapped it around the *escopeta*, hid it behind the tree, under the cluster of uprooted bushes, making it look as much like the surrounding undergrowth as she could.

"I'm going to sneak into the medical tents and get what we need. You are going to unlatch the specimen cages and then get out of there, without becoming a smilodon snack. Think you can do that?"

"You want me to create a diversion?"

"Yes. Then come back here." She stood and took a few steps back. They were far enough from the main road so that no one would notice the disturbed foliage unless they were looking for it, but close enough that they could easily find it again.

"What if something happens to you?" he asked.

She grabbed the pack and cast a reassuring smile over her shoulder as she headed towards the road. "Nothing will happen to me."

His lips pressed into a slight grimace, but he followed.

They hiked the muddy shoulder of the road. Several times she stopped to add to the muck already splattering their clothes so they looked like weary travelers too poor and downtrodden to bother with.

With his unkempt beard, Juan already looked like a Balboan colonist. Bright blue eyes were rare here, but not unheard of, and only a problem if someone already had reason to be suspicious.

"Keep your eyes down and don't speak," she said. "Shoulders hunched."

He slumped.

"A little more." She pulled his hat a forward a bit so it would hide his face better, and then did the same for hers.

She took the pack with their remaining supplies and slipped her arms through so it hung down over her belly. Then she rebuttoned her shirt around it and cradled her new "belly" like she'd seen pregnant women do. As they approached the entry, she added a realistic waddle.

The trio of bored soldiers didn't even spare them a look as they placed bets and rolled dice. Their rifles were stacked out of reach. Alcohol and drugs scented the surrounding air.

They shuffled past, heads down, like they made the trek every day.

Except for the buzz of many voices rising from the mess tent as the soldiers settled in for dinner, the camp was quiet. The occasional complaint of a smilodon cut the air and sent the trixies chattering.

Mitzi veered left and circled around the back of the Red Cross tents while Juan kept moving towards the staging area.

She peered through the clear plastic windows. The tents were dark, like they hadn't seen use in a while. She parted the entry flap and pulled it shut behind her.

Chilled air made the hairs on her arms rise. Rows of folding tables had been set up and draped with thin blue coverings. White privacy curtains were drawn back against the sag of curving walls. The floor had the odd feel of plastic tarp over bare ground.

Must be a recovery unit.

Swinging the pack onto her back, she crossed the length of the tent, seeking a surgery or pharmacy.

She passed through a juncture where four structures met. The morgue was to her right, completely dark. The resonant hum of a generator penetrated the walls. A pool of light escaped a gap of sheeting in front of her.

The surgical suite's equipment was set up and waiting, the puffy walls drooping slightly inward, but she couldn't make out anything that looked promising enough to risk creeping around the well-lit area.

A throaty purr rose and fell to her left. She froze, heart thundering in her chest. The purr rose and fell again. The staging area with the smilodon was off to the right and too far away. She held her breath and cocked her head, listening.

Something moved to her left. She crept along the wall and parted the flap. The purr grew louder.

A man reclined on what looked like a portable stretcher. His head was thrown back, spittle gurgling in the back of his throat. The low light seeping in through the windows cast him in shadow but she could tell he wasn't a sedated patient. His uniform jacket was carelessly thrown over a nearby chair and he'd slipped out of his boots. He stirred and resettled.

Some sort of guard, or an opportunistic grunt taking advantage of the chilled air, he looked unarmed but was no doubt head and shoulders taller and close to twice her size.

She bit her lip.

The tent was lined with tables on one side and shelves on the other. Something large and solid like a safe filled the far end. She inched along the wall opposite the snoring figure, hugging the shadows.

Her heart seemed to freeze along with her breath whenever he fell silent. As her vision adjusted, the dark revealed shelf upon shelf of bottles, bags, and boxes—a treasure trove, all neatly arrayed and labeled.

She moved towards the farthest shelves, hastily reading labels. She unzipped the pack, cringing as it whispered open. Antibiotics went in.

She moved as quickly as stealth allowed, turning her back on the purring. It rose and fell.

Moving to the next shelf, she found steroids. Purr . . . purr . . . purr . . .

She added syringes to the bottles of pills and liquids. Purr . . . purr . . .

The smooth surface of latched metal boxes. Purr . . .

Something for pain.

Something strong.

Silence.

She dropped to the floor and hugging the pack to her chest, rolled under one of the tables.

The snorer's sock-covered feet menaced by, a confident predator, stalking. "I know you're in here, little thief."

She drew the pack up to her chest and zipped it shut.

He stopped, turned. "I won't hurt you."

A full body tremor shook her and she squeezed her eyes shut. That *maricón*, Nyere, had taunted her with the same tone, the same promise.

"Come out, little thief."

Her eyes popped open, nostrils flaring.

He moved sideways, closing in.

She unsheathed her knife, breathing despite the pressure in her throat, her chest.

He moved towards the back of the tent once again.

Blood roared in her ears. She scrambled towards the entry.

In her desperate vision, the entry grew for one moment. And receded the next. The boonie cap's strap tightened like a noose snapping tight. She was yanked backwards. The pack dropped. She wrapped her fingers around the strap, trying to loosen it.

He yanked again, unbalancing her further, sending her sprawling towards the rear as her pack spun in the opposite direction. She got her knees and hands underneath her. For a second.

He grabbed her hair and the belt around her waist and lifted her as if she were a child.

The tent spun around her. Something hard slammed against her back and skull. Her vision tunneled. Pain lanced her wrist as she lost her grip on the knife. It clattered against something as her lungs drew anguished breaths.

A face blurred out of the dark spots and tunneling of her vision. "Nice."

The reek of rot and stale breath. Dark, soulless eyes. A leer. "Very nice."

He had her up against the wall safe, enormous hands wrapped around her throat. Her toes barely touched the ground.

His eyes widened, assessing. His grip shifted. He splayed a hand beneath the hollow of her throat and used the other to tear open her shirt.

"Quiet now. I don't want to share you. And you wouldn't like it much, either."

He pinned her shoulders back against the wall. Her heels touched the ground. There was a thin line of blood on his left forearm. She'd nicked him.

Sweat dripped down her back. Her chest heaved, straining.

He licked his lips. Twice. "You don't want me to share either, do you?" The look in his eyes promised nothing good.

Never again.

His face came closer.

Pulse racing, she smashed the heel of her palm into his nose.

He roared closer.

She slid her shoulder against the wall as she grabbed his head. With all her might, she slammed his head into the hinge protruding from the wall safe.

He connected with a squelching thud and liquid sprinkled her vision.

Long-held hatred rose within her, driving the heel of her palm into his bloodied face once more.

For her home.

Her friends.

Her freedom.

For each person his kind had hurt.

For each person she'd had to watch die.

A sack of meat left a streak of darkness as it slid down the wall safe. She stood over him, panting, wishing for a knife to end his life. She stomped on his groin.

Loosened hair tickled her face. Something dripped down her chin. She wiped it away and spit as she stepped over him. Retrieving her pack, she picked up her knife with a blood-slick hand.

Juan had left the smilodon's cage for last.

The trixies' crates had been easy. A simple slide of the latch and the doors could be pushed open. The clever little reptiles were already testing the doors, pushing against them with their beaks. They'd have them open in no time, and as soon as the moonbats came out, the trixies would take to the skies after their natural prey.

The smilodon stood at the back her cage. Her head almost reached his elbow and she eyed him with a wariness that had, no doubt, been bought with the cattle-prods he'd found nearby. He improvised a piece of pipe as a prybar, stuck it between latch and lock, and heaved.

The latch popped open.

He used the far end of the pipe to nudge the lock off and slide the bar aside. Once she was free she could bound into the jungle, although it was far more likely she'd go after whoever came to feed her scraps from the mess hall. That must be the distraction Mitzi was planning for—using the animals to cover any possible alarm her theft might raise.

Or maybe she's just keeping you out of her way.

He pushed his ego aside.

Wishing he could convince the smilodon to take off for the freedom of the jungle, he nevertheless backed away slowly until he was sure the beast wasn't going to pursue.

Shoving his hands into his pockets, he donned his hunched posture.

Mitzi emerged from the hospital tents, looking more "pregnant" than before, walking with purpose—a bit too much purpose.

He caught up to her. "Waddle," he whispered, and placed his arm around her shoulders.

She was trembling, but she slowed.

He snuck a sideways look. The buttons of her shirt were gone. The pack was no longer well-hidden. They veered into shadows, walking at an agonizingly slow pace.

His pulse thundered in his ears as they passed the sentries and made their way back up the winding road.

A roar tore through the air. Alarms shrieked to life.

Feeding time. *Hope she enjoys it.* He consoled himself with the singular thought that she was too valuable a specimen to kill outright and they'd use a tranquilizer gun.

Mitzi straightened and swung the pack onto her back. She threaded her arms through it, hefting it without effort, and used the shirt tails to keep the shirt closed. Her face lit up with a brilliant smile. Despite the blood splattered on her face and clothing, and the weight of the pack on her back she looked like a great burden had been lifted off her shoulders.

After retrieving the *escopeta*, they disappeared into the jungle.

Later that night, camped around a small fire well away from the uproar of the UN camp, Mitzi pulled out a map and frowned as though she didn't like what it was telling her.

He squatted beside her. "What's wrong?"

She rested her forefinger on a mark. "I left instructions to meet us here tomorrow"—her finger hopped to another mark—"or here the day after."

"Can we make the first rendezvous?" The sooner they got to Joe the better.

Her frown deepened, but she nodded.

They *had* to make the first rendezvous point, Mitzi told herself. Joe's life depended on it.

No, it doesn't. He'll be fine. He's young and healthy.

She slowed and drank from her canteen.

Juan passed her, carrying the pack up the footpath.

She envied the spring in his step, his eagerness. The next rendezvous point was farther, but safer.

Safer for you. Not Joe.

And just like that, they stepped out from underneath the jungle's protective canopy, into the open.

A suspension bridge made of rope and wood spanned the gorge that cut a great big scar through the mountain range. The calm day seemed suddenly violent as gusts swept up through the gorge.

Her hair swirled about her face. She shook from more than the chilling passage of air. The turmoil of running waters rode the breezes, swelling to an echoing roar.

Juan kept moving, obviously unconcerned, not even turning back to check on her, like the bridge was just another type of road.

She froze at the foot of the bridge. If she kept her eyes forward . . .

Her fingers curled around the handrail—a thick rope that seemed far too weathered for the task. Juan was already halfway across, and he was going to notice if she waited much longer.

It isn't that far, the logical part of Mitzi's mind insisted.

Far enough, the fearful part chimed in.

Despite the water she'd just chugged from her canteen, her throat felt dry and unyielding, and there was a swelling ache in her chest like someone was sitting on it.

Even as she filled her lungs, it felt like air was being denied her. Two someones parked themselves on her chest and beckoned— *Come, join us*—to some friends.

Move.

One step. More. Each one agony. A gust shook the bridge, making it creak. Her heart was in her throat. Her hand formed into a death's grip as the drop to the bottom of the gorge stretched into infinity beneath her.

Infinity means no landing, Logic reassured her.

It also means you'll fall forever, Fear insisted.

She closed her eyes. It took the edge off her vertigo. All that time she'd spent painfully working herself up to being able to stand on cliffs, wasted, after all.

The bridge swayed again, its creaking a thunderous, unceasing roar in her ears, fueling the spinning sensation that . . . Would. Not. Stop.

Warmth wrapped around her icy death-grip.

She opened her eyes. Juan stood in front of her, smiling. He'd ducked slightly and was looking right into her eyes.

"It'll be all right. Just look at me."

Her disobedient gaze dropped to the plank beneath her feet, the cracked one with the hole in the center, the one that tunneled into just how far down those sharp rocks really were.

Fear punched Logic in the throat and hurled the bitch into the gorge. *Oh, G—*

Juan's finger hooked her chin, forcing her gaze to his again. She swallowed the fist-sized lump of bile that had worked its way up her throat.

"I figured it out, you know." He pried one of her fingers loose and tugged the rest of her hand off the handrail. Her nails dug into his arm.

Fear used Father's voice to remind her, *Move, girl, or die.*

"It's Mariazinha," Juan said, bright smile sparkling.

She blinked.

"Your name," he added.

Her name? Silly, stupid, gringo. Joe was dying because she wasn't moving. More would die if she didn't—

Move, move, move.

The bridge swayed. The plank creaked. His kind eyes were blue.

"No?" His lips formed a musing pout. "Marjukka, then, it's gotta be Marjukka."

She dared not shake her head lest is set off the spinning sensation. This was no time for games.

Move.

"Malenka then, although it doesn't suit you."

They were like the sky, those eyes. Or a lake. Soothing. Serene.

"No? Good. I don't like that one. Mirelle?"

She bit her lip.

"Maritza, although that one sounds like a cat's name. Do you like cats?"

Cats? Was he crazy? Who wanted to talk about cats? "For a—"

The blue eyes smiled, crinkling the sunburned skin around them.

"—a smilodon," she stuttered. "Maybe."

"A big cat name, then. Mairwen."

She sank onto solid ground, relief crashing over her, anchoring her into the softness of bark and leaves and the undergrowth's earthy aroma. The cooling moisture drove the someones off her chest.

Juan's grip relaxed.

She pulled her hand away. Four carved furrows decorated his forearm. She'd drawn blood.

He shrugged: a careless, never-mind kind of gesture. "You can't mind scratches if you like cats."

Her breaths were still coming in fulfilling gasps as she looked over her shoulder. The bridge was still there. Behind her. And she was across it, not falling to her death.

He sat down, grinning like the idiot he was.

Silly, stupid, wonderful gringo.

"Were any of my guesses right?" he asked.

She shook her head. "Promise you won't laugh."

"I promise."

"Mitzilla." She waited for him to break his promise. Everyone did. Never mind that her name had been around longer than giant fictional lizards or that she wasn't prone to excessive or monsterlike qualities. Never mind that she wasn't into badassery of any kind.

"Mitzilla what?"

Oh? She took a deep, quivering breath. "Carrera."

There. He knew. And just like all the others, wouldn't touch *el jefe's* daughter. Even if she hadn't already been damaged goods.

"Juan Fernando Alvarez. Junior." He stuck his hand out.

She stared at it like it was some sort of steel-clawed trap.

"It's an honor to formally meet you, Miss Carrera." He brought her hand to his lips, smiling over her knuckles, and kissed her hand.

Delicious little jolts skated up her arm.

She let out a quivering breath.

Wow.

There was something about the way that Juan stood that told Mitzi not to even think about demanding her turn to carry the pack. He was so tall, this gringo. Even in the short time she'd known him, he'd changed, losing his boyish softness. More man than boy now. He offered her his hand.

She took it, allowing him to help her rise, despite the heat surging in her cheeks.

His grip remained firm.

No one touched *el jefe's* daughter. No one.

"This way?" he asked, smiling, and turned towards a fork that veered to the right.

The sun was more than halfway through its arc, and there'd been no sign of pursuit. Something was on their side—either good planning or dumb luck. Or self-interest. Perhaps her attacker wouldn't report letting a thief get the best of him.

She nodded.

Juan held her hand all the way to the rendezvous site, a clearing at the base of a tiered waterfall that spilled into a pond. The water flowed over the ledges like crystal veils piercing emerald silk.

The area around the pond was undisturbed, with no signs of recent use, no animal droppings, and no foot- or hoof-prints.

"Our people haven't been here yet," she said.

"I'll start a fire." He let go of her hand, set the pack down, and gathered stones for the fire pit.

She set the *escopeta* aside and shrugged out of the shirt to wash it. The scrubbing motion reawakened the pain in the heel of her palm. It throbbed, protesting any further tenderizing. She flexed her hand, testing it. She'd hit the would-be rapist hard enough to bruise. Hard enough to feel a pain like shin splints all along her forearm. And it had felt glorious. Freeing. Right.

Leaning over the placid water, she caught her reflection and grimaced. The bruise that circled her neck looked like she'd survived a hanging. She couldn't recall how she'd gotten the split in her lip. Or the cut above her brow. And she was still covered in mud and sweat.

Within moments she was out of her sandals and castoffs and underneath the waterfall. She tucked her head, letting the soothing water work the knots out of her back and shoulders. Combing her fingers through the fall of her hair, she closed her eyes and tilted her head.

The scent of clean, male musk flowed along the breeze. She opened her eyes to find Juan standing over her, wet hair slicked back, looking like some mythical sea god risen from his watery domain. His gaze met hers as his thumb traced her lip line, lingering at the cut there. Then the one at her brow. The blue eyes questioned in silence.

Her breath caught.

He leaned closer, thick dark lashes fanning a scorching gaze. His face hovered over hers for what seemed like an eternity as something deep inside her untangled to feed a rising, torturing anticipation.

His lips touched hers.

Her fingers tangled in his hair, drawing him in so he could devour and be devoured in turn. They shared breath after breath, touch after touch. Roughened hands anchored to her hips, he pulled her against him, leaving no doubt as to what she did to him. He wanted *her*.

Having tasted him, she broke their kiss to savor his scent, inhaling deeply, running her cheek against his roughened jaw. Despite the cooling water, his lips continued to trace a line of fire to her brow, then to the bruise circling her neck. He lingered there longest, soothing. A balm.

For all her pain.

Within easy reach, the *escopeta* rested behind Juan, as flames from the fire cast shadows that seemed to dance to the music of the waterfall. Mitzi lay in the shelter of his body, resting her head on a makeshift pillow. Her face was soft in sleep, the fall of her hair draping across her still-naked form. He could live out the rest of his life with nothing and no one else to look at, if he could only make this moment last so long.

He'd insisted on taking first watch, knowing he wouldn't be able to sleep. Even now, his heart drummed in his chest, like an untamed thing. A war drum. His thoughts were likewise, in turmoil.

What have I done?

He caressed the swell of her hip, admiring her curves. The softness of her skin belied the strength beneath, just like her silence had. She would not speak to him of what had happened, of the blood, the bruises. He hadn't pressed. When she was ready, she'd tell him. All that mattered was that she'd emerged victorious. He squeezed her hip and she snuggled closer. Greed tugged at him, wanting— demanding—more.

Mine.

He took a shuddering breath. His. She could be his. And he, hers. He would make a good husband.

Unlike his people who'd bought passage on the colonization ship, hers had been sentenced to their lives here. How would she feel about being uprooted once again? Would she even leave her family with the fight not won?

He could stay. They needed fighters. All he required was some training. He was willing to fight for them—for her. They had come here for that purpose—to fight for liberty. Their fates had been intertwined from the start.

Across a sky barely lit by the smallest of Terra Nova's moons— Bellona—distant guns thundered. Eyes wide, Mitzi jerked upright and pulled the thin blanket around her.

"It's all right," he said, pushing aside the netting as he sat up. "They're far away."

Her gaze traveled above the treetops, to where a sinister light pulsed and swelled against the distant horizon. A staccato of softer sounds was answered by a deeper boom. Cannons?

Mitzi rose, parted the netting around them, and retrieved the clothes that had been set to dry on rocks around the fire. She tugged her underclothes on with urgency, but fumbled for shirt buttons that were no longer there. She drew her pants over long legs, but her belt fought back when she tried to cinch it.

He followed and stepped into his pants.

Silence fell. Something like the faint call of a bugle echoed, barely there and receding. Even to his untrained ear it sounded like retreat.

She slipped into sandals.

There were tears in her eyes when she stood to face him. "Stay here," she said, going for the *escopeta* behind him.

"No." He grabbed her arm.

She tried to shake him off, but he pulled her into his embrace and held her. "If you think I'm letting you go off by yourself, you're crazy," he whispered into her ear.

"Someone needs to stay here, or all this will have been for nothing."

The token words had none of the determination with which she usually spoke. She knew. Knew as well as he did, that it was folly to go, that one or both of them would make no difference to whatever was going on out there. Not without the cargo they'd brought. The cargo that wasn't here yet.

"Then we both go."

Another distant roar. Her fingers dug into his arm. "Those are my people. My father."

"I know."

He held her as she flinched with every explosion. She buried her face in his chest.

"Everything will be fine, you'll see," he said as the noise and light ceased.

At some point she had relaxed against him.

"How do you *know*?"

"The stars are shining."

Morning greeted them without cannons, bugles or drums. Whatever her father had been doing, it was over. Mitzi studied her map, folded it, and paced. Unfolded it again. She had a good idea of where he could be, but uncertainty gnawed at her gut.

Juan snored softly atop their makeshift bedroll, his tossing and turning mimicking her own churning doubts. Would he stay? Could she convince him to stay? *Stay?* She huffed out a surprised breath. *She* wanted to stay.

The edges of the bruise on her palm were fading to green. For years she'd wished for the chance to escape this place and all its demons, tormented by the guilt that came with knowing that her family wouldn't be here if it hadn't been for her. She wouldn't have abandoned her family—not even in those selfish moments when being *el jefe's* daughter meant pretending she didn't hear the warnings the young men around her received as a matter of course—but she had wished that she could. And there was her opportunity for escape, on the bedroll, and she wanted him to stay.

Here. With her. For her.

One of Juan's shirts was still spread out on the rocks. Its fabric was soft and clean. She scrunched it up and buried her face in it, savoring the masculine scent lingering in its fibers. She'd never be satisfied with just the memory of him.

No more regrets. If she had to do the same again . . . she would. And she *would* make her father understand—whatever it took—and dare him to deny her.

A wicked smile crept across her face. She opened her eyes and cast a sideways glance at her still-sleeping man. She donned his shirt—*its* buttons still worked, after all. He could wear the damaged one, or better yet, go without.

She pushed the netting aside, knelt, and pressed a chaste kiss to his lips. He stirred, eyes fluttering, lips seeking hers even as she pulled away.

Rubbing the sleep from his eyes, he rolled to his side. "Good morni—"

The braying of a donkey bounced off the cliff face, a second before the source of the sound barreled through the foliage like a beast possessed, bee-lining for them like he was going to mow them down. Mitzi stepped out of the donkey's way just as Juan rolled, barely avoiding careless hooves.

Felix burst out of the jungle, shouting something that sounded very much like a curse. Eyes wide, he sprinted towards her and almost took her down with his enthusiasm.

"Mitzi, Mitzi, you made it." An instant later he stepped back, cheeks blazing at the taboo of having his wiry arms around her. His gaze lingered on her healing lip and brow. He frowned at the one on her neck. His hands, no longer awkwardly hanging at his side, tightened on the bow sling crossing his chest.

"So did you," she said. Smiling, she pulled him to her so she could kiss the top of his head before he could draw the wrong conclusions. She gave him a squeeze that made his eyes go even wider. He stepped back, his gaze darting, doubt and disbelief playing over his face, but he relaxed.

Juan was lacing up his boots as the donkey carelessly slurped at the water. A bell sounded in the distance accompanied by a chorus of nickers, snorts and a drawn-out neigh.

"Sorry we're late. We lost one of the mules," Felix said as the rest of their party emerged from the trees.

Mitzi and Juan reached Joe at the same time. He looked better than she'd expected. He was still riding in the litter, but he was propped up into a sitting position, rifle across his lap. The amount of sweat on his brow betrayed the lingering fever, but he was smiling at them.

Joe and Juan traded reports with the abbreviated bravado of old friends reassuring each other. There was a slight tremor in her hands as she prepared the antibiotic. She'd expected teasing and judging gazes. Her hands steadied as she shot the antibiotic into her patient's good arm.

"Ouch." Joe flinched at the sudden sting as she pushed down on the plunger, too hard and fast for comfort.

"You big baby." Carr's mocking voice was colored with relief as he gave Mitzi a grateful nod.

She checked the dressing. No infection. No tell-tale smell. They had kept it clean. She wished Esmeralda was here. Her little sister was the better medic, the gentler touch.

"Here," Mitzi said, handing Joe painkillers and steroids. She wasn't sure if she should up-dose him or not, given that so much time had passed, and that he was doing better, somehow, all on his own. Lucky gringo.

He gulped the pills down and joined the ongoing banter . . .

"Did you hear the explosions?"

"—smilodon, and—"

"What about the helicopters?"

"Helicopters? No. Cannons."

"How could you miss—"

A few hours later they were in the deep jungle again. Juan rode at her side, rifle in hand once more.

"I told you everything would be fine," Juan said.

She nodded, gaze intent on the path ahead. They were close. They had to be. Dread over facing her father, fear at finding that they were too late, relief that they had made it this far, all took their turn battering her.

It was Pedro, her father's best sniper, who found them.

"We're down to seventy-five men," Pedro told her as he assessed the reinforcements she'd brought. She could tell by his expression that he found the gringos wanting.

"Your father is thinking of surrendering," he added in a whisper as he took the mare's reins and led them towards the camp.

"I didn't think that word was in Father's vocabulary."

"He'd rather surrender to the honorable enemies than the *maricones*," Pedro said.

He meant the Gurkhas and Sikhs. Despite the fact that both of those groups were part of the contingent sent to hunt them all down and kill them, her father respected them for their adherence to honorable behaviors. Well, that and their guts, toughness, and discipline.

She hopped down so she could walk at Pedro's side. The gringos dismounted as well, as if she'd given some silent order.

Pedro shrugged. The little loin-clothed man walked on, his gaze intent on his bare feet as they walked into the center of camp. Ragged tents, cooking fires, and camouflage netting surrounded a handful of the supposed seventy-five fighting men who'd survived.

Exhausted faces greeted them, blinking in disbelief.

Juan was at her side, rifle slung over his shoulder. His arm found its place around her waist. She turned to catch his gaze. He smiled that blindingly optimistic smile of his.

Father emerged from a tent. His gaze came to rest on her mother's *escopeta* and his face hardened.

She must not let him think something had happened to her mother.

"Mom says 'hi.' She told me to lead these men to you. Even loaned me her shotgun for safety and I never would have expected her to do that." She cringed at the fumbling words. All it took was Father's presence to make her feel like a child again.

Juan's arm tightened around her waist.

Her father frowned past them, no doubt trying to make sense of the heavily laden mules and her mother's strange instructions.

Juan stepped forward, hand extended in greeting. "Are you Belisario Carrera?"

"I am." One piercing blue gaze met another as they shook hands.

"Sir, I'm Juan Alvarez, Jr., from down in Southern Columbia, and, sir, we've brought some things I think you maybe need."

INTERLUDE:
From Jimenez's *History of the Wars of Liberation*

Though we—all of us, all across the planet—should never lose sight or memory of the courage and determination of our ancestors, we also ought to remember that, absent help from certain safe areas, we'd still be under Old Earth.

Help, however, ran in two directions. If we, in Balboa, were the beneficiaries of *gringo* charity, no less was the UN the beneficiary of human capital from our own planet.

This came in several forms. One was obvious, corvee labor, more honestly called slave labor, from some aspects of our population. They had, too, informers galore, local women engaged in what we might euphemistically call "morale support," a number of whom were informers for us. There were also policemen who sometimes assisted them, if only by keeping peace in areas the UN had pacified, bureaucrats who did the important work of collecting taxes, usually in kind, to keep the UN troops fed, road builders, wood cutter, animal breeders, etc.

One of the more ambitious projects, however, involved the use of Uhuran mercenary troops in the exceedingly hot—in both senses—Cochin Front. . . .

7.
THE PANTHER MEN

Justin Watson[8]

FROM: MARSHALL HIMCHAN MOON, COMMANDER
UNITED NATIONS PEACEKEEPING FORCE–TERRA NOVA
TO: GENERAL JEAN-PAUL ARCAND, COMMANDER-UN
FORCES COCHINA
SUBJECT: UNACCEPTABLE

Jean-Paul, I have long defended your unorthodox decisions, but arming neo-barbarian Terra Novans with modern equipment? The SecGen himself is aware and annoyed that you've undertaken something so brazen without so much as a by-your-leave. Taking this in conjunction with the massacre of the Italian contingent and your disappointing opium harvest, there are elements on the council calling for your relief. Give me something, some justification for your actions, some reason why I can or should oppose the people howling for your head.

ACK ASAP
MOON

---

8 Justin Watson grew up an Army brat, living in Germany, Alabama, Texas, Korea, Colorado and Alaska, and fed on a steady diet of X-Men, Star Trek, Robert Heinlein, DragonLance, and Babylon 5. While attending West Point, he met his future wife, Michele, on an airplane, and soon began writing in earnest with her encouragement. In 2005 he graduated from West Point and served as a field artillery officer, completing combat tours in Iraq and Afghanistan, and earning the Bronze Star, Purple Heart and the Combat Action Badge.

Medically retired from the Army in 2015, Justin settled in Houston with Michele, their four children and an excessively friendly Old English Sheepdog.

FROM: GENERAL JEAN-PAUL ARCAND, COMMANDER-UN
FORCES COCHINA
TO: MARSHALL HIMCHAN MOON, COMMANDER UNITED
NATIONS PEACEKEEPING FORCE–TERRA NOVA
SUBJECT: RE: UNACCEPTABLE

The Italians were massacred because you appointed a useless, whore-mongering drunkard as their commander and refused to listen when I tried to have him relieved. The opium numbers for Lang Xan and Angkok were better than mine this year because the Cochinese Liberation Front simply buys safe haven from the cowardly incompetents you've placed in command there with stolen opium. As for why I'm arming Terra Novan neobarbs, that reasoning is simple; because it will work. I assure you my Zulu mercenaries make far better soldiers than the soft city boys and irredeemable criminal scum you've been sending me, and we don't have to pay the outrageous expense of transporting the Zulu on interstellar spaceships.

If you want to relieve me, you're welcome to come and try.

SCIPIO, OUT.

Thung Lung Xanh District
Cochin Colony, Terra Nova

Arcand's guts rippled unpleasantly as another volley of artillery shells landed on the redoubt four hundred meters to his front. The ring of hilltop fortifications was occluded by black-gray-brown clouds of fragmentation, smoke and upturned mud, but once the smoke cleared he could see the boxy shapes of the bunkers were un-deformed and defiant.

His Zulu mercenaries surrounded a trio of fortified hills rising from the middle of an island in the junction of the Green River Valley with the Snake and Horn Rivers. The island had long since been cleared of jungle. The hills guarded a compound of metal containerized housing units, wire and sandbags, once occupied by UN troops, now in the hands of Cochin Liberation Front resistance fighters.

The hilltops provided clear observation for miles along all three rivers. Given Cochina's lack of a road network, each water way was an essential vein of goods and information and vital to controlling the colony. Arcand had posted two companies of infantry to hold this island, with heavy fortifications and a full battery of mortars.

And STILL those worthless fucking Dagos managed to lose the damned base.

"*Merde*," Arcand said aloud, setting aside his field glasses for a moment.

The tall French officer stood in a chest-deep fighting position just below the crest on the forward slope of a small ridge. Two green eyes peered out from underneath his helmet on either side of a prominent Gallic nose, under which he kept a well-trimmed mustache. Next to him crouched his radioman, a long-service Foreign Legionnaire named Ngo. Originally from America rather than Vietnam on Old Earth, Ngo was a passable Vietnamese speaker due to his grandfather's efforts. On Arcand's other side stood his chief of staff, a short, stocky dark-haired German colonel named Karl-Heinz Schwartzengrosse who had also brought his radioman.

"Our guns can't reduce the bunkers." Arcand said.

"I should think not, *Herr General*," Schwartzengrosse said, sniffing at Arcand's frustration. "My pioneers built those bunkers, I would have them flogged if they collapsed under light guns."

"That's so helpful now that they're in enemy hands, *Herr Oberst*," Arcand said, tone dripping with acid.

"You cannot blame us for that, sir," Schwartzengrosse said with mock-wounded dignity. "It's pearls-before-swine to entrust good German fortifications to Italians. We've known that since 1943."

Arcand snorted, suppressing a smile.

Another volley of artillery fire punctuated their conversation. As soon as the smoke subsided, the insurgents continued to fire unabated upon the besieging Zulus.

"*Merde*," Arcand said, again. "All right, have the artillery lay in the smoke screen, have all mortars put HE on those bunkers. It will do even less than the artillery, but it should at least fuck with their aim. Tell the artillery to have their firing solution for Hill 392 prepared, as soon as Colonel nDlamini initiates his assault on Hill 371, start shelling Hill 392. That will suppress them while the Zulus are exposed on the other hillside."

Schwartzengrosse nodded, and took the hand microphone from his radioman. He began issuing orders over the artillery radio net. Arcand, in turn, turned Ngo's radio to his command frequency and raised the Zulu's company commander.

"Assegai, this is Scipio, prepare to advance."

One of the tallest and most heavily muscled Zulus led the rest into the attack. Four days of beard covered Alexander nDlamini's angular jaw and his large brown eyes were wide with adrenaline. The epaulettes of his green and black fatigues bore five brown stripes indicating his rank as a colonel.

Alexander sprinted up the side of the hill, more than a hundred of his men arrayed behind him and to either side. He made it about ten meters up before ten riflemen overtook him on their way up the slope, a massive man with a gray beard shouting at them the whole way.

"Move, you bastards," Adjutant-Chef Mjanwe screamed. "Will you let your prince do all your fighting for you?!"

Alexander smiled, a momentary flash of brilliant white against coal black skin. The hill was long and steep, with mud layered several inches thick. With each step the mud sucked at his boots. Rising with the clinging mud, the smell of rotting vegetation and death filled his nostrils. As the company plunged into the massive smoke cloud provided by the artillery, forms became indistinct while diffuse light lent everything on the hillside a surreal, nightmarish quality.

Alexander could barely see the men to his left and right, their dark green-gray-black uniforms blending them perfectly into the mist and mud. For several moments, all Alexander could hear was the squelch of his boots in the mud and his own ragged breathing as they trudged up the hill. Then the air was filled with the crack-thweet of bullets flying past them.

The shots were raggedly aimed, but they were close enough to cause Alexander's stomach to feel like it was simultaneously crawling to his shoes and leaping out of his throat.

"Stay on line!" he shouted. "Marching fire!"

Matching deed to word, Alexander raised his rifle to his hip and fired off a round every time his left foot hit the ground. Muzzle flashes burst through the fog on a long line to his left and right. The uneven but persistent cacophony of return-fire drove the enemies' heads down, even in their bunkers.

The angular outlines of the hillside bunkers loomed up out of the fog like massive headstones. Alexander looked around to see his subordinate officers and NCOs running about, positioning machine gun teams with oblique angles into the bunkers' firing slits and urging riflemen forward on their bellies, hopefully beneath the fire of both friend and foe.

"Thenjiwe," Alexander shouted, pulling his young radio operator down into a crater in the hill next to one of the machine gun teams. The boy, just turned seventeen, regarded him with wide eyes. With two metallic clacks, Alexander ejected his spent magazine and reloaded a fresh one as he spoke. "I won't need the radio for a minute, stay here with the machine guns."

Without waiting for a reply, Alexander joined the advancing riflemen, cradling his rifle across his arms so it stayed up and out of the mud even as the clinging, sticky terrain coated his uniform and invaded every crevice of his body. Enemy and friendly fire cracked and buzzed back and forth over his head.

Not ten meters to his left, a musket ball tore into a soldier's shoulder with a sucking, cracking sound, nearly ripping the man's arm off. The ruined limb hung by strips of skin and a shredded lattice work of ligament and bone that hardly resembled a shoulder socket. He began to scream, a terrible too-shrill sound. One of his fellows rolled laterally and began to work on him, Alexander could make out an injector in the man's hand and the wounded man's screams mercifully subsided after a thump-hiss sent an ampule of morphine coursing into his system.

Alexander rolled back over bumping against another soldier, a thin, younger man—

"Damn you, Thenjiwe," Alexander said. "I said I didn't need you!"

"Begging your pardon, *iNkosi*," the young man said, using the isiZulu address for a lord with a toothy grin despite the deluge of fire and carnage around them. "You said you didn't need the radio so I left it with one of the machine gun teams."

"This is insubord—" a pair of near misses buzzed over them like angry hornets. "*Eish!* Damn you, little Cousin, let's go."

An arrow thunked into the mud where Alexander's right foot had been just a moment earlier. They were now receiving volleys of arrows, modern small arms and black powder musketry all at once. At this range arrows and crossbow bolts could be just as dangerous as bullets. Perhaps more so, given that the insurgents probably dipped the arrowheads in shit and UN medical care, miraculous as it was, was still hours away from the front line.

The assault element reached a line of sandbags no more than five meters away from the bunkers. Alexander rolled onto his back, let his rifle lie across his chest, and retrieved a grenade from a pouch on his load-bearing vest.

"GRENADES!" He shouted.

Alexander pulled the pin on his grenade, let the metallic lever, colloquially known as the "spoon," fly and counted to two as slowly as his racing heart would let him.

"Three," he continued, as he propped up on an elbow but still low to the ground to avoid masking his own machine gunners' fire, and chucked the grenade into the nearest bunker. The trajectory was more like a baseball pitch than a classic lob, but it worked. He was close enough that he actually heard the grenade clang against the back wall of the bunker then clunk to its floor.

Pressing himself flat to the ground face down, he grabbed Thenjiwe to make sure the boy was prone too. The concussion of the blast washed over him and he felt debris clatter none-too-gently against the top of his helmet. His grenade's detonation was replicated in the hill's other two bunkers. The machine gunners ceased firing over their comrade's heads, knowing what was coming next.

Springing to his feet, Alexander sprinted toward the bunker, screaming one word, the same centuries-old battle cry that had shaken rival Nguni tribes, the Voortrekkers, the redcoats and communists alike; now revived on a new planet.

"*NGADLA!*"

The cry rose over the din of battle, echoed in dozens of throats as the Zulu charged the bunkers.

"*NGADLA! NGADLA!*"

Alexander, Thenjiwe close on his heels, sprinted around the side of the nearest bunker, and through its rear entrance. Only one man was still standing in the bunker. He was tall for a Cochin, and all Alexander could make out about him otherwise was that he was covered in blood and dirt, somehow still standing despite the grenade detonation. The insurgent stopped fumbling with a crossbow as Alexander burst through the back door. Dropping the weapon, the man pulled out a grenade, identical to the one Alexander had thrown seconds earlier.

The bloodied insurgent managed to get the pin out, but as his left hand came away from the metal sphere Alexander rammed his bayonet between the man's second and third ribs with all the force in his body. The insurgent's breath left him in a rasp and his bones cracked with his impact against the bunker wall, then Alexander twisted the rifle, changing his bayonet's orientation from perpendicular to parallel with his enemy's rib cage. Planting his foot on the man's thigh, he pulled the bayonet out with a cracking and squelching sound and a gush of blood and viscera.

"*NGADLA!*" Alexander screamed, but then the grenade rolled out of the eviscerated insurgent's hand.

Five, a detached piece of Alexander's mind registered the standard fuse time for a frag grenade. He could try to climb back out of the bunker, or dive for it.

Four, Alexander dove, hitting the ground with jarring force, his fingers brushed the grenade, but it rolled out of his grasp further into the bunker.

Three, snaking along the floor, Alexander reached again and managed to get a firm grip on the baseball sized metal sphere, batting it into a pit in the center of the bunker made for just such an occasion.

Two, Alexander grabbed the eviscerated insurgent, who'd lost enough blood that he offered no resistance. Alexander man-handled the dying man to the ground, right on top of the pit, curled himself into a ball atop his enemy, shut his eyes tight and held his hands over his ears.

One—THOOM!

The blast turned his victim into a vaguely cohesive pile of meat and sent Alexander flying several feet into the air and over onto his back. Alexander hit the concrete floor with a *huff* of air. For several seconds he lay still, allowing the buzzing in his ears to subside and his vision to clear.

When he could see again, he saw that Thenjiwe was sprawled on his back, covered in blood and guts, clearly dazed but breathing normally. After a few seconds, Alexander heard voices speaking isiZulu. They sounded as if they were speaking from the other end of a long metal funnel, but one addressed him directly and Alexander realized they were just outside.

"Colonel nDlamini, are you in there?"

"Yes, we're in here, this bunker is clear," Alexander shouted to the door, his own voice sounding muffled and distorted in his ears. He climbed painfully to his feet, wiping entrails away from his eyes. He offered his free hand to Thenjiwe.

"*Ngiybonga, sir,*" Thenjiwe said, as he accepted Alexander's hand.

"*Wamukelekile, imbongolo engenayo,*" Alexander said. *You're welcome, insubordinate ass.*

Alexander's adjutant-chef, Nkosiphindule Mjanwe, walked through the bunker door. The gnarled older warrior examined the carnage inside the bunker with aplomb. Seeing his commander coated in gore didn't seem to faze him.

"Sir, this hilltop is taken," he said, his voice matter of fact.

"Excellent, Adjutant-Chef," Alexander said, as he finished pulling his radioman to his feet. "Engage Hill 392 and tell the machine gun teams to hurry."

Mjanwe acknowledged the order with a crisp, "Yes, iNkosi," then strode off rapidly to carry out his orders.

Turning back to the firing slit, Alexander pulled a gray cylindrical grenade with green tape on it from a pouch on his chest. Pulling the pin, he tossed it just outside the bunker. A cloud of green smoke billowed out of the small canister; the predesignated visual signal for having taken a mission objective. That done, he turned to his young cousin.

"Are you all right, Thenjiwe?" He asked, looking into the boy's eyes, checking for signs of concussion.

"I'm fine, sir," Thenjiwe protested, drawing away. "I feel fine."

Alexander nodded.

"Good, because my radio is a hundred meters down the hill." Alexander waved out the bunker's firing slit. "And guess who's running down there to bring it to me?"

"But, Cousin," Thenjiwe said, looking balefully at Alexander. "Can't the gunners bring it up with them?"

"This is a, 'sir,' conversation, *Corporal*," Alexander said, eyes flashing with a good simulation of genuine anger. He jabbed a finger into the boy's chest. "Next time I tell you to stay put, you stay *put*. What would your *mother* say to me if you were killed to no good end?"

"As long as all my wounds were in my front, you know as well as I do that your aunt would say, 'well done.'"

Alexander patted his young cousin's shoulder and smiled at him. "Well spoken," he said. "But you're still going to go get my radio."

Headquarters, UN Forces-Cochina
Khoi Dau Moi, Capital
Cochina Colony, Terra Nova

Since she was not attending mass, Mai didn't bother with a more formal gown, or any of the western cut garb she wore while serving General Arcand. Her loose blue tunic and gray canvas pants marked her as any random peasant girl running errands, and though eschewing make-up couldn't make her plain, it did make her look less, "westernized."

Two green-and-black camo clad legionnaire nodded politely as she stepped out into the fog and humidity of the Cochinese morning, familiar with her routine. No guards followed her as she left the compound. If she tried to escape her father would die and her neighbors back in Thang Pho Xahn would suffer terrible retribution as well. Such restraints had proven more effective than sentinels or chains.

Mai monitored her gait, ensuring her stride was neither too bold nor too meek so as to draw the eye of bipedal predators. Mai loved her people, but she was under no illusion that the Cochinese were all good men. Despite the presence of sabretooth cats, cave bears and sundry other terrible carnivores on Terra Nova, Man had thus far proven himself the deadliest animal on two worlds.

The morning heat was already oppressive, rapidly coating Mai in sweat and soaking the armpits of her tunic and the crotch of her pants. The moist discomfort annoyed Mai, not for its own sake, but because it was a tactile reminder of how living in a climate-controlled cage had changed her.

With the general away on an operation, Mai had little to do at the compound. Not that her duties were all that onerous when he was present. She was a student of all things French and teacher of all things Cochinese, serving girl and social secretary, but only to Arcand himself and, unlike his predecessor, Arcand didn't expect sexual favors of her. Since the old Frenchman didn't have a boy to satiate his lust, either, Mai was unsure why she remained unmolested. Surely the UN had some miracle cure for impotence.

If he expected her loyalty in exchange for his unwillingness to rape her, he would be sadly disappointed. She'd willingly suffer a thousand more such indignities to rid her home of the godless Earthpigs.

Still, Arcand had been meticulously correct in his conduct toward her. He had even quelled misconduct from his subordinates towards her peers amongst the other captives. It was admirable enough that she was willing to pray that he died quickly when they finally drove the godless UN from Cochina. She believed such magnanimity to be her duty as a Christian.

The brackish smell of the river was heavily seasoned with the ammonia stench of dead fish as Mai approached Khoi Dau Moi's economic heart. Men and women of all ages, dressed much as she was, moved from bamboo stand to stand, trading hauls of fish for pottery or bushels of rice for a cut of gamey water-buffalo meat and perhaps a few grams of opium or black powder under the table.

Thus the haggling of the market went on, even under the pall of the occupation. The UN demand for opium hampered production of many other necessary agricultural goods, but it hadn't, quite, destroyed their barter economy.

Mai kept the crosses atop St. Christopher's Church in front of her. Five years ago, St. Christopher's had been the largest structure in Cochina, bigger than any governor's mansion, bigger even than the Buddhist shrine at Thành Phố Dôi Den. Now the ugly, synthetic monstrosities of the UN headquarters buildings all dwarfed it and everything else the Cochinese could construct with their own means.

The intended message of superiority, and permanence, was clear.

But as Mai approached the stone façade of her church, she noted that it still stood despite the shadow of the UN's tyranny.

A light shines in the darkness, she silently recited John's gospel. *And the darkness has not overcome it.*

She pushed the doors of the church open with a creak. There was no mass on Wednesday morning, so she found the pews empty. Fortunately, Father Duc was fiddling with something upon the altar. She was glad she'd caught him. When he wasn't actively engaged at his church, Duc spent his time out amongst his flock providing counseling, or simply lending a hand with this chore or that, despite his advanced years.

Since Duc considered every Cochinese he could reach on foot or cart part of his flock, he was popular with Buddhists as well as Christians, and even had the grudging respect of the communists in Khoi Dau Moi.

"Mai," Duc said, smiling. "What brings you to Church on a Wednesday morning? You can't have amassed so many sins in three days as to need confession again."

Mai bowed her head respectfully, but then put her hand out to shake his, a slightly more masculine gesture than was customary for a girl her age greeting a patriarchal figure. Duc showed no surprise at her extended hand, or at the thick slip of folded paper she passed when he grasped it.

"I was hoping I could join you on your rounds, today," she said. "I have no pressing duties at headquarters."

"Of course, child," Duc said, smiling. "I thank the Lord for your devotion to His ministry and your people."

On Approach to Thang Pho Xahn
Cochin Colony, Terra Nova

Alexander's stomach gave a little jolt as the helicopter's nose dipped below the horizon and negative gees pulled his rear off the canvas seat. The Zulu prince smirked a bit at the widening of Thenjiwe's eyes across from him. He and his younger cousin were the third generation of colonists in Northern Uruhu. While they had always known that flying machines were more than myth, the fact that neither they nor their parents had firsthand experience with them lent all aircraft an air of mystery, and for some of the colonists, terror.

Personally, Alexander thought flying was one of the best things about this war and if he weren't weighed down with the burden of his blood and the burden of command would've loved to become an aviator himself. Thenjiwe's paling knuckles and clenched jaw muscles indicated he didn't share his older cousin's enthusiasm. Out of the corner of his eye he could see Arcand's face remained impassive at the helicopter's sharp maneuvering.

The sun was sinking into the dark green hilltops, illuminating the jungle canopy in pink, orange and purple rays as the UN helicopters approached the district capital of Thang Pho Xahn. While a great deal larger than most Cochinese hamlets, "District Capital," still seemed a pretentious moniker for the town. It was mostly thatched roof and bamboo construction, but a few stone and even a couple of brick buildings stood out.

The bird flared out over a field just beyond the outskirt buildings of the village and settled gently on its wheels. Ten helicopters joined the one carrying Alexander and Arcand on the ground mere seconds later, having shifted from a vee to a diamond formation. C Company of the 1st Zulu Auxiliary Rifles poured out of the birds. Two platoons secured the landing zone forming a ring of green-and-black clad Zulus, rifles and machine guns pointed outward. The third platoon escorted the general and the prince into the town.

Arcand and Alexander followed a well-manicured flagstone path past some of the larger, more impressive bamboo huts to one of the brick buildings in the village. It was a two-story reddish-brown building with actual glass windows and an orange, two-tiered roof that sloped up to points at each of the buildings' corners.

The steps that led up to the building's main entrance were flanked by two sandstone guardian lions. Each was five feet tall, one held its massive paw over a globe, the other over a lion cub. A blue uniformed native trooper stood beside each lion. Both men snapped to and brought their flintlock rifles perpendicular to the ground, held in both hands and centered. Arcand returned their presentation of arms with a salute. Corporal Ngo, his radioman, stepped forward and spoke in Vietnamese to the guards. After a brief exchange, the younger guard nodded politely and walked up the stairs and into the house.

Governor Trung Thieu was a known quantity to the UN occupiers and had, from all reports, personally led his native troops in a successful defense of Thang Pho Xahn even as the Italians had failed to hold the river valley fortress. Arcand rewarded his competence and loyalty with a higher degree of autonomy than most of the district governors enjoyed.

The general, being a fair sort, didn't let his appreciation be tempered by the fact that Trung Thieu's loyalty was secured by his only daughter's presence as a de facto hostage at the UN headquarters. Virtually all of the local notables had given up beloved children to be "educated" by the benevolent UN forces charged with defending the colony from undesirable elements. No one, not even Arcand, used the word hostage aloud.

Alexander could feel Thenjiwe fidgeting next to him, compulsively running a hand across the back of his neck then wiping it on his pant leg. Alexander quelled the unnecessary motion with a cough and a flick of his eyes to the Legionnaires and Cochinese. Thenjiwe, receiving the message, straightened up and did his best to pretend the jungle heat and moisture weren't murdering his soul.

Fortunately, the guard did not take long to return.

"Sir," he said in thick French. "Governor Thieu will see you now."

As was proper, given that General Arcand was the de facto ruler of all Cochina, he entered Thieu's study first, even before their host. It was a positively cavernous room by colonial standards with both a writing desk and a green, rectangular conference table: an Old Earth antique, Alexander noted, made of plastic that none of the Terra Novan colonies were capable of making yet. The plain white walls were lined with book shelves.

Thieu joined them in short order. The governor was not a physically imposing man, but his posture was unbent and deep lines crossed his weathered face. Despite the state of his colony as an occupied territory, despite the fact that his only child remained in his occupier's custody, despite the ludicrous imbalance of power between the two men, he met Arcand's eyes steadily, with grave dignity.

"General," Thieu said, with a moderate bow. "I take it you have been victorious?"

"Yes, Governor," Arcand said, returning the bow with a shallower one. "The fortress has been retaken. I will be leaving more of my own troops to help you fend off any future incursions, as well as some reliable native troops levied from the Southern Districts."

Thieu's expression changed not one whit, but Alexander felt palpable disapproval radiating from the old man.

"As you wish, General," Thieu said, his tone as still as his features. "Please, have a seat."

They sat around the green plastic table, Alexander to Arcand's left, Thieu across from Arcand, the unoccupied side toward the door. Alexander ensured he had a clear view of the door, since Arcand had insisted Alexander's troops wait outside the mansion.

"I'm afraid there remains an unpleasantness to resolve," Arcand said.

The first visible sign of consternation, a small crease between the eyebrows, flitted across Thieu's face.

"What, 'unpleasantness,' remains? Was not the fortress the last major insurgent position in the district?"

"Yes," said Arcand. "It was, but there remains the task of discouraging further acts of rebellion. Given that more than two hundred Italians died and that a majority of the CLF regulars escaped across the border into Lang Xan with significant quantities of Italian weapons and munitions, enemy propaganda will certainly paint this as a victory. We must take measures to invalidate that perception, and to discourage others from joining the CLF cause."

The governor and the general stared, stone-faced, at one another for long, painful seconds. Alexander felt their war of wills as if it were tangible, as if he were back on the hillside, artillery impacting just a short distance away. Formidable as Arcand was, Alexander believed the old man might have won the contest had he a single card to play beyond his own resolve. Thieu rose a great deal in Alexander's estimation at that moment.

Since his position as supplicant was inalterable, though, the old man broke the silence first.

"General Arcand," Thieu said, slowly, carefully, as if probing a minefield with his words. "How would you discourage others? I think mass reprisals would be ineffective and counterproductive."

Underneath the table, Alexander's hand tightened on the butt of the pistol in his thigh holster. Thieu's native guards were just in the other room, much closer than Alexander's Zulus. Arcand, for his part, kept his hands folded calmly on the green plastic tabletop.

"I do not propose, Governor Thieu," Arcand said with a frosty edge to every word. "I command."

Arcand let that linger for several breaths before he continued.

"But no, I do not intend anything so indiscriminate. We have gathered genetic data on every single insurgent we killed or captured. We will systematically sweep every settlement in the district, starting with the capital, to find their relatives. Women and children will be moved to reeducation camps in the south and given meaningful work. Colonel nDlamini's men will execute the adult males."

Alexander missed several beats of conversation after that. Arcand, damn his arrogance, hadn't warned Alexander that his men were now to be executioners. The general had predicted, correctly, damn him again, that Alexander wouldn't contradict him in front of the governor. Furthermore, Alexander saw the balance of fury and cold logic at work in Arcand's solution and had to admit he appreciated it.

"General, I think, perhaps, that would be an overreaction," Thieu said, but even as he argued, Alexander noted his posture was fractionally more relaxed.

He's not willing to fight to the hilt to stop this, Alexander realized, with horror and admiration. Thieu was pragmatic enough to accept the UN rooting out his troublemakers for him.

"Two hundred of my men lie dead upon that hill," Arcand said, his voice rising for the first time in the conversation, as he pointed back down the valley. "Every single body was mutilated. I can only hope most of them were already dead when the vermin went to work on them. I will avenge them, and the people will learn that joining the insurgency will result in their death and the outright destruction of their families. Your people's only hope is in cooperation with us."

This response, though brutal, was measured and appropriate given the locals' imperatives. The Cochinese, like their Vietnamese ancestors, like Alexander's own people, were communal in a way most Europeans simply couldn't understand. The Terra Novan colonists were even more so, the primitive conditions of the new world having necessitated they embrace older and harsher ways just to survive.

By striking at specific family groups rather than rounding up random villagers, Arcand could instill fear and underscore his resolve without appearing capricious or driving the undecided into the insurgency's arms. If anything, he was showing generosity by allowing the women and children to live, albeit far away from their homes and under the burden of, "meaningful work."

Thieu was opening his mouth to make a counter point when the study's door swung open. Two white-uniformed locals carried in trays laden with tea and hors d'oeuvres. A flash of unconcealed anger drew Thieu's eyebrows together sharply.

"I did not call for—" his words fell off abruptly and confusion replaced anger on his countenance. Alexander felt a shard of ice in his gut as he realized what was going on.

Thieu doesn't recognize the servants.

The intruders dropped their trays. One of the men was shouting something in Vietnamese that sounded like, "chat fan boy!" Both of them produced black pistols from inside their uniforms. The men held the weapons one-handed instead of dropping into a supported two-handed stance, but at conversational distance their lack of form wouldn't matter. Alexander saw the pistols coming up as if in slow motion.

The Zulu prince was in motion before the tea cups hit the floor. The tabletop wouldn't stop even the smallest caliber bullets, but its lightness also made it a serviceable projectile. Alexander sprang to his feet, flipped the table onto its side and kicked it at the attackers in one smooth motion. The table took both men in the legs, doubling them over and driving the muzzles of their pistols towards the floor. Their first shots punched holes through the tawny smilodon fur rug and into the wooden flooring. The sound was deafening in the enclosed space.

Alexander threw himself forward, following through as his right foot hit the floor to leap into a dive tackle at the nearest gunman. His left shoulder plowed into the man's mid-section and his momentum and far greater mass drove the thin assassin violently back into the door frame. Alexander heard the man's bones crack. As they slid down the door jamb to the floor, Alexander heard a second and then a third shot but he couldn't see what came of them.

The insurgent he grappled still held the sleek, Italian pistol in his right hand. Alexander immediately clamped his enemy's gun hand with both of his and slammed his wrist against the door jamb with a crack, then again, and then a third time before the pistol fell from the man's numb grasp. Rather than go for his own sidearm, Alexander launched into a full assault on the man's unprotected face, raining elbows and fists on his head until he went limp.

Someone was shouting his name from a distance, but the fury for which his people were renowned had taken Alexander and he continued to beat the insurgent's face into a pulp. He didn't stop until he felt a hand on his shoulder. Whirling, his fists skinned and covered in blood, Alexander turned to face the second attacker with wide reddened eyes. Instead he found Arcand standing there, his pistol not *exactly* pointed at Alexander, a look of caution on his face.

"We want that one alive," Arcand said, nodding at the sodden heap of assailant Alexander had left on the floor.

Alexander took several deep breaths.

"Yes, sir," he said, stepping away from the man as Ngo and Thenjiwe crowded forward.

Only then did he notice that the other attacker was lying on the floor with the pink and gray contents of his skull sprayed across one of the governor's nice book cases. Alexander looked from the body to where Arcand was coolly returning his pistol to its holster. The body had one neat red entry wound in its cheek and another just over the eye cavity. It had been good shooting on Arcand's part under stress, even at point blank range.

Alexander hauled the man he had beaten to his feet. The man's eyes fluttered open and he stared at the large young Zulu in unabashed fear. He muttered something through his swollen lips that sounded like, "nan con bay-oh."

"Take him to the medics," Alexander said to Thenjiwe. "Make sure he lives and can talk."

"And tell the interrogators to add both men's DNA to the purge list," Arcand added.

Fantastic, Alexander thought. *More men for me to murder.*

Arcand stared hard at Alexander for a moment, as if reading his thoughts.

Rather than chastise his subordinate, Arcand shrugged, communicating his own thoughts to Alexander quite clearly.

C'est la guerre.

Arcand turned to Thieu.

"Governor, while I am only modestly conversant in your beautiful language," he said. "I do believe, '*Chate phan boi*,' translates to something like, 'die traitor.' I note also, that the insurgents managed to smuggle two captured pistols into your very house."

Thieu inclined his head slightly. If he was rattled by the attempt on his life, it was not apparent in his demeanor.

"Just so, General."

"It appears you have just as much reason to suppress future attempts at treason as I do," Arcand said. "That being the case, I'll expect your full cooperation."

Thieu's stony expression moved not a millimeter for three uncomfortable seconds. Then he nodded his acquiescence.

"It will be as you say, General."

"Thank you, Governor," said Arcand. "I'll bring in my staff to go over details in two hours. In the meantime, Colonel nDlamini and I will take our leave. I'm sure you have much to do."

"Of course," said Thieu. "Until next time."

Arcand, Alexander and their troops made for the front door, but Alexander paused a moment in front of the governor.

"Governor Thieu?"

The stoic old man's face evinced clear surprise at being directly addressed by the big black mercenary.

"Yes, Colonel, what is it?"

"The man we captured, he said, 'nan con bay,' " Alexander said. "What does it mean?"

"Nam con bao," Thieu said. "It means, more or less, 'Panther Men.'"

Thang Pho Xahn
Three Days Later

"Chúa ơi, không!"

"Xin đừng! Anh ta không phải là một tên khủng bố!"

The wails of wives, mothers, and children assaulted his senses, but Alexander pushed them firmly out of his mind as he walked amongst the prone forms of the condemned. He stood in a ditch amongst a dozen dead and dying Cochinese men, his pistol in his hand. Only he and his officers carried out the reprisals. While his men were not at all squeamish about killing, there was little honor in shooting bound, defenseless men. His officers were carrying out their prince's direct orders and thus had some moral top cover, and he ensured his enlisted men need not touch the task and thus remained unsullied.

The great kings Cetshwayo and Shaka would've impaled these men *and* their families without losing a second of sleep. Alexander knew it and took great pride in the fierceness of his distant ancestors all the same, but they had not *believed* as he did. Alexander respected the traditions of his people, but his Catholicism was more than window dressing. While Christians throughout history hadn't shied away from atrocity themselves, the young Zulu prince knew what the teachings of Christ dictated, and this was not it.

And yet, the insurgents were themselves indiscriminate killers and rapists. They predated upon the very people they claimed to be liberating. They *had* to be stopped and moral platitudes were insufficient to the task.

Already insects were gathering around the corpses and the heat and stench were visibly affecting even his staunchest officers.

An old man with thick gray hair and mustache was at his feet. Looking up at the young Uruhuan prince, gasping, he seemed to be pleading for something. The rifle bullets hadn't killed him outright.

Leveling his pistol and aiming so as to sever the old man's brain stem, Alexander squeezed the trigger. The crack of the .45 caliber round carried through the syrupy air. The bullet ripped out the back of the man's cranial cavity and buried itself into the soft jungle floor.

Heavenly Father, I cannot even pray for forgiveness. I simply pray that this is not in vain.

Holstering his pistol, Alexander turned to his soldiers and motioned for them to bring in the next group of condemned men.

St. Christopher's Church
Khoi Dau Moi
Cochin Colony, Terra Nova

It was late Sunday afternoon and the sun's slanting rays still kept the interior of the church uncomfortably hot. The air in the cramped confessional booth was stifling and damp, pressing on Mai's words as she hissed them through the privacy screen to Father Duc. Mai could hear the soft footsteps of acolytes moving about the sanctuary, cleaning up after the last Mass, so she kept her voice low despite her fury.

"They tried to murder my father," She said, her hands clenched into fists in her lap. "I will not give you another scrap of information."

Silence reigned for three full seconds, the only exceptions being Mai's rapid heartbeat in her ears and the old priest's breathing. She could see nothing of his expression through the screen and the encompassing darkness of the booth.

"I'm sorry, Mai," Duc said, breaking the silence. "The operation wasn't sanctioned by the Committee. An independent cadre commander ordered the assassination attempt without consulting his superiors."

"I want that commander dead," Mai said in a low, rage-filled growl. "Or no more intelligence from inside the headquarters. Furthermore, I will tell them that my very own priest tried to recruit me for the resistance. I wonder how long it would take Arcand's interrogators to break you."

"Mai, you don't mean that," Duc said in the same gentle, understanding tone she usually found so comforting, but which only heightened her anger now.

"If the resistance can't protect my father, what do I owe them?"

"It's not about what you owe them, Mai," Duc said. "It's about what you owe yourself. You don't want to live as a quisling."

"I want my father murdered even less," Mai said. "And a collaborator is quite comfortable under Arcand's regime."

"I understand your anger, but have you considered that it is actually more likely your father will survive to the end of the war now?" Duc said, his voice still maddeningly conciliatory. "His position with Arcand is more secure than ever and the CLF doesn't have the people for another serious attempt. The Committee knew they'd be sacrificing just about all of their local assets to take the Italian base and get their heavy weapons across the border into Lang Xan. Thang Pho Xahn will be quiet for a long time."

"I want a protective order put on my father from the Committee," Mai said.

Duc sighed.

"Think, child," Duc said, a note of impatience finally creeping into his tone. "If they issue such an order, every operative who hears it is a possible point of discovery for the UN. You'd be putting him in more danger, not less."

Mai sat wordlessly for several painful seconds, her anger and fear pounding at her ribcage, twisting her stomach, fingernails digging into her sweat-slick palms.

"All right, Father, I'll still spy for you. But allow me to be clear," Mai said, finally. "If he dies, we die."

"I understand, Mai," Duc said. "And I accept."

Headquarters, UN Forces-Cochina
Khoi Dau Moi
Cochin Colony, Terra Nova
Three Weeks Later

Arcand's mood was blacker than the storm clouds that gathered over the colonial capital. The bleak, sodden view out his office window only fed his frustration. He glowered at the sheets of rain pummeling the courtyard, a sheet of paper crumpled in his hand. The drumming of the deluge on the roof was a cadence for his own infuriated pulse.

He kept his working office a simpler affair than most of his peers. Even so, the walls were dominated by full book cases and the flags of his former commands, so much so that the light green paint of the walls was barely visible. Most prominently, the colors of the 2nd Regiment *Etranger Parachutiste* decorated the wall behind him.

Why the hell am I even bothering with this? He asked himself. *If the sonofabitch doesn't want the stupid medal—*

The door opened, interrupting his thoughts. Trung Mai, dressed in a white blouse and blue skirt of western cut, entered.

"Sir, Colonel nDlamini to see you," the Cochin girl said. Even the lovely sight of Mai and her normally soothing soprano voice did nothing to take the edge off Arcand's anger.

"Yes, send him in," Arcand said, placing his hands, fingers interlocked, upon the desk top.

Mai closed the door behind her. A few seconds later three sharp raps sounded on the door.

"*Entrez*," Arcand said.

Alexander nDlamini, less-than-resplendent in dirty battle dress uniform, marched into his office. Halting three paces away from Arcand's desk, he came to rigid attention and saluted crisply.

"Colonel nDlamini reports to the commanding general, as ordered, sir!" he barked.

Arcand returned the salute casually. He was not upset at Alexander's wet, mud-encrusted uniform or the fact that he smelled like an incontinent goat. He had, after all, summoned the young officer directly from a field training exercise.

Having blooded platoons, and now a company, they were currently working on fielding a full-strength battalion of Zulus. Alexander was getting closer to a colonel in responsibility as well as title and the Zulu Rifles were rapidly, as far as such things go, becoming an actual regiment.

So his filthy appearance was beside the point, what *did* piss Arcand off was the defiant anger in Alexander's eyes. Arcand recognized Alexander's expression only too well, having directed his own version of it at superior, peer, and subordinate alike over the years.

Oh, I'm wasting your time calling you in out of the field, you little shit? Is that it?

Arcand did not put Alexander at ease, but let him stand at attention. Taking up the itinerary in his hands again, he held it up so Alexander could see it.

"Colonel, would you care to tell me what the fuck this is all about?" Arcand dived right into the crux of the matter.

"Sir, I've no issues with the awards ceremony schedule save those already noted," Alexander kept his voice studiously neutral, his posture rigid and unnaturally still.

"Cut the horseshit," Arcand said. "Why have you refused acceptance of the Military Medal? Don't give me false modesty; we both know you deserve the fucking thing as much as anyone."

Alexander was quiet for a long moment, his eyes fixed on a point several inches above Arcand's head.

"Sir, I am afraid I can give no answer which wouldn't constitute insubordination by the terms of our contract," Alexander said.

Arcand glared a second longer, then shook his head and let out a sharp bark of laughter. He leaned back in his chair and gave Alexander a look that held as much empathy as exasperation.

"It's about the reprisals, is it not?" Arcand asked.

Alexander exhaled sharply once and swallowed.

"Yes, sir."

Arcand nodded.

"Oh, at ease, Colonel," the Frenchman said, with a wave. "In fact, sit down."

Alexander looked back at the proffered leather-upholstered chair.

"Sir, I would soil it," he protested.

"Shut up and sit down, Alexander," Arcand said, rising from his own chair to come around his desk. "I'm going to tell you a story. A true story about a young officer I served with back in Darkest Africa, some thousands of kilometers north of your ancestral home."

Alexander sank into the chair, looking confused.

"I was then a lowly brigadier general," Arcand continued, leaning back against the front of his desk. "I commanded seven thousand, 'peace-keepers,' in Eastern Africa. In reality we were securing mineral and fuel concerns for the benefit of the European Commonwealth, but we tried to do some good along the way.

"The local insurgents, a hash of Marxists, local animists, and Islamists, were particularly nasty even by the standards of the region. After we cleared them out of a key tritium-producing province, I ordered all commands to execute every adult male relative of the insurgents we could lay our hands on. Just as I ordered you to do.

"One company commander refused. He was my best, so I didn't slap him down, but feigned ignorance of his disobedience. It was the biggest mistake of my life, and his. When we had to shift his company to another region for a time, it took the insurgency about a month to grow back like the cancer it was. When he returned, he found hundreds of the locals who had supported us raped, murdered, mutilated. Some had been eaten by the insurgents, oh, not by the Muslims, credit where it's due, they'd have none of that, but some of the animists had no such compunctions.

"So this time, having learned his lesson, he did as I ordered," Arcand said, and his voice broke just audibly, his eyes flicking to a picture on one of his bookshelves for just a split second. "And allowed himself to be overcome with the guilt of both having failed to do what was necessary the first time, and of having executed men whose guilt was uncertain the second. This distraction proved fatal, as a month later he led a patrol into an ambush he should've spotted. But he managed to lead them out again before he died of his wounds."

Arcand paused and took a deep, steadying breath before continuing.

"That company, previously my most aggressive formation in battle, was fit only for guard duty after that. Not because a popular commander died, though that always hurts, but because they'd seen him broken and wracked by guilt. His doubt and indecision cost me a company of paratroopers, just as it cost my son his life."

Arcand ground these last words out, closing his eyes for a moment. When he opened them, Alexander was regarding him gravely with wide eyes.

"I apologize," Arcand said. "I did not intend to become emotional, but you must learn from his mistake. Only the truly twisted enjoy being executioners, but it's a virtual certainty that most of those men were active or tacit supporters of the CLF anyway."

"It's nearly as certain that a minority weren't," Alexander insisted.

"Statistically, yes," Arcand said. "It's also statistically certain that if you fight a war of any duration and intensity, an artillery barrage, a bombing sortie, an ill-placed grenade or machine gun burst is going to kill someone who isn't an enemy combatant. This is no different, and if you treat it differently, if you act as if a tragic necessity has irrevocably tarnished your honor, you will undercut your men's morale. Without morale, their discipline will break and you will find yourself ruling over a rabble rather than a formation. Rabble dies on the battlefield, young prince.

"With any luck, our next major operation will be the invasion of Lang Xan. The complexity and ferocity of the battle will dwarf the Green Valley campaign. Your men must enter into the operation assured of themselves and of you.

"So, Colonel nDlamini, you will stand in front of me and accept your personal decoration for valor, just before your company accepts its unit decoration. You will do so regardless of your personal feelings, for the sake of your men and the mission you have contractually agreed to fulfill. Am I clear?"

Alexander frowned, but Arcand could see the wheels turning in the young prince's eyes. He knew he'd made his points.

"Yes, sir," Alexander said, at last. "For the sake of my people, and fulfilling our contract, I will comply."

Officer Club, UN HQ
Khoi Dau Moi
Cochina Colony
Two Days Later

The rain had abated, leaving a clear, lovely view of the night sky. Eris and Hecate, two of Terra Nova's moons, were up and bathing the headquarters' central courtyard in silvery light. Alone, leaning on the railing of the O Club patio, Alexander stared up at the stars, completely oblivious to the sounds of music and merriment behind him.

He was clad in the dark blue, red and silver trimmed dress uniform that Arcand had gifted to all the officers of the 1st Zulu Auxiliary Rifles. His pistol was secured in a highly polished black leather shoulder-and-waist belt opposite the Iklwah short spear scabbarded on his left leg. Arcand had commissioned special leaf-bladed bayonets so that the Zulus wouldn't drop their rifles in melee, but neither Alexander nor his men would fully abandon their ancestral weaponry.

Two freshly acquired accoutrements adorned his uniform tonight: a green-black-blue fouragerres encircled his left shoulder, the symbol of his unit's Croix de Guerre for an extra-planetary theater, and a golden medal suspended by a green and yellow ribbon gleamed on his breast; his own Military Medal.

Alexander's nightmares were still littered with crying widows and orphans and the watery eyes of an old man whose lungs were filling with blood. Nevertheless, he'd accepted the damned medal, and smiled, proudly. It wasn't a sham, per se; he *was* immeasurably proud. Yet he was simultaneously ridden with shame. He simply chose which emotion he displayed for his men. At least, that's how he rationalized it. And if war was teaching him anything, it was the fine art of rationalization.

It was with no small amount of self-recrimination that he recalled the council where he'd pushed so damned hard to make this deal, to provide Arcand with troops.

He remembered how King Matthew Credo nDlamini, third regnant sovereign of New Zululand, sat rigidly upon his throne, tension in his shoulders and forearms belying his calm façade. His feet rested on the tawny pelt of a pack-alpha scimitar cat he'd killed himself, his head crowned with the burnished brown antlers of a magnificent buck sivatherium.

To King Matthew's right stood his sons, Jacob, a thinner reedier version of his older brother, and Alexander. To his left stood Nkosiphindule Mjanwe and Father Piter van Graef, a portly old man with a great white beard, who was New Zululand's only Catholic priest and one of its few resident white men.

"King Matthew," Alexander said, formally, "It is clear to me on both moral and practical grounds that we should take his offer. We saw the video and pictures that the Frenchman brought with him. The Cochinese insurgents are raping, torturing, and slaughtering their own people wholesale. It is our Christian duty to oppose such evil. Furthermore, the advantages we stand to gain in industry, medicine and military power are significant."

Mjanwe frowned at Alexander from the king's left, but it was Alexander's half-brother, Jacob, who spoke next. They were of a height, but Jacob's frame was more sparsely muscled, indicating a life focused on negotiation and study rather than hunting and fighting.

"Your Majesty," Jacob said. "Prince Alexander is right; we cannot afford to pass up this opportunity. What Arcand can grant could leapfrog us generations ahead of our current standard of living, and with modern weapons and ammunition and spare parts to keep them operational, we would be unchallenged, militarily."

Alexander looked at Jacob in surprise. The half-brothers rarely agreed. But Mjanwe could take no more and spoke before Alexander had a chance.

"We are already militarily dominant," he snapped. "Would you cut a deal with the devil just for more comfort and some trinkets?"

"The technologies on his list are more than trinkets," Alexander said, heat in his voice. "Many of them could save hundreds, thousands of lives, and the videos—"

"The videos are likely a digital fiction," Mjanwe said. "Or Arcand had some of his Asian Foreign Legionnaires dress up in local garb and go on a killing spree."

"Unlikely," said Father Piter, wiping sweat from around his collar. "The extent of the evidence defies fabrication. Still, your instincts are good. Beware Frenchmen bearing gifts."

"Father Piter," Alexander said. "Surely you can't countenance such slaughter if it is within our power to stop it?"

The old priest shook his head.

"Nik is right to mistrust them. Under normal circumstances I would advise you to avoid this bargain."

"Under normal circumstances?" Mjanwe's eyebrows furrowed in suspicion.

Father Piter sighed.

"Your Majesty," Piter said, turning to King Matthew. "If you refuse him, Arcand will find another source for his mercenaries. It is possible he will go far afield, and whoever accepts his offer will not be our problem. But what if he picks a rival tribe from over the mountains? Or what if, God forbid, he extends this offer to the Yithrabi?"

For long seconds, King Matthew considered each of them. Then he spoke, his voice carrying the full weight of royal command.

"We will negotiate," he said. "Assuming we can secure sufficient safeguards, we will make the deal and send our soldiers to fight in return for what has been promised."

"Excellent, Father," Jacob said. "I would lead this regiment myself, if it is your wish."

"It is not," King Matthew said, coldly. "Alexander will command our expeditionary regiment. Nkosiphindule, you will go as his chief advisor."

"Prince Alexander," Matthew said, rising and putting a hand on Alexander's shoulder. "You cannot trust Arcand and you certainly can't trust his masters. Fulfill our contract, win his war for him, by all means, but never forget that while our goals and his may overlap, they are not identical. Protect your honor, and place your realm first."

Have I done that? Alexander asked himself, his thoughts returning to the present, staring out at the moonlit courtyard. *Have I protected my honor?*

"You know," a Cochin accented, sweetly feminine voice slid through his dark memories like a knife. "It won't be long until everyone is wondering where the hero of the hour is."

Alexander turned slowly, unsurprised to see Trung Mai standing on the patio with him. Tall for a Cochin girl at five foot six, her French heels barely raised the crown of her head to Alexander's shoulder. She was dressed in a conservative but well-fitted green evening gown with amber accents that complimented her dark, almond shaped eyes.

Alexander found Arcand's personal hostage an achingly beautiful sight on a normal day. In her current state, she was breathtaking. Where his Faith would not quietly accept brutal military necessity, it also prohibited him from taking advantage of the carefully vetted brothels available to his men. Mai's silk-clad curves drew his imagination off on tortuously pleasant excursions.

"Ms. Mai." Alexander bowed politely, tamping down on the surge of lust. "You look lovely this evening."

"Thank you, Your Highness," she said, returning his bow with a smile and a curtsey. "You look quite dashing yourself, despite your obvious perplexity."

"Perplexity?" Alexander said. "I'm afraid I do not know this word."

"You look troubled, Your Highness," Mai said. "And you are missing your own party."

"It is nothing," Alexander lied. "The battle to liberate your home district was intense and our training scheduled since hasn't allowed for much rest. I'm simply tired."

"Of course," Mai said, her tone laden with polite disbelief.

"And why are you foregoing the party?" Alexander said. "I'm sure there are many who would be overjoyed at your company."

"That was an exceedingly polite way to tell me to leave you alone," Mai said, her smile broadening into a grin.

He couldn't stop a quiet laugh. Mai had become a friend of sorts. Alexander, who credited himself for his maturity in this matter, knew they could not be more than friends, and that even their friendship must have limits.

"Besides," Mai continued. "Perhaps I just prefer the company of my fellow captives."

Alexander's smile vanished, replaced by a frown.

Limits.

"I am not a captive," Alexander said.

"Of course you aren't." Anger fell in beside the mockery in Mai's tone. "Free men often fight for tyrannical occupiers against people who have done nothing to them."

"Done nothing to *my* people, yes," Alexander said. "But I've seen the, 'freedom fighters,' deeds with my own eyes. They nearly murdered your father and they would violate and murder you and your entire family with no more hesitation."

Alexander cut himself off. He'd let her get to him again. To his surprise, Mai didn't press her attack after striking an exposed nerve.

"Of course, Prince Alexander," she said, and she appeared genuinely contrite. "I apologize. We all do our duty as best we see fit."

"Your apology is unnecessary," Alexander mustered another smile. "But if you would honor me with a dance, the matter would be forgotten even more easily."

Alexander held out a hand. Mai's troubled expression cleared and blossomed into another smile, less mischievous than her initial expression.

"Of course, Your Highness," she said, then her eyes glinted with humor again. "Try not to step on my toes this time."

"I will do my humble best."

Arcand was on his sixth glass of cognac. The potent drink had a flora and citrus zest to it as he swirled it on his tongue. It was an extravagant expenditure of booze as he had only had a half-dozen bottles of genuine French cognac on this planet, but his war was going well for the first time in more than a year. That called for a special libation.

Seeing Alexander with Mai furthered his good cheer. He'd noticed Alexander brooding out on the balcony at the beginning of the reception and worried that he would have to coax the prince back into the party to fulfill his social obligations. Mai's intervention had not only saved Arcand from that unpleasant duty, her result was a less sullen compliance.

Schwartzengrosse appeared at his elbow. The short, stocky

German colonel was drinking a double measure of something golden and fragrant. Following Arcand's gaze, Schwartzengrosse's eyebrows quirked, betraying his skepticism.

"Forgive me, *Herr General*," he said, his breath reeking of fermented apples. "I wasn't aware we were in the matchmaking business. I was under the impression we were occupying a rebellious colony."

Arcand snorted.

"You are an unfeeling Hun without a milligram of poetry in your soul," Arcand said.

"*Das ist richtig, mein General*," Schwartzengrosse said. "But I suppose as hobbies go, mating your Uruhuan mercenaries with your Cochin hostages is more interesting than breeding horses or dogs."

Arcand drained his glass and reached for the cognac again.

"You really don't see it, do you?"

"See what, sir? Two attractive young people falling in love? *Ja, wunderbahr*. Let's put aside our weapons and write a play about it. Perhaps we can make up our opium shortfalls in ticket sales."

"No, you dull Boche," Arcand said as he emptied the ovoid shaped bottle into his glass. "Oh, yes, I have a few more shreds of my soul left than you have, so I can appreciate the romance of it, but put sentimentality aside. They are our future."

"General," Schwartzengrosse's eyes widened then narrowed. "The only future I'm interested in is one where we win this fucking war and go home, to Earth."

Arcand was already shaking his head before Schwartzengrosse finished his sentence.

"*No, non, nein*," Arcand paused to take another drink before continuing. "You think the spineless faggots on the Security Council will let us return home? We are two of perhaps a half-dozen senior officers worth a shit in combat in the entire UNPF. We command the hardest sonsofbitches our countries have left. We are dangerous."

"Exactly," the German insisted. "That's why they need us; to do the work their gelded lackeys can't."

"And that work is here, my friend," Arcand said. "They have exported everyone with a spine to this world. There's no real fighting to be done back on Earth, so what are we but a liability to them if we return?

"We are conquerors, and we have a kingdom to claim, right here, practically laid at our feet, but we'll need to normalize our rule and create a nobility to help us rule it. Surely you remember the tale of the Sabine women?"

"*Jawohl, Herr General*," Schwartzengrosse said. "But you've been excruciatingly clear that our men aren't to rape anyone, so I don't see the relevance."

"I'm not talking about the rape," Arcand said. "I'm talking about the same assimilation process that eventually made the Sabines into Romans, but a touch more civilized.

"Our officers marry Cochina's most prominent daughters en masse. They create a new de facto ruling class, a legitimate one to the Cochin. The new generation will be familiar with their ways, but schooled and indoctrinated to ours. Prince Alexander and Trung Mai are only the first.

"We have sixty years of life, easy, before we need rejuvenation. That's two to three generations we can personally oversee before we even need to arrange a trip back to Earth. And once we've solidified our rule here, I see no reason not to expand outward."

"Tabling your insanity for the moment," Schwartzengrosse said. "Why a mercenary? Why not one of our own to inaugurate your strategic dating service?"

"Ah, that's just it," Arcand said. "Alexander is a born and bred prince. He has been trained not only in how to fight, but how to rule. We'll need that, and by the time we've pacified Cochina, he will be one of our own. His prominence will also solidify a permanent alliance with the Zulu, enabling us to field even more regiments of their fine warriors. In time, he will succeed his father, and then our alliance will be all the stronger with him in New Zululand on his throne. We'll have a stable base and the finest fighting force on the planet."

"You really think the Cochinese will ever accept a Frog as their king?" Schwartzengrosse shook his head. "Much less the Angkokians and Lang Xanese, or, God forbid, the Zhong or the Yamatans?"

Arcand lifted his chin.

"The Swedes germinated their royal line with French seed," he said with a sniff. "Why should good taste be confined to Scandinavia?"

Schwartzengrosse stared at his commander for three long seconds, then reached out for Arcand's glass. The move took Arcand by surprise; so much so that he did not stop the German as he drank Arcand's Remy Martin cognac in an appalling, uncivilized gulp.

"What the hell are you doing?" Arcand said.

"I haven't had nearly enough, and you've had entirely too much," the German said, his voice deadpan. "I'm doing what I can to remedy that situation."

Arcand started laughing, a hearty laugh that came from his gut.

The laughter came to an abrupt halt when Schwartzengrosse pointed out the Headquarters duty officer, still in green and black battle dress, coming through the back doors of the Officer's Club. The young captain was trying to be subtle, but he was clearly in a hurry, a half-page of paper in his hand. Taking the floor in long strides, he came to attention just two feet from Arcand and Schwartzengrosse.

"General Arcand, sir," he said, in a low voice. "I apologize for disrupting the reception, but this came in Flash priority from the Security Council."

He proffered the paper to his commanding general, Arcand took it and, after taking a moment to focus, started reading. His expression lit into a smile, then immediately fell. Looking back up at the captain, he handed the paper to his German chief of staff to read.

"Who has seen this?" Arcand demanded of the captain.

"Myself, sir, one of our enlisted cryptologists and our chief of signals," he answered, his voice betraying nerves.

"Keep them all in the command center until I get there. You and they are to speak to no one until I've talked to all of you in one room," Arcand said in a low, dangerous voice. "This is to be kept utmost secret. If this leaks, I will have all three of you shot, just to be sure I got the one responsible. Clear, Captain?"

"Yes, sir," the young officer said, blanching.

"Dismissed," Arcand said.

Schwartzengrosse was just finishing the missive when Arcand turned to him.

"*Scheiss*," he murmured. "What are we going to do with this?"

"To the first matter, the obvious, we attack as soon as possible," Arcand said. "To the second, we ensure there is no chance of the news getting to Colonel nDlamini or his men until we're ready to mitigate the consequences."

Alexander found his worries returning after the reception dispersed.

At one in the morning, Alexander, accompanied by his personal guard, left the party and began to wander the streets of Khoi Dau Moi. He wasn't sure what he was looking for, and he felt bad for the soldiers who were forced to follow him in his vague search for some kind of . . . he wasn't even sure, serenity, perhaps? Though KDM was the most pacified of Cochina's settlements, it would still be stupid for any UN soldier to wander off by themselves, thus the fire team trailing him.

Perhaps subconsciously guided, perhaps because it was the largest structure outside the UN compound, Alexander unknowingly mirrored Mai's path to St. Christopher's church. Despite having frequently attended Father Piter's services back home, Alexander hadn't set foot inside a church since deploying to Cochina.

He had two solid excuses for this lapse; the UN didn't have chaplains or chapels, while local Cochinese services were held in the Vietnamese language. He'd picked up some of the language from his interpreters and more from Mai, but he was not nearly proficient enough to follow a Mass in the local tongue yet.

A part of him recoiled as they approached the church's ornamental façade. Arcand had convinced him of the necessity of putting on a brave face despite his personal misgivings, but bending to that imperative wasn't the same as believing that his actions were just in the eyes of God.

Don't be a coward, he told himself. *If you can't face your Lord and account for your sins, of what worth is your faith?*

Taking a deep breath, he approached St. Christopher's wooden double doors.

"Wait here," he told his guards, who did not look happy, but complied.

The church appeared empty, much as he had expected at one in the morning. Walking up to the front of the church, Alexander crossed himself and genuflected in front of the altar before sitting in the front pew. Despite the turmoil in his soul, Alexander felt peace seep into his being as he sat in church, gazing upon the cross. He resented it, knowing how dreadfully undeserved that peace was. Acknowledging God's presence and authority now was an anti-septic poured into his open wounds.

"Can I help you, son?"

Alexander started at an old man's voice behind him. Rising out of the pew and turning rapidly, he just managed to stay his hand from reaching for his pistol.

An old Cochinese man in priestly robes and collar stood in the middle aisle a few pews behind Alexander. Stooped, withered, and more than a foot shorter than Alexander, the priest regarded the Zulu mercenary prince with a mild expression completely devoid of trepidation.

"Good evening, Father," Alexander schooled his voice to calm courtesy. "I just came to sit and pray. I'm sorry if I've intruded."

"This is the House of the Lord." The priest smiled gently. "No one who seeks God here is an intruder. I'd heard some of you Uruhuans were Catholic. I'm glad to see you here."

"You're very kind, but I'm not so sure you'd say that if you knew what I've done," said Alexander.

"I'd say it if you'd murdered my own children," the priest said, his voice ringing with conviction. "Because that is the duty I owe the Lord."

The power of the old man's faith cowed and shamed Alexander. After a few seconds of silence, he picked up on something odd the old Cochinese had said.

"Children?" Alexander asked, confused.

"I wasn't always a priest, son," the priest said, smiling, his tone mild once again. "But now, I am Father Duc."

Father Duc held out his hand. Alexander took it firmly but not with undue force. The reciprocal grip was still strong, indicating a life spent doing more than studying scripture and preaching.

"I am Alexander nDlamini," Alexander said. "Thank you for allowing me to pray here, and for your warm welcome."

"Ah, sit, please," Duc said. "You are the Zulu prince, if I hear correctly. No wonder the Lord brought you here."

"Why do you say that, Father?" Alexander asked as he settled back into the pew beside Duc, trying to keep suspicion out of his voice.

"I've fought wars, my son," Duc said. "I know what it can do to a soul. You are a young man entrusted with a terrible burden. It is only natural you seek spiritual guidance in the midst of it all, perhaps even absolution?"

When Alexander didn't respond and didn't make eye contact, Father Duc persisted.

"I assure you the seal of confession applies to anything you tell me, in or out of the booth," Duc said, gently. "Neither your enemies nor your employers will have access to anything you say inside these walls."

Alexander shook his head again.

"Thank you, Father, truly," he said. "But even if I could talk about it, I can't truly repent."

"You don't feel guilt for whatever it is that troubles you?" Duc asked, his voice still mild.

"Immense guilt," Alexander said, the image of bound, lifeless bodies and grieving, red-eyed women and children fixed in his mind's eye. "But I may have to do it again. If I cannot make an honest effort to refrain from my sins, then my repentance is false and you cannot intervene on my behalf for Christ's absolution."

Father Duc nodded.

"You've been rightly instructed in this matter," he said. "But it still might help you to talk about it."

Alexander began to shake his head, but then he stopped. It wasn't as if his actions were a secret. Arcand had ordered it all done as an abject lesson to the locals.

"I saw terrible things during the battles in the Green Valley," Alexander said. "In three of the villages the CLF managed to occupy, everyone who'd cooperated with us was murdered, usually alongside their families, their children. Many of the CLF irregulars raped the women and girls first, sometimes for hours, from what the survivors told us. The main force regulars were more disciplined, for whatever that's worth."

Alexander paused, taking a deep breath.

"I vowed that I would do whatever I needed to do to destroy the CLF after the first village we recaptured," Alexander continued. "So when General Arcand ordered us to kill every living male relative of the resistance fighters, I did it. And I thought I could live with it, after all, it's not so different from how my ancestors used to take care of enemies."

"It's not that different from how everyone's ancestors took care of enemies," Father Duc said. "No one tribe, state or nation bears unique shame for that, nor are many innocent of it."

"But it eats at me," Alexander continued as if Duc hadn't spoken. "Many of those men probably had nothing to do with the resistance. Many probably tried to dissuade their brothers, sons, cousins from fighting, but we killed them all the same and turned their women and children into little more than slaves. My men and I made more than a thousand widows and orphans . . . not in battle, but in executions.

"But the worst part is that I *am* living with it. I continue to function as a prince and commander because I can do nothing else, and if I have to kill another thousand bound and helpless men to win this goddamned war, I will. To do anything else is to condemn my men to hideous deaths and deprive my homeland of almost two thousand of its finest warriors, all for nothing."

The Zulu prince's head sank into his hands.

"Essentially, I am damned no matter what," Alexander said through his fingers. "If I survive this war, can I truly repent even then, knowing that I would blacken my soul again if I felt my duty to my people required it?"

He felt a thin, strong hand on his shoulder.

"Alexander, what does your duty as a prince require? Is it merely that your people survive, or do you need to lead them to something better?" Father Duc said. "I don't have an easy answer to that, but I beg you to pray and meditate on the matter. You are right in that, if you won't repent, I can't grant you absolution. I offer you but one small comfort; you would not feel such pain if you did not have an intact soul to be wounded. God loves you and wants you to embrace your salvation."

Before Alexander could respond, the doors of the church opened and Mjanwe's boots thumped on the wooden floor up the aisle toward them. The grizzled NCO nodded politely to the priest and came to attention in front of Alexander.

"I beg your pardon for interrupting, *iNkosi*," Mjanwe's voice was clear and devoid of slur despite the copious amounts of whiskey

Alexander had watched him consume earlier that evening. "But General Arcand requests your presence at Headquarters."

"Excuse me, Father," Alexander said, standing to leave, somewhat dazed that he had unburdened himself so freely to a stranger, priest or not. "Thank you for your conversation and counsel."

"It was my pleasure, Prince Alexander," Duc said. "I hope you will come see me again."

Alexander paused for a moment, half turned to the door. Turning back to Duc he said, "I just may. Thank you again."

When he reached headquarters, Alexander was ushered into the main operations room. A familiar terrain model dominated the room on a large, low table in its center. It depicted a large swath of river valley and adjacent hills, with two towns, one fishing hamlet and one walled village dominating. Alexander had already studied it extensively. It represented the CLF's largest base area in Lang Xan. Though only he and Mjanwe knew it, his battalion's entire training regimen had been geared towards preparations for attacking it.

The regimental level commanders and other independent battalions were all there as well. Arcand regarded them all from the north end of the terrain model. He made eye contact with Alexander briefly and for a moment Alexander thought he could see something resigned, even melancholy in the Frenchman's expression. It was gone rapidly, if it had even really been there, and Arcand appeared confident, excited, even a bit triumphant.

Realization dawned on Alexander a second before Arcand began to talk.

"Gentlemen," he said. "Operation North Wind is approved. As soon as the monsoons end in the central region, we will invade Lang Xan."

Khoi Dau Moi

The evening was notably cooler and pleasant in Khoi Dau Moi as service at St. Christopher's let out. An odd, diverse crowd emerged from the great wooden doors. The congregation was still predominantly locals, but several faces had complexions ranging from dark tan to flat black, their height and uniforms further distinguishing from the mass of Catholic Cochinese villagers. The conversation in the evening air was a polyglot hum of Vietnamese, French and isiZulu.

There had been tension at first, when Alexander and a handful of his men began attending evening mass at St. Christopher's. After several weeks, though, their presence was a normal thing. A few tentative friendships, beyond Mai's and Alexander's, formed in those weeks.

Even a few pale white faces broke up the crowd, though admittedly some of these were more or less open spies. Mai hoped some of them might hear and receive the Word of the Lord in good faith regardless; that way their souls wouldn't be eternally damned when the resistance killed them all.

Alexander and his Zulus were resplendent in their blue dress uniforms with matching kepi. Mai couldn't help but cast an admiring gaze at Alexander in particular as she looped a hand through his arm. Objectively, he wasn't all that handsome, but he was tall and strong, and every decoration on his uniform was for valor, not some petty recognition of bureaucratic excellence.

The sheathed short spear and holstered pistol on his shoulder-and-waist belt completed the image of dash and danger. Furthermore, even in the heat of Cochina in a heavy uniform, he smelled right.

Such an unladylike thought, Mai chastised herself mockingly.

As had become their custom after evening Mass, Alexander walked Mai back to the Compound with only his personal guards and Adjutant-Chef Mjanwe trailing at a respectable distance. The guards were the only Zulus in battle dress rather than the ornate blue dress uniforms, and each man carried a rifle at the low-ready.

The old Zulu warrior always stood at the back of the Church throughout Mass, joining Alexander as he departed. He remained politely quiet but refused to take communion or otherwise participate. When Mai asked Alexander about this, he'd told her that while many of his men blended Christianity with the traditional Nguni beliefs, Mjanwe remained a hard line believer in the old ways. He only set foot in a Christian church out of loyalty to his earthly lord, not because he put any stock in Christ's claim to divine Lordship.

Mai thought that sad, as she rather liked the grizzled old warrior, seeing many of the virtues of huntsmen she'd grown up with from her own district in his demeanor.

Their journey terminated at the steps to Arcand's personal domicile, a grand white mansion with stone steps leading to a sweeping porch. The structure wouldn't have looked out of place in Vietnam before Dien Bien Phu, but was nevertheless reinforced with modern materials and technologies to make it sturdier, more defensible.

The Cochinese girl and the Zulu prince stood awkwardly for several seconds before the first stair, neither wanting to go, neither having anything more to say.

"I will be gone in the morning," Alexander said, finally. "It may be an extended absence."

Mai picked up something about his tone.

"This is it, isn't it?" She asked. "The big mission you've been training for."

"You know I can't—" Alexander began.

"Of course you can't," Mai said, holding up a forestalling hand. "If the general doesn't need anything, I'll go to sleep myself. I'll look forward to your return."

A brief flicker of something, distaste, anger, perhaps even jealousy crossed Alexander's face when she mentioned the possibility of General Arcand needing something. She'd seen it before and assumed it was just annoyance with his employer. It just then occurred to her that in the months she'd known Alexander, she'd never clarified something important.

"Alexander, you know that General Arcand doesn't, eh, take liberties with me, don't you?"

"Oh, good," Alexander said, his face brightening. Realizing that he'd betrayed more emotion than he'd intended, his expression fell into something sheepish, and very young. A trill of musical laughter escaped Mai's lips.

I giggle now? She thought, confounded.

"I suppose that it isn't properly my concern," Alexander said, looking at his boots.

On impulse, Mai closed the distance between them and reached a hand up to his cheek.

"Isn't it?" she asked.

When Alexander met her eyes, she felt all his warmth and passion in his gaze like a wave washing over her. Though she'd been intentionally stirring his emotions for weeks now, they still overwhelmed her in their intensity and honesty. This man cared for her and wanted her for more than a transitory pleasure, as surely as she breathed.

At five foot six, Mai was tall for a Cochin girl, but she still had to go up on tip toe and pull his head down toward her to kiss him lightly on the corner of his mouth before rapidly stepping back out of his personal space.

"Take care, Prince Alexander. I would be most aggrieved at the loss of your company."

She caught a glimpse of Adjutant-Chef Mjanwe's grin as she turned to leave, and the casual touch of his hand to his Kepi, but she acknowledged neither. Instead she fled up the stone steps of Arcand's quarters, silently berating herself with every step.

Stupid, foolish girl! She berated herself. *How does this end? How does this end in any other way than with one or both of you dead? You idiotic little twat!*

Her feet carried her automatically through the front door and to Arcand's private office as the stream of verbal abuse spewed like a firehose of degradation in her mind. Just before the threshold of Arcand's inner sanctum, she had the presence of mind to stop and collect herself. She saw light under the door, after a deep breath she opened the door softly and entered.

Arcand's office was actually little different from his study, which was in turn, little different from his library; all lined with bookshelves and with every horizontal surface holding at least one volume, a bottle of liquor or both, including his desk. Mai had been allowed, required even, to read many of the books; especially those concerning politics, sociology and history.

The general wasn't present, so she reached to turn the lights off and leave. But her hand froze in mid-air when she noticed a map on his desk. That was odd, as he usually kept that sort of thing in the operations shop. He must have been reviewing some last minute details for whatever big mission was in the offing.

Mai's pulse quickened. She'd reported the UN's increased activity to the resistance, but perhaps here she could determine some details.

Looking around and confirming she was alone in the office, Mai approached the desk. She had to stifle a gasp at what she saw.

It was a map of Lang Xan. The entire resistance depended on the safe havens afforded by the indescribably corrupt UN forces there. Not only did they leave the CLF bases alone, they conveniently, "lost," their military hardware in a roughly equal mass to what opium made its way into their hands, over and above the standard protection shipments, of course. The ability to retreat across the border, reconstitute bloodied units and train new recruits had enabled the Cochinese to resist a power with a technological edge of centuries far longer than they would have been able otherwise.

Mai wasn't fluent in the military graphics Arcand had drawn over the map's topography, and the southwest quadrant was covered by a pile of papers she dare not disturb, but the gist was exceedingly clear. This was a massive incursion, accomplished by helicopter and riverine insertion.

Alexander said he's leaving tomorrow, she thought. *It's already too late . . . No, wait, they won't launch the attack directly from here, he'll have to go to a staging area closer to the border. We have a day . . . maybe two. If Father Duc can get a runner on the road tonight, we might get word there in time.*

Despite the risk, Mai retrieved a small note pad and pen from a pocket in her dress and began to write down six-digit grid coordinates to the landing zones marked on Arcand's map. She'd kept her ability to read topographic maps one of her most closely guarded secrets since the first days of her captivity. There were many CLF victories due in part to the fact that Arcand's predecessor had been careless with classified maps around her. Arcand had always been more conscientious, until tonight.

"Mai, child, is that you?"

Arcand's voice, slow and fatigued, scared Mai out of several years of life. She stifled a yelp.

"Yes, General," Mai managed to say calmly. "I came to see if you needed anything before I turned in."

Arcand appeared in the doorframe between office and study. He was composed and upright, but his eyes held a slightly glassy quality. He was not sloppily drunk, she had never seen him thus, but he had clearly been at the bottle.

After months on end of concealing her emotions, Mai should've easily been able to pass scrutiny given his current condition, but the intensity of her interaction with Alexander, the revelation of the UN's impending invasion of Lang Xan and being on the edge of being found out put a subtle flush on her cheeks.

"Are you alright, Mai?" Arcand asked, and for the moment his voice sounded solicitous rather than suspicious.

"Yes, General," she said. "I just returned from evening service with Colonel nDlamini."

"Ah," Arcand smiled, a genuine expression, but tinged with sadness. "Of course. Good, very good. I imagine he'll need you very much in the coming months."

"General?" Mai said, confused.

"It's nothing," Arcand gave a graceful, Gallic wave of negation. "Come, sit, have a drink with me."

Confusion warred with terror for Mai's emotions. Arcand had always treated her correctly, even cordially, but he'd never been so informal. Was he trying to get her drunk because he was finally planning on breaking his self-enforced celibacy?

This is a hell of a night for his chivalry to fail him!

Arcand poured a glass of purplish red wine and set it on an end table next to a comfortable leather chair. He poured a glass for himself as well, and took the chair opposite hers, gesturing for her to sit. She did so, unable to hide her confusion. Fortunately, that was in character for spy and hostage-servant alike in this case. Arcand said nothing for many seconds, merely drinking his wine and staring out the window.

"General," Mai said, tentatively. "It's late and you seem tired—"

"I seem drunk," Arcand interrupted her with a raspy chuckle. "Because I am. But don't worry, I don't have anything nefarious in mind for you. I just wanted to talk to you."

Mai was extremely confused now.

"What do you want to talk about, General?"

"I'm sorry, you know," Arcand said. "For how you were treated. It was wrong, I'm glad the sonofabitch is dead. Every Army has its beasts, but I don't let them run amuck in my command."

"I know that, General," Mai admitted.

"Do you still hate us?" Arcand said. "It's all right if you do, I would hate us if I were you."

Mai considered the Frenchman opposite her carefully. His words were clear, his voice steady and his eyes focused on her; nonetheless he was clearly drunk. Any answer could end her life.

Tell the truth and shame the devil.

"I don't hate you, personally, General," she said. "But I wish you'd all go away."

Arcand barked a sharp laugh, startling Mai again.

"Including Alexander?" Arcand asked. Mai said nothing, but blushed.

"No need to answer that, of course. Thank you for being honest, Mai," he said, then drained his glass again. She noted several empty bottles on the low coffee table.

"I understand why you hate us, but I wanted to tell you that everything I do, no matter how cruel it seems, is to a good end," Arcand said. "The world I'm going to give you and Alexander, and your people, it will be better. I swear it will be better. I know you don't believe me, but I'll prove it to you in the end."

Mai said nothing, merely regarding her captor in shock.

He means it, it isn't just the wine, she thought. *Is this what war does to men of conscience? Drives them insane in their own spiraling rationalizations? Is this what Alexander will be like some day?*

Seeing her shock, Arcand regained himself with a visible effort. Leaning back in his chair, he closed his eyes and sighed.

"Thank you, Mai," he said, quietly. "You're right, it is late. You may go now."

"You should rest, too, General," Mai said.

"I will, child," he said, his voice gentle. "Go on, now."

Mai stood and left the room, taking care not to appear hurried as she went to help kill two men who cared for her.

On Approach to LZ Black
Lang Xan Colony, Terra Nova

Alexander scanned the landscape below the helicopter with night optics that turned the dark jungle canopy textured green-gray. Oddly, Alexander was one of only three Zulus aboard, the others being his RTO Thenjiwe and Adjutant-Chef Mjanwe. The other seven occupants were German combat engineers from the pioneer platoon that had been attached to his battalion for this operation. Wanting to keep his line platoons intact, Alexander had willingly stuffed his battalion headquarters personnel, himself included, wherever they could fit on the helicopters, as long as they were headed to the right LZ.

The helicopters attempted very few sharp maneuvers as more than half of them carried sling loads of wire, ammunition, and mines, the gray-green bags looking for all the world like canvas scrotums swaying beneath the advancing helicopters.

Underneath his calm demeanor, Alexander obsessively reviewed the plan for this operation. His battalion, plus German attachments, was headed for three landing zones on a peninsula formed by a massive oxbow in the Lang Xanese branch of the Green River. The fishing town of Savannakhet occupied the banks of the peninsula, and though its kilometer-long expanse of wooden docks were unassuming, primitive things, they were pivotal to Arcand's plan. With no feasible overland line of supply and communication, airmobile and riverine transport were the only way the UN could support sustained operations in this region of Lang Xan. For this shitty little brushfire war, Savannakhet was the equivalent of a deep water port.

Alpha and Bravo companies were occupying LZ's Red and White, from which they could isolate the peninsula from the main land. They would establish, as rapidly as possible, westward facing battle positions to defend against any reaction from the CLF main force, which was garrisoned eight kilometers away at the walled city of Champasak. Charlie Company, the German Pioneers, and Alexander's battalion headquarters element would make landfall at LZ Black, on the peninsula itself, behind LZs Red and White, and capture Savannakhet.

A flotilla of riverboats of every size and description was already underway from KDM up the Green River. With luck, the flotilla should reach Savannakhet's docks shortly after the second sortie of helicopters brought resupply plus reinforcements from the German contingent.

Depending on the enemy's reaction time, the Zulus and their German allies would either be defending their own lines or advancing against Champasak, attempting to draw out and fix the bulk of the CLF's modern-armed main battle force, thought to be of roughly regimental strength. It was extremely unlikely the Zulus could conquer Champasak alone, but once the bulk of the CLF's combat power was concentrated on Alexander's force, Arcand would initiate phase two of Operation North Wind.

Having secured enough fixed wing craft from UNPFTN to loft the entire 2nd Regiment *Etranger Parachutiste* of the Legion, Arcand intended to jump them into drop zones to the southwest of Champasak. Once they were reorganized following the jump, the entire regiment would march on Champasak.

If the enemy refused to take the Zulus as bait, the alternate plan was to link up with the 2REP, surround Champasak, and wait for resupply and reinforcements via subsequent helicopter and riverine sorties. Once every available unit was in Lang Xan and fully supplied, they would then have to siege and probably storm Champasak while it was fully garrisoned, at much greater cost in lives. Alexander devoutly hoped it wouldn't come to that.

"Two minutes out, Colonel," the pilot's laconic French voice sounded in Alexander's headphones.

"Acknowledged," Alexander said, his voice equally calm.

Turning to the rest of the helicopter's occupants from his perch near the open door, Alexander held up two fingers. The Germans and Zulus nodded acknowledgement and checked that their weapons were chambered and their equipment secure to disembark the helicopter. Alexander removed the headset and secured his own helmet.

The helicopter formation split into three distinct sections headed for their specific LZs with the unladen birds leading the way and unloading their troops first. The gray-green-white ground outside the helicopter grew closer and closer in Alexander's night-vision monocle until he felt the wheels hit the jungle floor. He did not need to give orders. His chalk flowed out the sides of the helicopter, avoiding the forward area of the rotor cone so as not to receive a fatal haircut.

Alexander kneeled next to a tree and turned inward, watching the gray-white thermal shapes of his men encircling the LZ, going to the prone or kneeling in the bush and pointing their rifles and machine guns outward. NCOs and officers communicated with hand and arm signals as the rotor wash stirred the wet night air into a constant thrum.

Mjanwe alone stood straight up, a chem-light in one hand and a radio hand mic pressed to his ear with the other. He was the only Zulu soldier old enough to have experienced helicopter operations back on Earth, which was why the Legionnaires had chosen him for advanced training in LZ control.

Under Mjanwe's careful guidance, the first slung-load helicopter came to a hover just meters above the ground and sank, slowly, towards the jungle clearing. The helicopter's engines strained to stay aloft in ground effect in the humidity. Slowly the canvas bag settled to the ground and the cables holding the bag slackened and then dropped to the ground. The canvas fell aside revealing a pallet of razor wire and pickets.

They repeated the process five times to get the rest of their palletized equipment and ammunition onto the LZ. All told, it took less than an hour. Alexander allowed himself a grin of satisfaction at his men's efficiency as the last of the helicopters, unburdened, turned north and headed back for the border.

"What the fuck is that?" One of his troops shouted.

The random exclamation and a series of flashes drew Alexander's eyes left, faint orange trails of smoke rose from the jungle.

"Oh, shit," he said. "Thenjiwe, give me the aviation net, now!"

It took his cousin less than a second to flip the frequency knob and hand the hand mic over to Alexander.

"Dragon Elements, SAMs at your six, say again, SAMs at your six, go evasive!"

The helicopters broke and dipped, scattering their neat formation in a dozen directions, but it was too late for two of the aircraft. The nearest helicopter was over the river when the missile intersected its flight-path. It was consumed in a brilliant orange flash and reduced to twisted and burning metal, plummeting, its forward momentum carrying it to the opposite bank. The explosion washed out Alexander's night optics for a moment, but flash-suppression safeguards prevented him from being blinded.

Alexander turned to his operations officer, Commandant Bongani, not as grizzled as Adjutant-Chef Mjanwe, Bongani was still visibly older than the other Zulu officer though not yet middle-aged. Although Bongani was hobbled from an unfortunate encounter with a scimitar cat, Alexander found the older man's intellect and maturity indispensable despite his physical limitations.

"Bongani," Alexander said, as the remainder of the helicopters moved away unscathed, "Inform Scipio of confirmed SAM threat."

"Yes, sir," Bongani said, turning to his RTO.

"How the hell did they get SAMs? We don't even have SAMs," Thenjiwe said.

"From the UN contingent here, obviously," Alexander said.

"But why would the UN soldiers here have brought them in the first place?" Captain Kwanele, the Charlie Company commander jogged up and joined the conversation. He was an exceedingly handsome young officer with chiseled jaw and serious dark eyes. "The insurgents can't put up a kite, much less a helicopter."

"They have them to sell them to the insurgents, of course, sir," Adjutant-Chef Mjanwe said, his expression grim.

"Come on," Alexander said. "It just became even more vital we secure those docks. We may not see another helicopter for some time."

To the east, gunfire and explosions punctuated his words.

Two Kilometers Southeast of Savannakhet

It was zero-five hundred and the sun's weak rays were just beginning to creep across the jungle floor, scattering light on a textbook clusterfuck.

Leaving Commandant Bongani with the headquarters troops and the Germans to set up the battalion operations center and hold the docks, Alexander led Kwanele and his men through the mounting morning heat toward the sound of the guns. Alpha and Bravo were still southeast of the neck of the peninsula formed by the oxbow, arrayed in a roughly vee shape.

They had already sacrificed a kilometer of jungle to avoid becoming encircled or overrun. There were only four more kilometers left to Savannakhet. And while they were holding, there was a gap between them they couldn't close. It was up to Kwanele's Charlie Company to seal it off.

There's no way the CLF moved a force this size and had them ready to attack so quickly without prior warning, Alexander thought. *We had an operational security breach.*

The rattle of automatic weapons fire was suddenly much more immediate.

"Contact front!" Alexander could hear the spot reports as his Zulus began to return fire. "Five men, two hundred meters, engaging!"

"Contact front, three men, one-fifty, engaging!"

"Contact front, one squad, two hundred, engaging!"

Alexander checked himself from snapping out orders, allowing Kwanele and his platoon leaders to manage the immediate fight. He relayed the development to Bongani for report to higher. He stayed close enough to the battle to see what was going on with his own eyes, but far enough back to avoid become decisively engaged himself.

Alexander watched as two Charlie company soldiers hit the jungle floor on their bellies. One calmly sighted in his grenade launcher, while the other, a light machine gunner, triggered controlled bursts at the enemy ahead of them. The grenadier sent a 40mm high explosive grenade hurling into the enemy, shredding an entire fire team that had been clumped together. The Zulus crawled forward a few feet, then sprung up and sprinted to another decent sized tree before repeating the process.

Their advance was replicated all along Charlie's line. The CLF regulars, no longer facing the Zulu with overwhelming numerical superiority, lost their momentum.

A tight group of three soldiers in CLF khaki stayed on their feet two seconds longer than they should have, allowing one of Charlie's medium machine gun teams to cut them down with a well-aimed burst. Another enemy fire team lay in the prone in one clump of trees without moving, thinking themselves concealed, but ultimately inviting a fragmentation grenade right on top of their position.

The gray burst of metal fragments killed two of the men instantly, two others lay on the ground, screaming in pain, their entrails lying on the roots of the trees they'd been hiding behind.

Alexander paused for a moment, brought his rifle to his shoulder and squeezed the trigger twice, ending one man's suffering with a controlled pair that left two neat entry wounds in his chest and softball sized exit wounds in his back. The young prince tracked to the left slightly to put the other man out of his misery, but two loud cracks from Thenjiwe's rifle eliminated the necessity.

The slaughter culminated as the dense jungle vegetation died off into a clear area leading up to a rocky ridge that stretched a kilometer across most of the neck of the Savannakhet peninsula. The fleeing CLF fighters fell one by one, shot in the back as they attempted to make it to the threadbare safety of the rocks. Once again the gunfire was distant, the immediate area quiet. Alexander noticed, for the first time, the whistle of mortars flying from LZ Black, over their head, east to where Alpha and Bravo were locked in combat with enemy's main body.

Finally! Alexander grinned as the detonations sounded over the ridge. Not sparing a moment to relax, Alexander sprinted to find Kwanele. He started issuing orders as soon as he found him.

"Get your company arrayed on the forward slope of that ridge," he said. "I'm going to Alpha and get them to reorient their line to tie in with your position, send your XO to Bravo Company to collect their XO and adjutant, then have them all meet me here."

"Yes, sir," Kwanele said. "Why do you want the XOs and adjutants?"

"They're going to help me lay out our next defensive position here and tie in the obstacles the Germans will lay out," Alexander said. "After the ridge line, this clearing is the only decent-sized engagement area we've got before we're back in the town. You've got to hold the enemy as long as possible to give us the chance to prep the next line of defense."

UN Headquarters, Khoi Dau Moi

The operations center in Arcand's headquarters was arrayed in a bowl of work stations around a central situation map table where Schwartzengrosse and Arcand stood. Those without an immediate task listened intently to Arcand's conversation with the Zulu's commander.

"Assegai, this is Scipio," Arcand said, keying his hand mic. "Confirm you have engaged the enemy's main force."

When the radio crackled to life small arms fire and explosions were audible over Alexander's tinny, distorted voice.

"Scipio, Assegai," he said, and even over the EM spectrum, Arcand could hear tension and annoyance lacing the call-signs. "We are engaged by an enemy force of at least regimental strength or higher, equipped with Italian small arms and other unidentified modern small arms, over."

"Roger, Assegai," Arcand paused, took a deep breath. "How long can you hold?"

The radio was silent for several seconds. Arcand resisted the urge to key his mic again, knowing that jostling the commander in the field was not merely impolite, but potentially dangerous.

"Scipio, at this rate I estimate we can hold this ridge for the rest of the day. If we can make it until nightfall we'll withdraw to hasty fortifications to the northwest. We should be able to hold there for twenty-four hours, unless the enemy decides to overwhelm us with a sheer frontal assault. Beyond that I don't know."

Arcand looked at Schwartzengrosse for a long moment, silently seeking his chief of staff's advice. The German officer's face was motionless, deathly serious for a long moment. Then he nodded once, firmly.

"Assegai," Arcand keyed the mic again. "Do what you can. I'm accelerating our time table. I'll be on the ground with 2 REP tonight."

"Roger, Scip—"

Alexander's transmission was cut off abruptly by a thunderous explosion.

"Assegai! Assegai," Arcand shouted into the mic. "Alexander, what was that? Report!"

"They've brought those heavy Italian mortars into play," Alexander said. "I have to go. Contact my Operations Center for further updates. Assegai, out."

The Ridge, Southeast of Savvanakhet

The dirt and grass, trees and rocks beneath his battalion appeared gray-white-green once again through Alexander's night optics as he watched the men of his Alpha and Bravo Companies creeping past Charlie Company's lines. The enemy had, perhaps wisely, refused to press the attack at night given that every single Zulu was equipped and trained with their night optics while the enemy only had a handful of captured devices still working.

Alexander sat with his back against a rock, half-eaten field ration in his hand. Thenjiwe lay fast asleep less than a meter away, his head tilted back over the radio in his assault pack. They had held the line against almost continual attack through the day as Alexander had said they would. More than half of them were wounded, half of that too badly to fight, and nearly a quarter of his men on the ground were dead, but they'd held, and inflicted far more death then they'd been dealt.

Unfortunately, the enemy had reinforced faster than Alexander's Zulus had been able to attrit them. Even though they had massacred the first regiment they'd made contact with two more fresh regiments. Intel's estimates were that it would take the enemy at least three days to mass that large a force on Savannakhet.

Alexander had ordered a methodical, subtle withdrawal under cover of night. Alpha and Bravo, holding the flanks, sent their left and right most fire teams, respectively, back through their lines to Charlie Company. From there their own XOs and adjutant-chefs guided them down the back of the ridge to their new battle positions, through the wire and mine belts that the Germans had been placing all day. The rest of the companies followed, at staggered intervals, by teams, crews, and platoons.

Kwanele found him almost an hour after the withdrawal began.

"Sir," he said in a low voice. "You should go. Alpha and Bravo have completed their withdrawal. We'll begin ours as soon as we receive word they're through the obstacle belt."

Kwanele, like Alexander, was covered in dust from shattered rock, mass quantities of sweat having drawn irregular lines in the coating. He was, additionally, peppered with minor wounds from fragmentation and stone splinters. He'd been superb in command of the defense, remaining calm and unflappable, even as the last CLF assault had come within hand grenade range of their lines. It wasn't as if Kwanele *needed* his battalion commander there.

But there was nowhere else Alexander needed to be more, at the moment, and no place where things could go wrong as quickly as at the point of withdrawal. Beyond that, Alexander remembered something, a scrap of dialogue from a book of allegorical fantasy Father Piter had shared with him:

"For this is what it means to be king; to be first in every desperate attack and last in every desperate retreat . . . "

Alexander shook his head.

"No, Kwanele," he said. "I will remain until you are ready to withdraw. If the enemy detects our movement, this will be the decisive point."

"As you wish, *iNkosi*," Kwanele said.

"Why is it my subordinates always resort to my royal title when they think I'm being a stubborn ass?" Alexander said.

"Sir, I wouldn't dare suggest a thing of either my prince or my commander," Kwanele said, grinning.

"I might," a new voice entered the conversation from the darkness. Mjanwe joined the two officers, careful to stay low and avoid casting a human silhouette against the rocky hillside.

"Well, adjutant-chefs have privileges a mere captain dare not usurp," Kwanele said with mock solemnity.

"You're damn right you don't, sir," Mjanwe said with a snort. "The last elements of Alpha and Bravo are in position down the hill. We have forward-slope observers hidden and set in the jungle on both flanks, everyone else is withdrawn."

"Excellent," Alexander nodded in satisfaction. "Captain Kwanele, you may begin your withdrawal."

Kwanele and Mjanwe moved off to begin coordinating the withdrawal. Alexander kicked his RTO gently on the shoulder. Thenjiwe awoke with a start, looking around groggily.

"Whaazzat, I wasn't sleeping, cousin . . . "

"Of course you weren't," said Alexander, so tired he didn't correct the familial address. "Get up, we are leaving."

To his credit, Thenjiwe was ready to move in less than a minute. He looked around perplexed.

"Hey," Thenjiwe said. "Why did they stop shelling us?"

"Limited ammunition," Alexander said. "They aren't good at adjusting fire in daylight; they would be wasting rounds at night."

"Oh," Thenjiwe said, nodding.

Each step down the rocky hillside was a trial as, under full pack, Alexander tried his best to move quietly and rapidly while small stones crunched and slid out from underfoot and larger ones clacked against each other and attempted to catch his ankles. Alexander wasn't, quite, the last man down, but he and Thenjiwe traveled with the last squad off the line. So focused was Alexander on his footing that he didn't notice Mjanwe traveling next to him until the old warrior spoke.

"Fall in behind me, sir," he said. "There's only one lane through the minefield. Thenjiwe, pick up the flags as we go through."

Thenjiwe did as he was ordered, clearing the flags that marked the safe path through the minefield as they passed through. Every second he was still standing out in the open, surrounded by mines on either side was pure hell on Alexander's nerves. If the enemy put it together that the Zulu had completely abandoned the ridge and surrounding jungle, they could be up on top and firing down at the exposed rear of the column any second.

Alexander breathed a sigh of relief as they crossed the last set of flags. They were still fifty meters from the woodline of the jungle and he could barely make out the closest fighting positions. As he got close enough to discern them, he could see that the positions were dug in chest deep and most had at least some overhead cover in the form of cut down tree trunks.

The Germans and Alexander's headquarters troopers had done yeoman's work preparing the battalion's battle position, but already he could see a glaring flaw. While the battle positions were well placed, he could tell, even under night optics, that there were no alternate or supplementary positions for the battalion. If the enemy did get their position registered for their mortars, the Zulu would have no choice but to stay in their holes and take it.

Then again, it occurred to Alexander as he, Thenjiwe and Mjanwe slipped into a bigger hole slightly back from most of the other positions. *Our position may not have enough depth for alternate and supplementary fighting positions anyway.*

We've made bricks without straw, that's for sure. But will it be enough to stop a force nearly ten times our size?

Drop Zone Green
5 Kilometers Southwest of Champasak

Fuckfuckfuckfuckfuck, Arcand thought as he struggled with the risers on his parachute.

The shimmering black water of the river was surprisingly cold as Arcand, despite his best efforts to side slip away, plunged into it. He had to fight off panic as the water went right up his nostrils and the impact forced the air from his lungs.

Schwartzengrosse had begged him not to jump with the 2 REP, but Arcand had insisted. There was little he could do to affect the battle from his headquarters in KDM anymore. He might do some good out on the ground with the regiment. It was his job as the commander to be present to affect the battle at the decisive point.

"Besides," he'd said, with patently Gallic nonchalance. "I have more than a dozen combat jumps, I'll be fine."

Didn't mention that your last combat jump was twelve years ago, you arrogant fuck, did you?

The struggling general managed to get his parachute released before it tangled, bunched and started to drag him under, but in his flailing motions, he managed to release his rifle and everything not secured to his load-bearing vest as well. The current was not overwhelming, but it was fast enough to carry weapon and pack away from him rapidly and into the muck of the river bottom.

Merde.

Arcand thought about diving for it, but the river was pitch black, and his night optics, while water-proofed, were of little use in seeing under water in moonlight. He began to sidestroke for the shore, hoping his flailing hadn't attracted a crocodile or some other carnivorous megafauna that wouldn't find the entire magazine of his pistol ticklish, much less fatal.

His limbs were burning from pulling himself through the water by the time his boots dragged on the first pebbles of the shallows, and he nearly sobbed in relief as he waded up and out of the water. Out of shape and scared shitless though he might be, he had the presence of mind to get into the woodline, flip his night vision monocle down and start scanning for an IR strobe, the prearranged marker for an assembly area.

The chill of the river water receded rapidly as Arcand made his way through the jungle vegetation, checking his wrist GPS to ensure he stayed on course for the nearest assembly area. His sweat ensured that his uniform stayed damp. With a mildly shaking hand he unsnapped his holster and pulled out his pistol.

After some minutes moving by himself, Arcand spotted a singular IR strobe.

Better to travel with friends, Arcand altered his course toward the strobe.

Arcand estimated he was less than thirty meters from the strobe when the beam of an infrared laser sight, invisible to the naked eye but bright and terrible in his own night optics, slashed through the jungle scape to settle on his chest.

"Cannae!" A harsh, low voice growled at him.

"Zama!" Arcand responded immediately, his hands going up, palms out reflexively.

"Advance and be recognized," the voice said.

Zeroing in on the voice, Arcand could now make out the legionnaire kneeling amidst an array of palm fronds, rifle leveled at him. The general took a few careful steps forward. Once he was within three meters, the legionnaire stood up, lowering his rifle.

"General Arcand, sir?" The rifleman had a Turkish accent to his French, and his voice sounded much younger now than the initial challenge had.

"That's right," Arcand said, his voice low. "Do you have a squad assembled yet?"

"No, sir," the soldier said. "Corporal Mushki told me to pull security this direction until we did. We were waiting on one or two more."

"Well, I'm one more," Arcand said. "Let's get your squad leader and head to the nearest assembly area. What's your name, Legionnaire?"

"Yavuz, sir," he said. "Sir, where's your rifle?"

Arcand drew himself up and scoffed, making a show of returning his pistol to its holster.

"I've got you, Yavuz, why would I need a rifle?"

1st ZAR Main Line of Resistance

Thenjiwe's radio crackled to life, the voice that came through it was low, but clear.

"Assegai Six, this is Oh-Pee Three," the whispering voice said. "I estimate enemy strength as two-thousand plus. Maybe half modern arms, half crossbow or musket. Lots of movement, I think they're going to attack soon."

Alexander took the proffered mic from Thenjiwe and keyed it, hoping his forward observer had remembered to put his ear piece in and put the radio on whisper mode.

"Oh-Pee-Three, Six," Alexander said, his own voice unconsciously low. "Roger. How are they arrayed; can you identify where the advance will be weighted?"

"They are arrayed evenly across the base of the ridge, Six," the observer reported. "Expect frontal assault."

"Understood, Oh-Pee-Three," Alexander said. "Remain silent unless you have to report something vital. God be with you."

"And with you, Six."

"Six, out," Alexander said. He let go of the transmit button and took a deep breath. He'd feared the CLF would attempt this. If they'd committed to this course of action yesterday, or even this morning, there would've been no question they could crush the Zulu lines with simple weight of numbers. Oh, their own formation would have been devastated and incapable of follow on operations for quite some time afterward, but that would've been little comfort to the Zulus.

Alexander turned to Mjanwe.

"You heard," he said.

"Yes, sir."

Alexander thought furiously for several seconds, but he couldn't think of a preparation he hadn't made. He couldn't think of a further adjustment to their position or plan that was an objective improvement and not just busy work. He looked into Mjanwe's eyes, saw the old man's recognition of his fear and uncertainty and looked down in shame.

He felt the old warrior's strong, gnarled hand grip his shoulder and looked up. Mjanwe smiled at him, the expression nearly cracking his visage.

"Prince Alexander, you have done all you can," said Mjanwe. "If we die here today, it is not due to any lack of courage or competence. You are every ounce your father's son, and it has been an honor to serve you."

Alexander, despite the heat, despite his thirst, despite the possibility of his impending death and the death or capture of his men, felt his heart swell at Mjanwe's words. Never, in all his life, had Nkosiphindule Mjanwe dispensed such praise in Alexander's earshot.

"Sir," Thenjiwe said, handing him the radio mic again. Alexander took it and smiled his gratitude at both men before keying the mic to talk.

"Guidons, guidons," Alexander said, a traditional term to call for his subordinate commanders' attention. "Prepare to receive the enemy. Keep fire discipline and be prepared for close combat. They're not stopping this time, so we're just going to have to kill every last one of the *malebe*. Six, out."

The Walls of Champasak

Champasak lay in a clearing amongst the jungle-coated hills. Its walls were twelve feet high and made of thick plastered adobe and anchored with stone pillars at regular intervals. The city's defenses had been designed, initially, to protect it from Zhong marauders from the South. Ironically, those same marauders were a cornerstone of the UN's publicly stated casus belli for occupying the colonies of Northwest Urania. Arcand hadn't considered the UN's propaganda in months, but he snorted a bit at the hypocrisy of it all just then, moments before he would likely give the order to storm the colonists' safe haven from the depredators the UN avowed they were protecting them against.

Since the CLF had secured the walled city as their base of operations, the primitive adobe walls had been supplemented with wire obstacles and minefields. Arcand's men were poised all around the walled town with mine-clearing charges, Bangalore torpedoes for the wire, and breaching charges for the walls. But he was going to try something else first.

Corporal Mushki and his squad had stayed close throughout the advance. Now, Yavuz, the young Turkish legionnaire, held aloft a white flag affixed to his rifle to signify truce, he marched out beside Arcand in plain view of the CLF insurgents manning the walls.

"Why *me*, sir?" Yavuz whispered.

Arcand stifled a grin.

"Think before you point a rifle at your general next time," he said, giving the young soldier a wink.

Turning to the walls, Arcand raised his voice to a bellow.

"I am General Arcand," he shouted. "I would speak with your commander."

Many of the defenders stirred on the walls. They could just shoot him, but he hoped their leaders, at least, would be smart enough to know that killing one man, even a general, would do nothing to improve their odds of survival and might, indeed, doom them. Arcand and Yavuz stood in the midday sun of Lang Xan, sweat pouring down their faces leaving streaks in the grime they'd accumulated fighting through the jungle, before someone finally spoke.

"I am Colonel Nguyen," a cochin man of indeterminate years climbed up onto the wall in front of them. "Speak."

"Colonel, I have your fortress surrounded. My mortars are trained on your position while your indirect fire assets are forward near Savannakhet, I possess the means to breach your defenses in minutes and I estimate we outnumber your force by a ratio of ten to one. Also, I suspect you have little in the way of modern armaments while all of my men are armed with semi-automatic and automatic weaponry.

"Given the military reality of the situation, further bloodshed would be meaningless. I implore you to consider surrender," Arcand said.

"You've been imploring us to surrender for years, yet we're still here," Nguyen said. There were a few laughs on the wall at that, but to Arcand they sounded half-hearted.

"Your courage and skill are unquestioned, Colonel," Arcand said sincerely. "But due to that skill, I know you recognize the truth of my words. Forcing me to storm Champasak will cost me lives, yes, but ultimately it will do nothing to aid your cause, and all your men will die for nothing. It may surprise you to know I do not want that any more than you do."

There was another long silence.

"What terms do you offer?"

"First," Arcand said. "Are the men and women you captured at the Green Valley firebase alive and unharmed?"

"Yes," Nguyen said. "We are not animals. Though I cannot, of course, guarantee their safety should you storm the fortress."

Not animals my ass, Arcand thought of his mutilated men angrily, but he quickly shoved the emotion aside. Righteous outrage wouldn't help him accomplish his mission today.

"That is good," Arcand said. "My terms are simple; first you will return my captured personnel, unharmed and alive. Second, you will lay down your arms and submit yourselves to captivity. Neither you nor your men will be tortured or executed, you will be treated as legal combatants, even though your status as such is dubious."

Nguyen stared at them, his face inscrutable.

"We will give you our answer by sundown," Nguyen said.

No, "Colonel," genuine anger coursed through Arcand's veins. *No stalling.*

"You will give me your answer in the next five minutes," Arcand shouted back, his voice filled with cold fury. "Or I will order my men to storm your fortress and kill you all. And if your prisoners are harmed in the assault, I will ensure that you, personally, Colonel, are taken alive. You and any other captives we have when Champasak falls will take several weeks to die. Before you die, I will see to the death of every single relative and friend we identify from your blood and the words we wring from you and your men.

"Your spies are competent, so you know I make no idle threats. Surrender now and live out the war in, if not comfortable, then safe captivity with your wives, children, parents and siblings unmolested. Fuck with me and I won't simply kill you all, I will erase all trace of your existence from this world.

"Choose wisely, Colonel."

1st ZAR Main Line of Resistance

The enemy's main force crested the ridge in black rivulets of men, like streams of angry ants pouring down the rocky forward slope. Alexander's men held their fire, keeping their positions concealed from these fresh troops and waiting to expend their ammunition to maximum effect as the enemy closed the range between them.

"Mortars," Alexander said into the radio. "Stand by to fire Target Group Tango-One-Fox."

"Mortars, ready," Alexander's mortar platoon leader said. For this operation, both the battalion's and each individual company's eighty-one millimeter mortar platoons were concentrated in Savannakhet, the better to mass fires on the attackers, totaling fifteen tubes.

Alexander gauged the enemy's rate of advance versus the small rise that delineated the targets. Ideally, he would match their speed with the time of flight of the mortar rounds so that the bulk of the barrage caught the main body of the enemy in the open.

Right . . . about . . . now.

"Fire Tango-One-Fox," Alexander commanded.

"Shot, over."

Crumps and booms shook the thick, afternoon air, followed by whistles and freight-car shrieks as the rounds sailed overhead toward the advancing enemy. The rivulets of CLF infantry slowed to a trickle under the fire, creating a separation in the echelons of the attack, just as Alexander had intended.

CLF riflemen and machine gunners on the ridgeline poured fire over the heads of their advancing comrades onto the Zulu line. If their marksmanship training wasn't as good as the Zulus, what they lacked in quality they accounted for in quantity.

A mixed horde of uniformed and civilian clothed men began tossing grenades while still more than a hundred meters from the ZAR's forward-most position. Alexander stared in befuddlement for a moment; it was too long a pitch for the strongest men to reach the Zulu battle line. Then the pitiful smoke laid by the enemy's mortars began to build higher and he understood.

Smoke grenades.

Through the smoke, Alexander could see dozens of man-shapes within meters of the wire obstacles. They were avoiding the obvious avenue of approach the engineers left in between the wire, correctly guessing it to be mined.

With a series of muted booms, six gray clouds blossomed just above the enemy smoke screen, and released a deluge of steel rain on the attackers. Through his binoculars, Alexander saw insurgents flattened by overpressure, eviscerated by jagged steel shards. Devastating as the mortar fire was, though, there were simply too many attackers and too few tubes to stop them.

"Guidons, Six," Alexander said. "Weapons Free, fire at will."

Two seconds later, the entire front line of the ZAR erupted in gunfire. They interlocked as best they could, the right side of the line sweeping the left wire strands, the left targeting the right.

The first attacker to reach the razor wire was an old, white-haired man in baggy peasant tunic, sprinting onward even though his left arm ended in a bloody stump. He carried no weapon but flung himself bodily on the wire. The entire first line, rank would be too orderly a word, of attackers followed him in falling to their bellies on the wire, allowing its blades to lacerate them through their thin, ragged peasants' clothes.

For a wild second, Alexander thought the combined weight of direct and indirect fire had broken the first wave of the advance, but then it dawned upon him what he was seeing.

A body-breach en masse, he thought. *I'll be damned.*

At a lack for demolition charges or other sapper equipment to breach the wire, the CLF was using what they had; expendable bodies. Alexander noted that none of their modern-equipped troops were on their bellies being shredded by the razor wire. It was a ruthless and intelligent tactic.

The second and third lines of attackers reached the wire seconds after their comrades. These troops were younger, fitter, most wielded modern rifles. They trampled the older men without hesitation.

Their smoke screen was a bare curtain of wisps, but it didn't matter. Alexander watched as grazing fire from his machine guns ripped the guts out of a uniformed rifleman in a spray of gore less than a soccer pitch from his own line, but he was replaced by three more. Every meter of ground cost dozens of CLF lives, and yet they pressed.

The cacophony of the battle was like a living thing assaulting his senses. The acrid stenches of spent gun powder and fresh corpses laced the thick air around him. The staccato rattle of the machine guns, the crump and boom of the mortars, the screams of rage, and the screams of the dying all pressed in on him; driving his heart rate higher and higher. Alexander was overcome by contradictory urges to laugh wildly or to crumble to the ground and bury his head in his hands.

The sharp clack of a rifle bolt locking back right next to his ear brought Alexander back to his sense. Mjanwe had just run another magazine dry. The old warrior patted his magazine pouches frantically, but they were empty.

"I'm out!" He shouted.

Alexander tossed him one of his own magazines, then picked up his hand mic as the human tide before him cleared the obstacle belt. All along the line he saw the same thing repeated. Even aiming every burst, every shot, his riflemen were running out of magazines, gunners were down to their last drum.

"Mortars, this is Assegai Six," Alexander said. "Fire the FPF."

In seconds the mortars began falling in a sheet of steel rain on a line almost four hundred meters across, adding to the long ragged columns of dead and maimed enemy. The massive display of fire shook the ground around him with each volley and occasional pieces of fragmentation zipped overhead past his position. The term danger-close was a memory; they were within critical risk-estimate-distances now. It wasn't a matter of if the mortars caused friendly casualties, but how many.

It was a calculated, reasonable risk, but it was not without consequence. Even as the enemy continued to rush the Zulu line over their own maimed and dying comrades, an errant chunk of fragmentation whistled into Alexander's own foxhole, shattering his radio hand mic and ripping through Thenjiwe's face in the bargain.

The young man fell silently to the muddy bottom of their fighting position, his face above the left cheek bone a ruined, bloody mass.

"Thenjiwe!" Alexander shouted, dropping to a knee beside Thenjiwe and going reflexively into casualty treatment. His cousin was still breathing, but he was out cold and bleeding profusely—

Mjanwe stopped him.

"I have him, sir, command the battalion!"

Alexander nodded, standing back up even as Mjanwe began treating the wound whilst screaming for a medic.

The enemy was within one hundred meters now. Torn by steel, shaken by concussion, covered in their own blood and the blood of their comrades, still they advanced. All about him, Alexander's men were reaching the end of their ammunition.

But not the end of their courage.

Taking a deep breath, Alexander screamed from the bottom of his gut and gave what he expected to be the last orders of his life.

"FIX BAYONETS! KILL THEM ALL! NGADLA!"

His riflemen snapped their leaf shaped bayonets in place, his machine gunners and other troops without bayonet lugs on their weapons drew their traditional Iklwah short spears. *Oberleutnant* Mueller and his engineers affixed bayonets or prepared to gut the enemy with sharpened entrenching tools.

A medic slid into their foxhole and began to work on Thenjiwe. Alexander rapidly split the last of his magazines with Mjanwe as the old man stood to join him. Alexander's ammo load was relatively full due to the fact that he'd been busy talking on the radio rather than shooting.

Moving targets were harder to hit, but the enemy was running straight toward them, simplifying the task a bit. Alexander placed his rifle on single shot, lined up the holographic crosshairs on the lead insurgent, less than fifty meters from his foxhole, and squeezed, his rifle jolted into his shoulder and—CRACK—the man tumbled to the ground.

The next bravest insurgent followed his friend to the ground, Alexander missed the third shot, and the fourth, but finally felled that target with a controlled pair—CRACK-CRACK. Mjanwe and Alexander stacked a dozen men in front of their foxhole, but then the gap was closed. Three men, uniformed and armed with Italian rifles were on the forward lip of their position.

The rightmost died instantly, Mjanwe blew off the back of his skull at point blank. The center man was on Mjanwe before the old warrior could shift his muzzle to bear. Mjanwe barely managed to parry the man's bayonet lunge with his own rifle. The two collided, falling back against the rear of the command hole, grunting and cursing as they struggled for advantage.

Alexander drove his bayonet into the leftmost man's guts and pulled the trigger on his still loaded rifle, blowing the man's innards and a chunk of his spine out onto a nearby palm. The insurgent's eyes widened in shock and pain; he slid to the jungle floor just in front of their foxhole and clutched his guts. Alexander placed his rifle muzzle to the back of the man's head and pulled the trigger before turning to plunge his bayonet into the man who attacked Mjanwe.

The blade pierced the remaining attacker's kidney, black blood spreading across the back of his uniform like an ink stain. He exhaled sharply, arched his back and screamed. Mjanwe took the opportunity to stab the man in the gut as he fell forward, knocking them both to the floor of the foxhole. Both Zulus screamed the ancient battle cry, "NGADLA!"

Alexander kicked the dead insurgent off his adjutant-chef and offered the older man his hand. Mjanwe took it, springing back to his feet with Alexander's help.

"Than—"

The expression of gratitude died in a rush of air and a gurgle, an arrow protruded from Mjanwe's throat, blood welling out of the puncture.

"NO!"

Alexander whirled to see a boy, in his early teens at most, kneeling less than ten meters away and reloading a crossbow. Enraged, Alexander leveled his rifle and cranked off five shots. Perfect trigger squeeze was hardly needed at that range, the boy's reedy frame jerked as each bullet caught him in the chest.

The medic shifted his attention from Thenjiwe, who was now bandaged, to Mjanwe. Alexander, knowing his duty, kept to the fight. Three more insurgents died before reaching his foxhole and were not immediately replaced by a new threat. Alexander took the second of respite to load his last magazine and try to regain situational awareness.

The indirect fire had ceased from both sides, without a radio to check, he assumed that his mortars had burned through their entire load of ammunition. The enemy were only trickling through the human-carpeted gaps in the wire now, but his lines were already infested, overwhelmed by CLF, more than a thousand of them, he estimated.

The 1st Battalion of the 1st Zulu Auxiliary Rifles was dying hard, but it *was* dying.

Movement to his front drew his attention. A squad of non-uniformed, flintlock-armed insurgents appeared in front of his foxhole, kneeling and aiming, at him!

Alexander threw himself flat to the ground, pulling the medic down with him as a volley of lead balls flew overhead, ripping large divots out of the mud at the front of his foxhole but passing overhead without harming him or his comrades. Alexander popped back up immediately and returned fire.

Rather than try to reload, the squad of musketeers charged. Five fell to Alexander's rifle before they reached his hole, but four jumped into his foxhole, swinging their heavy wooden muskets like clubs. One attacker swung at the medic, who tried to dodge but took the brunt of it on his left leg. He collapsed to the floor screaming.

Alexander batted aside the first swing aimed at him and kicked that man in the balls as hard he could, but the move left his right leg exposed and another insurgent managed to hit the back of his knee. A flash of intense pain surged through his entire right side when the wooden stock made impact with a meaty thwack. The force of it bent his joint, thankfully in the right direction, and buckled Alexander to kneeling.

In pain, but still aware, Alexander lunged awkwardly and managed to slash at that attacker's belly with his bayonet, drawing a stream of blood and a howl of pain. He tried to whirl in time to close the gap in his defense opened by the lunge, but a third attacker landed a crushing over-hand blow on his shoulder, dislocating his arm with a sickly wrenching noise. Alexander's rifle fell from his grasp and another buttstock hit him squarely in the chest, knocking him sprawling on his back at the bottom of the foxhole and driving the air from his lungs.

Time dilated for Alexander, the insurgents' muskets cast unnaturally long shadows as his enemies raised their weapons, preparing to club him to death. But just as the muskets reached the aphelion of their deadly arcs, the angry hornet sound of bullets flying nearby and accompanying thump-squelches of impact broke the moment. Alexander's attackers jerked as bullets ripped through them and they fell limp against the sides of the foxhole.

His breath returning to him, Alexander lurched to his feet. The medic was by his side, supporting him, his own assailant also lay dead at the bottom of the foxhole. Alexander hadn't noticed the boy was German, not Zulu, until just then.

"*Danke*," Alexander said.

"*Bitte*," the blue-eyed boy said, panting.

Zulu prince and German private looked around for their saviors. Alexander first saw his own mortarmen joining the fray. Good lads, when they'd run dry of ammo they'd marched to the main line of battle. But also—

More than four hundred fully kitted infantrymen in lighter green fatigues than Alexander's Zulus. The entire remainder of Cochina's German contingent, and approaching his foxhole was a familiar, short boxy figure. Colonel Karl-Heinz Schwartzengrosse, armed with a rifle, clad in helmet and body armor, walked casually to Alexander's foxhole as his Germans joined the fray.

"*Guten Tag, Oberst* nDlamini," he said. "Thank you for saving some insurgents for us."

Alexander gave a harsh chuckle, leaning against the side of his foxhole.

"It was kind of you to come, *Herr Oberst*," he said simply. "Most welcome . . . *most* welcome."

Alexander looked up and down the line, saw the CLF attack breaking like waves upon rock. His own people had still been fighting fiercely when the Germans arrived. Facing a full battalion of reinforcements, the attackers' morale shattered. Some ran, but they were easily gunned down. The rest were killed or captured in minutes.

While Schwartzengrosse and his fresh troops cleared off the ridgeline, supported by resupplied mortars and newly-arrived light artillery, the Zulus and Pioneers tended to their dead and wounded, drank deeply from the freshly arrived water stores, and slept.

Arcand with 2d REP met the remainder of the CLF main battle force attempting to flee into the hills towards Champasak in the foothills. Less than forty-eight hours from the day Alexander first set foot in Lang Xan, there were still follow-on operations to conduct, but the campaign was decided.

They had won.

Savannakhet, Lang Xan Colony
D+3

Another sortie of helicopters lifted from the field just south of Savannakhet. They carried the last and most lightly wounded of Alexander's troops. The dead would start next. On the docks, lines of hundreds of prisoners awaited transport via boat to prison camps in Cochina. Non-expectant wounded took priority over them.

The prisoners were segregated into two groups; all those captured by 2 REP at the surrender of Champasak along with the uniformed combatants from the Battle of Savannakhet were one group. The second were those fighting out of uniform against Alexander's Zulus. The first group Arcand ordered treated as legal combatants, entitled to the protections accorded prisoners of war by law and custom. Those fighting without proper uniform or identifying insignia at Savannakhet Arcand marked for thorough and brutal interrogation, followed by execution or reeducation on a case by case basis.

Arcand stood on the roof of the Savannakhet port authority watching it all. It was a great victory, but it was soured by the next task he had before him. The early evening was still oppressively hot and humid, but it was better than the day, and at least up here it was quiet for a moment.

"We didn't get them all, you know," Schwartzengrosse said.

Arcand turned to see the short, blocky German climbing crude wooden stairs to the roof.

"Had it occurred to you, Karl," Arcand said. "That I came up here because I don't want company?"

"Of course you don't, sir," Schwartzengrosse said. "But waiting isn't going to make it any better. You need to tell him."

Arcand's gaze shifted south again, to where Colonel Prince Alexander Dumanisi nDlamini stood amongst the rows of his dead, his left arm still in a highly visible white sling. The rule of thumb was that a unit broke somewhere around thirty-percent casualties, combined dead and wounded. Alexander's command had suffered forty percent killed in action and another forty percent seriously wounded, and virtually no one in the defense of Savannakhet had gotten away completely unbloodied. They'd still been fighting like rabid wolverines when the Germans relieved them.

And at the cost of two hundred and five dead, and two hundred seven wounded, Alexander had killed three thousand of the CLF's best fighters. Schwartzengrosse, with only light casualties amongst his Germans, had captured another thousand.

"His legend, the Zulu legend, grows," Schwartzengrosse said, nodding south to the rocky ridge that straddled the neck of the Savannakhet peninsula. "The locals are already calling it, 'Panther Ridge.'"

"It's deserved," Arcand said. "We may not have gotten them all, my friend, but we got enough. Also, the amount of materiel here and at Champasak is damning. I will be able to use it to unseat Mgabe and unify Lang Xan and Angkok under my command."

"I'll send Mgabe my condolences on his impending, 'suicide,'" Schwartzengrosse said, knowing how the UN liked to dispose of an aristocrat once he was too thoroughly discredited. "But if we're going to pacify two more colonies, we're going to need that boy commanding his other two battalions. How do you plan to arrange that?"

"I'm not sure," Arcand said, turning toward the stairs. "I'll think of something."

"I should have listened, Nik," Alexander said.

Nkosiphindule Mjanwe did not answer his prince's words, lying as he did in eternal repose amongst the ranks of the 1st Zulu Rifles' fallen. Zulu, German and Frenchman lay side by side in long rows. It was an awful, hallowed sight.

"You didn't want this war," Alexander said. "You told us not to come, and I insisted. I killed you and all these . . . my people."

Alexander fell silent, unable to do anything but stand, grieving and suffering for the butcher's bill they'd incurred.

Thenjiwe was back in Khoi Dau Moi by now. He'd still been unconscious when they'd loaded him on the medevac bird. Commandant Bongani was laid out two rows down from Mjanwe. All of Charlie Company's lieutenants were dead, as were two out of the three of the officers of Alpha, Bravo and the battalion staff. The NCOs had been similarly winnowed; more of them lay dead in raw numbers, though their survival rate was somewhat better as a ratio compared to their lieutenants and captains.

A cough interrupted his thoughts. Alexander turned to find General Arcand regarding him. The general's expression was carefully still, but Alexander thought he could detect something unusual, chagrin, or perhaps even shame, in the Frenchman's eyes.

Alexander's grief pivoted sharply into anger. This man had fed an entire battalion of his people into a slaughterhouse while his own legionnaires had a comparatively uneventful stroll through the jungle, culminating in accepting the enemy's surrender without a fight.

"How?" Alexander said, the French word coming out unnaturally clipped and harsh.

Arcand didn't need elaboration.

"According to Colonel Schwartzengrosse," Arcand said. "They found a janitor trying to smuggle classified documents out of the Ops section yesterday. The counterintel specialists are still sweating him, we'll ferret out the rest of his network. I've already reprimanded the Operations section for lax security."

"I want to execute the spies," Alexander said. "You've ordered me to kill men who've done me no wrong. I will have the blood of the men responsible for all this."

Arcand nodded. The two men stood in awkward silence for several long seconds.

"Was there something else, General?"

"Colonel," Arcand said, but then shut his mouth, starting over. "Alexander, I know you've been through hell these last two days, but I'm afraid I have more bad news."

"What is it?" Alexander said, his face a mask of anger and fatigue. The resignation in his voice told Arcand that the young prince didn't believe it could get much worse. Arcand desperately wished that was true.

"Prince Jacob nDlamini has assumed the throne of New Zululand," Arcand said, he faltered for a moment at the expression of horror that crossed Alexander's face, but then he plowed on.

"He deposed your father and executed him for crimes against humanity, along with most of your uncles and your mother," Arcand said.

Alexander's nostrils flared and his breath was coming in gasps, his right hand rested on the butt of his pistol. Arcand cursed himself silently. He'd allowed his guilt and sentimentality to cloud his judgment. He'd seen Alexander beat an insurgent half to death with his own hands; it was entirely possible the young Zulu warrior might kill Arcand now, and damn the consequences.

Arcand did not reach for his own pistol, but gazed unwaveringly at Alexander, waiting on him.

"What is the UN going to do about it?" Alexander said between gritted teeth.

"The change in regime was entirely the result of internal factors," Alexander said. "And the UN has no vital interest in the region. King Jacob has promised to abide by the agreements your father enacted and even extend them. The UN will not authorize my intervention."

"And you asked to intervene, of course," Alexander said, every word dripping with bitter irony.

"I would if I could, Alexander," Arcand insisted. "Perhaps someday, I can. After this victory I think I will be able to solidify the entire region under my command. Once I have the resources, it's just a matter of finding a pretext—"

"Spare me the pipe dream," Alexander snapped. "I suppose you will now hand me and my surviving family over to my bastard half-brother? Take one of his lackeys as a replacement commander for your expendable kaffirs?"

"No!" Arcand said, sharply. "I have secured amnesty for you and all your men, including your cousins. You will continue to serve here, free, fully paid contractors and completely unharmed."

"Except for the occasional massacre," Alexander said jerking his head toward the rows of corpses. "Is this how you plan to dispose of us? Why fight us when you can just expend us on suicide missions."

"I had no idea that we had a leak in our security," Arcand said. "I swear I would not have just sent you in to Savannakhet if I'd known two full regiments were waiting for you."

"But you knew my parents had been murdered before we embarked for this mission," Alexander said. "Did you not?"

Arcand stood stock still, for three seconds, then nodded once.

"You expect us to keep fighting for you after this?" Alexander said. "How can I ever trust you again?"

"I did the best I could with a shit situation," Arcand said. "I have never wished you ill. Stay, fight for me, and I promise you and your people will always have a place of honor here."

"This is not our home!"

"MAKE IT YOUR HOME," Arcand shouted. "Kingdoms go to those with the strength, cunning and courage to take and keep them, Prince Alexander. Your old throne is lost to you, take a new one here!"

"Won't you be occupying that particular chair?" Alexander said.

When Arcand answered there was a fervent, desperate gleam in his eyes.

"I will need a lieutenant and eventual heir," Arcand said. "Schwartzengrosse and I are old men, and none of my other officers have your ability to lead, much less to rule. Think about it, with the medicine at my disposal, you could live for centuries more, perhaps, with Mai at your side."

Alexander's face was a study in mixed emotions, confusion, rage, fear, grief all played across his expression openly.

"Besides, Prince Alexander," Arcand said, the manic light fading from his eyes. "What choice do you have? If you kill me, our men will fall upon one another. Mine will win, albeit at great cost, and then what hope will you and yours have? At least in my service you are alive, free and able to fight."

Alexander's expression smoothed, the grief and confusion, the fear and even the rage replaced with a look of cold calculation. Slowly, he removed his hand from his pistol.

"You will ensure my people don't find out until I can gather them together to tell them," Alexander said. "I will consult with my officers back in Khoi Dau Moi. Any attempt to disarm or detain my troops will be taken as a declaration of war. I will give you my decision tomorrow night."

St. Christopher's Church
Khoi Dau Moi
One Day Later

Flashes of lightning illuminated the crosses atop St. Christopher's at irregular but frequent intervals. The bolts were close enough that the sheets of rain pummeling Alexander didn't mute the peals of thunder that accompanied each of them short seconds behind.

He'd told his officers to have all the men, including those just returned from Lang Xan, turned out, armed and ready to defend their part of the compound, to admit no other UN troops, not even Arcand himself, until Alexander returned. Having taken such prudent precautions, Alexander immediately followed them with a stupid decision.

Not entirely sure why it couldn't wait, Alexander decided he needed to talk to Mai. He had a half-baked notion that if worse came to worst, he wanted to spirit her away from Arcand to avoid having her harmed or used as leverage against him. In reality, for all his martial virtue, he was a young man who had nearly died multiple times in the last four days and, worse, lost most of what mattered to him in the world. Imperatives much older than duty drove him to seek out the woman he loved.

She wasn't at Arcand's quarters, so he'd set out for the church, alone. Fortunately, anyone wishing him ill was also sensible enough to be inside in the middle of a thunderstorm. It was a long, sodden journey to get to St. Christopher's. His path brought him to the side, rather than the magnificent façade of the church. He pushed open the modest single wooden door and found himself in the hallway outside Duc's private office.

The storm must have covered his entrance because he heard voices in Vietnamese coming from the sanctuary as if they hadn't heard anything unusual. Alexander was relieved to hear Mai's lovely soprano and Duc's deeper voice replying. He realized it would be good to talk to both of them.

Mai had been working on his Vietnamese, and while he was still shy of fully fluent, he was able to pick up on the gist of their conversation.

". . . lived with myself . . . he died . . . but . . . do we do now?" Mai was saying.

"Earthpigs . . . casualties . . . as bad, proportion . . . not decisive. We can't give up," Duc said.

Alexander stopped dead in his tracks, straining to hear more.

". . . so many dead . . . get the . . . I gave you in time?" Mai said.

Alexander's heart thudded painfully against his chest and chill went though him. They had betrayed him. Both of them. No hapless janitor had gotten the plan for Operation North Wind to the CLF, it had been Arcand's personal servant.

". . . did, didn't see parachute place . . ." Duc was saying. ". . . and Alexander . . . men fought too well."

It was enough, Alexander drew his pistol, he had only one hand available but it was enough for this work. He strode into the sanctuary, pistol leveled. Mai, soaked to the bone through her dress, and Father Duc, in his plain priestly robes, stood just in front of the altar.

"I trusted you, Father," Alexander said, his voice steady and strange in his own ears. The front sight of the pistol shifted to Mai. "And I loved you. And you tried to murder me."

Neither cowered; Duc looked grave and sad, Mai cried, but did not look away, guilt, grief and resolve warring for her lovely face.

Not for my men, Alexander thought, willing his heart to harden. *For her terrorists.*

"I'm so sorry, Alexander," Mai spoke first. "I never wanted to hurt you, but don't you see; you've been fighting the wrong people. Look what they did to your own family!"

"You knew about that, too?" Alexander said, his sight post steadied right between Mai's breasts.

"Only after you'd already left," she said. "But Arcand's superiors ordered it done, and Arcand did nothing about it, just fed you and your men into a slaughterhouse, knowing he'd already betrayed you."

The truth of it hammered at Alexander. He had no allies. The UN was complicit in his family's murder. His own blood had murdered their father. Mai and Duc had helped slaughter his men and nearly gotten him killed. There were no options.

"How about you, Father?" Alexander asked, shifting the gun to cover Duc. "Do you have any rationalizations for putting a knife in my back?"

"I fight for my people's freedom," Duc said, gravely shaking his head. "I resist the godless UN just as any Christian should. But I never betrayed your confidence, Alexander. I was your confessor, nothing you ever told me, nothing I observed while ministering to you ever made its way to the resistance."

"So what do we do now?" Alexander said.

"You're the one with the gun, son," Duc said.

"All of you have betrayed me on every front," Alexander said. "What is left for me but revenge?"

"No," Mai said. "Alexander, don't do this, you can be on the right side. Join us! Your men are the best soldiers in this war, fight the UN. Take back your freedom, help us regain ours."

"You should've made that argument before you betrayed me and helped kill my men," Alexander said, the pistol shifting back to Mai.

"Son, you know what you're doing is wrong," Duc said. "Arcand works for petty exploiters and tyrants. If anyone on this planet is ever to be free, we have to be rid of them. Put aside your personal feelings;

if the Zulu are ever to rule themselves for truth, who should you fight?"

Peals of thunder punctuated Duc's words, and the lightning cast the scene in flashes of brilliance. Alexander's indecision tore at him. What madness cast the treacherous priest's words as a ray of terrible truth in the midst of this hurricane of betrayal and tragedy?

The massive double doors at the front of the sanctuary swung open with a BANG, Arcand swept in through the deluge, flanked on either side by two legionnaires, their rifles to their shoulders and leveled. Alexander looked behind him for only a brief moment, but Duc moved surprisingly fast for such an old man. Producing a knife from under his robes, he wrapped one arm around Mai's shoulders and placed the point of the knife against the side of her throat.

"Stop right there or I'll slit this traitor's throat," Duc shouted in French.

Arcand held up a hand, and he and his fire team stopped halfway up the center aisle.

"There's nowhere to go," Arcand said. "The janitor gave you up. If you surrender and cooperate, I promise your sentence will be much lighter."

Duc ignored the French general. Instead, he stared straight at Alexander and shouted something. The tone was angry, belying the words, the pronunciation less than ideal, but Alexander realized that Duc was speaking isiZulu.

"Do it, Alexander," he barked. "Soul ready. Take care Mai."

As the priest spoke he shifted his head away from Mai's, creating a larger gap between them. Alexander aligned the sights right on the juncture of the priest's nose and forehead and squeezed the trigger. The single supersonic crack of the pistol rang louder than thunder through the sanctuary. The priest's head snapped back in a flash of gray hair, the back of his skull exploded outward, blood and brain matter splattered the altar of Christ.

Mai turned as Duc's mortal remains collapsed to the floor in a heap. She covered her mouth with her hands, her eyes locked on the old priest's body.

For several seconds, all Alexander could hear were the thunder and his own heart beating. Then Arcand's booted footsteps broke the silence as he approached.

"What happened?" Arcand said. "Why did you have your gun on him already?"

Alexander thought furiously, frowning. He'd killed a true priest, a good man who had, nevertheless, betrayed him.

Is there nothing true in this world?

Alexander looked at Mai, standing petrified, just a bit of blood and bone flecking the shoulder of her dress, staring at the shriveled body of her confessor.

"He was trying to recruit Mai and me for the resistance," Alexander said. "We tried to convince him to turn himself in; that we'd beg for clemency for him. He became agitated, desperate so I pulled my pistol on him. You saw the rest."

Mai looked away from the body, finally, her eyes shimmering once again with tears. She took a hesitant step toward Alexander, staring into his eyes like a drowning woman staring at a life raft.

Alexander holstered his pistol, stepped forward and held out his good arm. Mai buried her face in his chest and wept bitterly.

"What was that he said at the last?" Arcand said. "It wasn't Vietnamese."

"No, it was the Zulu tongue," Alexander said. "Apparently he's been learning it. He said that Mai and I are both going to hell. How did you know to be here, now?"

"I had you followed," Arcand said. "For your own safety, of course, when you took off like a damned fool by yourself. I ordered my men to give you your distance but not let anything happen to you. When the janitor finally cracked and gave up Duc, I realized where you and Mai were and came myself to make sure you were all right."

Alexander said nothing, merely held Mai and stared blankly at Arcand.

"Alexander, I hope this illustrates what I've been telling you, the CLF will stop at nothing," he said. "We've scored a major victory, but we have to finish them if we're to bring order here. Please, stay, fight with me. You can still do good here."

Alexander looked at the bloodstained altar for a moment, then down at Mai, still sobbing in his arms. She was now burden and comfort, beloved and betrayer. But she was real, and if she'd acted against him, she'd done so trying to keep faith with something higher.

Something higher.

"Clearly this war isn't done with us," Alexander said. "The Panther Men will stay, and we will fight."

INTERLUDE:
From Jimenez's *History of the Wars of Liberation*

Cochin was not the only place on Terra Nova, the inhabitants of which had brought with them a long tradition of resistance to foreign rule, lengthy lists of heroes of that resistance, and martyrs of the same. Indeed, a quick scan of the names of our nations will reveal that at least a fifth of them were named for heroes from resistance movements of Old Earth.

How could it not then happen that there would spring up resistance movements here?

Still, there were subjective factors in the likelihood of any given area being thrown into rebellion. One of the larger of these, fully equal to the tradition of rebellion, was the extent to which the area was exploited and overtaxed by the UN, itself. This took the form not only of money seized, but more commonly food, and, far too commonly, women and girls.

Cochin, rapidly evolving into a productive rice culture, was one such. Aguinaldo, some eleven hundred kilometers to Cochin's west, was another . . .

8.
DESERTION

Kacey Ezell[9]

Captain Lele Campbell took a deep breath, careful not to let it make her chest rise as she reminded herself for the thousandth time that it wasn't generally considered polite to stab one's commanding officer in the face.

"Thanks for handling that, Lele," Major Alcasar said with his customary leering grin. "Could you run by the DFAC and have them send over a cup of coffee on your way out, too, sweetling? That's my girl."

Another deep breath, down into the belly so as not to draw his eyes and make him feel invited. A crisp nod and an unreturned salute. Turn on the heel and go. Get the hell out of this man's office before doing something regrettable. *I am not your girl.*

Out into the marginally cooler Terra Novan dusk. Lele looked up as the local sun slid behind the horizon, backlighting the high cloud layers in spectacular pinks and oranges. At the sight of it she drew in another breath, this time not bothering to try to hide that she was, in

9 Kacey Ezell is an active duty USAF instructor pilot with 2500+ hours in the UH-1N Huey and Mi-171 helicopters. When not teaching young pilots to beat the air into submission, she writes sci-fi/fantasy/horror/noir/alternate history fiction. Her first novel, *Minds of Men*, was a Dragon Award Finalist for Best Alternate History. She's contributed to multiple Baen anthologies and has twice been selected for inclusion in the Year's Best Military and Adventure Science Fiction compilation. In 2018, her story "Family Over Blood" won the Year's Best Military and Adventure Science Fiction Readers' Choice Award. In addition to writing for Baen, she has published several novels and short stories with independent publisher Chris Kennedy Publishing. She is married with two daughters. You can find out more and join her mailing list at www.kaceyezell.net.

fact, a girl. *Almost worth putting up with the son of a bitch for this. Almost . . . not quite.* She'd gotten out of the major's office just in time. Any longer, and he'd likely have thought she was angling to stay for the night.

Some island bird chittered in the trees that crowded close against the perimeter of their camp. No matter how often they sent defoliation teams out to clear the fenceline, the insanely aggressive Terra Novan flora just continued its creeping, green assault toward the cleared area, and the perimeter barrier of concrete T-walls.

Inside the T-walls, armed security forces patrolled, their tiger-striped uniforms indistinguishable from Lele's unless one got close enough to see the patches of a civilian security contractor on their shoulders. They would leer and catcall if she got too close, but as they mostly kept to their own billets near the front gate, Lele found them easy enough to avoid.

Which was good, because the camp itself wasn't very big. Besides the operations area near the flightline, there were really just two areas: the supply depot, and the living area. The living area consisted of a maze of shipping containers that had been converted into billets. They even came with a cute name: CHU, for "Containerized Housing Unit." Lele's own CHU sat at the corner of the maze, directly across a pitted, muddy street from their dining facility, or DFAC. Next to the warehouse-sized DFAC (which never made sense to Lele. Supposedly, it was so big in case they had to use their base as a staging point. That was also why they had a two-mile-long runway. But no one ever landed there, and the DFAC was never full, at least not that she'd ever seen), while a long, low temporary building housed the gym, with a decent selection of free weights and other fitness gear.

Eat. Sleep. Workout. Fly. So far, that had been the theme of this deployment. Oh, that and avoiding the attentions of Major Alcasar.

The flat, greasy scent of the dining facility wafted over to her, overlaying the thick, wet scent of the jungle and bringing her back to the here and now.

Time for chow. She turned, boots crunching on gravel, and began walking toward the prefab building which had shipped to Terra Nova flat and been set up by some Navy SeaBees seconded to the UN.

A few moments later, more crunching gravel heralded the arrival of her copilot.

"The major giving you trouble again, ma'am?" Jack asked quietly.

Lele summoned a tired smile and looked up at him. Way up, as it happened.

Lieutenant Jack Ackerman was a throwback to his Nordic ancestors. A muscular 6'3" with blond hair and blue eyes, he'd been the backup quarterback for the Brigham Young University Cougars in his college days. He hadn't played either the political or athletic game well enough to get picked up to play pro ball, and so had joined the military to feed his family. His wife was as blonde and beautiful as he was, and so were their angelic-faced, demon-tempered children. All six of them, at last count.

Lele herself took after her Filipina grandmother in both looks and temperament, and so she was certain that she and Jack made a comical sight together. But Jack was a good pilot, a solid crewman, and a dedicated family man. Which meant that he'd have her back. And that was something Lele treasured more than gold.

"Not really," she said, speaking of the major. "At least, not overly so."

Jack gave her a skeptical look.

"Okay, well not more than usual. You know how it is. Be his bitch or be his Bitch, but at least he's not insistent. Excuse me, I gotta send him some coffee," she said as they entered the hand washing area right outside the DFAC entrance. Try as she might, she couldn't entirely keep the look of disgust off her face.

"Airman," Lele said, approaching a group of young enlisted security forces troops washing up. "Major Alcasar needs a pot of coffee taken to his office. Not you," she said, pointing at the one female airman in their group. "You two go. Tell the cooks Captain Campbell authorized it. Now, please. You can make sure your buddies don't lose their place in line," she added to the female, whose name she knew was Baxter.

"I'll save you seats," Airman Baxter said to her friends, then gave an infinitesimal nod to Lele. The two men saluted. The captain returned it, and they all went inside about their various tasks.

"What was that all about?" Jack asked as the two of them got their trays and headed for the end of the line.

"What?"

"The thing with the males going, but not the female."

Lele looked up at Jack again, wondering how under the stars someone with six kids could be so naive.

"Alcasar's pretty much one hundred percent het from what I can tell," she said quietly. "If I had let Baxter go, he might have interpreted that as me sending her in my place. She might not have thought she could refuse. Better to avoid the whole thing entirely."

Jack's face went blank, which Lele had learned to interpret as him covering up some kind of strong emotion. She gave him a tiny smile and a shrug, then stepped forward as the person in front of them moved closer to the food.

"It doesn't seem right," Lele heard him mutter.

"Right or wrong, that's the way things are."

"Yeah, but you shouldn't have to—"

She turned around, making a slashing motion with her hand.

"Enough," she said. "I don't have to. That's the point. I don't have to, and so I'm not, and this is *not* the time or place for this discussion."

Jack pressed his lips together firmly and stared at her. She stared right back until he exhaled noisily and nodded.

Lele let her shoulders sag, and exhaustion hit her full force. She reached out and touched Jack's arm lightly.

"Look, Jack. I know how you feel. And I appreciate your concern. But you have to be careful. You can't apply your religious morals to other people, especially not your superior officers, all right? That kind of thing can get you in all kinds of trouble. So just keep your head down and do your job. Feed your family. All seven of them."

"Eight," he said quietly, looking down at the floor. Lele gaped, and then saw the corners of his mouth turn up.

Something ugly and mean twisted deep inside her, cramping in her chest, driving out the air. She gasped, and a few people at a table nearby turned to look. By sheer force of will, she managed to make her mouth stretch in a smile.

"Truly?" she asked, her voice trembling only a little. "Another? Congratulations."

"Thanks," Jack said, lifting his gaze from the floor and smiling at her. The joy-filled expression and softness in his eyes made her own eyes want to fill. She took one hand off her tray and shoved it into her pocket, where she could dig her fingernails into her palm.

"When?" she asked. Better to get it all out now.

"Almost exactly nine months after we left. Remember, I was almost late for the shuttle?" He said with a grin and a blush. "Anyway . . . Another boy. He's about five now. She named him Samuel. I just got word the other day."

"That's really terrific," Lele said, forcing the words out. "You know, I . . . I'm actually not feeling very well. Probably shouldn't have had the gumbo for lunch. I think I'm going to head back to my room."

"Oh!" Jack said, the beatific smile disappearing in lieu of a look of deep concern. "Sure. Um . . . do you need help? Want me to take you to the clinic?"

"No, I'm fine, I just need to go. I'll get something later."

"Uh, okay, ma'am. I'll . . . see you tomorrow . . . I guess?"

Lele nodded and turned away, shoving her tray onto a nearby table and nearly bolting for the door. She had to get out of the DFAC before she threw up from the effort it took not to lose control of her emotions.

Outside, it had fallen fully dark with not even the smallest of the planet's three moons showing. Some native beastie sang out either a mating or a hunting cry; she thought in sounded like a trixie on the trail of an *antania*.

Lele broke into a run, gravel rolling and slipping under her boots. She had to get back to her room, she had to get out of sight. She was going to lose control, and she couldn't let anyone see her do it.

The tears started to blur her vision as she fumbled with the key. She blinked furiously and shoved the key home, then turned the knob and flung herself inside. Luckily for her, she kept her shower bucket on her desk next to the door. This wasn't going to be a quick cry. This one was going to take a while and leave telltale scarlet marks on her face. She was going to have to take it to the showers.

Bucket in hand, she ducked her head down so that her tears were less obvious and turned back for the communal shower trailer at the center of the mass of containers that constituted their camp's billets. As she walked, she whispered pleas that she didn't encounter anyone on the way to, or in the shower trailer. Not that she believed anyone was listening, but it was a habit.

Divine intervention or not, Lele was in luck. The shower trailer stood empty and close with the steam of a recently departed bather.

She took herself to the stall at the very back and started to undress. The first sob broke past her lips as she untied her boots. *Keep it together, almost there . . .*

A crank on the lever and hot water, scalded by the alien sun, poured down through the showerhead. Lele ducked under the spray and opened her mouth in a silent scream of agonizing grief.

Water flooded over her, blotching her tan skin red where it hit. She could feel the heat running down over her stomach, flowing between her thighs like the blood had done that last time, and all three of the times before. Red, hot, sticky hell boiling out of her, burning away her dreams, her love, her faith.

Arms crossed over her chest, eyes closed as the tears ran, Lele sank to her knees under the spray, letting the anger and grief for her four lost babies flow like the water down the shower drain.

"Feeling better?" Jack asked the next morning. He plunked his tray down next to hers and slid onto the trestle bench. The DFAC was emptier than usual, and Lele had been enjoying the quiet as she sipped her mediocre coffee.

"Yeah, I am," she said. "Thanks. Sorry about that. I just suddenly . . . "

"It happens," Jack said. "Strange planet, strange food. I'm just glad you're okay. Rumor has it that we're going to be briefed on something big at the O-nine-hundred. I heard it could be the big mish."

"I heard that, too," Lele said. "I'm interested to see what Alcasar's got up his sleeve."

Despite his ongoing offer of "quid pro quo," Major Alcasar wasn't a terrible tactical air commander. He wasn't a particularly gifted pilot, but he at least had a grasp of how one should employ rotary wing assets in a given environment for a particular mission. Lele's major beef with him was that he knew he was on the fast track for promotion, and he had every intention of staying there. In other words, he was a consummate "yes" man, regardless of whether or not those yesses were actually sound decisions for his mission and his people.

This, of course, was complicated by the questions of just *what* their mission was and just *who* were his people.

Officially, they were the 2629th Expeditionary Helicopter

Squadron, though they barely had the numbers to make up a "real world" flight, if that. Part of that fast track for Major Alcasar was that he was given command of a "squadron," even if it only held about fifty people. Though they were USAF personnel, they'd been chopped to the UN for the Counterinsurgency Peacekeeping mission here on Terra Nova. Typically, they supported ground units drawn from all over Earth here to do the same. Despite the advances in interstellar travel, nothing beat an old-fashioned helicopter for putting people with guns into remote locations. The USAF had an aging fleet of cheap, reliable UH-1Z2 Iroquois II "Duey" helicopters left over from their strategic missile support mission. While the missiles were now under the direct control of the UN, and therefore no longer required rotary-wing security assets, the machines and crews still functioned as well as they ever had, so they got farmed out to meet the U.S.' commitment to the UN.

So far, they'd hauled a lot of guys and gear from point A to point B in their old school Dueys, but that was about it. It reminded Lele of old vids she'd seen about a war in southeastern Asia. That war had featured the Duey's ancestor bird, the storied Huey. As an on-again, off-again student of aviation history, Lele appreciated that symmetry. Her ex-husband would have loved it, she thought with a twinge.

"What'd you eat this morning?" Jack was asking. "You're not going to get sick on me again are you?"

"Toast and eggs," Lele answered, grateful for the excuse to think about something else. She definitely didn't need to be thinking about her ex when a possible mission was in the offing. "And coffee. I think I'm good."

"Hmph. I suppose. You'd be better off if those were real eggs, though," Jack said, muttering as he dug into his own bowl of cereal.

Lele laughed. Jack's dietary prejudices were a running joke between the two of them.

"C'mon, Jack, you know they can't do that. They'd offend the vegans."

"I don't protest that they serve coffee, do I? I just don't drink it. Maybe the vegans could do the same."

"You Mormons are too polite. You should protest. Make a little more noise."

"No, thanks," he said. "Last time that got us persecuted, our prophet killed and our church exiled across a continent. Being polite is a much better option compared to that . . . hey! Maybe we should start persecuting vegans!"

Lele fought to keep from snorting hot coffee through her nose and just shook her head, grateful that no one was sitting near enough to hear her copilot's anti-social sense of humor.

They continued to banter while Jack ate his breakfast. He finished with just enough time for the two of them to make it to the 0900 mass briefing without rushing, so they went straight there after dumping their trays in the appropriate receptacles for trash, recyclables, and compost.

The 0900 mass briefing was held in another prefab building not far from the DFAC, in the operations section. This structure served as a combination auditorium and conference room. Like the DFAC, it was ugly, beige, and smelled faintly of mildew and cleaner. Lele and Jack arrived with a few minutes to spare, and found seats together near the front of the room.

"Room, tench-HUTT!" the squadron's first sergeant called out, causing the predictable rumble as the gathered crews came to their feet. Lele could hear Major Alcasar walking in from the back of the room. He did enjoy his pomp and circumstance.

"Please be seated," the major said as he reached the plywood podium at the front of the room. He nodded regally (or what Lele thought he must *imagine* "regally" looked like) at the two-striper in the corner, and a glowing rectangle appeared on the wall behind him.

"Yesss!" Jack breathed. "Death by PowerPoint! My favorite!"

"Shut. Up." Lele whispered, using the toe of her boot to kick her copilot in the ankle.

"Yes ma'am," Jack responded. "Anything you say, ma'am."

"Idiot."

"Ladies and gentlemen," Major Alcasar said, throwing his voice a bit deeper than usual as he tried to project across the room. *He seems to be feeling full of gravitas*, Lele thought. *This must be a doozy of a mission.*

"Welcome to the daily stand up brief. As of right now, all day flights are canceled due to a higher priority mission. At the conclusion of this briefing, all crews will leave this briefing room and enter crew rest as of ten hundred hours local. Showtime is twenty-two hundred local for an air assault mission here."

Alcasar gestured grandly to the slideshow projected behind him. The slide changed from a blank white to a satellite image of a narrow valley between two mountain ridges, with a lake at one end. The major gestured to his slide-flipper, and the image zoomed in on the southern shore of the lake. "This, here, is the village of Lawa Bundok, population about three hundred. Recent intelligence reports have highlighted this location as a critical node in the insurgents' communication network. In addition, we have a credible report that at least one High Value Target may be located within the confines of the village. And don't ask me which one, none of you have the need to know," the major said with a smirk. Meaning, of course, that *he* knew. Naturally.

"Our portion of the mission is simple. The smallest moon rises at twenty-three hundred hours, giving us optimal light approximately an hour later. We will take off from the base at midnight, loaded with assault teams of approximately four to six individuals per aircraft. Flights will then proceed in elements of two aircraft apiece to the target location and insert where directed by the assault teams. These men are trained to operate on helicopters, so they should be familiar with your capabilities. You can trust them to choose workable landing zones."

I'll just bet we can, Lele thought cynically. He wasn't telling them where these "operators" originated, which meant that they probably weren't U.S. Best case was that they were from another member nation that worked well with U.S. aircrews. Worst case: they were highly incompetent and would do their best to get her killed. It was anyone's guess what they'd get on that spectrum.

"Once the insert is complete, you are to remain in location for rapid exfil of our forces. Indications are that there is no credible ground to air threat other than small arms, so each aircraft will be carrying two M-240s. In order to maintain the maximum lift capability for the customer, the firing systems have been slaved forward to the pilot's control panel on the collective head. You'll be using the head down display, but your three hundred and sixty degree forward looking infrared will give you ample warning of anyone approaching your helicopter. Please make sure that you don't shoot our customers," he added dryly, and then paused for long enough that it was clear people were supposed to laugh at this terrible joke.

Lele's estimation of the major's capabilities slid further and further downward as the briefing went on. He spent far too much time on inconsequential minutia and not nearly enough on the important stuff, like contingencies and detailed communications plans. Something in the back of her mind started to pull at her, but she tiredly pushed it away. It wasn't as if she had a choice in the matter, after all. This was the mission, she would have to go. No matter how much of a clusterfuck it seemed destined to become.

When Alcasar finally finished up and dismissed them, they filed out into the morning light. Some headed for the DFAC, but most of the crews veered for the CHUs. As usual, Jack fell into step beside her, shortening his long stride to do so.

"Well," he said softly. "That was interesting."

"Mmmhmm," she replied, unwilling to speak openly while they were in the midst of all the other crews. Most of them were good people, but it wouldn't do to put them in a position of having to choose between informing on her and Jack or not. Besides, she was certain most of them shared her thoughts about Major Alcasar's briefing. It had all the hallmarks of something dictated from above by someone who had no idea what they were doing . . . and naturally, Alcasar hadn't had the balls to say no.

"You okay?" Jack asked her, apropos of nothing, as they entered the maze of CHUs.

"Hmm? Oh. Yeah," she said. "Just thinking."

"Okay, well . . . I'm here," he said, sounding tentative. She gave him a tiny smile.

"I'm fine, Jack. Get some rest. I'll see you tonight."

Even the weather seemed to think this mission was a bad idea.

Lele swore as the first fat drops of rain started to patter down onto the tarmac beside her bird. The clouds were low and thick, but not low enough or thick enough to scrub the mission. Rain would reduce their visibility too, but again, likely not enough to cancel. It was her least favorite kind of situation: shitty weather blocking any moon- or starlight, making it dark as the devil's armpit, but not *quite* dark or shitty enough to keep them from flying.

Perfect. That ground-based navigation beacon better be working . . . not that it'll do any good once we get into the mountain valleys. Fuck.

With a last scowling shrug, she pulled herself into the right seat of the Duey and strapped in. Jack was already in place, helmet on, running the startup sequence. Lele pulled her own helmet on and toggled the intercom switch on her cyclic.

"Pilot's up," she said.

"Loud and clear," Jack replied. "Before starting engines checklist completed. Starting engines checklist. Engine One."

"Engaged," Lele said, and pressed the switch to make it so. The first of the Duey's two turboshaft engines started to turn, letting out a low rumble and whine as the drive train engaged the main rotor and the blades started to spin.

"Engine started," she reported, as the Duey gave a shudder and began to vibrate in its usual way.

"Oil pressures?"

"Within limits."

"Generator."

"On."

"Second Engine."

"Engaged," Lele said, and repeated the process with Engine Number Two. Within a few moments, they had the bird completely spun up and ready to go. She glanced down at her dimly green-lit gauges for one last check just as the major's voice came through her headset on the interplane frequency.

"KILGOR Flight Check, Interplane."

"Two," Lele answered, then listened as the other aircraft checked in with their respective callsigns in order. Somehow, she'd ended up as Major Alcasar's wingman for the mission. She'd have preferred to lead her own element, of course, though the truth was that she was far less likely to come to bodily harm by following Alcasar. He wasn't known for being in the thick of things, command notwithstanding. She was actually a little surprised that he'd chosen to fly this mission himself. He must expect it to be fairly visible by someone with clout. He'd probably get a medal out of it.

"KILGOR Flight, This is Lead. Pitch pull in Five. Proceed as briefed. Let's go get 'em, boys and girls!"

Lele fixed her eyes on the lead bird's tailboom and counted slowly backwards from five. When she reached zero, she saw the tell-tale tail wag through her night vision goggles as Alcasar pulled in collective. She followed suit and their skids lifted off the ground near simultaneously. The rain on her windscreen intensified, and Jack toggled on the windshield wipers without being asked. Because of the high humidity, all of the light sources at their base carried blooming halos of green in the goggles.

"Keep an eye underneath your goggles," she said on the intercom. "Let's not let get dragged into the weather."

"Amen," Jack replied. "Safe altitude around here is Eleven-Two. Thirteen-Five in the mountains."

"Got it," she said, and silently hoped that they didn't have to go that route. But if Alcasar dragged them into the clouds, the only way to ensure that they didn't hit the rising terrain would be to climb that high. It would be intensely cold, there was the risk of ice accumulation on their rotor blades, and they didn't have supplemental oxygen, so hypoxia could be a factor. Bad day all around. Better to stay under it, even if it meant not staying in super tight formation.

I may not have a hell of a lot to live for, but I'll be damned if I let Alcasar kill me, she thought, her lips curving at her own dark humor.

Per the major's brief, the various formation elements flew several thousand feet above the terrain during the enroute portion. About forty-five minutes into the flight, they reached the ridge that abutted the lake, and Alcasar gave the radio command to ingress into the low-level environment. Lele dropped her collective and fed in forward cyclic, and the Duey's fully articulated rotor system sliced down through the air as they dropped to a few feet above the treetops. Lele felt the lightness in her stomach and ass as the aircraft "went negative."

The air felt warmer down here, and the thick sweet scent of vegetation rose around them as they beat their way up the valley toward the lake and the little village. She heard a clicking on the intercom, and then an unfamiliar voice spoke in heavily accented English. Lele couldn't place the origin, but she thought it sounded vaguely European.

"You will make land beside the shore, yes? I will direct."

"As long as you direct an LZ that works," Lele said, her tone hard and unyielding. She wasn't going to let this guy kill her, either.

"Next to large building on lakeshore, there is large field. Good LZ."

"No wires?"

"No wires," he said, and Lele thought she heard laughter in his voice. Maybe the people out here weren't at the point of having electricity in their villages. Some of these colonies had regressed dramatically since coming to Terra Nova. In the back of her mind, something that might have been pity stirred. She shoved it away with all the rest of her emotions and focused on staying tight on lead.

"You show me, and if I can land there, I will," she said.

"Okay, Yes. Good," the man said, and that was all. At least he knew better than to clutter up her intercom with chatter. She checked her clock and the orbital timestamp. Almost there.

"One minute," she said into the intercom. She felt, more than heard, the teams getting positioned for their infil. Next to her, Jack toggled the arming switches for their defensive systems and ran through a preliminary diagnostic check from his side.

"Sonofabitch," she muttered then. Lead had started his approach, but he'd done it badly. Rather than staying low and doing a smooth, level deceleration, Alcasar or his copilot had cranked back on the cyclic without reducing the power, which resulted in a nose-high climb and rapid decel. Rather than follow him into a bad situation, she kept her nose down and took a small bid out to the right.

"Two's going around, right side," she transmitted, aware that she was going to catch hell for it later on. Going around was *not*, typically speaking, a tactically sound maneuver. It was, however, better than crashing, which is what she would have done if she'd have allowed lead to drag her into that crap approach path.

"This is LZ, Two O'Clock low," the team lead in the back said. Lele banked the bird up to the right and caught sight of the field in question. It was open and rectangular, like a soccer green, and it sat next to a long, low-slung building.

"Got it, on the approach," Lele said, her voice empty of emotion. She eased back on the cyclic, lifting the nose while sliding the collective to the floor.

"Ninety knots, power's out, sink's nil," Jack replied with his own empty voice. Lele continued her aft cyclic, letting the airspeed bleed off in a level deceleration. When the airframe started to shudder in the classic "burble" that signaled effective translational lift, she relaxed her aft pressure and let the nose come down to a level attitude. Then, just as smoothly as she'd put it down, pulled in collective with her left hand in order to cushion her landing to the flat, level surface of the field.

"Team's cleared out," she said.

"Good flying!" the team lead's voice came back through the intercom. He sounded excited and joyful. Lele looked over her shoulder to see him and his buddies unass the aircraft, and then she got on the interplane frequency.

"Lead, this is two. Be advised, customer directed an LZ forward and to your two o'clock. We're down, awaiting further orders."

"As briefed," Alcasar's voice came back. "Hold for my takeoff. Clear to rejoin on me once we pass you."

Lele clicked her mic switch twice in rapid succession, then looked over at Jack and shook her head. She didn't dare say anything out loud, lest it later be downloaded from the cockpit voice recorder, but this was without a doubt the most ill-planned op she'd ever participated in. The interplane frequency started blowing up with various elements talking to one another to coordinate not crashing, because nothing had been briefed in enough detail. It was piss-poor planning, and there wasn't anything she or anyone else could do about it.

In the middle of these dark thoughts, a blinding flash of light stabbed into her eyes, gaining down her goggles to nothing and causing Jack to let out a swear word she'd never heard from him before.

"What was that?" he asked, just before another explosion and bright light hit. Lele twisted in her seat as best she could, but all she could make out was the flash of gunfire in the buildings behind her.

"Locals must be resisting," she said. "Maybe one of the high-value targets is here. Get ready with that FL—"

She broke off, then squinted at the heads down display screen in the console that showed the image from her forward looking infrared, or FLIR. On the screen, she could just make out the silhouettes of four figures creeping toward the building in front of her. She blinked and looked up at the painted sign over the door.

Eskuwela. School. What the . . . ?

As she watched, one of the men she'd inserted fixed a breaching charge to the door at the short end of the long, low building. She closed her eyes and waited for the explosion, and then opened them in mounting horror. The four figures slipped inside, and the sounds of gunfire soon followed. The FLIR picked up brief flashes through the windows as the team marched, room by room, down the length of the building.

"Oh no," Jack said, sounding sick. "No, no . . ." A coppery taste filled Lele's mouth. She'd bitten through her lip. Blood on her chin, blood on her hands, blood on her thighs . . . Her mind filled up with the red thickness of it, drowned her, pulled her under.

"Run," Jack said. His voice on the intercom sounded very faint over the rushing of blood in Lele's ears. "They're climbing out of the windows at the far end of the building. Oh my hell, they're so little! C'mon, kids, *run!*"

"Jack," Lele said, her voice empty as it had been on the approach. Now was not the time to feel. Now was the time to act. She flipped on the force trim, reached up with her left hand to stabilize the cyclic, and drew her service pistol from the holster on her survival vest with the right.

"Lele! What—?" Jack asked.

She turned in her seat as much as she could and pointed the gun at his head.

"Get out," she said.

"What are you doing?" he asked, sounding hysterical. "Lele, put the gun away! I'm your friend!"

"That's why I'm doing this," she said. The words started to gather more steam as she spoke, as more tiny bodies slipped out of windows and the end door of the building and went running off into the dubious safety of the night. Too bad she and those she'd brought with her could see in the dark.

"I don't understand," Jack said. "Lele—"

"No. You have a family to go back to. There's no going back from this. So I am forcing you, at gunpoint, out of my aircraft. Do you hear me? That's what you tell them. I held a gun to your head and made you get out. Now. Get. Out."

Comprehension dawned on his face in the dim glow cast by his goggles. He pressed his lips together, and then nodded once. She kept the gun steady on him as he released the catch on his harness and slipped out of the seat. He looked as if he would say something, but she cut her eyes to the cockpit voice recorder, and he desisted. She watched him unhook his comm cord from his helmet, and then shouted, barely audible over the rotor noise.

"I'll get them on board for you! Good Luck, Ma'am!"

Before she could say anything, he took off running for the school, scooping up small bodies as he ran. Lele held her breath and prayed that the team of killers she'd delivered would remain occupied inside for just a little while longer.

Jack brought them back by twos and threes, and a tiny detached corner of Lele's mind wondered how he'd managed to convince the scattering children that he was not to be feared. She kept her head and the FLIR on a swivel as he loaded the aircraft, until a small voice spoke in shaky Tagalog on her intercom.

"You will help us?"

"I will," she said in the same language, blessing her grandmother for forcing her to learn all those years ago. "Make sure the little ones are sitting down and holding on. And make sure the doors are closed."

"Your big man closed them. We are ready."

"All right," she said, as she advanced the throttles from flight idle to military power. The rotor's beat accelerated in return, getting louder and throwing out more wash. Jack stepped up to the door, saluted, and then stepped back with his hands raised ostentatiously high.

With no clue what she was doing, Lele switched off her aircraft's transponder, and pulled the circuit breaker from the panel above her head. Then she pulled in to a hover and swiveled the guns to point at the lone man standing in the field. Then she put the nose down and accelerated up and over the lake. Her best bet was to get out of there as fast as she could, before someone could take off and follow her.

The rain that she'd earlier cursed had suddenly become her best ally. It started to pour down in heavier sheets, as if the night itself were weeping for the destruction of the little village. Lele flew toward the far slope of the valley, hoping to find a pass below the level of the lurking clouds. She'd thought she'd seen something during that abortion of a briefing yesterday . . .

There! It wasn't much, merely a dip in the ridgeline, but she could clearly see the cloud layer above it, thanks to the flames that had started back in the village. She made for the pass, trying not to hear the sounds of the children crying in the cabin behind her.

"Are you still on comm?" she asked.

"Yes, lady?" the girl who'd spoken before answered. She didn't sound very old. Ten at most.

"What is your name?"

"Mirabel."

"Mirabel. I'm Lele. How old are you?"

"Eight."

Eight years old. You poor baby. What the hell am I doing?

"Are you the oldest?"

"Yes. The older ones are gone or dead," Mirabel said, her voice matter-of-fact and growing steadier by the minute. "We were small enough to get out through the window."

"I'm so sorry, Mirabel," Lele said. "I can't . . . I am just so sorry. I want to help you, but I . . . I'm not sure where to go."

"Can you take us to *Mga Yungib*?" Mirabel asked. "My parents are hiding there."

"The Caves? What Caves?"

"In the next valley. You are going the right way. Just over this mountain, and then on the backside. It is a long trip by mule, but we are going much faster than a mule can go."

"How do you know this? How to get there, where it is?"

"Everyone knows. When the soldiers come, that is where you must flee, if you can."

When the soldiers come. So this has happened before? It wasn't just a colossal fuck up? What is going on here?

Lele didn't really have time to figure it out just then, as they were rapidly approaching that mountain pass. It looked like a solid wall of darkness beyond, which made Lele's insides clench in fear, but going back was simply not an option. So she dropped down to the level of the trees, slowed her speed significantly, and began picking her way through the mountains. The whole time, she felt as if someone had a weapon pointed at her six, as if she were about to be shot out of the sky at any moment.

Maybe she was. Even more reason to push forward into the

darkness like an insane person. Because, clearly, that's what she'd become.

"Mirabel, do you know anything more about where these caves are?" she asked.

"They told us to come halfway down the mountain, and we would see them in the rock face," she said.

"*In* the rock face? Okay . . ." as the crested the shoulder of the peak, the ambient light decreased dramatically. Lele began to think seriously about finding a place just to land and spend the night, then trying to find these caves in the light of day. The problem, of course, was that if she could see to find them, so could anyone else. And while Alcasar and his Intel buddies might not know to look for a rock face with caves in it, they would most certainly pay attention to a rogue Duey flying around.

"Missile, missile." The silky-seductive tones of the Duey's audio warning system purred in Lele's ear, while a blinding flash of light gained her goggles down to nothing as the aircraft's automatic flare dispensers did their thing.

"Shit!" Lele cursed, and jerked the aircraft into a bank in a last-ditch maneuver to force the threat to miss them. She was low and slow, and didn't have much energy to work with, so she hauled up on the collective, and prayed that the Duey's engines would spool quick enough to save their asses.

The engines shrieked, but delivered. She felt a kick in the seat of her pants, and watched as a corkscrew trail of smoke streaked by them.

"That's us!" Mirabel said over the intercom. "The missile came from the caves!"

"Of course it did," Lele muttered. "If only we could tell your families not to shoot at . . ."

The Loudhailer.

"Mirabel!" Lele said as she righted the aircraft and brought it back around . . . toward the threat, but she was deliberately not thinking about that at the moment. On this crazy night, what was one more crazy action? The fingers of her collective hand flew across the switches on the overhead console panel, and a shielded green light that she'd almost never seen flipped on. A static hum joined the sound of the rotors and the engines in her ears.

"Lady?" Mirabel asked, her little voice scared. Lele didn't even want to think about how much she and the other little ones were being jostled around with her flying.

"When I say, I need you to talk into your microphone. I need you to call out your parents names, your name. The names of the other children. I need you to tell them that you're all on this bird, okay? I need you to tell them not to shoot at us, but that we need to land!"

Lele pulled her nose up and banked the bird over hard to reverse course and head back toward the cliff face and whoever it was that had launched the missile at them.

"Okay, lady," Mirabel said, sounding doubtful. Lele nearly laughed, because she felt the same way.

"Now, Mirabel!" she said, and hit the "broadcast" switch on the loudhailer.

"Mama, papa! It's Mirabel! And Baby, and Angel, and Rizal, and Arvin, and . . . "

Lele felt the words of a half-remembered prayer slip through her lips as she flew closer, and closer to the cliff. With every second, her options for evading another shot decreased, but she flew on, putting her faith in a God she didn't think existed . . . and in the sing-song sound of a child's voice.

Lightning cracked overhead, and rain continued to pour down, but the mountain stayed still. Unsure of what else to do, Lele slowed, feeding in power, and coming to a hover over the dark-shrouded jungle canopy that covered the slope.

A light appeared below, then another. Lele slewed the FLIR over to look, and saw several figures moving in the trees ahead. As she watched, they appeared to roll the canopy back, as if it were nothing but a curtain. Underneath, a wide, open field beckoned invitingly.

"Mirabel, tell them that if they want us to land there, they should move the two lights together, and then separate them by the width of a house." Lele didn't know how wide a typical house was, but she figured that that amount of separation should be enough for her to see and respond appropriately.

The little girl relayed this instruction, and sure enough, the two lights came together, and then split apart. From her hover approximately a hundred feet above the ground (and maybe twenty feet above the level of the surrounding trees), Lele started her approach. By the time she felt her skids touch the spongy surface of the field, she was certain that this whole thing must be a dream. Had she really just done all of that?

Unable to think of anything else to do, she cut the engines and let the rotor idle to a stop. As soon as the blades stopped turning, a woman broke through the crowd gathered in the treeline and sprinted toward the aircraft.

"Mirabel!" the woman cried, her arms outstretched. In the light from the torches that had been used to mark the impromptu LZ, Lele could see tearmarks that glistened down the woman's face.

"Mama!" the little girl cried from the back, and Lele felt a series of thumps and clangs as the child fought free of the seatbelt that Jack had cinched around her and two others. With that same sense of dreamlike unreality, Lele unstrapped herself and opened the door of the Duey. The woman had been joined by four or five more people, presumably parents of the children inside. They cried their children's names and pounded on the plexiglass windows of the bird in their haste.

"Move back," Lele said in Tagalog. "Let me open the door."

The parents fell silent and turned to stare at her. Lele couldn't imagine what they must think. Here she was, helmeted, armed, wearing a UN uniform and insignia, and yet she spoke Tagalog, and had brought their children to them. She stepped up to the door, and tugged on the old-fashioned style handle, then slid the door back to let the crying children spill out into their parents' arms.

The kids' voices tumbled all over one another as they each related the tale as they'd experienced it. First one, than another, then several more adults let out shrieks and heartrending wails of denial as they learned that their children hadn't been among the ones she'd rescued.

Lele watched for a moment, safe behind the shield of her helmet and night vision goggles, and then turned to go back to the cockpit. Accompanied only by the familiar ache of loss, she climbed back into her seat and completed the shutdown sequence.

When she was finished, she removed her helmet and hung it on the hook above her seat. Then she took a moment to retie her hair back into a neat bun before stepping out of the aircraft again.

"Mama, this is her. This is Lady Lele." Lele blinked, and focused on the small, skinny girl who spoke. After a moment of blankness, she realized suddenly that this tiny child could only be Mirabel, the brave little voice from the back.

"Lady Lele," Mirabel's mother said, and her voice and her eyes filled with tears once more. Lele found herself drawn into a chokingly tight embrace as the woman wailed over her. More and more arms wrapped around her, and Lele felt as if she would be smothered by the gratitude that rolled off of these people.

"Step back, step back. Let the woman breathe!" The voice that spoke was male, and carried that faint quaver that bespoke great age. The suffocating hugs eased, and one by one the people stepped away. Somewhere nearby, another torch flared, and the flickering light played over the figure of a wizened older man.

"Grandfather," Lele said respectfully, as her grandmother would have expected.

"You are Filipina?" the man asked, his face stern.

"My grandmother was. She taught me the language. I'm from California."

"What is your name?"

"Leonora Cristina Adalynne Reyes Campbell. But . . . please call me Lele."

"Lele. You are a UN officer."

"I am . . . was. Sort of. My government ordered me and some others to work for them."

"Your unit attacked our village."

Lele swallowed hard and nodded. Was this it, then? Would they execute her for the actions of her unit? To be honest, she wasn't entirely sure she could blame them if they did. The memory of gunshots in a school echoed through her head.

"My unit did," she said, when it appeared that the old man required more of an explanation. "We were told that it was a communication node for the insurgency."

"It was a place to send our children. A place for them to get schooling."

"Yes," she said softly. "I know that now. It is not what we were told. When I realized . . . my copilot grabbed as many of the kids as he could and I ran with them. Mirabel brought me here."

The old man looked at her for a long moment. Lele stood uncomfortably under his gaze and didn't look away. She could hear the snap of the flame on the torches, and patter of the continuing rain. Far away, thunder rumbled. The storm was passing them by, finally.

"What will you do now?" he asked.

The dreamlike feeling faded, leaving Lele weak-kneed with fatigue. She felt like sagging, collapsing to the ground. So she pulled herself straighter.

"I don't know," she said. "If I go back, they will likely kill me for desertion. After they interrogate me to find out the location of this place. It would be better if you killed me here, first."

"Why?" he asked.

"Because . . . I don't want to betray you . . ." Lele said slowly, not really understanding why he was asking. She'd thought she'd been pretty clear.

"No, child. Why did you save our children?"

Oh.

Wind gusted, and a fresh curtain of warm jungle rain poured down like blood from the sky. *Blood on her hands, spilling from her thighs . . .*

"Because," she whispered, "I couldn't save my own."

"Ah," the old man said. Slowly, he smiled. Lele wavered, and the world closed in from the edges.

Her face was hot. Lele squinted her eyes open and realized why. She lay next to an open window, and the brutal equatorial Terra Novan sun blazed in through a hole in the concealing canopy.

Lele sat up and looked out of the window, which was really just a square hole cut into the crude wooden wall of a shack. From this angle, she could clearly see the clever net arrangement that the people used to camouflage the wide field in front of the caves. They'd even managed to tie living plants in pots up among the nets, so as to hide from chlorophyll sensitive recon cameras. From the air, it would just look like so much jungle. But underneath, an entire village teemed with life and activity.

Instinct had her looking for her aircraft. She leaned out of the window and craned her neck until she saw it at the far end of the field. Someone had strung a rope around it, and no one appeared inclined to cross this barrier.

"You're awake!"

Lele turned to see the woman from the night before, Mirabel's mother, walking into the small shelter where she'd been sleeping. Like Lele, she was small and slight. But Lele remembered this woman's crushing hug, and knew that her delicate body contained a wiry strength that typically came from leading some kind of an interesting life.

"I . . . yes," Lele said. She put a self-conscious hand to her hair. "I'm not exactly sure what happened."

"You fainted, and then you slept. For most of the day, really. The sun will set in a few hours. That's fine, though. You needed your rest, after a flight like that. Mirabel told us all about it. Such a storyteller, that girl!" the woman spoke with a mother's pride. Lele found herself smiling, even through the familiar pain.

"She's a brave girl," she said.

"Yes," her mother agreed. She came and sat on the bed next to Lele, and took one of Lele's hands in hers. "She is. My name is Eva. How many?"

"What?"

"Miscarriages? Our doctor examined you after you fainted. She said you'd had at least one, probably more. Those were the babies you couldn't save, weren't they? How many?"

"Four," Lele breathed on a wave of agony. Eva nodded.

"I lost two before Mirabel. She is my miracle baby. Proof of God's love."

"God's love?" Lele asked. Her voice turned sharp, brittle. "How can that be? What kind of God kills children in the womb?" *Or allows them to be murdered by men with guns?* "How can that be love?"

"How can it be otherwise? Look at all the children you saved last night. Would you have been here had you not lost those poor babies? So they wait for you in heaven while you do your work here. Then, when you die, they will welcome you to heaven."

"I wish I believed that," Lele said.

Eva smiled and patted her cheek.

"You will see. God loves you very much, Lady Lele. That is why he brought you to us. You left behind a home filled with pain. Now this is your home, and you can be free."

"In what way?"

"In all ways! You can stay, you can go. This is not like the UN, where your fate is tied to your place in society. You can do what you want, be what you want."

"I want . . ." Lele trailed off, closed her mouth so hard it hurt her lips.

Eva reached out and stroked her hair.

"What, sister? What do you want? What is it that you want to be?"

"A mother," she breathed, and the dam broke. Great wracking sobs erupted from deep within her chest. Tears ran in scalding lines from her eyes. She crumpled around herself and felt the unending grief well up as it had done so many times before.

This time, though, there was someone there.

Always before, she'd been alone. Her ex-husband hadn't wanted to deal with the blood and the mess of it. He'd been too busy with his own pain, and his anger at her inability to do this simple thing right. After the divorce, she'd cried in secret, lest anyone else learn of her failure and her shame. It had seemed safer, since she knew that this agony would never go away.

But not this time. Eva wrapped her arms around Lele's shaking shoulders and drew her head down onto her generous chest. Unlike the hardness of last night's embrace, this was soft, gentle. Comforting. When Lele's sobs quieted, Eva didn't let up, but simply crooned soft words in the grieving woman's ear.

"That's it, my sister. Cry it out. I cry for my lost babes too, even after my Mirabel. You cry as much as you need. There is peace and healing in tears, you know."

Lele sniffled a laugh at that and sat up.

"Not for me," she said swiping at her eyes. "Tears are shameful and weak."

"That is nonsense," Eva scoffed. "Tears are what make us human. You cry, and then you feel better. This is the way of things."

"You wanted something, when you came in here. I'm sorry to have distracted you," Lele said, eager to talk about something else. She felt strange. Hollow and light, as if her tears had emptied her, at least temporarily, of the raging grief. It didn't usually work that way. Usually, she cried herself to exhaustion, then she snuck back to her room and passed out.

"Oh! Yes. I was going to ask you if you would help me. Some of the little ones you saved . . . well . . . their parents were in the village. We haven't heard from them. There is hope yet, but . . ." she gave an eloquent shrug.

"Anyway, they need someone to cuddle them and get them to eat a little something. I thought perhaps if you weren't too tired, you might be able to get a response out of them. They all know that you saved them, you see. You are their Lady Lele. Their angel in a helicopter."

Lele froze, and searched the other woman's face. Mirabel's mother smiled softly, her eyes full of the knowledge of just what she was offering.

"All right," Lele whispered.

"All right," Eva said, getting up. She held out her hands and helped Lele to her feet. "Let's go. Your children are waiting."

INTERLUDE:
From Jimenez's *History of the Wars of Liberation*

And so, to the list of heroes of revolution and resistance on Old Earth, were added new names from Terra Nova's guerilla history. On the *Isla Real*, for example, we have coastal defense batteries named for Pedro, called "el cholo," for Mitzilla Carrera de Alvarez, daughter of Belisario Carrera, for her husband, Juan Alvarez, and for Mendoza, whose first name we do not know. In addition, there are coast defense batteries named for UN deserters to our cause Amita Kaur Bhago and Nandi Mkhize. Near the capital of Aguinaldo is a park named after General Lele Campbell. Gaul has its Citadelle Madalene La Pen, as Sachsen has its more generally named Freiheitkaempferstrasse, a highway connecting the north with the capital in the south.

But amidst all of that heroism and self-sacrifice, there was a shadier side.

Not everyone who came to Terra Nova came here voluntarily. Not everyone came without a considerable number of police on their tail. In addition to the heroes, we also received more than our share of villains, ranging from the corrupt rich to political terrorists from Old Earth, eager, this time, "to do it right."

9.
BLOOD, SWEAT, AND TEARS

Christopher L. Smith[10]

Marko followed the assistant through the heavy, ornately carved wooden door into the Shah's office.

Silverwood, he thought, casting an appraising eye over the workmanship, *No expense spared here.*

Scenes of nymphs cavorting gaily through a forest of tranzitrees were well crafted, their delicate features skillfully carved down to the smallest detail. Individual leaves, blades of grass, vines—they all spoke volumes towards the artist's skill. The gold filigree covering it all, however, spoke volumes towards the owner's lack of good taste.

Marko made sure his face remained expressionless. His opinion on art wasn't the reason he was here.

The Shah loved to remind the people of his wealth. From his limo—the only one of its kind on Terra Nova, as far as Marko

---

10 A native Texan by birth (if not geography), Chris Smith moved "home" as soon as he could.

While there, he also met a wonderful lady who somehow found him to be funny, charming, and worth marrying. (She has since changed her mind on the funny and charming, but figures he's still a keeper.)

Chris began writing fiction in 2012. His short stories can be found in the following anthologies: "Bad Blood and Old Silver," (*Luna's Children:Stranger Worlds*, Dark Oak Press), "Isaac Crane and the Ancient Hunger" (*Dark Corners* Anthology, Fantom Enterprises); "200 miles to Huntsville" (*Black Tide Rising*, Baen); "What Manner of Fool" (*Sha'Daa: Inked*, Copper Dog Publishing); "Case Hardened" (*Forged in Blood*, Baen); and "Velut Luna" (*The Good, The Bad, and The Merc*, Seventh Seal Press).

He has co-written two novels, *Kraken Mare* (Severed Press) with Jason Cordova, and *Gunpowder and Embers—Last Judgement's Fire Book 1* (Baen, Forthcoming) with John Ringo and Kacey Ezell. A solo urban fantasy novel is currently under construction.

His cats allow his family and three dogs to reside with them outside of San Antonio.

knew—to the massive ceremonies for visiting officials, the Shah made everyone aware of exactly how poor they were in comparison. For some, it seemed to inspire them. For Marko, it served as an object lesson. Hard work and diligence was its own reward. Money could go away with bad decisions. Pride and respect for yourself was harder to lose.

"Ah—Marko Saavedra!," the Shah said, spreading his arms and smiling, "My friend! It is good you have accepted my offer to join me!"

Marko bowed, careful to keep his eyes turned to the floor as he did so. He held the bow slightly longer than was technically proper, to the Shah's apparent amusement.

"No need for that, my friend," the Shah said, expression making his words a lie. He was smugly pleased by the gesture, Marko could tell. He waved to the overstuffed leather chairs in front of his desk. "Please, sit. Would you care for a drink?"

"Thank you, sir. I would."

"Fruit juice for my friend, and water," the Shah said to his assistant. "And please be quick about it."

The young man left, gently closing the door behind him. The Shah turned back, still smiling.

"How may I help you, today, sir?" Marko said, "I must say that I was surprised by your invitation."

"Ah . . . Straight to the heart of the matter. I like that in a man," the Shah said. Again, his face didn't match the words or tone. The Shah's reputation was that of a man who liked to make an entrance, draw out the production, make people wait.

"I have a visitor arriving in sixteen days," he said, leaning closer. A heavy cloud of perfume followed him. "Whom, I can't say, but it is someone I'm anxious to impress."

"I'm certain that you will not fail to do so, sir."

"Ah! But that is my dilemma, Marko. This visitor is not so easily impressed as the local dignitaries. I need to show them what a man of my stature has at his beck and call. That is where you come in."

"Sir? I'm not sure how I can help? I'm a simple builder."

"But what you do is not so simple, is it?" the Shah said, sitting back again. He was interrupted by the return of the assistant. The man came in carrying a silver tray, on which were four crystal goblets, a decanter of water, and another decanter of dark red juice. "Thank you, Ali, you may go."

As the door closed again, the Shah poured the drinks and continued.

"I'm told you are the best in the city, Marko. That you can accomplish quality works with a small crew in a short amount of time. This is what I need."

"What are you thinking of, sir?" Marko said, mentally gathering a list of names. "Depending on the project, I'm not sure it can be accomplished in your time frame."

"What I need is a fountain. One that will be a centerpiece of the reception."

"A fountain? That shouldn't be too difficult, for any one of many tradesmen in the city."

"Ah—but this fountain is special. I need it pour not water—but wine, liquor, and beer. My guest and their entourage are not bound by the same traditions as we are, and will appreciate the gesture."

Marko sipped his juice, turning the idea over in his head. A hollow structure, utilizing tubing inside and some kind of pump . . . it didn't seem like a difficult project.

"The liquid must also be chilled."

Marko started slightly, barely catching himself before he choked. He cleared his throat and looked at the man across from him. The Shah was serious.

"I'm sorry sir, did you say 'chilled'?"

"Yes! What better way to refresh yourself after a long trip across the stars than by indulging in a cold beverage?" His smile grew wider. "I'm told that you can do this, no?"

"I . . . I suppose it could be done, sir," Marko said, frowning slightly, "It just hasn't been done before."

"And that is why I must have it!"

"You do realize that this can't be done cheaply? Not in the time frame you have set?"

"Bah! Money is no object. You will be given what amounts to unlimited funds to do this." Reaching into a desk drawer, the Shah produced a ledger and fountain pen. Both with gold inlay, Marko noted. "Here is a deposit, should you accept. I believe one hundred thousand dirhem should be enough to start?"

With a flourish, he signed the paper and tore it from the book. He held it towards Marko. Marko leaned forward, taking the other end. The Shah didn't let go.

"I must add," he said, face losing all joviality, "that if you are unable to complete this project, you will have a very difficult time finding work again."

Sweat made Marko's hand suddenly very slick. Acceptance meant taking care of his family for the foreseeable future. To reject it would likely bring the same fate as failure. There was only one response.

"Sir, I will do my absolute best."

He took the check.

It wouldn't be easy, but it also wasn't impossible. One week for demo and building the support pieces, one week to install the fountain and fine tune everything. Refrigeration was easy—he'd been on several projects with large walk-in coolers. The main thing would be getting that refrigeration method to cool the fountain. Still, that was just re-purposing existing equipment for something new.

The challenge would be getting the crews in place to do all the work, and getting that fountain built.

Especially the fountain. Artisans are a flaky bunch on the best days, He thought. Adding a short time frame and pressure could really bite him in the ass. He took another look at his notes about what the Shah wanted.

Six different types of beverages would require as many spouts, and all the individual workings to make that happen. Cooling it all would require the additional copper tubing and connections. Making it all appear, as though magically, in the center of the ballroom—that would take some effort.

Marko began listing the different components, and who the best choices for the work were for each, with alternates.

Tomorrow would be busy, getting in touch with all of them. And the clock was ticking. He leaned back in his chair, lacing his fingers behind his head. Focusing on a point beyond the ceiling, he inhaled slowly.

"Papa!" His youngest daughter's piping voice startled him, his heart leaping in his chest. While the distraction cost him his relaxation technique, it was a welcome one. He reveled in the feeling that, at least for a few more years, his child was excited to see him. There would be time for work, later, after the house was asleep.

"Hello little Estrella," he said, bracing himself for her inevitable pounce into his lap. "How was school today? OOF!"

"It was terrible, Papa!" she said, pouting. "Julio pulled my hair, and Selina just laughed!"

"Ah, that means Julio likes you, little one, and I thought Selina was your best friend?"

"Not anymore, she isn't," Estrella said fiercely, shaking her head. Droplets of water landed on his desk, her damp hair smelling of the rose petal soap her mother preferred. "She likes Julio, and wants him to like her too, so she's being mean to me."

Ah, the Mercurial relationships of six-year-olds. His oldest had been the same at this age. Marko stifled the smile, and allowed his face to take a stern expression. It was hard to do, but he'd had practice.

"Well, that's just not right," he said, hugging her. "Friends like that aren't worth having."

"Estrella," His wife's voice came from the doorway. "It's time for bed."

"Yes, Mama, I was just telling Papa about Selina and Julio."

"I know, dear heart, but Papa is busy, and you have to be up early." Isabelle said, smiling. "Now tell Papa goodnight, and off to bed."

"Goodnight, Papa, I love you."

"And I you, little Star." Marko said, giving her one last, tight squeeze. "Now go sleep so you can shine brightly tomorrow."

He watched her leave, his wife lingering in the doorway.

"How much more do you have to do tonight?" Her question, delivered in a husky tone, was loaded. "I need to discuss a matter of some urgency with you."

"Maybe ten minutes?" Marko felt himself grinning like a fool.

"Make it five."

The look in Isabelle's eyes made him promise himself it would be no more than three.

Marko sipped his coffee, savoring the few moments of peace before things got rolling. He had been able to get a lot done, surprising himself with how smoothly everything had gone. The tradesmen he'd contacted had jumped at the chance to join the team, committing themselves to this job over any others for the next two weeks. His initial site walk with the demo and rebuild team was first thing in the morning, with actual labor scheduled to begin that night.

The fountain itself was still somewhat worrisome, as the sculptor had been dubious of the time frame. Marko knew the man would come through, however, as this was his standard method of getting more money from the buyer. Still, the amount of intricate internal tubing could cause friction between the artiste and the engineers. He was confident that a few large sums of money would smooth over any issues between the two. That meeting was set for tomorrow as well.

He checked his list. So far so good, only a few other minor details to attend to before the big push. As this was his project, sleep would be a precious commodity over the next few weeks.

"Mr. Saavedra, I need to speak to you," a man at his side said, sliding into the booth across from him. "It is about your project."

Marko took a moment to examine the man. He had the look of a banker, dressed casually in slacks and a light cotton shirt. Middle-sized, his lightly tanned face lacking wrinkles, it was hard to believe this person had worked outside much in his career, if ever.

Word traveled fast in the industry, so Marko showed little surprise at the man's words. He did allow himself to raise an eyebrow at his impertinence.

"Oh?" he said, sipping the cooling coffee. "And what exactly would you like to discuss?"

"I'd like to join your crew," the man said, leaning forward and dropping his voice. "However, the details are best left for a quieter location."

The man stood, dropping a note on the table, more than enough to cover Marko's bill.

"If you could come with me, please?"

"I'm really busy, Mr . . . ?"

"Mister is just fine for right now, and I'm afraid I must insist that you come, quietly." The man held out one hand in a "right this way" gesture while pulling back the corner of his untucked shirt with the other.

Marko could easily make out the grip of a small pistol holstered in the man's waistband. His heart raced, sweat coating his palms. He took a deep breath, releasing it slowly. Something told him it wouldn't be wise to show fear.

"Funny," he said, sliding to the edge of the booth, "I wouldn't think kidnappers would usually pay for their victim's meal."

The man leaned in again, keeping his voice low at Marko's ear.

"Please don't try anything or make a scene. There are several others nearby that won't be quite as polite as I am. I assure you, no harm will come to you."

Marko took another slow breath, trying to keep his voice from shaking.

"Well, as it seems I have no choice, please lead the way."

The canvas bag over his head was clean, at least. The muted daylight filtering through it showed no signs of being used for any other less fortunate victims. All things considered, Marko had been treated well—no violence, or threats, or even anything less than a firm politeness. Whoever these guys were, they acted with a stoic professionalism that gave him some hope. He kept his breathing slow and deep, and his hands in his lap. It helped to keep his racing heart from jumping into his throat.

Thirty minutes of riding, with multiple twists, turns, and nothing but the sound of horse-hooves had him thoroughly confused as to their destination. Just as he was about to ask how much longer they would be, the carriage creaked to a stop. Marko held his tongue as he was helped out of the coach and led up what felt like a dirt path.

"Watch your step, Mr. Saavedra, there are six stairs in front of you."

At the top, after crossing a threshold, the bag was removed from his head, his nose assaulted with the smell of human waste. The old house had obviously been home to transients in the past, and hadn't been cleaned by its new occupants. Marko found himself wishing for the bag again.

"Mr. Saavedra," the man from the cafe said, "if you will please come this way."

Marko followed the man into what appeared to be the kitchen, thankfully clean, bare except for a few chairs and a table. A coffee pot sat on a counter, half full, its aroma filling the small space.

The man motioned for Marko to sit, and poured three mugs of

the dark brew. He brought all three to the table, placing one in front of Marko.

"I apologize for interrupting you earlier, Mr. Saavedra. While I realize that a cup of coffee falls far short of making up for these circumstances, it is the best I can do right now."

"It's something, at least," Marko said, taking a careful sip of the hot liquid. Strong, pleasantly bitter, with a slight acidity, it was high quality. "I would like to know what I'm doing here, though."

"Of course. All will be explained, shortly. We're only waiting for my employer to join us."

At his words, a door opened out of Marko's line of sight. Footsteps came down a hall around the corner.

A man appeared, dressed in a non-descript beige business suit. Slightly balding, hair at his temples graying, the man could've been any mid-level manager at any white collar business. Lean, but not emaciated, aged anywhere between forty and sixty, he was the walking definition of "average."

"Mr. Saavedra, it is a pleasure to meet you," the man said, mopping sweat from his forehead with a linen handkerchief. "I apologize for the less than ideal methods used to bring you here, but one can never be too careful."

Marko nodded, not trusting himself to say anything. He had an idea of who he was dealing with, but nothing more than vague rumors and scuttlebutt. None of which helped his nerves.

"I'll spare you any more pleasantries and idle chit chat, Mr. Saavedra," he said, taking a seat. "I have brought you here because we need your help. It has come to our attention that the Shah has hired you to do a job, one that ensure that you will be in the mansion when a certain guest arrives."

Marko nodded again.

"My organization needs to make a statement. One that undermines the Shah's absolute control over the people of this country. We need you to facilitate this statement."

"I'm not sure what you're asking of me, sir," Marko said.

"Allow me to explain, in as much detail as I feel is appropriate for your safety: The statement is related to the visitor your project is supposed to impress. Our needs are simple—we need one of our men to join your crew, in order make this statement. That is all."

"It's never 'all,' sir," Marko said, "I realize there's more to this, so let me be blunt: I will not fail at a job I've accepted. I've essentially made a promise, to not fulfill it would damage my reputation, as well as violate my own personal ethics."

"We wouldn't be asking you to fail on purpose, Mr. Saavedra. In fact, we want you to succeed, and will do what we can to help you do so. In fact, it is of vital importance that you *do* succeed. All we ask is that our man be allowed access to the Shah's mansion."

"Forgive me for seeming selfish, but what do I get out of this deal?"

"Your family will never want again, Mr. Saavedra. I understand that you have a daughter about to go to University?" At Marko's hesitant nod, the man continued. "We can make sure that she is not only accepted, but will receive a substantial scholarship."

"And if I refuse?"

"Well, I'd hate to imply that anything bad will happen . . . "

"But."

". . . but, one can't be certain of security of those that one deems important."

"Security?" Marko's temper flared. "Are you threatening my family's safety?"

"Don't be crass, Mr. Saavedra. We would never stoop to threatening physical harm to innocents." The man smiled, tight lipped. "However, accidents do happen."

Marko jumped to his feet, white-knuckled hands gripping the table, vision narrowing down to tight focus on the man. The men around him snapped to attention. Something cold and metallic pressed against the back of his neck. Immediately, his rational mind took over, suppressing the anger coursing through him.

"Mr. Saavedra," the man from the cafe said softly, "I'd consider your next moves very carefully."

Marko inhaled slowly, staring coldly at the man in front of him. He sat down.

"I don't appreciate being bullied or threatened, sir."

"And I appreciate that, Mr. Saavedra," the man said. "However, the circumstances require a certain, ah, forcefulness of our offer."

"Well, then," Marko said, fuming, "it appears we have an agreement."

"Excellent!" the man said, standing. "My associate will escort you back to the cafe, and give you further contact information. Good day, Mr. Saavedra."

"Not that good," Marko said under his breath.

Marko passed his hand over his eyes, feeling the beginning of a stress headache forming. The sculptor and the engineer were arguing—again—over the inclusion of the internal tubing.

"It's ruining the lines of the piece!" The artist, Cristobal Almeria, shouted, waving a lit cutting torch. "This *plebian* doesn't understand how it will affect the emotional effect!"

He turned to Marko.

"I can't work under these conditions, Marko!"

"If it is to pour correctly," the engineer said calmly, "this is where and how the lines must run. I can't have that many turns in steel tubing in such a short space."

"But it looks *hideous!*"

Marko dropped his hand, throwing a quick glance at his shadow for the last three days. After delivering him, unharmed as promised, back at the cafe, the man had introduced himself as Ricardo Ivey. Since then, he'd been Marko's constant companion, posing as project manager. To his credit, the man had quietly kept out of the way, only interjecting occasionally to ask pointed questions at the right moments, then making notes on a small pad.

Marko understood, but hated, the look of mild amusement on Ivey's face.

"Gentlemen," Marko said, "there is always a solution to a problem. Let's take a step back, breathe deeply, and discuss this calmly."

He held up a hand to stall Almeria's reply. In his experience with the man, it would be passionate, long-winded, and pig-headed.

"Deep breaths, Cristobal. I won't let you speak until I see you take them."

The engineer made an obvious effort to do just that, though in Marko's opinion, he wasn't the one that needed to relax. Marko nodded slightly, to show him he appreciated the gesture, then watched the artist.

Cristobal rolled his eyes, then took several overly exaggerated lungfuls of air.

"Happy?"

Marko made a motion for him to proceed.

"If the tubing doesn't bend here, it won't allow me to make the weld look right," he said. "It would be akin to a boil on a beautiful woman's face. It's a flaw that wouldn't just be noticeable to the trained eye, but a deformity that any layman would see."

"I understand," Marko said, gesturing to the engineer. "And you say that it won't function properly if it bends?"

"Mostly correct, Mr. Saavedra. What he's suggesting, it restricts the flow, and could cause cracks in the steel."

Marko nodded, moving over to the drawings of the fountain at the table. It would be a beautiful piece of work, once finished. Bronzed birds, in various poses of action or inaction, formed the body of the statue. Their open mouths would dispense the drinks—doves for beer, raptors for the liquor, and birds of paradise for the wines. If he could get the two men to agree, that is. He studied to the areas of contention.

"If we moved this slightly," he said, pointing to one of the doves, "angling its neck upwards more, would that reduce the sweep of the bend, and allow the weld to be made properly?"

The engineer squinted slightly as he thought. After a few seconds, he nodded.

The artist, did the same, begrudgingly.

"Yes, that could work," Almeria said, "but it would change the stance, and therefore the *meaning*. The dove represents peace, which is shown through his passive body language. This would make them appear challenging."

"Ah, but true peace is only gained through some aggression, is it not?" Ivey said, breaking his silence. "It seems to me, that by giving your dove a more challenging appearance, that a dichotomy of ideals is achieved."

Almeria's lip curled as he raised a hand to wave dismissively. He stopped short, squinting at the piece, then turned to look at Ivey.

"You . . . you have a point. I hadn't thought of that," he said. His demeanor changed abruptly, a smile replacing the sneer. "I have come to the brilliant deduction that this dove's aggressive stance represents the struggle of the human condition—to be ready for violence even while working for peace. I, am a genius!"

Marko turned slightly, rolling his eyes. The others were more or less having the same reaction, hiding smiles behind their hands and stifling "coughs."

Artists, Marko thought.

"It is unquestionably genius," Ivey said, "and genius should be rewarded, don't you think, Mr. Saavedra?"

"Oh, by all means," Marko said, nodding. He reached into his pocket for the checkbook. "I believe a bonus is definitely in order, to encourage more bursts of inspiration that resolve issues."

He quickly wrote two checks, one for the artist, and one for the engineer.

"Thank you, gentlemen, for your willingness to discuss this rationally, and come to a swift conclusion. I assume that the project will progress on time?"

Both men nodded, seemingly satisfied with the amounts.

"Excellent. I will return in a week for the finished piece." He nodded to Ivey. "We should leave these two to their project."

"That was impressive," Marko said, sitting in his office facing Ivey. "I wouldn't have considered you an art critic."

"You learn more about people and culture by studying their art," he said. "The more you know about them, the easier it is to infiltrate, manipulate, and further your own goals."

"That's a ruthless slant to take."

"Yes, it is," Ivey said, shrugging. "We live in a ruthless world. I'm a ruthless person. I survive and further my agenda."

"Let's talk about that," Marko said, leaning forward slightly. "I'm not clear what it is I'm supposed to help you with."

"It's none of your concern, at this point."

"I'd beg to differ, sir," Marko said, meeting the man's eyes. "This is my family and livelihood at stake. I don't see what could concern me more."

"You are only an end to a means. If you do as we request, you will have nothing to worry about."

"And what exactly is that request?"

"Get me access to the Shah's mansion, and stay out of my way."

"To what end?"

"Again, none of your concern. Should everything go as planned, you will not be implicated."

"Implicated. That doesn't fill me with confidence."

"You have an appointment in an hour at the mansion," Ivey said, checking his watch. "I'd dare say that is more important than this line of discussion."

Marko glared at him, only to be met with stone faced silence. With a snort, he stood and walked to the door. Ivey followed shortly after.

Security at the mansion was tight, as was to be expected. The guard at the gate held a clipboard, flipping through a list of names slowly, comparing Marko's ID to each in turn. Marko was thankful for the warm day and bright sun, as it made the cold sweat on his brow less out of place.

"Mr. Saavedra, you're cleared, but your . . ." the guard stopped, looking at Ivey suspiciously. ". . . companion isn't. I'll need to run a security scan."

"How long will this take?" Marko said, frowning. "We have an appointment in less than twenty minutes."

The guard shrugged, apparently not knowing or caring what the answer might be.

Great, Marko thought, *this could be trouble if Ivey can't come in.*

"Don't worry, Mr. Saavedra, I took the liberty of filing the paperwork with the head of security yesterday," Ivey said. "I'm sure it's just a minor oversight."

The guard picked up a handset, and after a few moments, spoke to someone on the other end. Marko could hear clicks and hissing, even a meter away. He kept his voice low enough that Marko couldn't make out what he was saying, and his face gave no indication of, well, anything. Kid had good control, or this was routine enough that it didn't warrant any thought on his part.

Probably the latter.

After a minute of silence, a few questions, and several requests to repeat the last statement, the guard hung up.

"You're clear, sirs," he said, turning back to them with two badges. One, marked "temporary" he gave to Ivey, the other had Marko's name and picture on it. He nodded at Ivey. "You will need to visit the guard station inside to get a picture taken. These badges will be returned to this gate when you exit."

They took them, clipped them to their shirts, and walked into the building.

The demolition team had been busy, working in shifts around the clock to prepare for the install team. The ballroom's floor had been cordoned off, keeping most of the more curious staff at bay, as well as providing a more or less "safe perimeter" for the workers. Nothing would slow down the work like a staff member getting hurt on-site.

Things were proceeding well, and more importantly, on schedule. The area where the fountain would sit had been stripped down to the bare concrete, with twenty centimeter holes bored in three separate locations, roughly equidistant from each other. These would match up with the location of the beverage tubing.

The fountain itself would sit over the top, covering all the inner workings from view, and the wood flooring would be replaced to make the whole thing seamless.

Marko found the demo supervisor, a tired looking man holding a large cup of coffee and a clipboard. His expression showed tension, satisfaction, and exhaustion in equal measures.

"Berto," Marko said, approaching. "How are we looking?"

"*I'm* looking like hammered shit, Marko." the man said, grinning. "*You're* looking like someone that has actually gotten a few hours' sleep."

"Only for now, my friend," Marko said, "Only for now. Next week, you'll see a different man."

He took the proffered clipboard from Berto and glanced through the pages. Things were progressing as they should, with the demo team scheduled to finish soon.

"This looks good," he said. "The install team will be here in a few hours, to pick up where you left off. Anything they need to worry about?"

"Nothing major, the floor will need bracing under the fountain, of course, and there is a small water leak near where you'll be putting the refrigeration unit, but that's easily fixed."

"Excellent." Marko said, handing the clipboard back. "Keep up the good work. I'm going to show Mr. Ivey around, and bring him up to speed."

Berto nodded, clapped Marko on the shoulder, and returned his focus to the proceedings.

Marko beckoned to Ivey, walking in the direction of the security office. Twenty minutes later, they both walked out, Ivey clipping his brand new badge to his shirt. The bored looking security guard at the desk had barely glanced at the man's ID before punching his information into the difference engine. Incorrectly. Twice. By the time they had everything correct, the guard was visibly annoyed, handing the final badge across the desk with a snarl.

Marko passed the elevator, preferring to take the stairs to the basement storage area. Ivey remained silent, but the few times Marko glanced at him, seemed to be taking mental notes about their surroundings. Given that he still had no idea what the man's purpose in this was, Marko tried to put it out of his mind, focusing on *his* purpose.

He continued on down the narrow corridor to the main storage area, mentally measuring the width of the hallway and comparing it to the size of the equipment that would be carted down it. The demo team had done a good job of clearing the hallway of the assorted accumulated stuff that had cluttered it previously. Give a person space to put something, and it would inevitably get filled. Junk drawer writ large. He'd check the various rooms leading off the hallway on the way back.

As they entered the large storage room, he saw that his team had marked the floor with neon pink paint, laying out the dimensions and location of the large walk-in cooler, and the supporting equipment. Marko nodded in satisfaction, before turning to examine the walls.

Several holes were cut into the walls, just below the ceiling level, each about fifteen centimeters in diameter. The beverage lines would be fed through those, leading into the rooms they had passed previously, eventually terminating under the fountain. Smaller holes had been drilled into the walls as well, spaced throughout the room. Marko nodded—All appeared to be in order.

Ivey seemed interested in the smaller penetrations.

"These holes," he said, "What are they to be used for?"

"Electrical, drain lines, compressor lines," Marko said, looking at the man. This was the most he'd asked about the actual operations since he'd met him. "Why?"

"I assume these components will be run from a central location, say a breaker box, or something similar?"

"Yes, and to the compressor located on the roof of the building."

"Excellent. I'll need to see them."

"I don't see why."

"It's none of your concern at the moment. I need to see these areas, and you will show them to me."

"I don't like your tone, Mr. Ivey."

"I don't care, Mr. Saavedra." Ivey gave him a cold stare. "I have a job to do. You have an agreement to facilitate that job. It occurs to me that, in the normal course of your responsibilities here, examining these systems would be completely natural, and shouldn't raise any issues."

"I'm not arguing that, Mr. Ivey. I'm arguing that I'm not your servant, nor in your employ." Marko crossed his arms. "I deserve more respect from you than you are providing, and I need that to change."

"Mr. Saavedra," Ivey said, a tight smile pulling the corners of his lips up slightly. "Would you be so kind as to escort me to the locations I desire to examine? Pretty please. With sugar on top."

"Since you asked so politely, Mr. Ivey, I'd be happy to do so."

"Thank you," Ivey said. "It would've been unhelpful to have had to kill you."

Marko had no doubt Ivey meant it.

Isabelle looked at him from across the table.

"What's wrong, dearest?"

Marko steeled himself. He'd been putting the subject off throughout dinner, knowing that he couldn't hide anything from his wife. He'd been silent since he'd sat down, barely tasting his meal. Normally, he'd relish each bite, never failing to be amazed at Isabelle's skill with simple ingredients. Tonight, however, his mind was elsewhere.

"Marko, I know something is bothering you," she said. "You haven't been with us this evening."

He glanced at Estrella and her older sister, Alessandra, both enjoying fresh cream and berries. Isabelle noticed, nodded, and turned to their daughters.

"Alessandra, why don't you show your sister your new dress? You may take your desserts with you."

Their oldest, familiar with her mother's hints, nodded.

"Yes, Mama," she said, gathering up her dish. "Come on, Little Star, we can play dress up."

"Now Marko," Isabelle said when they had left. "Tell me what's on your mind."

"I need you to take the children to your mother's until I finish this project."

"I don't understand, Marko," she said, frowning. "You've never asked us to leave before, no matter how stressed you were."

"It isn't that, beloved," he smiled, hoping that it would look sincere. "It's just that I'll be working nights, and needing to sleep during the day."

"I understand," she said, with a sly grin. "And I know you'll be less inclined to sleep if we are home alone."

Marko chuckled. She was right, no matter how tired he'd be, having the house to themselves would be a strong temptation to stay awake.

"It isn't any farther from Estrella's school, I don't see any issue there," she said, tapping a finger to her smooth cheek. "And, I have been promising Mother a visit for weeks, now."

She nodded, signaling the decision was made. A stray lock of brown hair, still untouched by gray, fell forward over her brow. Marko reached forward to brush it back, gently.

I wish I could tell you, dearest, that my fears outweigh any need for rest, he thought, as his wife pressed her head into his palm.

The truth of the matter was that he didn't know what Ivey's plans entailed. He'd insisted on delivering the fountain himself, and had been extremely curious about the installation process. Marko had found nothing out of the ordinary with the piece afterwards, but still had a nagging suspicion.

Ivey was dangerous, ruthless, and determined. Something told him that his "statement" could invite repercussions. And if, somehow, Marko was held to blame for any failure of the man's mission, well, the implied threat against his family had been made.

"Well," Isabelle said, "if I'm not to see you for a while, I should make sure you remember me."

She stood, taking his hand and leading him away from the table. As they walked through the house towards their bedroom, he could hear Estrella's laughter. Her sister would keep her occupied for the time being.

Isabelle entered their room, turning to face him. She ran her hands through his hair as she leaned into him, her soft lips finding his. Marko gently nudged the door closed behind them.

Marko started, the heavy pounding on his door dragging him unceremoniously from his dreams. He checked the clock—only four hours since he'd fallen into bed, exhausted. The last several days had been long, a minimum of eighteen hours on site, if not more. Out of the last thirty-six hours, he'd been able to catch three hours sleep, one hour at a time.

What the hell? he thought. *There must be some mistake.*

He racked his brain as he staggered upright, trying to determine exactly why someone would be here at this hour.

"I'm coming, dammit, don't beat it down!"

As he worked the locks on the sturdy, heavily reinforced wood, he congratulated himself for his foresight in replacing the original frame and structure. What had been here when he'd moved in all those years ago would've come crashing down at the first set of blows.

And people criticize me for overbuilding?

He swung the door open to see Ivey, staring at him with his cold eyes, tool bag slung across his body.

"Oh, it's you," Marko said, sighing heavily. "What could possibly be so urgent that you couldn't let me get a full night's sleep?"

"It's noon, Mr. Saavedra. You've been asleep for sixteen hours," Ivey said flatly. "Look carefully."

Marko blinked slowly, comprehension dawning. The hazy light from the overcast day didn't help to reconcile his internal clock, but he could now hear bird song mixed in with the sounds of a neighborhood going about its daily business.

"Why are you here, Ivey?" Marko scowled at the man in front of him. "My debt is paid, you got the access you needed."

"There's an issue. A malfunction, if you will, in the plan." Ivey said. "Access is limited to critical personnel only. As you are listed as critical in case of emergency, your presence is needed."

"How is this my problem?"

"I'm making it your problem. I can't get in if you don't get me in.

Access, Mr. Saavedra, that is what you agreed to provide. You will provide it or you will be in violation of your agreement," Ivey's eyes were flat. "And all that entails."

"I get that you're on some secret mission here, but lack of planning on your part does not constitute an emergency on mine." Marko started to shut the door.

"Talked to your wife and children, lately, Saavedra?"

"What are you implying?"

"Nothing. Just curious how they are doing at Isabelle's mother's house."

"How did you know that?" Marko had told no one where they were going, and had urged Isabelle to leave after dark.

Ivey continued staring at him, his only expression a small uptick in the corner of his mouth. Marko desperately wanted to slap it off him, but had a strong hunch about what would happen if he tried.

Ivey seemed to read something in his face.

"Shall we, Mr. Saavedra?"

Marko nodded.

"Name?" the bored-looking guard said, glancing up from his clipboard.

"Marko Saavedra and Richard Ivey," Marko said.

"Purpose of visit?"

"I was told there's an issue with my equipment, and it needs immediate attention."

"The fireworks begin in thirty minutes, sir, the reception shortly after," the guard said, emotionlessly.

"Exactly," Marko said, "I need to get this fixed now. We wouldn't want the Shah to be upset, would we?"

Any resolve the guard had faded at his employers title. Orders or no, the risk of retribution from the Shah overrode any possible punishment from a superior officer.

"Your assistant is prohibited, sir."

"There's equipment that weighs over two hundred kilos. Do you expect me to move it myself?"

"Sir, other guards will be available . . . "

"And do these guards know exactly how to fix the machinery? Or what tools I'll need to use?" Marko's exasperation was only half feigned. "You said it yourself, there's only a short time before the reception. Less, now. I need Mr. Ivey to get this fixed quickly. His badge is next to mine. He's been cleared for the last week. Why is now any different?"

After a short hesitation, the guard nodded.

"You have forty-five minutes. Then you will be escorted from the grounds. Sabir will show you the way."

"And if it takes longer?"

"Make sure it doesn't." He handed over the badges. "I'll need to look inside that bag."

"It's just tools," Marko said, exasperated. In truth, he hoped his expression would cover his nervousness. "The same tools we've carried in for the last week."

"I'll need to search the bag," the guard said again, "No entry without search."

Marko glanced at Ivey, who seemed unaffected by the situation, maintaining his usual level of stoic silence. He did, however, slip the bag's strap off his shoulder and hand it to the guard.

This did nothing to lessen Marko's tension, until, after a few seconds of poking around inside, the guard passed the bag back.

"Proceed."

Sabir led them into the building, stopping just inside the door of the servant's entrance.

"Where to, sirs?" he said.

"We need to go into the basement," Ivey said. "Where the refrigeration equipment is located."

Sabir looked at Marko for assurance.

"That's a good place to start," Marko said nodding. He moved to the side slightly as a group of children passed them, giggling as they ran.

Sabir in the lead, the trio made their way down the stairs and into the basement hallway. Moments later, they approached the locked door to the storage room. Their escort unlocked the door, swinging it open and standing just inside as Marko and Ivey walked in.

Marko made a show of looking inside the cooler, examining the pressure regulators and dispense equipment.

"Odd, nothing seems to be out of place in here," he said. "Ricardo, do you see anything wrong?"

Ivey walked past the guard to stand next to Marko, leaning past him as though examining a regulator. His breath buzzed in Marko's ear.

"I need you to distract our escort," he whispered. Louder, he said, "Everything looks okay to me. Shall we check the cooling unit?"

Marko nodded, exiting the cooler and moving to the refrigeration device. Both pumps hummed softly as he squatted next to the machine, slowly running his hands over the steel body.

"I think there's something . . . Excuse me, Sabir, could I have you shine your flashlight over here? It's hard to see."

Sabir said nothing, but removed his compact light from its pouch next to his sidearm, clicking the button as he did so. Bright, focused light momentarily blinded Marko before he could turn away.

"Aah," he said, holding up a hand to shade his eyes. "Thank you, but I need it over here."

Sabir snickered slightly, apparently amused at Marko's discomfort, but took two steps forward.

"Hm," Marko said, "still can't quite make out . . . Could you bring the light a little bit closer please?"

He pointed at the far corner of the square unit, waving the guard over with his other hand.

"It's just back here, if you look, you can see exactly what I need." Sabir stood next to him, leaning over the unit slightly, playing the light back and forth over the machine. "That's it, right there. Now hold it steady . . . "

Sabir grunted in surprise as Ivey's forearm slid around his throat, followed by a sharp gasp. The young guard went limp, and Ivey slowly lowered him to the floor, withdrawing the knife from the man's back as he did so. After quickly cleaning and resheathing the blade, Ivey took the guard's sidearm, spare magazine, and keys as Marko looked on in shock.

"What have you done?" he said, softly.

"I've eliminated an obstacle to my success."

"No, you've committed murder. That means I'm an accomplice. My family will suffer for this, and I'll be put to death!"

"That is a chance I'm willing to take. Besides, he's still alive." Ivey looked down at the guard, whose mouth opened and closed silently. With a quick movement, he cut the man's throat. "Now it's murder."

"Are you serious?" Marko stared at Ivey, feeling his eyes widen as his jaw dropped. "This is no time for joking! I fulfilled my part of this deal, well beyond what any reasonable man in my position would."

"This reminds me of an old saying," Ivey said, smirking. "I am altering the deal, pray I do not alter it further."

"No," Marko said, shaking his head, "I'm done with this. I won't be a part of this madness."

Ivey's eyes grew hard, his voice dropping as he leaned forward.

"Listen to me very carefully, Mr. Saavedra—I will succeed in my mission. You can continue to live, or I can dispose of you as I would any other obstacle. You're only alive *at this moment* because you may still prove to be useful."

The guard's pistol appeared in his hand, held at his thigh, pointing at the floor.

For now. Marko thought.

"You'll notice I didn't use the word essential."

Marko felt his shoulders slump. Ivey was right, there was no option but to do what the man demanded.

For now.

"I'm glad we have an understanding, Mr. Saavedra," Ivey said. "Please take Sabir's feet and help me put him in the cooler."

The young guard's body was heavier than he expected, but they were able to wrestle it into the walk-in, locking the door when they were finished with Marko's master key. Marko kept his eyes firmly on the young man's belt buckle, and not the trail of blood on the floor. Or the guard's eyes.

"There," Ivey said, checking his clothes for any obvious stains. "Now, I need to visit the area immediately under the fountain itself. I'm sure you understand that you'll be leading the way, and why."

They made their way down the hall, following the beverage tubing running along the ceiling. Marko both prayed and feared that they would encounter someone while they walked. Discovery would absolve him of any wrongs, however, it could also mean his death at Ivey's hand.

The insulated bundle of tubing took a sharp turn above a door, disappearing into the room beyond. At Ivey's nod, Marko tried to open the door, his hand slipping on the steel knob. He wiped his palms on his pants, finally getting it open on the second try. He ignored Ivey's smirk as he entered the room, closing the door after Ivey brushed past.

"Now, Mr. Saavedra, since I can't have you do this part, I'm going to politely request you stand at the far side of the room, and raise your hands. Be assured that any attempt to move will be considered negative, and I'll respond accordingly."

Marko nodded, moving close to the shelving as far from Ivey as possible, and raised his arms above his head. The room itself was small, barely three meters end to end, and under two meters wide. The shelf took up most of its corner, haphazardly filled with cleaning supplies in large buckets and jugs. Ivey took one of the buckets from the middle shelf, grunting with the effort.

Marko felt the shelf sway slightly. He placed one hand on the top to steady it.

Ivey carefully placed the pistol in easy reach while reaching into his shoulder bag with the other. He removed what looked like a multimeter, two wire leads with alligator clips attached, and a roll of black tape. Standing on the bucket, he reached above his head to the bundle.

Short work with the knife, and he'd cut open the insulation, feeling around inside with one hand. A few seconds later, he produced two wires. In moments, he'd attached the device to the insulated bundle, several wraps of tape holding it in place. He then attached the clips to the wires.

"There. Now, Mr. Saavedra, we are free to leave." He checked his watch after retrieving the pistol. "And still have time left before the deadline expires. Well done."

Marko said nothing, keeping his expression flat.

"Oh, and just in case you're wondering, the device can't be removed without setting it off, unless you know the proper sequence to remove the wires." Ivey said, again pointing the pistol at him. "I can see it in your eyes, Marko, that this is distasteful to you, and you're trying to figure out how to stop me. Trust me when I say you can't. Do you understand?"

Marko nodded.

"Excellent." Keeping the gun steady, Ivey nodded towards the door. "Shall we, then? As much as I'm willing to die for my cause, it's not high on my list of preferred outcomes."

Marko stayed motionless, both hands raised, one still on the shelf.

"Mr. Saavedra, I would like to vacate the premises before the device detonates," Ivey said, taking a step forward and lowering the pistol. "You may lower your hands now."

Several muffled explosions came from above them. Ivey glanced upward. Marko pulled hard on the shelf, upsetting its balance and causing it to topple forward.

"Shit!" Ivey raised his hands instinctively to cover his face as hundreds of kilos of shelf and chemicals fell on him, knocking him to the floor. The gun hit the floor, skittering a few feet away. Lunging, Marko grabbed it and stepped to the door, stuffing the pistol into his waistband as he did so.

Marko threw the door open, barreling into the hall as fast as he could, heading for the staircase. Though the attendees and some staff would be outside watching the fireworks, the Shah's palace would have at least a hundred others in the building for a reception of this size.

I need to clear everyone that I can. Marko's thoughts were punctuated by more explosions. He stopped at the top of the stairs, looking up and down the hallway.

There! A fire alarm switch was on the wall about ten meters from his location. *It may get anyone inside to vacate, and keep the crowd outside from re-entering.*

He ran down the hall, covering the distance as fast as possible. The thought of not getting the warning out in time sent a burst of adrenaline through his veins. He yanked the handle down hard, the claxon-like warning buzzer immediately blasting through the formerly quiet building.

A crowd appeared at the far end of the corridor; kitchen staff by their uniforms. Human nature being what it was, Marko knew that if no one smelled smoke or saw fire, they would tend to ignore the alarm and stay put.

"This is not a drill!" he shouted, making "this way" motions with his arms. "You need to get out of the building immediately! There's a fire in the basement!"

The group looked confused, not moving, and whispering amongst themselves.

"NOW, PEOPLE! I'm not kidding!"

Human nature tended to make people listen to someone that

appeared to be an authority. As Marko was the loudest, and most commanding person in the immediate area, the staff started walking towards him on their way to the front door. A few men and women hesitated, looking back and forth between themselves. Marko started towards them.

"You lot, what part didn't you understand?"

"It's not that," one young woman, her coat and apron identifying her as a chef, "It's just that . . ."

It hit him as she trailed off.

"You all have children?" At their nods, he continued, "Are they in the building?"

"Yes," the chef said, somehow becoming the group's spokesperson. "We all do, and they weren't allowed to watch the fireworks from the lawn."

"Right," Marko said, "get them and pass the word on to any others with children. But go quickly, I don't know how long we have."

He turned from the group and started running towards the ballroom. Ivey had said the device couldn't be disconnected, but, there was a chance he was lying. The wires had been in the tubing bundle, which meant whatever he had planted was inside the fountain. Marko had made the connections himself, and hadn't seen anything out of the ordinary, but Ivey had watched the process, and could've come back afterwards.

But what would trigger the device? What Ivey installed downstairs had no timer or readout that Marko could see.

A statement. He'd wanted to make a definitive statement. What would make the most impact?

Marko ran his hands over the fountain, thoughts churning. Obviously, it had to be related to the visiting dignitary. The Shah would want his guest to be impressed, and flattered by the thoughtful gesture. He looked at each tap—Which one?

Space voyage. Wine and liquor could be served room temperature. His eyes locked on the beer tap.

"I see you've figured it out," Ivey's voice came from behind him. Marko whipped around to see the man walking towards him, limping slightly. The knife he'd used on Sabir was in his hand. Marko pulled the pistol from behind his back, hands shaking as he raised the weapon.

"You've never used one of those, Mr. Saavedra," Ivey said, rolling his eyes. "Better men than you have tried to kill me, and failed. I'm almost insulted."

Marko's finger tightened on the trigger.

"Mr. Saavedra," Ivey said, continuing to close the gap between them, "while there's no doubt in my mind that you're capable of pulling the trigger, I highly doubt you'll hit me."

Marko's hesitation allowed Ivey to take two more steps, stopping when Marko thumbed the hammer back. At four half meters, he didn't think he could miss.

"Please, Mr. Ivey," he said, trying to keep his hand steady, "I don't want to shoot you, but I will if I have to."

"Think about the consequences if you do, Marko," Ivey said, standing almost casually. "Killing me puts your family at risk—my employers will consider their arrangement null and void."

He was right. No matter what he did, the chance was there that he'd be implicated. Even if he was able to kill Ivey and remove the explosive, the Shah would consider him an accomplice that lost his nerve. Neither a long term in prison, or a quick execution, would be a desirable outcome. Not to mention what it would mean to his family's name. His assets would be frozen, his property confiscated. Isabelle and the children would die as paupers.

As to the other group, it wouldn't take them long to figure out who'd foiled their plans, especially if Ivey lived. Killing him would not be beneficial, as it would erase any doubt as to whom was responsible for the failure. Retribution would be swift, he was sure. The thought of living without his family crushed his soul. Marko lowered the pistol, shoulders slumping.

Ivey rushed forward, covering the distance between them faster than Marko thought possible. Ivey was on him before he could raise the pistol, a single shot plowing into the wooden paneling of the floor harmlessly several feet wide. Lights flashed before his eyes as Ivey's fist crashed into his jaw, staggering him. He reeled, falling backwards onto the sculpture, it's metal body the only thing keeping him from hitting the floor. Ivey's knife blade pressed into his throat.

"Now, Marko, you have two options. Die, knowing that your death does nothing to stop tonight's 'unfortunate' event. Or, live, make our escape, and see your children again."

Steel pressed into Marko's back, the sharp point of the dove's defiantly raised beak close to breaking the skin. There was another option, one that would fulfill his agreement with the conspirators, and possibly shield his family from the Shah's wrath. He raised his hands slowly.

"Good choice, Mr. Saavedra."

Marko pulled sharply on the tap handle, honey-colored liquid flowing into the drain below it. Ivey's eyes went wide.

Marko's last thought flew through his mind as the explosion ripped through his body.

It poured perfectly.

INTERLUDE:
From Jimenez's *History of the Wars of Liberation*

One of the problems besetting the United Nations' efforts to suppress the liberation movements on Terra Nova was that not only was every movement initially unique as to temperament, time, and place, but every movement was also different as to technique. Thus, there was no perfect answer to the UN's problems, while forces seconded from Earth's armies tended to use whatever technique was in vogue back home, even if it was a supremely imperfect approach for the area to which they were deployed.

There were, basically, four different kinds of insurgency taking place on Terra Nova. In the area of western Taurania, amidst and adjacent to the colonies we now call "Cochin" and "Ming Zhong Guo," the emphasis was on outgoverning the governments, on setting up entire shadow governments from criminal courts to tax collectors, and especially the latter, to support the insurgent companies, battalions, regiments, and the political cadres they advanced and defended. In Central Columbia, supported by the colonies that would someday join to form the Federated States, the emphasis was on establishing safe zones in which to build more or less conventional formations, relying on the sea and local agriculture for food, and then invade en masse. In Uhuru, it was from the beginning a campaign of terrorism directed at the UN's bureaucracy and the UN-supporting farmers to get them to pack up and leave, leaving the reins of power in insurgent hands.

And then there were the places where there wasn't much insurgency, where the UN saw one that wasn't there, and where the UN's actions created an insurgency where none had yet arisen . . .

10.
WELLINGTON

Alexander Macris[11]

Roy Wyatt could see the shadow of the man through the doorway of the sheepfold. The rock walls were too high to see over, but he knew he was in there. He felt against his hip for the reassuring weight of the revolver. It was an Old Earth model, .45 long colt, double action, six shots. He fingered the hammer back and called out. "I know you're inside, mate. Why don't you come out? You won't be harmed."

There was no response from within. Wyatt looked over at Blake. The old sheep farmer had spotted the stranger that morning when he was heading towards the pasture. There'd been blood smeared on the door—enough of it cause Blake to get himself worked up. Now it was Wyatt's job to sort it out.

"Listen. I'm local sheriff here at New Bend. The owner radioed me about a trespasser. Showed me the blood on the door. You hurt?"

"You with the UN?"

"The UN?" *In New Bend?* United Nations Peacekeepers seemed to be everywhere on Terra Nova these days, but they sure weren't here. Secluded in a valley in the Cloud Mountains, New Bend rarely even got visitors at all. That's why folks came to New Bend in the first place—to get away from the stifling crowds of Old Earth and find a place of their own. "No one here's UN, mate. Not much need for the

---

11 Alexander Macris is an entrepreneur, executive, lawyer, and game designer. He currently serves as studio head of Autarch LLC, a tabletop game company, which publishes his best-selling *Adventurer Conqueror King System*.

UN in New Bend. I don't need PKs to stop drunks from fighting over sheep."

There was a choked laugh from within. "Okay." Then a pause. "I'm hurt."

"Sorry to hear that. I'm going to come in. I'll come in real slow and you keep it easy, okay? No shooting."

"Don't have a gun."

"Good to know. I'm still going to take it slow. Here I am. Walking in." Wyatt stepped into the doorway of the sheepfold. He could see the stranger clearly now. He was in his mid thirties. He had the brown skin and dark hair of a Maori, but his eyes were green and his nose was aquiline. The stranger had equipped himself with a hay fork, but looked to be using it as a crutch more than a weapon. A crude bandage, stained black with blood, was wrapped around his left thigh.

Wyatt showed his palms. He'd left the service revolver in its holster. "I'm Sheriff Roy Wyatt. You can call me Roy, or Sheriff. Or Wyatt. Most folks go with Wyatt."

"My name's Jim. Jim Geary. Didn't mean to stuff things up for ya, Sheriff." The stranger offered up a smile. Wyatt thought he looked embarrassed.

"No worries, Jim. Why don't you come with me down to the station? We'll give Mr. Blake his sheepfold back and my deputy can see you right."

The man looked down at his feet for a moment, and then he looked up and gave a half smile. He started limping forward. Wyatt led him out. They passed Blake, still standing outside the sheepfold.

"Sorry about the blood," said Geary. He shrugged ruefully.

Wyatt eyeballed the stranger. Geary was leaning back in the cell, feet up on the pallet, enjoying a sandwich and a fizzy drink. He had a fresh white bandage around his wound. Steve Remi, the deputy, had been an army medic back in New Zealand before the Old Earth demilitarization. Even with Remi's training it hadn't been easy to clean up Geary's leg—the man had taken a hit from a 10mm flechette round, and it was a messy wound. That kind of high-tech ammo wasn't exactly common in Wellington. It wasn't even common on the *planet*.

"So what brought you to New Bend, mate?" Wyatt asked.

"Just passing through," said Geary.

"Yeah. But passing through to where?"

"Well, I was heading south to the tunnel in Griffon Peak. To get some material. But I had to take a detour." Geary massaged his wounded leg.

Wyatt frowned. The Griffon Peak tunnel went from nowhere to nowhere and was used by no one. UN planners had once envisioned a whole series of interlocking underground thoroughfares that would carry automotive traffic below the Cloud Mountains and protect the precious alpine biome above. Then the Old Earth bureaucrats had realized the colony didn't have any automotive traffic. The project had been "indefinitely suspended" and the construction material abandoned in place. Nowadays the place was a ruin.

"Probably better off. Tunnel's not safe to—" Wyatt was interrupted by the sound of the station door opening. A pair of dark-suited figures entered. The first was an icy blonde woman with cold blue eyes. Her companion was an Asian man with the bland face of a dentist, or a serial killer.

The blonde spoke. "I am Special Agent Nikita Bogin and this is Special Agent Vinh Hue." She had a thick Russian accent, and it took Wyatt a moment to process her words. "We are here to demand extradition of prisoner James H. Geary." She gestured at the jail cell.

Geary made a face, stomped a foot, and shouted *"Haere noa!"* *Freedom.* The agents affected not to notice and kept their icy stares directed at Wyatt. Remi cracked his knuckles nervously at his desk. Wyatt decided he'd better fill the silence before Geary decided to perform a haka from his jail cell.

"G'day . . . Sheriff Roy Wyatt." He walked over and offered his hand to Bogin. She left him hanging so rather than let it get awkward he pivoted his hand to point back at the cell. "Mr. Geary here is my prisoner. Got him on charges of trespassing over at the Blake farm. What do you need with him?"

"Mr. Geary is wanted on charges of resisting arrest, subversion, destruction of government property, and hate speech," said Hue. "He's a known terrorist." The Asian man read off the litany of charges with a condescending tone that made Wyatt grit his teeth.

"Hate speech. Well, that does sound dangerous. But I guess we should ask to see some identification. You understand. We don't see too much in the way of UN big shots here at New Bend. Actually I don't think we've ever seen UN big shots." He paused and eyed them suspiciously. "Are you big shots?" Remi laughed from the back of the station.

Wordlessly, the two agents produced badges from inside black leather coats. He gave them a once over. Bronze, UN logo— Peacekeeping Force. *Legit.* When Wyatt nodded, the badges vanished back behind the leather coats.

"He's likely to be released in a couple days if Blake doesn't press charges. So why don't you come back then?"

"We'll take him now, if you please," said Hue.

"And if I hand over Mr. Geary to you, what happens to him?"

The Russian, Bogin, answered. "That is none of your concern, Mr. Wyatt." The way she said his name made it sound like a disease.

"That's *Sheriff* Wyatt. And it is my concern. He's my prisoner. I'm not in the habit of just handing people over to the first space cops that come through the door." He offered them a toothy smile. "I know you think it's all bush justice here on Terra Nova, but we've still got a little bit of process . . . I'm going to need some transfer paperwork."

"Sheriff Wyatt," said Bogin. "I can assure you that Mr. Geary will be treated with all due process. But under United Nations Regulation F-403c(32) we are not required to file extradition paperwork for category V, VI, or VII perpetrator. Mr. Geary qualifies as all three." She stepped in close—close enough that Wyatt could smell the scent of a perfume that cost more than his monthly salary. Close enough that he could identify the Steyr Mannlicher 10mm flechette pistol in her shoulder holster. "That is not going to be problem, is it?"

Wyatt sniffed the air again for her perfume. It was almost too fragrant against the sweaty smell of the sheriff's office.

"I don't have a problem," he said. Wyatt looked back at his deputy. Remi offered him a cool smile. The big man had his own reasons to hate the UN—before his forced deportation he'd had a good life on Old Earth, a career, a woman he'd loved. "I just don't remember New Bend being part of the UN. We on the Security Council, Steve?" he asked.

Remi called back from his deck. "No, Sheriff, sure don't recall being on the Security Council."

"No, me neither," said Wyatt. He turned back to the agents. "And besides, you haven't answered my question. What's going to happen to Mr. Geary if I turn him over to you?"

Her partner's hand glided towards his holster, but Bogin was placatory. "You are proceduralist. I understand," she said. "So am I. Mr. Geary will be taken unharmed to our vessel, *UNS Robert Mugabe*. There he will be tried by judge in special tribunal. If found guilty by judge, he will be sentenced to appropriate psychological reconditioning and detained in service facility until such time as he has paid his debt to society."

"So he won't be tried by a jury?" Wyatt frowned.

She smiled. *One proceduralist to another.* "Of course not! We are not barbarians, Sheriff Wyatt. Obviously a random assortment of ignorant jurors cannot guarantee society justice any more than unregulated capitalist economy can guarantee society stability." She waved a hand. The Asian relaxed his grip on his pistol. "Everything will be efficiently handled by trained judicial administrator."

Wyatt took a deep breath. "I think you mistook my meaning, ma'am. Here at New Bend, we're very old fashioned. We don't have many experts. But we reckon jurors—you, know, regular folk—might actually know something."

Bogin stepped back like his words had shoved her.

"And we reckon that when a man looks to be taken off his home world to get brainwashed at work camp, it deserves a little more than the say-so of some foreign agents," Wyatt continued. "So I think, with all due respect, that I'll need a chance to research this myself before I decide to hand him over to you."

The special agents said nothing, but Hue slipped his hand back on his pistol. Then metal grated on tile—Remi had pushed back his chair and stood up. The deputy walked over to Wyatt. He was a big man. Wyatt felt the balance of power in the room tilt in his favor.

Apparently, so did the special agents. Bogin gave a curt nod. "As you wish, Sheriff Wyatt," she said. "We will return tomorrow at noon. We will be accompanied by security officers in order to assure that there are no inconvenient disruptions. I assume fifteen hours will afford you sufficient time to familiarize yourself with pertinent regulations?"

"Seems like enough time."

Bogin nodded, and the Asian held out a business card. *United*

Nations Peacekeeping Force—Wellington. Wyatt moved to take the card, but the agent didn't immediately relinquish it. "I hope we'll be able to report to headquarters that New Bend is in accord with the UN and supports progress for Terra Nova."

"We're all Kiwis here. Very progressive," Wyatt said, and smiled amiably. After a moment, Agent Hue let him take the card. Wyatt put it in his wallet, then walked with them to the exit. When the agents were gone, he closed the door and leaned on the closed frame.

Cocking his head to one side, folding his arms, Wyatt looked intently at the prisoner. "Okay, Geary," he said. "You're going to tell me everything. Starting with why the UN shot you."

At precisely noon the next day, Agents Hue and Bogin rode into the valley with a troop of blue-helmeted security officers wearing armor and carrying combat rifles. From his desk at the window, Wyatt had a clear line of sight to their posse. He counted their numbers as they approached and dismounted: Four security officers and two special agents. He wondered how bad it was going to be.

The special agents walked in. Wyatt stood up to meet them. "We're here to collect the prisoner James Geary," said Hue.

Wyatt tried to look sheepish. "He ain't here. Little bugger must have had a lock pick hidden up his bum. He cracked the jail gate and did a runner while I was napping."

"That is unacc—" said Agent Bogin.

Hue interrupted. "Did you pursue?"

"Well, when I woke up and saw he was gone I went after him. But he nicked a horse and I couldn't find him in the dark. From his tracks it looked like he was making for the mountains." Wyatt paused. "You think there's a terrorist base up there or something?"

The two special agents looked at each other, then at him. He made eye contact with both, shrugged, then looked past them. Through the window, Wyatt could see the lunch time crowds moving down Main Street. Office workers on break were mingling with sweaty farmhands pausing from their labors. A wagon with a half-dozen workmen drawn by a team of sleek horses was rolling in from the west. His townsfolk were nodding amiably to each other, but keeping their distance from the security officers outside his station. *Please just leave my town in peace,* he prayed.

The prayer didn't work. "You don't seriously expect me to believe that story, do you?" said Hue.

"What do you mean?"

"I looked you up, Sheriff Wyatt. Twenty years of service. A spotless record. Multiple commendations at every job. But suddenly, when a terrorist falls into your lap, you become a fuck-up?"

Wyatt glowered. "I expect you to believe my story *because* I'm an officer of twenty years experience with a spotless record. My record should count for something."

"I'm afraid it does not, Sheriff Wyatt," said Hue, subtly shaking his head. Somehow the flechette gun was in his hand and pointed at Wyatt. "Your firearm. Your jail keys. Put them on the floor."

That went south quickly. Wyatt eased his revolver out of its holster and lowered it to the floor gently. Then he fished his keys from his pocket and dropped them, too.

"Now, if you wouldn't mind." Hue waved the barrel of his pistol towards the jail cell. "Because I certainly wouldn't." Hue's finger touched the trigger.

Wyatt's nostrils flared. He held his hands up in surrender, but in his head the sheriff was already visualizing how it could go. *Step forward—lock the pistol down with my left, right elbow to his throat; then use the pistol to dispatch the sheila . . .*

Hue must have sensed his anger because he stepped out of arm's reach. "You dirtside locals are all the same," he sneered. "Trapped in your primitive paradigms of tribal loyalty and antisocial violence. On Earth, we have a word for people like you. We call you—"

"Assholes? No, wait—that's the word for people like you."

"Troglodytes. In the cell, Sheriff." Wyatt stepped behind the bars. Hue kept his pistol pointed at Wyatt while Bogin collected his revolver and keys from the floor. Wyatt glared at her while she locked him in.

"While you were looking me up, I looked up Geary," Wyatt said. "He was an anti-UN pundit whose words made you mad. That's it. You made him a criminal when you went after him and his family."

"Mr. Geary's words were calls for violence and subversion. He deserves what he will get. So do you." Hue glanced at the Russian. "Tell Officer Mirkovitch to bring in the interrogation equipment." Bogin stepped out the door and signaled to the security offers to come inside.

Then came the crack and flash of gunfire. Screams of pain and terror erupted and the lunch time crowd devolved into bedlam. Bogin ducked back through the door hastily.

The gun shots were coming from the wagon on the street. The workmen had exited on the far side and were using the carriage for cover while they fired hunting rifles at the UN troops. Bolt actions worked frantically. Three of the blue helmeted figures had already toppled.

The fourth had taken cover behind a barrel. His combat rifle blazed. A horse screamed as its flank was riddled with flechettes. It started pulling on its harness, and the wagon rolled forward. Now one of the insurgents was exposed. It was Steve Remi.

Before Remi could find new cover, the security officer fired a second burst. Remi's blood spattered across Main Street and formed tiny red puddles in the cracks of the cobblestones.

The insurgent closest to Remi stopped shooting and bound over to the downed man. The rest continued to lay down fire. The insurgent had just gotten to Remi when the last security officer went down. The streets of New Bend went quiet.

Inside the jailhouse, the two special agents had taken up a covered position just below the front window. Wyatt, from his cell, could see both them and the wagon outside. And he could hear the familiar voice of Jim Geary.

"We know you have Sheriff Wyatt in there," Jim yelled. "We want him, and we want your weapons. Hand them over."

Hue shouted back. "And if we don't?"

"Then you'll join your comrades out here in whatever hell God has reserved for bureaucrats and communists."

Outside, the insurgents were working quickly. One was cutting the harness that bound the horses to the wagon. Several others were saddling up the peacekeeper's horses by the door. The last was providing first aid to his fallen friend. "He's in real bad shape, Jim," the insurgent hollered. "We got to get him back to Doc."

Wyatt felt ill. *Why did you even get involved, you big lunk?* He'd told Remi to stay out of it, but the man saw too much of his own suffering in Geary's story. "I served my country as a medic!" he'd said. "And I had a girl. And the UN deported me. Fuck the UN." *And now you've gone and gotten yourself all fucked up.*

Hue's voice broke his reverie. "Looks like you're going to lose a man," the agent called out.

Geary shouted back. "You've already lost four. We can make this six and two if that's how you want this to play out. This ends either with both of you dead—or with your guns and your prisoner in our hands. Your choice."

"What assurance do we have that if we hand over our weapons you won't kill us on the spot?" Hue's voice was flat. He could have been discussing quarterly reports.

"We're the good guys," Geary answered. "That's your fucking assurance, you space Nazi."

Hue looked at Wyatt and then at Bogin. He made a pow-pow sign with his finger at the sheriff. Bogin shook her head and pointed to the sky. He nodded, then yelled out to Geary. "Fine. We're going to toss our weapons to the floor."

"Smart man," Geary called back. "Pop the mags out, put the guns on safety, and kick them to the door." He paused. "Hey, sheriff, can you hear me?"

"I hear you, Geary," he rumbled.

"When they've disarmed themselves, give us a little shout, okay?"

"Will do."

Wyatt watched as the special agents popped the magazines out of their guns, pulled the slides to clear the chambers, and dropped them to the floor. Grudgingly they kicked them towards the doorway.

Hue shot a look of hate at Wyatt. "The UN has a long memory. And a long arm. We'll find you."

"You better hope you don't." Wyatt raised his voice. "They've disarmed. Weapons are in the doorway."

"Okay, we're coming in." Geary and the insurgents strode in and took over. In a few moments Wyatt was out of the cell and holstering his revolver at his hip. Hue and Bogin were locked up. Their faces were expressionless, almost placid.

Wyatt barely stopped himself from gloating over the change of circumstances. Then he thought about Remi, and his face grew dark. *I should shoot them.* Geary interrupted his reverie. "Come on, let's get out of here."

Outside, the insurgents had saddled up the three uninjured horses from the wagon team, and rounded up the six that the UN posse had ridden in on. With Wyatt, Geary, four insurgents, and one casualty, that left two horses extra to swap out if anybody's mount went lame. Wyatt ended up on a Palomino mare. They tied Remi to a large bay gelding. The big man was barely conscious, so Wyatt took the bay's lead.

"Where to, Geary?" he asked.

"There's a resistance camp about ten miles up in the mountains. It's got a doctor. We can get there in an hour if we ride hard."

He looked at Remi. "Let's do that."

Geary extended his hand. "I appreciate you not handing me in."

"I appreciate you coming back for me." They shook.

"Welcome to the resistance, Sheriff."

The resistance fighters rode west, out of the valley and into the lower slopes of the Cloud Mountains. There was heavy forest cover, pine and oak, and the going was slower than Wyatt liked, but the heavy canopy meant they'd be invisible to the implacable eyes of the UN's overhead satellites.

After an hour of hard riding, Wyatt's horse was nearly blown. Wyatt had been a horseman all his life, and he felt the horse lover's anguish at having to push a mount too hard. He had paid a price for the exertion, too, of course. He was covered in sweat and his thighs were chafing through his jeans. But Remi was worse. The big man was slumped over his horse like a corpse and he was exuding a smell that Wyatt didn't like at all. Remi didn't have much time left.

At the front of the line, Geary signaled for the band to slow down. The resistance leader trotted off the trail they'd been riding and into the underbrush. Wyatt followed suit, bringing up Remi's horse just behind. The others formed a queue and followed. After a minute, a voice rang out from the trees: "Desert!"

"Peace!" Geary called back. They'd made it.

The resistance camp was a cluster of low green tents, perhaps a dozen in all, arranged in a semi circle. The main avenue of approach was guarded by a rampart of broken brush reinforced with sandbags.

The riders began to dismount, and Wyatt turned his attention to Remi. The big man's body was slumped over his horse, only the ropes they'd tied keeping him mounted. Remi was too big for Wyatt to safely handle, but Geary made a signal with his hand and a couple of sturdy-looking camp dwellers were soon hustling to help get the big man off the horse.

They worked together to carry Remi into one of the tents. It was cluttered with medical supplies and smelled of antiseptic. The men deposited Remi on a clean pallet. He barely fit. One of the camp dwellers called out. "Kathleen! Need you!"

A woman entered. She was older than the other insurgents, but her hands had an ageless agility. "What happened to him?" Kathleen began cutting off the bloodied bandages to examine Remi's wounds.

"He got shot. Burst of UN flechettes to the shoulder," said Wyatt.

"He's lost a lot of blood," she said, applying firm pressure to the wound after a quick assessment of the injury. "Bing, get me iodine, forceps, gauze, a unit of O neg, and two units of saline. And bring that light over here, I need to see this up close." One of the other insurgents—Bing, he assumed—started rummaging through the supplies and gathering what was needed. Wyatt looked on with appreciation as the woman deftly went to work.

"Where'd you get your medical training?"

"On sheep," she said, without a trace of sheepishness. "I'm a vet. Hold the pressure here, would you . . . Bing, hand me the tourniquet." Remi's face was as white as a sheet and he was moaning softly, as if from somewhere far away. The doc found a vein and tapped it with practiced ease, starting an IV line to replace the fluids Remy had lost along the treacherous ride. She then scrubbed the site of the wound, soaking up the excess blood and revealing the mangled flesh beneath. Her forceps navigated the injury with careful precision. Wyatt watched, feeling powerless.

"I think that's it," she said finally. Bing pumped a fist. Wyatt let out a breath he didn't know he'd been holding.

"Looks like you know your way around a gun shot, Doc."

"Learned on the job." She picked up a half-inch long sliver of plastic she'd dug out of Remi's shoulder and held it up. "Your friend is lucky none of these fragments hit a major artery." She dropped the sliver on the table and began to stitch him up.

Wyatt laughed. "You should see him play poker. So he's going to be okay?"

"Well, his career as a major league pitcher is over." She tied the suture off, cut the excess, and began to neatly dress the wound. "But yeah."

Another man had come into the tent while they were talking. His face was a mass of scar tissue. "Doc, I need to do a scan," the scarred man said. He held up a palm-sized plastic contraption with a digital screen. "The UN sometimes plants nano-trackers in its bullets."

"Go to it, Tene," she said. "I'm about finished up."

Tene walked up and waved the scanner over the flechette slivers. It made a soft beep. He frowned, sending the scars on his face into twisting fractals. He looked at Wyatt and pointed the scanner at him. It made a louder beep.

"Did you get shot?"

Wyatt didn't like the way Tene was looking at him. "No. I sure didn't." The scarred man stepped closer. BEEP.

"GEARY!" shouted Tene. "He's carrying a tracker!"

Wyatt was surprised at how quickly the doctor could move. One moment she was putting away bandages, the next moment she was pointing a carbine at him. Bing drew a gun, too. Tene just stood there, holding the scanner next to him. BEEP. BEEP. BEEP.

The tent flap opened and Geary entered. He looked at the scene and his face contorted into a grimace. He grabbed Wyatt by the shirt. "I trusted you," Geary spat.

"I know." Wyatt held his hands palms out. "Look, I don't know what's happening here but I swear to you . . . I'm not some sort of UN spy."

The scanner wouldn't stop beeping. "He's lying," Tene said. "This fucker has led them right to us."

Wyatt pointed at the pallet. "Remi's my best mate. You think I arranged for him to get shot?" Remi groaned at the sound of his name. Geary relaxed his hold and stepped back.

"Okay, so then what happened?"

Wyatt closed his eyes. His mind raced. *Think. Maybe they implanted something on me. On my revolver? In my clothes?* Then he knew. He fumbled for his wallet. Produced the business card—Hue's business card. He held it in front of the scanner. BE-BE-BE-BE-BE-BEEP.

"Motherfuckers," said Geary. "I watched them give it to you."

"So now what?" said Wyatt.

Bing spoke up. "Standard doctrine will be to follow up with an air assault at nightfall. They'll come in by chopper looking to take us at a camp or base."

"Yeah, thanks, Mister UN. That's where we are," said Tene. "Our camp. I say we leave the tracker here and start moving right now."

The doctor looked over at Remi. "This guy's in no shape to move."

"Fine. He can stay behind," said Tene. "So can his friend."

"It's not going to go down like that," said Geary. "And it's a stupid idea. If the PKs get to the camp, they'll just follow our trail. This many horses and men, moving fast? We'll have a head start but it won't be enough. They've got—"

"What if the PKs don't come to the camp?" said Wyatt.

Tene waved the scanner at him. "You already led them here!"

"Hear me out. I haven't been here long. Not long enough to establish this as a camp. I'll saddle up a fresh mount and ride off right now with the tracker still in my pocket. As far as the PKs know, all I did was stop here and eat a bite. I'll circle around to the south. By the time they come at me, I'll be miles away, and they won't have any idea where our paths diverged."

"That could work," said Tene. "If you don't mind dying."

"It's not high on my to do list. But you let me worry about that. I just need a fresh horse." Wyatt scanned the crowd, waiting for someone to challenge him.

No one did. After a moment, Geary nodded. "Okay then."

Bing led him over to a dapple gray gelding. "This is Argus," he said.

Wyatt reached out and stroked the horse's muscled neck. He leaned forward, speaking in low tones, and blew his breath gently into the horse's nostril. Argus pricked his ears, flared his nostrils, and blew short, rapid breaths. Wyatt recognized it as an equine greeting. *This is my breath, this is who I am.* It was a brief but intimate exchange that built trust between rider and mount. Wyatt would need that trust for the ride ahead. "Let's get you saddled up, Argus."

He started tacking up his mount. Geary limped over with some saddlebags of water and food. "You don't have to do this, you know," he said. "I've avoided UN patrols before."

Wyatt shook his head. "Tene's plan won't work. And Remi can't ride. It'd be a death sentence for him."

"Let me do it," said Geary. "It's me they want."

Wyatt paused and pointed to Geary's wounded thigh. The bandages were stained with blood. "If you keep riding hard on that leg, you'll be in worse shape than Remi. Look—just see my mate right, eh? Besides, it's not just you they want anymore."

"I will." There was nothing else to say, so they finished tacking up the horse in silence.

Wyatt left the camp and rode south. The forest was dense, and the trails twisted through rugged foothills and perilous cliffs. But the sky overhead was a clean azure without clouds, and the westering sun was painting the rocky canyons the hue of amethyst. Argus had a powerful stride and soon the redoubt was miles behind them.

They kept up a good pace throughout the day. Even with the shade of the trees, it was hot and he and Argus were soaked with sweat. Wyatt wasn't quite sure which of them smelled more rotten— either way, it was pretty bad. The chafing on his legs from the unfamiliar saddle was worse.

He stopped to water Argus a few minutes before sundown. That was when he heard the throbbing sound of rotors in the distance. A moment after, he saw it, coming in from the east, a small black speck in the darkening sky.

Wyatt knew he had the benefit of the tree cover to keep the helicopter from seeing him easily. They'd be relying on electronic navigation—and they didn't know the land. That would be their mistake. Wyatt left the trail and started heading southwest towards Gorson's Gorge and the Griffon Peak tunnel.

After a few minutes, he came to the edge of the tree canopy, near the banks of a stream that cut through the middle of Gorson's Gorge. The stream was easy to ford here but doing so would expose him to aerial observation. *No way around it. Just do it fast.* He urged Argus forward. Water splashed up the horse's legs as they cantered through the ford. He spotted the UN chopper, a bare few hundred yards away, and it spotted him. The chopper shifted its vector and began to get rapidly closer.

He rode into the canopy cover on the far side of the stream, then veered the horse into a sharp right hand turn so they were cantering along the edge of the bank. Soon they connected with the abandoned road to the tunnel. He was wide out into the open now but Griffon

Peak was just ahead. He could see the cutaway of the old tunnel, a black maw opening into the mountain face. It was time to gallop.

Argus snorted, sweat foaming his neck, his hooves pounding on the old road. The helicopter was only two hundred yards away and closing. There was a rat-a-tat-tat of machine gun fire. Bullets exploded on the cracked pavement. He knew they needed to weave and dodge to throw off the machine-gunner's aim but it was hard at full gallop. *Run in a straight line and die. Decelerate and die.* He decided to die sprinting and kicked Argus on to even faster speed.

The tunnel was only twenty yards away now. Ten yards. Five yards. The helicopter had maneuvered again and a hail of gunfire was now spraying ahead of him—across the face of the tunnel, cutting him off. There was nothing to do but ride through it and pray.

His heart raced with his horse. He felt the heat and pressure of bullets whizzing past him at supersonic speeds. Argus stumbled and for a moment Wyatt thought they were going to die at the tunnel entrance. Then they were in!

Inside, the Griffon Peak tunnel was on the edge of collapse. The shoddy UN-sponsored construction was not aging well. The rock faces of the corridor were badly cracked and already overgrown with sickly gray-green vines. Chunks of the wall and ceiling littered the floor by the entrance. The helicopter wouldn't be able to follow, and he imagined the UN troops would be cautious about advancing into a half-collapsed tunnel in the darkness. He was counting on their cowardice.

Wyatt had only advanced a few yards when Argus lurched again. A moment later the horse fell, and Wyatt fell alongside him. The sheriff rose to a crouch and examined his horse. Blood was gushing from Argus's flanks. A burst of high-caliber flechette rounds had savaged the horse. The proud gelding had kept on galloping until he had gotten his rider to safety.

Argus looked up at him with soulful black eyes. The horse was beginning to spasm in agony. Wyatt laid a soothing hand on Argus's muzzle. With his other hand, he drew his revolver. "Easy, boy. Easy. Rest now." He pulled the trigger. The sound was loud in the tunnel, loud enough to muffle his choked cry.

When the horse was still, he stood up and ran into the darkness. As he ran, he flicked on a torch and began casting its pale spotlight onto the floor ahead, searching, searching. Behind him, he could hear the rumbling thunder of the chopper approaching.

Fifty yards down the tunnel he found what he was looking for. He got to work.

By the time Wyatt was finished, the rotor blades of the chopper had stopped humming. The sun was behind the mountain, so the chopper crew had brought the vehicle down right next to the entrance, where its spotlights could illuminate the tunnel.

A voiced called out. "It does not have to end like this, Wyatt." It was Bogin. "Today's *indiscretion* can be . . . overlooked. Just tell us where we can find resistance camp."

Wyatt said nothing. He was well back from the entrance, crouched behind an old dump wagon still loaded with debris. He listened, and waited for a familiar voice.

"If you make us do this the hard way, it will be very unpleasant for you," Hue called out. "But very pleasant for me."

There it was. The sheriff thumbed back the hammer on his revolver and peeked around the edge of the dump wagon. He counted eight black silhouettes against the chopper's spotlight—six with rifles and two with pistols. They'd reached the body of his horse, just a few yards inside the tunnel mouth. Wyatt watched as one of the figures—Hue, he thought—bent down and picked something up. Wyatt smiled. He'd left the business card on the horse as a going away present.

He'd left something else there, too. Something abandoned thirty years ago and nowadays very unstable.

"I told you not to find me," Wyatt called. Hue looked up just as the sheriff fired. His bullets slammed into the dynamite he'd tucked beneath the horse's body. There was a crash like thunder—then blackness.

Wyatt woke to a quiet world. He groaned, and his voice sounded muffled to his ears. A thick patina of dust billowed off his body as he stood up. There was dried blood around his nostrils and ears and his head pounded. *This is going to be the mother of all headaches.* Even so, he was intact. The dump wagon had sheltered him from the worst of the blast.

The same couldn't be said for the PKs. There was nothing left of them at all. The east end of the Griffon Peak tunnel was entirely choked with fallen rock and rubble. The tunnel entrance had become a tomb. Given its proximity, the helicopter outside had probably been wrecked, too. The sheriff surveyed his work with satisfaction. *I gave you a good burial, Argus.*

He began to lope slowly towards the western exit. The sun had risen by the time he made it out of the darkness, and he smiled as the light warmed his face.

INTERLUDE:
From Jimenez's *History of the Wars of Liberation*

Merely overplaying their hand and their power was not the limit of UN personnel foraying into criminality and vice. Indeed, the latter was much more common than the former, even if the former was common enough. Beyond turning ten- and eleven-year-olds of both sexes into prostitutes, smuggling of rare and precious metals, illegal hunting of Noah-preserved flora and fauna, many of them, including many of the very highest rank, involved themselves in drug smuggling.

In many ways, of course, drugs were ideal. This was especially true of huánuco, a close cognate of cocaine and derived from a plant that was an ancestor of old Earth's coca plant. While a suitcase full of refined gold might be found out because the of the weight's tendency to derange calculations for shuttle flight back to the Earth fleet, or from a ship back down to Old Earth, to say nothing of the suspicious way such a satchel had to be carried aboard, a satchel full of the drug in purest form was even more valuable and weighed no more than the clothing it displaced.

Among Old Earth's neo-aristocrats, moreover, the drug had a special snob appeal, because only the very connected, indeed, could obtain it.

11.
HUÁNUCO

Lawrence Railey[12]

Tijuana, Mexico

At first, Thomas Romano thought the incessant pounding was the effects of previous night's tequila throbbing in his skull. Blurry images of that night started replaying in his mind, downing shot after shot with his roommate, dancing with some pretty local girl whose name couldn't quite penetrate the brain fog, stumbling outside and falling on the cold stone. He couldn't even quite recall how he'd made it home.

The knocking became more urgent. "Immigration! Open up!" Someone yelled in accented English.

"Tom, Tom, wake up! It's the *federales!*" his roommate David exclaimed annoyingly. The thought didn't quite compute in Tom's liquor-addled mind. What would the federals want with him? People came to Tijuana all the time to drink and act like idiots. Had he done something else last night? He couldn't remember enough to be sure.

Tom groaned and tried to get to his feet, stumbling, a cold spike of fear acting to sober him just enough to avoid falling back onto his bed. An empty beer bottle rolled off the bed with him and crashed to the floor.

---

12 Lawrence Railey is a software engineer, musician, amateur historian, and part-time pundit. His attentions are split between writing software, producing various forms of electronic music, and writing speculative commentaries on Late Antiquity, the fall of the Roman Empire, and the Byzantine period that followed. His musings on the decline of the modern West can be found at *thedeclination.com*.

The door flew in suddenly, and Tom's eyes grew wide. David stood frozen somewhere between panic and fear, his arms in the air.

"Thomas Romano, David Doherty." The officer spoke in confident, if heavily accented English. It was not a question. Behind him, a trio of well-armed officers stood ready. Tom's brain was slow to compute this, but realization came eventually. *This is fucking serious, if these were locals, they'd wouldn't know our names, they wouldn't be speaking English. What the hell did we do?*

"Yes, sir." Tom managed, his body battling between adrenaline overload and lethargic hangover. "That's us . . . "

David nodded, sweat dripping from his brow, whether from the fear, or from the effects of the recent UN-enforced air-conditioning ban, Tom couldn't be sure.

The officer smiled cruelly, and Tom knew that the excrement was about to encounter an air circulation device.

"You are currently residing in Mexico illegally. Your visas have expired as of last month, July Twelfth."

Shit, Tom thought. Their visas *had* expired. Getting them renewed had been an impossibility. UN flunkies didn't care much for people movement, unless they were the right people going to the right places. He and Dave didn't fall into either category. It had just been too expensive to stay in the United States on a developer's salary. Mexico, at least, had a long tradition of neglectful government. Neither of them had seriously expected the authorities to actually *enforce* the law, especially with American dollars smoothing the way.

American dollars, Tom realized, that might smooth his way out of this, too. He gestured to a small stack of crumpled bills on his workstation. "If you'll just allow us to . . ." he realized he had to be careful. Bribery, or *la mordida* as it was often called here, was an art in Mexico. "Well, we can pay the fines straight away, sir. And then we'll go get our papers in order . . . "

The officer smirked with wry amusement, his black mustache twitching slightly. Tom felt a fresh surge of anxiety. *It isn't going to work this time.*

"You do not have enough for that, *gringo*." He looked at the wad of crumpled up cash and made a quick mental calculation. There were several c-notes in that pile. "But, you may each have a few minutes to get your things. One bag only."

Fortunately, Tom thought, everything of value he had probably would fit in his backpack, and it was likewise for David. He nodded, carefully reaching for his bag, the officers tracking his movements. They looked itchy enough, Tom decided, best to be slow and obvious. Getting deported was bad enough. Getting shot by a corrupt cop was much worse.

His tablet computer was the first to go into his bag. It was the only thing he owned that was really worth anything. It wasn't the latest model, of course. It was a decade out of date, scratched up rather badly, and had a thin crack splitting the gorilla glass. But technological advancement had slowed to a crawl in recent years. It was still plenty fast and portable enough.

More importantly, without his rig, he couldn't earn anything. A pair of headphones, a quick selection of clothes, a solar charger, for Mexican power was never exactly reliable, and a few basic toiletries followed into the bag. The officer looked at him impatiently. The stack of bills that had been on David's workstation had already disappeared. In some things, even the Mexican authorities were quite efficient.

An ailing multicolored bus idled outside, coughing with a cloud of noxious diesel smoke. The trio of *federales* herded them inside. Stifling heat beat down from the late morning sun, and the bus was even worse, smelling of sweat and farts. The officer smiled again, and Tom felt the fear return. He had an inexplicable feeling that the worst was yet to come.

"Have a nice trip, *amigo*." The officer said ominously, remaining behind as the other three boarded the bus, facing the involuntary passengers.

David looked up and grinned wryly. "We aren't dead. So, we've got that, which is nice."

"Do you have a movie quote for everything?" Tom said, rubbing his temples, trying to banish the headache and his anxiety, and failing at both. "No, strike that. I already know the answer."

Sweat was soaking his T-shirt within minutes, and the guards offered no water.

Wherever we're going, we better get there soon, I was already dehydrated. And the road is doing my stomach no favors, either.

It was bad enough that even the thought of the local tap water wasn't as unappealing as it should have been. Decaying and half-abandoned towns dotted the sides of the cracked pavement of the freeway. In America, islands of relative prosperity still existed in some rural areas despite the crushing taxes. In Mexico, the countryside looked like a war zone. Parts of it probably were. UN levies stripped whole towns bare.

After two hours of stifling misery, the bus slowed and turned off the dusty, pothole-strewn highway. Tom forced himself to look out the window, the sunlight making his head pound. A large shuttle, silvery gray, sparkled under the sun, a self-propelled loading crane looming large beside it. UN markings covered the rocket, save for a small Mexican flag painted crudely in one corner. The booster rockets alone were bigger than tankers. The main body, cargo module, and personnel modules were larger, still.

It was only then that Tom realized what had been so amusing to the *federales*. They weren't getting deported from Mexico, they were being deported from *Earth*.

Tom turned to face the guards as David stared, mouth agape with a mixture of wonder and horror. "There must be a mistake. Send us back to America, not . . . this!" Bile curdled up in his throat, and he fought the urge to hurl, wishing the whole thing was some terrible liquor-infused nightmare.

One of the guards laughed. "No mistake, *gringo*." He leaned forward, a predatory expression on his face. "You may not know this, but we don't really like you Americans. You come here, you fuck our women, drink our beer, always party-party with you. And now the party is over. Time to pay your tab, *señor*."

David turned around, pleading. "If it's money you want, we can get more. Yes, we are good developers. Experienced. The best. We can get much more. We'll pay you as much as you want!"

The guard shook his head. "If you had the money, you wouldn't be here. Since you don't . . ." He shrugged and muttered something to the driver. The conversation was over.

Heat rose like a mirage from the scorching tarmac. Tom's headache worsened appreciably as he tried to shield his eyes from the sun's ruthless glare. His stomach chose this particular moment to give up its see-saw battle against projectile vomiting, and he hurled all over the tarmac. *Federales* around him pointed and laughed. UN technicians hurried about them as a Mexican UN official stood still throughout the seeming chaos, staring at the small crowd of unfortunates. Most of those around him were thoroughly Mexican, but there were a few other foreigners in the bunch, too.

"Sir, there has to be some mistake," Tom pleaded. "We're Americans we're supposed to be . . . well deported I guess, but not in that!"

The official laughed. "You are here illegally," he pronounced, "Mexico takes a dim view of this, *gringo*. We could have sent you to prison, but this is better I think. Enjoy your trip." That he apparently viewed Terra Nova as *worse* than a Mexican prison bode ill for their future. His cruel grin stretched from ear to ear as they were lined up with the rest of the malcontents and pushed toward the spacecraft.

As the hatch shut behind them, Tom realized he would never set foot on Earth again. UN livery covered his field of view. Everything in the spacecraft was covered in cheap blue United Nations fashion, and he felt hatred surge up within him. For Mexico, for the UN, for cheap Tijuana liquor, for the cultural and economic decay that drove them out of America in the first place.

David was fighting the shock, a stoic expression on his face, mumbling something that sounded vaguely like an appeal to God. Tom merely stowed his bag in the provided compartment, and sat quietly in his assigned seat, fastening the restraints under the watchful eyes of the guards. It was all surreal to him, like a nightmare he kept expecting to wake up from. Groans echoed around him from the other passengers. Concentrated human misery filled the ship. Few, if any, of the passengers appeared to be volunteers.

The spacecraft itself was spartan in the extreme. Whichever UN agency had built it had thought little about luxuries. It appeared to have been constructed to get as many people into orbit as quickly and cheaply as possible. Where, Tom knew from the Internet videos, a starship would be waiting to take them through the crossing to Terra Nova.

Nobody ever came back from Terra Nova, Tom thought.

Soon, the massive engines pushed him into his seat. He found himself blacking out, the combination of shock, g-forces, and lingering hangover too much for his stressed mind to handle any longer.

Constancia, Cienfuegos, Terra Nova

Tom scanned the rock-hard bread in his hand like a miner inspecting a piece of rock for the slightest hint of gold. If there was any nutritional value in the morsel, he couldn't detect it. The bread was almost as dirty as his leathery, sun-battered skin.

"I'm tired of this rock, I'm tired of Cienfuegos, I'm tired of the same goddamned stale bread, the heat, the water that makes a man shit his body weight if he neglects to boil it. Most of all, I'm tired of living on the UN's people landfill in space." Tom finished his complaint and flicked the morsel of stale bread into his mouth. *Waste not,* he thought sourly as he chewed the sorry excuse for food.

Looking to David, he shielded his eyes from the glare of sunlight creeping in through their mud hut's open-air windows. David had once been a rather portly fellow, a man of many beers and pizzas. Pizza delivery, of course, did not exist on Terra Nova, and when beer could be found, it was usually rotgut. All of David's excess fat had long since disappeared. His Irish constitution had once been fair and freckled, but now, in the places it wasn't burned, it was almost as tan as Tom's own Mediterranean tone. Still, there could be no doubt that David was poorly suited to Cienfuegos. Tom could at least sometimes pass for a local if he kept his mouth shut.

David looked up from his tablet computer and nodded his agreement. "Yeah. I miss it, too. The work sucks; my back is *killing* me. The beer is shit. But the women at least . . . they aren't all batshit crazy." If there was anything in life that motivated David more than food and booze, it was women. *Not,* Tom chuckled to himself, *that David is any good with them.* But knocking shops were the one thing Cienfuegos had in abundance, and every once in a while, even David could afford an hour or two.

The smile faded. They'd been lucky to keep their tablets and solar chargers. No one else appeared to have managed even that much. The stored movies, music, and books had kept both of them at least partially sane, despite the brutal farm work they'd scored. Life on Terra Nova was a curious mix of the modern and the medieval, with scraps of technology scavenged from the UN or smuggled in by the colonists themselves present here and there in a society otherwise sent back to the late Iron Age.

"The quota's gone up this week, you know," David mentioned as he finished the last of his bread. "Gotta keep the drug lord in his drugs."

Tom frowned. "You shouldn't call him that."

"Why not?" David asked. "Everyone else does."

"He grows tobacco. And Terra Novan tobacco is almost harmless. It's not the same thing."

"Eh, whatever. He still looks like a drug lord. And you know the rumors around the village. Some cocaine-like shit he's growing for the Earthers on the side. Locals call it *huánuco*."

"I don't want to know about that, and neither do you." Tom replied. *Because if any of those rumors are true, we don't want to end up dead. Nobody on Terra Nova could afford it; that would mean the only potential buyers would be blue helmets.*

Soon their shift would start, and it didn't do well to be late for work on Carlos's fields. Drug lord or not, he did not have a reputation for excessive tolerance.

"Well, we need to eat. Or at least I do, anyway," David quipped, standing up and sliding on his ratty excuse for a shirt, for what mediocre protection it might provide against the sun. "Even if it tastes like purified ass."

Tom stepped outside their meager hut into a view straight from a tourist's dream. Sandy beach stretched out to clear blue water, so clean you could see the bottom. Luscious palms graced the sides of the beach, swaying gently in the morning breeze. It was the kind of view, Tom noted, that millionaires and UN high hats would have paid a pretty penny for back on Earth.

And I'd give all of it up in a second for some air conditioning and a cold beer, Thomas thought, though it felt hollow despite the truth of it. What he really wanted, he realized, was to stop being the universe's butt monkey. He'd fled America because of high cost of living. No choice in the matter. He'd been exiled to Terra Nova because of the UN, and he'd had no choice in that either. Now he was farming tobacco in a tropical hellhole, and there wasn't any more choice in that than there had been in the rest.

I've never thought of myself as a fatalist, but Terra Nova is gonna wind up converting me.

A soft tune carried on in his ear buds, as he enjoyed one last song before a hard day slaving away in the fields. He could almost imagine, just for a moment, lying back on the beach in Tijuana, staring absently at some pretty girl, sipping on a margarita. Tom dropped his tablet and solar charger into his bag and strapped it to his belt. Time for reality.

The sand was hot and crept over the top of the Terra Novan sandals he wore. His new Nikes, and David's own Adidas, had been among the first things to go after they were dumped onto this rock. Their enormous value had kept them in food and drink just long enough to land a job in Carlos's fields and avoid complete starvation. So, the walk to the fields was long and uncomfortable. Somebody, somewhere in the village of Constancia, was an awful lot more comfortable than he was at the moment.

Tom frowned as he approached the gate to Carlos's plantation. Burly enforcers were waiting for him, and one of them barred his way.

"Stop," the man said simply, in accented English. The handgun of Earth manufacture on his hip suggested that disagreement was unwise.

David stopped, almost too late to avoid running into Tom.

"Hey pay attention to—what? What's going on?"

"Carlos wants to talk to both of you. You will come with me."

Tom nodded, cursing another situation in which he was no more than a passenger. David trudged along behind and whispered. "See, I told you he was a drug lord." Tom elbowed David's now nonexistent gut.

"Shuttup you moron. You're gonna get us shot."

Slipping back into her robe, Captain Pamela Andego dipped her finger in the *huánuco* bowl and pondered how she wound up in the ass-end of space, serving as the high admiral's personal plaything. There were benefits, of course. Rumored youth extension treatments, an endless vacation, the sort of life she'd always felt was her due but had somehow remained just out of reach. Serve another tour over Terra Nova, do what had to be done, they said, and it could all be hers. An endless carrot dangling in front of her like she was a human donkey. Somehow, it never came true. But the high admiral came to ride her anyway.

High Admiral Hortzmann was already done with her, leaving without much fuss. Scents of wine, sweat, and sex started to fade as the cabin air circulators wafted it all away. Equipment and toys had vanished into their respective cubbies. She felt cleaner then, the whole thing distant; a mere memory. With the *huánuco* high hitting her, Pam could *almost* forget any of it had happened.

Far beyond, the distant flare of a main engine burn caught her attention. The scheduled colony ship making was her final orbital insertion. She sighed heavily.

New colonists, new problems, she thought. *Maybe I can use a few of them as compensation for all my troubles. Better them than the high admiral, anyway.*

More importantly, however, the cargo holds of the returning ships would serve nicely for her own purposes. She had to be frugal with the space, she knew. The margin of error for space travel was exceedingly small. But enough of the *huánuco* could be smuggled back to Earth to pad her accounts sufficiently.

A few more trips, and I'll have enough to escape even the reach of the high admiral's lechery, she thought, grinning with anticipation.

The comm receiver chirped and she tapped the controls, lightly touching the key for "encrypted." A familiar, slimy, scarred face greeted her. Some men were ugly because of age. Others were endearing, despite otherwise gross physical features. Still others possessed a big, trollish, intimidating ugliness. Lieutenant Slade Cranston was just slimy, without even a trace of anything salvageable. She tried to ignore the bruised, half-naked local woman strung up in the background. Cranston didn't even care to pan the camera away.

"What do you want, Lieutenant?" She asked, inspecting her nails absently for traces of the drug. She had assigned the lieutenant planet-side on Cienfuegos, ostensibly to ride herd on her sailors when they rotated down for shore leave and entertainment of the sort even sailors in space seemed addicted to. But his real assignment was to run her smuggling operation on the ground. That it also kept him far away from her was a definite bonus. Some took occupation duty out of ambition, others out of boredom, or to escape political disfavor back on Earth. Cranston had clearly volunteered for it out of sadistic glee, the chance to work his will in a place as devoid of law as any that had ever existed.

"We've received the *huánuco*. It's ready for transport. Containers loaded into our shuttle and ready for transfer. Carlos did good this time, we're ahead of the estimated quota by around ten percent."

Pamela didn't want to think about what Cranston had done to get that extra ten percent out of Carlos. It was probably better for her conscience not to know, what she *did* know of his methods utterly disgusted her. If he hadn't been so useful, she would have been tempted to throw the slimy little man out of an airlock.

"Use auto pilot when you send the load up. I don't need one of your idiot flyboys getting high and drawing attention to himself this time." She cut the line before he could say anything else. That particular incident had been close. Too close to discovery for her comfort. Drug smuggling, she knew, was highly illegal in a technical sense, but it was common enough among the occupation forces, and was generally tolerated within reasonable limits *if one was discreet about it*. A *huánuco*-addled pilot nearly crashing into the main drive of the *Angela Merkel* certainly didn't count as particularly discreet.

For a moment she took in the vastness of space, the creeping terminator of the planet below, and imagined that she was returning home laden with spoils and political appointments, far away from drug deals, brewing revolutions, unruly reactionaries, and imposing high admirals.

Her comlink chirped. "Captain to the bridge."

She sighed.

Carlos's plantation manor loomed ahead of them, a sad little structure by Earther standards, but a veritable mansion to Terra Novan eyes. Most of it was even made of stone and stucco instead of the usual dried mud and half-rotten wood.

Tom took in the foyer, marveling for a moment that it was so cool inside the structure. A water fountain bubbled in the center, sucking heat from the air and making the temperature almost bearable. How they managed that without electricity, he could not say. But it was luxurious after months of slaving away under the heat of an alien sun.

Carlos appeared from around the corner, his modern linen suit crisp and clean, despite a couple of well-hidden patches. In a world of rags, he was the stand-out exception. While he was rather short, and well-fed by Terra Nova standards, the drug lord was quite fit, possessing a pair of broad shoulders and arms that looked like they could crush a man's neck with ease. If his hair was more gray than brown, he was still quite intimidating. But despite his deadly reputation in the village, it was not an unfriendly face which greeted them. A hard face, Tom realized, but not unfriendly.

He extended his hand in welcome. "*Ah, como estas, señores.* Come in, come in. Here, sit." His English was clear, pleasant, and only slightly accented. Sitting down next to the cool fountain, he motioned for the pair to join him. A beautiful olive-skinned young woman approached, setting down a tray with fresh fruits, a rough green bottle and some freshly rolled and clipped cigars. *If she's a servant,* Tom thought, *I'm an Oscar Mayer hot dog.* She had the look of a hardened woman, and the long bowie knife strapped to her hip only accentuated that observation. Nonetheless she, like Carlos, was not unfriendly.

"My daughter, Elena," Carlos explained. "Fruit? Cigars? Rum?" He offered generously.

David, naturally, was smitten by Elena almost immediately, despite the deadly seriousness of the situation. Carlos's eyebrow rose slightly, but if it bothered him, he said nothing. *Don't be a fucking idiot, David,* Tom thought.

Tom nodded quickly, wondering if they were going to be rewarded for something, or if they were about to be executed. Something wasn't right. And there were plenty of stories in the village about Carlos that involved murder, and worse.

Just what in the hell does he want from us?

The chief enforcer held up a priceless butane lighter of Earth manufacture as Tom puffed lightly on the cigar, trying to keep his hands from trembling, and failing miserably. Apparently oblivious to the danger, David merely smiled and accepted his own graciously.

Carlos smiled comfortingly. "*Señor,* I do not know what they say of me in the village, but you have nothing to fear from me. You have done me no wrong."

Tom tried to return the smile. "I thought well . . . maybe . . . we are not so good at farming and . . ." They needed the job. It wasn't like they could dial a recruiter on Terra Nova. It was work the fields or starve to death. Or worse. Rumors of guerrilla bands outside the village were legion. They did not have a reputation for liking anybody, much less two fish-out-of-water gringos.

"No, no *señor*. We already knew that." He waved his hands as if it were a mere trifle. "It is okay. You are getting better. You do not shirk your work, which is better than some." The woman offered a glass of rum to both developers. "No ice. And the rum is not so good as on Earth. But it is something."

Taking a sip, Tom tried not to gag. It was indeed rather foul, though somewhat less terrible than the usual Terra Novan fare. Carlos chuckled. The beautiful-yet-dangerous woman sauntered away, and David was clearly torn by a desire to check out her ample posterior, and the common sense that doing it in front of the "drug lord" was probably an efficient way to commit suicide. Common sense won, Tom noted as he watched his friend's struggle out of the corner of his eye, but only just.

"Yes, *señor*, my opinion of the rum is the same as yours. But now to business." He puffed on his own cigar lightly and set it down on his ashtray. "You are both IT people, right?"

David nodded, his attention restored. "Well, we were once. Not like they're hiring down here though."

Stroking his chin, Tom pondered that for a moment. *What could he possibly want us to do. Unless . . .* It hit him suddenly. *He knows we have the computers. Shit, he must want them,* he thought anxiously. They had been careful to hide the machines from prying eyes, as they both knew they could be killed for the things. Tablets surely had immense value to the locals and evidently they had not been careful enough in hiding them. Carlos had many eyes in the village. The fear returned. It was the last real link they had to old Earth. The last piece of technology on this twisted Gilligan's Island in space.

"Ah! Very good!" Carlos grinned. "You have your own devices, no?"

David's grin fell away, coming late to the same realization, and he glanced at Tom warily.

Cat's out of the bag, I guess, Tom thought, noting Carlos's men around the manor, *it's not like I have a choice here.* He nodded reluctantly. "Yes, we have them." Giving them up would be a terrible blow. The music, games, and old movies stored on them were about the only things that kept him sane.

"Good. I have a better job for you then, a way you can earn much more than the scraps you get for harvesting my crop." The grin on Carlos's face fell away, and a predatory expression flashed for a moment.

"The *pitufos*. Smurfs in your language. Blue helmets. You worked for them on Earth once, yes?"

David took that one. "Yeah. Much good it did us. The blue helmets kicked us off Earth. Or at least their Mexican lackeys did."

"I have heard your story from the other workers, yes. Good. I need your help with them." He picked up his cigar and took a long drag, the cloud of smoke obscuring his face for a moment. "The *pitufos*, they come and take . . . things. My best cigars, of course, but sometimes . . . they take other things. Tell us to do things at gunpoint." His expression was pained and dangerous, and Tom saw murder in his eyes, mixed with a strange sadness that smoldered through the hazy cigar smoke like the eyes of the Devil himself. Tom almost flinched despite himself. "You know how it is with them."

As David fished absently through the fruit left by the woman, Tom's thoughts sifted through those words. If the rumors in the village were true, he was probably supplying UN smugglers with alien drugs. *But that's not the issue,* Tom's thoughts were confused, *why would a drug lord want to kill off his buyers?* There was something personal in all this, something very precious that had been taken by the smurfs. Something that transcended profit.

"I understand." He really didn't, but Tom felt there was no other choice but to go along for the moment.

"Good. Know this." Carlos downed the remaining rum in his glass in one quick shot. "We are done with the *pitufos*. Not even here, on this world, will they leave us in peace. We must rid ourselves of them. But they have ships up there," he pointed casually toward the sky. "They have drones, and radios, and sensors. Many things. And they record everything. This has made it difficult for us."

"Do you have radios of your own?" Tom asked cautiously.

"*Sí*. But they don't do us much good. They can find us when we use them and send men and aircraft to hunt us. So, we rarely use them. We can trick some of their sensors and drones, but it's difficult. And we don't know what their ships can really do. This is why you are here."

"What do you want us to do?" David asked, having cleared most of the provided snacks.

"Disrupt them. Annoy them. Demoralize them. Break their communications. Make them pay less attention to us or think we are somewhere else. Tell us what you can of their capabilities. I don't know exactly—but whatever you can do. Cause as much trouble for them as you can. We will do the rest." Rage simmered beneath Carlos's demeanor. Tom knew he didn't really have a choice here either, and he sighed. A casual glance confirmed the enforcers were still watching the exchange. There was no way the plantation master was going to let them live with this information if they did not agree to work for him.

But then, Tom thought wryly, *we already work for him. What difference does it make if we pick tobacco or fuck with blue helmets? At least this won't suck as badly as slaving away in the sun.*

Carlos continued. "If you do this, you will eat and drink well. You will have favor with us, no one in the village will touch you. You may even have these back." He presented them with their original shoes, priceless treasures despite the extra wear they had clearly suffered. David gasped in shock. Tom merely held Carlos's gaze and gave a slight nod of appreciation. The blisters on his feet already seemed to feel better just *looking* at their original shoes. On Terra Nova, these were worth *months* of food.

Carlos continued. "And if you wish it, I can have you taken all the way to the *gringo* sector when your task is done, 'South Columbia,' they call it. It is not an easy journey, but I will get you there safely if you want."

Tom didn't want to know what the penalty for saying no would be. Such a death might be quick. But it was an offer he would've accepted regardless of the implied threat, and Carlos probably knew that. For his part, David merely nodded enthusiastically. Anything that didn't involve slow starvation was sure to be popular with David. Juice trickled down his chin, and Tom wondered briefly if he'd fatten up again now that decent food was back on the menu.

"Yes . . . we will help you." Tom agreed. *Besides,* Tom thought, *this will be fun. Fuck the smurfs, and the ship they flew us in on.*

Anxiety was still there, but there was a hint of excitement, too. He puffed nervously on the cigar, wondering where all this would lead. The UN might kill them, Carlos might tire of them and have them killed, or things might go relatively well, and they'd be fighting a war against the UN with nothing more than two tablets and a few armed thugs. And he *still* had no choice in anything, not really.

At least it was better than stale bread and shitty shoes, though.

It was one thing to agree to cause trouble for Carlos's smurfs, it was quite another to actually do it, Tom realized. He worked the laser-projected virtual keyboard that folded out from his tablet. He looked up and motioned for David to come over. "Check this out."

Tom pulled up a photoshop of the high admiral being interviewed by an AP journalist, with several loincloth-covered, which is to say bare-breasted, Terra Novan women of various ethnicities behind him, captioned with "of course I support diversity, haven't you seen my harem?" The view count was through the roof, though most of the occupation force was far too savvy to actually share the meme openly.

Most of the occupiers were on a much smaller facsimile of the Internet, scaled down, with the comm relays in major bases and orbiting starships serving as backbones. Security was generally quite poor, for the UN hadn't seen much need for it when most of the devices even capable of accessing the network were in the hands of their people. For weeks, Tom had composed memes and posted long anti-UN screeds under anonymous burner accounts. David had spent his time digging around for deeper levels of access.

At first Carlos had seemed quite amused with their antics. The major network hub for Cienfuegos was the starship *Angela Merkel*, in geosynchronous orbit above. Most traffic went through there, and so he had presented Carlos with a meme based on the ship's insanely hot captain.

Tom had sketched out "The Smurfs of Terra Nova" in old pinup style using a picture of Pamela Andego, the captain of the *Angela Merkel*. He altered her into a smurf with a provocative little bikini and a suggestive smile, her hands on her hips and breasts thrust prominently forward, her bikini barely holding her breasts in. An army of slobbering, hungry smurf soldiers drooled behind her, tongues lolling out. Each featured a blue helmet with "UN" emblazoned on it. That one *did* merit several shares.

Carlos's grin when he saw it was both hateful and amused. *Maybe he won't murder us in our sleep and take back our shoes after all,* Tom had thought. *Probably not, anyway.*

After a moment, Carlos had decided to explain a little of his hostility. "You know, with enough beer, the sailors sometimes tell our whores that the captain is also a whore. She sold her body to get her command, they say. Perhaps you can use that."

After that, a steady stream of memes had resulted, and two weeks had passed with little results other than shitposts. David, naturally, had been the first to notice that the once plentiful food and drink was starting to thin out a little. There were more enforcers hanging around them, too. *Carlos isn't going to wait much longer. We need a big win, and we need it soon,* Tom realized.

Some of the enforcers had even been making bets on how long they would survive. "Meg bait in a week," Enrique had said. Jose had disagreed. He figured they had a whole two weeks before Carlos tired of them. Everybody else thought both were being extremely optimistic. The key, Tom knew, was the VPN. That was where the juicy information would be.

Getting on the wireless network and worming their way into the occupation's social media networks had been an easy enough task for David, who had been a first-rate network engineer back on old Earth. And Tom's memes were doing *something*. The overall tone of social media had changed dramatically since the anonymous posts began. Demoralization was definitely happening at *some* level, he could tell. But the overall effect was difficult to quantify in any real way. It wasn't enough.

"We've got news, web forums, social media, public chats, hell there's even an imageboard on here. The whole damned occupation force is on this shit. Even the sailors." He had explained to Carlos after David cracked the semi-public network.

Much chaos could be sown on an imageboard, he knew. UN censors had been after the "wretched hives" of cisheteropatriarchal hate speech for decades, but Tom had always been able to find them on the dark web. Terra Novan networks, far away from the professional bureaucrats in the Department of Economic and Social Affairs, were far more lax in their censorship campaigns. He'd found the imageboards on the first day.

And he had. Pointing out the hypocrisy of the occupiers was easy enough. Carlos had even supplied a list of rapes, murders, and all manner of drunken sexual antics and drug crimes committed by the *pitufos*. It was a *very* long list. And that had been in Cienfuegos and neighboring areas alone. Some of the soldiers were of a decent sort, but the reality of the occupation was wearing upon them. Others didn't care and used the locals as playthings and drug suppliers, but that was useful information in itself.

Still, without access to the secured network, it was hopeless, and Carlos would surely cast them aside sooner or later.

"I give up, man. I can't even get in the fucking VPN. I don't even *see* the network. I know it's there, but . . ." Exasperated, Tom turned to David. If there was going to be a network miracle, it would have to come from him.

"I think I figured it out," David said optimistically. "I'm pretty sure it's just using a standard token generator. Real basic shit. But I can't brute force it. Not with this hardware. I've tried, and it just isn't working." he gestured to his tablet. "If we got our hands on a physical device, maybe then I could do something . . . but I've no idea how the fuck we do that, dude."

Social engineering was Tom's domain. There had to be a way to get his hands on one of the sailor's devices. After a few hours, the idea came to him. It was simple enough, but if Carlos didn't like it, they were probably screwed.

Before he could lose his nerve, he turned to the chief goon, Enrique. "I need to speak to Carlos. I think I have a way to get him what he wants." The burly guard nodded silently and vanished. His ability to move so quietly despite his muscular bulk was always unnerving to both programmers.

Carlos entered a few moments later. The friendly expression had worn thin, and Tom could detect impatience in the man's gaze. Though the drug lord said nothing, he got the message loud and clear: *don't waste any more of my time.*

Tom dived right into it. "Sir, David cracked their local social media network, but there's nothing big in it. We've caused a lot of mischief in there with memes and social media. Some disinformation, demoralization and that kind of shit. But we could do more if we could get deeper access. The other network is protected by two-factor authentication." He fumbled a moment trying to think of how to explain it.

David continued for him, catching on to the idea. The two of them had always made a good development team, as they tended to think along similar lines. "Some of their senior officers will probably have an access token which generates rotating random keys, usually on their smartphones." Tom frowned, they weren't exactly smartphones, but he supposed the description was close enough to do. "If we got our hands on one, we might gain some access to the *Angela Merkel*'s network, at least at some basic level, since the local uplink is connected to that vessel. Give me a couple hours with one, and we could probably crack it. But only if they don't know it's been taken. If they know it's lost or stolen, they will cut off the access."

Tom nodded his agreement. "We need this if we're going to take this to the next level, sir."

Carlos considered this for a few moments then nodded gravely. "I will see what I can do. But if I do this for you, I expect a return on my investment. Soon."

Tom nodded his agreement quickly.

"Now let me see what I can do."

Not just any whore would do for this job.

Martina Garcia's hut, however neat it was, stank of sweat and sex, a smell that had overwhelmed even the native odors of Terra Nova. A gold cross dangled from her neck, her only possession of value if one didn't count her physical attributes. For a woman who had spent most of her youth on Terra Nova, she retained a great deal of beauty. Large, firm breasts topped a tiny, supple waist, in a traditional hourglass shape. These had served her well enough, as had her . . . flexibility with her clients.

"Martina," Carlos asked, glancing sideways at the unusually large Christian symbol fastened to one wall of her hut, "do you have among your clientele any of the . . ." Carlos pointed his finger skyward, in misplaced but perfectly understandable paranoia.

The hooker cast her eyes low. "You know I do, Don Carlos, many of them. A girl's got to . . . "

He made a gentle shushing motion. "No shame, child, no shame. Yes, a girl's got to eat. But how do you know when to schedule them? How do you know to free up the time?"

Without a word she reached fingers down in between breasts

ample and firm, pulling out a small and thin grayish device, a UN communicator. "They gave me this," she said, brightly.

"Child," said Carlos, "for this be all thy sins forgiven. Now tell me about your . . . mmm . . . your clients."

"Well, you know, Don Carlos, men need to talk . . ."

There were other pretty girls near the local base that might compete with her more effectively, were it not for her specialty. Even here, far away from Earth, there were those sailors who had peculiar desires. For them was the other, far larger, wooden cross tied up on the other side of her modest hut. This one was constructed in the manner of a Saint Andrews cross, and it was mostly used to service those among the sailors who possessed a sadomasochistic streak.

Her flogger cracked, and the man tied to her cross moaned, enjoying the pain. She walked around it to face him on the other side of the cross, giving the sailor an enticing view of her naked body. His attention was fully upon her, overwhelmed with lust, but to make sure, her fingers traced along his shoulders and his back, where the skin was warmed by the impact of the flogger. He shivered intensely.

"I have a special treat for you . . ." she said seductively, her hand reaching lower.

Her eyes flicked only for the briefest of moments as a small child rifled through the man's pants and escaped with the smartphone. *Viva la revolucion!* she thought. *Viva libertad!*

Thanks to Carlos, David had managed to image the smartphone before the kid ran off to slip it back to wherever he had nabbed it.

"How did the kid . . ." David began to ask before Carlos shushed him with a very serious, "You don't really wanna know."

No matter; they had a working image of the device running in a virtual machine, and the security token worked as promised. The access hadn't been cut. That would do well enough.

This is amazing, Tom thought to himself, parsing through the owner's files, *everything I need is in here.* Whoever Samuel Ellis had been, besides an unwilling stooge, he had a decent amount of access to the communications systems, both at the local base and on board the *Angela Merkel*. Tom recognized a kindred, if somewhat unimaginative, mind in the man's e-mails and communications. The patsy was some kind of mid-level IT flunky. While Carlos probably would have preferred control over the ship's weapons or something, a thing that would *never* have been possible via network control unless the ship builders were utter morons, which they generally weren't, Tom was still very pleased with this. There was much mischief that could be caused from Samuel's position.

Not the least of which was a bit of social engineering.

Carlos watched them work from behind, and it was quite unnerving for both of them. Hours went by as both developers poured through the VPN and the device image, looking for potential avenues for mischief. Since the patsy had been a network admin, there had to be something . . .

David grinned. "Yes! I've got access to their e-mail server! Now . . . what could I do with that . . . "

"We could send an order or something." Tom suggested helpfully. "Normally nobody would ever take orders via an e-mail. At least I'm pretty sure that's standard military protocol. But look, if some dumb grunt gets an order from the high admiral in an e-mail, is he really going to say no?"

"Go on," Carlos said with a hint of interest.

Tom continued. "This is the kind of trick that might only work once. We spoof the high admiral's e-mail using his own admin credentials, get Samuel to do something you need that we don't have direct access to. Since he's a network admin, he'd have control over the comms. Now, if and when he figures out the order is fake . . . "

". . . then it won't work again," Carlos finished, tapping his ashes out on a small ashtray. "They will know better." Carlos didn't say, but silently wondered, *Unless, of course, the stooge keeps it secret to cover his own ass.*

"Yes, they'll send some communication reminding people not to do dumb shit like that, and it won't work again. So, what do you want? What can we give you from the comm system that would help you and your men?"

Carlos relaxed, putting out his cigar and leaning back in his chair. His expression was relaxed and contemplative. Tom felt an inexplicable wave of relief wash over him.

"I'm glad you asked, *señor*. As I said before, they keep tracking our radios—not just mine, but all the fighters on Cienfuegos—and so we have stopped using them. But that makes problems for us because we can't coordinate well over long distances and communications rely upon runners who are sometimes caught, and . . . "

. . . and so, Petty Officer Ellis, I will need you to disable radio monitoring for the frequencies listed in the attached spreadsheet, in the Angela Merkel's *zone of responsibility. Now, the reasons for this are to remain on a strictly need-to-know basis. Do not share this with any other crew aboard the* Angela Merkel, *and if anyone asks why the monitoring of these frequencies has been disabled, you will explain that the order came directly from me and to contact me directly if verification is required. Do not say anything else, or the communications tests we are conducting will be unduly delayed. You have been chosen out of all others because of your high marks on our aptitude tests and your dedication to duty.*

High Admiral Justin Hortzmann . . .

David finished reading the high admiral's e-mail signature and smiled. "Hopefully this works. It's pretty risky."

Tom nodded and took a long pull from the rum bottle as he sent the email. For the first time in a while he felt in control of his situation, if only a little bit. The food and drink had returned since they'd started reading the *Angela Merkel*'s email. That had won favor with Carlos almost immediately, for the intelligence buried in it had proven helpful in ways Tom really didn't want to know. He was sure it was going to get some blue helmets killed somewhere, somehow. And this little social engineering trick, if it worked, ought to buy even more favor.

It feels good, he thought. *Terra Nova sucks, but as far as life on this planet goes, this isn't so bad. Sure, maybe he kills us, maybe he doesn't, but at least it's not tobacco farming.* He felt a sudden, purely psychosomatic, twinge of the agony-in-the-back that was part and parcel of pulling tobacco from the beds before it was transplanted.

"Yes, I know it's risky, but this guy looks to be both arrogant and stupid. He might really believe the high admiral chose him for some hush-hush op because he's super smart or some shit. Anyway, if it works, the all the fighters in Cienfuegos will be able to use their radios again. They'll have a whole list of safe frequencies to use. It'll be a big win." Tom almost felt bad for the guy, but thought better of it. Samuel Ellis was a tool, another faceless smurf in an army of them, part of the system that had exiled them across the universe. *Assuming we're even in the same universe.* And he *was* an arrogant ass who thought he was some kind of super genius. Every e-mail and social media post oozed with self-importance.

"What do you think the guerillas will do, if they can use their radios again?" David asked.

Tom shrugged. "I don't know, and I don't want to know. The less we know about what they do, the less chance of us ending up dead."

Behind them, Enrique shuffled his feet, getting their attention. You never knew if he was lurking nearby. "We will use this to kill *pitufos, señor.* Lots of them. Help us plan attacks. Coordinate." His English was thickly accented, and the last word was mangled pretty badly. "What more do you need to know? But this is good. We do not have to cut you up and make you into meg bait." Enrique's smile looked a little *too* eager. Carlos waved him away distractedly, but Tom noted that the drug lord didn't contradict Enrique, either.

David laughed, thinking it was a joke. Tom wasn't so sure, yet. At the very least, he had no desire to put the supposed joke to the test. Carlos vanished, off to whatever drug lord business he attended to when he wasn't monitoring their progress.

"Fine with me," David began. "Anyway, that reminds me. They'll want us dead for this, too." His smile turned into a smirk, and he pointed to his own machine. "I was pinging all cameras on the ship and seeing which ones I could get access to. Unfortunately, most of the original cameras were heavily secured, and most of the private cameras were . . . well, not very useful to me. However, the captain has one in her quarters. We can tap into it, see what we can see . . . "

"A watch party then," Tom said, motioning toward Carlos's men. He explained it to them. They would watch for a while, on and off, and see if they could catch anything interesting and useful. They couldn't save every bit of video from the cameras, they didn't have the disk space, Tom knew. But they could run a twenty-four hour rolling backup in case they caught anything interesting.

The captain walked into her quarters a few hours later, and she started stripping down. *That* got the attention of Carlos's men.

"We've got bush . . . we've got bush . . ." David quoted. Tom knew it had to be from some ancient movie in David's collection. Everything was movie quotes with him, it was a habit that had long annoyed Tom, but it was part and parcel of having David for a coworker and roommate. Sure enough, the captain was soon naked, and changing into some lingerie outfit that looked vaguely kinky.

"She is pretty hot . . ." Tom observed. An older man entered her quarters, and began stripping down himself. That drew groans and complaints from the guards.

"*Si*. She is sexy. But why is she with that old man?" Enrique wondered aloud. "Is it true that the captain is a whore?"

Tom watched as the old man produced a flogger from his bag, and began twirling it around in his hand to some kind of cadence. The whole thing appeared to require a great deal of skill. Periodically, it slammed against the captain's ample—and very red—ass. He turned to face the camera, reaching for another implement.

Tom pulled a screenshot and enhanced it. "It can't be. No fucking way . . ." He zoomed in to the face, recognizing it from the memes he'd been posting all over social media.

David nodded in sudden, excited recognition. "It is. It's HIM. The high-fucking-admiral. Holy shit. Pull up the social media feeds, this shit is going viral!"

Normally the view counts on their posts were high, but the shares were few. Nobody wanted to be seen making a career-limiting social media post sharing some shitpost meme. Sure, they'd *view* it, maybe even tell their buddies about it. But few were willing to share it or post it on their walls.

The sex tape made the rounds anyway. Shares exploded all over the network. It was too juicy *not* to share. And once a few did it, the rest figured they had some kind of group immunity.

After a couple of days, Tom wasn't sure there was any smurf on Terra Nova who *hadn't* seen the video.

She wasn't sure which was worse, the embarrassment of having her entire crew see the sex tape in perfect high definition, color-corrected detail, or knowing that the high admiral would soon be calling her, wondering why their tryst was being broadcast to the entire UN presence on and around Terra Nova.

Either way, the dread in the pit of her stomach was overwhelming.

And she couldn't help wondering if every crew member she interacted with was mentally undressing her. She could think of little else. Whoever had distributed the video had known his business. Even the *huánuco* was doing nothing to soothe her, now.

The communicator chimed, and the dread multiplied. She held back the tears and the tremors, but just barely. The face of the high admiral appeared.

"Captain. You undoubtedly know why I've called." His face was stoic and unreadable. That he had called her by her rank, and not her first name, boded ill.

But he was the one who wanted me to record everything and send the video to him, she wanted to protest. The high admiral got off on it, she supposed.

She nodded and tried to keep her voice level. "Yes, sir. I can explain, there's been a series of strange incidents on social media recently, some kind of anonymous traitor or something who has been demoralizing our forces, and . . . "

"Don't bother, I'm apprised of the situation. We've been looking into it too." He took a deep breath and looked like he was steeling himself for something. "I'm not having you relieved of command, if that's what you're worrying about. Being frank, it looks as bad for me as it does for you. We're going to bury this thing as much as we can. Fortunately, the few on Earth who could make an issue out of this aren't likely to care, and in any event, I'm blocking the drone-carried return social feeds to Earth for a while. You got rid of the camera, I'm assuming."

Pamela nodded and let out a deep sigh of relief. But the dread in her stomach did not subside completely. There would be a price for this consideration, she knew. But she could handle his needs, at least when things calmed down, anyway. "Thank you, sir." She said simply, blinking quickly to avoid crying.

The high admiral waved his hand distractedly and continued. "This saboteur needs to be dealt with, Captain. And we now have evidence that he has some kind of access to your ship. First the social media memes, now this. He's escalating his game."

"I don't think we have a traitor on board, sir. We've had monitoring in place on everybody, both in the base down on Cienfuegos and on board the ship. I've had people monitoring the people doing the monitoring. There's nothing, sir! I don't know who is sending out all this hate speech!"

Stroking his chin, the High Admiral thought about it for a moment. He gestured downward. "Yes, we've considered this. There's one place you're not looking."

"The colonists, sir?"

He nodded his agreement. "The colonists. There's an uplink in Cienfuegos. So, if someone on the surface got access to the uplink somehow, everything that's happened so far would make sense."

"That shouldn't be possible, sir." She thought about it for a moment. "They'd need a late-model system, a wideband Wi-Fi transmitter, and a way to power it all. Such equipment is restricted and it's not like they can just make it here. And they'd need VPN access. That means having a token tied to a user's device ID. We've accounted for all of them, manually! I've had eyes on every device."

The high admiral frowned, and Pamela felt the dread returning to her stomach. She quickly recovered. "But maybe I should check the recent colonization manifests against the latest drone-datastream from Earth. Just in case anything stands out."

"Yes, perhaps you should . . ." The high admiral agreed. His expression changed, and Pamela saw the spark of lust in his eyes. "We'll keep things quiet for a while, Pam. But when this has blown over, I expect you will make it up to me."

"Yes, sir."

Hortzmann disconnected, and Pamela considered her options. A few mostly gratitude-driven tears welled up and inched down her cheeks. She wiped away her tears and steeled herself before tapping the comm. If it was someone on Cienfuegos, she had some idea of a potential source.

Cranston's ugly mug greeted here. "Ma'am?" His voice was vaguely patronizing, and his eyes were roaming where they probably shouldn't be. *He's seen the tape*, she realized suddenly.

"I need you to start questioning people in Constancia, Lieutenant. I need answers, and I think Carlos might have something to do with what's been going on."

Cranston rubbed his chin, "Why would Carlos do something like that?"

"Don't pretend to *me,* Lieutenant. You know full well. *You* killed her."

Cranston grinned, and Pamela repressed an instinctive shiver. "Oh, well yeah, I suppose he could still be mad about that. What do you want me to do?"

"Just ask around. Get me some information. If somebody in Carlos's employ is doing this, I want to know about it. *Capiche?*"

"Yes, ma'am!" Cranston said, perhaps too eagerly. She cut the comm channel before she succumbed to the temptation to have him taken out behind the base and shot.

Mirthful laughter echoed in the villa as Carlos nearly spit out his trademark cigar. The high admiral had the captain bent over as he applied a series of spankings to her repeated cries of "yes, daddy!" It had been the third time this week that the video had topped the social media charts. It was both an excellent meme, and basically pornography, which was always popular on *any* network.

"Good, good. That will keep them busy for a while. They will be looking for whoever posted this. We can use this time to do more." Attacks had exploded all over Cienfuegos and the surrounding areas. Carlos was not short on contacts among guerrilla bands, it seemed.

Tom's face fell. *Shit, I didn't think about that. Might as well have painted a bullseye on my ass.* From the sound of things, Cienfuegos heaved with rebellious activity. Certainly, the local UN base was on lockdown. Knocking shops were nearly empty, and sailors came down in heavily armed groups, now. Only Cranston and his band of smurf thugs were still regular patrons, though they had been making extensive use of them. Whores all throughout the town were up in arms over *that.* Nobody wanted Cranston or his merry men, as David had termed them, as customers.

They were going to be looking for the perpetrators, and while it was unlikely their counterparts in orbit would be able to track them, for David had always been a master of his craft, Tom knew, it was still disconcerting. The UN occupiers would surely kill them if they ever found out.

Still, Carlos remained generous with his food and drink, and the woman from before sauntered in carrying a small box of cigars.

David's gaze lingered, looking for a moment into those deep

brown eyes, traveling down to the long, dark blond hair that flowed almost to her tiny waist. The combination was highly exotic. At least David had the sense to keep his gaze somewhat discreet.

Tom detected a certain family resemblance to Carlos and kept his focus on the proffered cigars. David was less careful, as was usually the case with him. He grinned at her, but somehow managed to be almost charming.

"*Gracias*," David said, smiling widely. She smiled sweetly at him in return and opened the cigar box. There was something hard in her eyes, though, and the knife was still there, on her hip. No, she was not one to be messed with at all. David was either unaware, however, or more likely just didn't care.

"We celebrate, *amigos*." Carlos, seemingly oblivious to the byplay, flicked open his precious lighter as Tom leaned in. "The *pitufo* whore has been deeply shamed. Perhaps they will even remove her from her ship."

David shook his head but lit up his cigar anyway and took a long drag, washing it down with a shot of rum. "No, doesn't look that way. Comm traffic up there is crazy, but I've seen nothing even hinting at a change in command. Only a mass broadcast to find whomever is broadcasting sexist hate speech and slut-shaming the captain for her sexual preferences. The usual UN agitprop, man. Peace, love, diversity, and a lot of weird sex—while on a starship, no less. But we did piss them off. It's a mess up there."

And that worries me too, Tom thought, lighting up his own cigar. *The person we cribbed the token from might suspect something. Either way, they're going to have to start looking planetside soon if they aren't complete idiots.*

Carlos nodded, satisfied. "You have done well for me. I have a new task for you. Do you know how to work on drones?"

Tom nodded, "I do."

"Good, good," Carlos patted him on the back, nearly dislodging the celebratory cigar from his mouth. The gringo wizards had done so much now that he was totally unsurprised. "This should be fun for you."

"You keep using that word," David quoted. "I do not think it means what you think it means."

Tom had to resist the urge to facepalm. It was a bad quote, even for David. Enrique, on the other hand, thought it was hilarious, his deep belly laugh filling the room. Who knew that one had to fly all the way to the ass-end of the universe to find someone who hadn't seen *The Princess Bride*? But that, he knew, was something he could correct during the next movie night.

The dining room was luxurious by Terra Novan standards, which were admittedly stuck somewhere in late antiquity. Tom pulled a splinter out of his hand, courtesy of the rough-finished live edge dining table. People on old Earth used to pay extra money for pieces they regarded as more authentic, hand-crafted. Here on Terra Nova, the splinters were free.

He glanced at his old roommate and tried to figure out how all of this had happened to them, and where he intended to go from here, provided the universe saw fit to supply him with a choice. So far, it had declined to provide him with such opportunities. *Or*, he thought, *maybe I he was just too blind to see them.*

He cut into the chicken on his plate and speared a piece on his stolen UN fork. Carlos had seen fit to supply them with some trappings of civilization, at least.

"What are we going to do, man? Where the hell do we go after all this, supposing Carlos lets us live? The American sector, maybe? That's what I'm thinking." Tom wondered aloud.

David met his gaze, and pondered that for a moment, his face torn in indecision. "Go? If we can't get back to Earth, this place is as good as any. Better than most, I think. I'm staying."

"You crazy? Is it the woman? You always were stupid around them," Tom replied, acid in his voice. The jealousy came and went, and he felt bad almost immediately. "I'm sorry, that was wrong."

David nodded his agreement. "Yeah, it was. But look, Tom . . . when have we ever meant anything to anybody? Here I'm somebody, you know? An engineer. A hacker. Somebody's trusted minion. I don't know. But somebody. It's different. I'm done being some shy geek."

Tom smiled. It was true, David had changed. Where once there was only pudge, now there was wiry muscle. His fair constitution had darkened with the relentless alien sunlight. There was an edge to him now. David of old wouldn't have hurt a fly. David of Terra Nova had a predatory expression not unlike one of Carlos's goons. This David could kill, would kill, Tom knew, if the situation called for it. *Or to get revenge for his girl's young sister. Or to make the dead girl's older sister his own.*

"It's not only Elena," David said. "To be honest, man, I don't know if she likes me at all, or if I'm just the amusing gringo from the skies, a fad to be forgotten in a week. But since when have I ever really interested anybody?" He finished the last of his chicken and stood up. Enrique had been training both of them in basic martial arts. Nothing fancy, but enough to get them by if the circumstances called for it. Tom wondered if he looked as different now as David did.

Tom finished his own plate of food and washed it down with some of the local rotgut, this time without even so much as a grimace. He smiled in anticipation.

"Time to shitpost the world, dude. Then build a flying bomb."

Sweat dripped from Tom's brow. It wasn't like he had ever done anything quite like this before. David's computer was connected to the drone's receiving unit as he reprogrammed the access tokens, leaving Tom with the duty of attempting to jury rig the detonator. He'd built many homebrew drones before, but this was different, and he didn't even have most of the tools he needed, only what scraps Carlos and his contacts had managed to scrounge up.

He didn't even have a soldering iron or even any way to power one, but at least there was a generous supply of electrical tape and wire nuts, and a Pringles can one of Carlos's goons had pilfered from a UN commissary to beef up the antenna on the stolen controller rig. Pringles canning was an ancient range-extension trick that dated back to the earliest days of wireless networking, and the stale-tasting chips were a staple of UN commissaries around the planet due to ease of transport. Carlos had been oddly confused when they requested one, but had obtained one anyway.

It would be the sorriest drone build he'd ever done, but it would work.

Probably work, anyway.

A mid-size, four-rotor drone with a heavy-duty rechargeable battery sat on his makeshift workbench. It would take *weeks* with their tiny solar chargers to fully trickle-charge the thing. Nobody had a real generator around here except the smurfs. The rotors had been badly bent, but Tom had hammered them straight, hopefully straight enough to fly. The balance was tricky. He thumbed the controller and the drone powered up, beginning to hover. It wobbled but didn't lose stability entirely.

"How did you guys manage to get an intact drone from the smurfs?" Tom faced Enrique as the drone settled back on the table and shut down.

"Birds. The weird ones," he said.

"Ah, Archaeopteryx?" Tom replied.

"*Si*. Those. We trained some to attack the drones that were always spying on us. This drone got caught in the trees and wasn't badly broken." Enrique answered. "I was there. It was funny."

"Funny? Why?" David looked up from his work.

"We didn't know this drone had metal . . . what is the word . . ." He twirled his index finger around in a circle, emulating a helicopter.

"Rotors?" Tom supplied helpfully.

"*Si*. Metal rotors. The bird died. It was funny." Enrique grinned, showing a row of fearsome looking teeth. "It attacked the drone as we trained it to do, then squawked, and blood flew all over the place. We ate well that night." He shrugged.

"That's gotta be weird," Tom began. "I mean, eating a dinosaur bird that was supposed to be extinct millions of years ago. What did it taste like?"

Enrique rubbed his chin, thinking back on it. "*Pollo*," he decided.

"Speaking of which," David smiled as Elena entered into the room with their lunch. There was some breaded chicken, positively luxurious, and a bottle of the ubiquitous and atrocious local rum. She returned the smile, setting the bottle down on David's makeshift work bench. David had been spending a little off time with her, and Carlos had so far said nothing untoward to either of them.

"My father says this batch of rum tastes much better than the others. I don't know. It is still bad." She said in fluent, if accented, English.

She continued, her voice soft and sweet but her expression terrible and full of simmering hatred. It was a curious contrast. "You are helping us fight the *pitufos*?"

Tom nodded. She burned hot with righteous Latin fury. She was

more disconcerting, in her own way, than even Carlos. Her almost
demure demeanor changed to one nearly as murderous as one of
guerrillas frequently seen around the plantation. Tom found himself
wondering again just what had happened.

"Good. They will pay for my sister."

Tom dropped the screwdriver he'd been holding in his other hand,
his task forgotten for the moment.

"What happened?" David asked cautiously. "I mean, your father
said as much, sort of, but . . . "

"The captain came for tribute from my father," she began. "She
wanted him to grow the *huánuco* for them. He told them he didn't do
that anymore."

"Wait, they *forced* him to make it?" David asked stupidly.

Elena hesitated for a moment and looked at Enrique. But he didn't
seem to care. The cat probably had to come out of the bag sooner or
later. *An unwilling drug lord*, Tom thought wryly, *now I really have
heard it all.*

"He was. Drugs were the family business on Earth, and it went
badly for us. My father tried to get us out of the business. We could
either flee here or die. He vowed he was done with it all, after that.
He would grow tobacco. Make rum too, maybe. We would start over
as a family. But the *pitufo* captain, she knew who he was, and wanted
him to grow *huánuco*. It is kind of like your cocaine, and rich
Earthers pay well to have it. When my father refused, Cranston took
my sister hostage, to make him do it."

"Why did she want your father do it? Why didn't she just pay
someone else to grow it?" Tom asked, intensely curious despite the
risk involved in knowing too much.

"She couldn't manage it herself. Nobody else had the respect of
the village. Her sailors only come down for a short time. Enough to
pick up the *huánuco*, but not to run the whole operation. Only her
man Cranston stays for very long. I don't think it is legal for them,
even if many of them do smuggle things."

"When my father refused, and the captain put pressure on her
men to get it done, Cranston took my sister at gunpoint to make us
do it. He used her, did things to her. When we could see her, she
showed us the bruises. But there was nothing we could do. We didn't
have the guns back then, or enough men. So we made the *huánuco*

for them. And when our first crop was not enough to satisfy Cranston, he killed my sister. Said she tried to escape, but we know he lied. He enjoys killing, especially when he takes the *huánuco*. He told us the same might happen to me if he didn't get enough next time. And the captain lets him do it, so long as she gets her money. When we made enough money selling some extra crops on the side, we bought guns from other *pitufo* smugglers."

Elena's eyes were red, but it was hard to tell if it was from sadness or hatred, or more likely, some undefined mixture of both.

David was slow to register; "They raped her and killed her?" Shock crossed his features, followed by that look Tom knew all too well. David wanted to do something heroic and stupid for no good reason whatsoever, except that a beautiful woman had told him she'd been horribly wronged. He'd have to deal with that impetuous naivety soon enough, Tom knew.

No choice at all, he thought.

Elena nodded, her gaze lingering on David for a moment, a quizzical, almost judgmental look crossing her features. Apparently, she decided she was satisfied, and so she smiled sweetly at him again. She was quite expressive, and her mood, though hot-tempered, had faded quickly into something else. Tom got the distinct sense that she was fully aware of David's interest, and intended to use it for her own purposes. Not that David would've been put off by that anyway.

"How long ago?" David wondered.

"A few years ago."

"How did you avoid them?"

"Some of the *pitufos* like the younger girls better." Elena said disgustedly. "That doesn't matter though. It could have been me, instead. It should have been me. I was older. I was stronger."

"Older?" David echoed. "How old was your sister?"

"Twelve." At the memory, Elena shuddered and poured herself a small cup of the local rum and took a sip. She gulped the rest, then smiled at David and looked at the drone. "I hope whatever you are building, it kills many *pitufos*."

David grinned wickedly. "It will, miss. It sure will."

Tom felt a small pang of jealousy as Elena, hips swaying, walked out, for she looked very pleased with David's reply. And as Tom noted, the last of David's beer gut had vanished utterly. Tom could see the change in him. Even the shyness was fading away. Elena saw a very different man than he did. She saw an engineer building weapons for her father, a man who was honored with a high place in his councils, not some geek gringo slumming it in Tijuana for cheap beer, who couldn't even find the courage to talk to a woman when he was stone drunk.

Then again, Tom noted as his attention shifted back to the makeshift detonator, he'd changed too. He had a certain detached coldness and sense of purpose that hadn't been there before. The purpose was satisfying in a way his wanderlust back on Earth hadn't been. He had something *important* to do for once. Not just writing crappy code for software for some out-of-touch bureaucrat a thousand miles away who would probably waste it and throw it all away just to start over again in six months. No more droning mission statements and diversity meetings. This was *something*.

Enrique patted Tom on the back, nearly dislodging the cigar from his mouth, and smiled. The other goons were coming around, too. Tom suspected that was at least partly because of the movies the two would pull up on their machines when taking breaks. Carlos's men would crowd around and watch whatever movies the two had cribbed from the local UN social media networks. The sight was almost comical, seeing a bunch of thugs and guerrillas crowding around a paltry fourteen inch screen to watch ancient films. But it was top notch entertainment on this planet, and a luxury almost nobody else on this ball of dirt possessed.

The odds on their survival were improving. Most thought they'd last at least a month. One optimistic fellow thought they might last the whole summer, at least if the smurfs didn't kill everybody before then. Enrique still suggested they were going to be meg bait, but it could possibly have been a joke.

Possibly.

Lieutenant Slade Cranston zipped up his pants and unceremoniously kicked the prostitute out of his villa. It had been a fun few days, but she no longer amused him. Martina evidently preferred the Domme role, and there were some who rotated down from the *Angela Merkel* and took advantage of her services. Cranston had other tastes, and the whore limped out of the villa covered in bruises, her tattered dress torn and stained. Little pleased him more than breaking a Domme to her proper role as a submissive.

Still, the whore had stepped out first when he'd stopped by the brothel for an extended outcall, paid with *huánuco*, naturally. Most of the rest had been too frightened of him. He grinned. *She must really need the money,* he thought. All of it had been worth putting off his trip up to the *Angela Merkel* for a few days. He sat in the rocking chair on the front porch of the villa and finished off his beer. Not one of the local rotgut varieties, but a genuine cold one shipped all the way from Earth. He didn't even want to know what it cost to get it out this far. He gulped down the cold brew and lobbed the empty can in the general direction of the whore, still shuffling toward the gate.

Some hated duty down on Terra Nova, but for Cranston, the opportunities to sate his appetites more than made up for the disgusting primitiveness of the place. On Earth, he'd have had few such opportunities. He wasn't rich enough or connected enough to get away with it. But here, things were different. It was *his* ant farm to run. He ran his finger through a bowl of *huánuco* paste and finished it off. The high was pleasant and familiar, especially coming after such an entertaining afternoon.

"Ten percent," he chuckled to himself. He'd gotten close to twenty percent more out of Carlos. The captain, of course, didn't need to know that. On Earth, his *huánuco* habit would have cost him more than he could make in a lifetime. Here, it was practically free.

At first, he thought the buzzing was in his head. *huánuco* could do that sometimes. But it grew louder and closer.

It had taken the better part of a month to fully repair, reprogram, and outfit the drone with their sorry excuse for tools. "Stone knives and bearskins," David had called it. But, stone age tools or not, the job had been done at last. Carlos had used that time to collect many seriously unsavory characters for some kind of ambush. They were hard men, human predators that looked at the two developers like a wolf might consider a wounded deer. But Carlos had pronounced them off limits, and that protection seemed to hold real weight with the goons.

While David had always been the better network engineer, Tom was the superior drone pilot. In the days before their exile, drone racing had been a hobby of his, tinkering with them for speed and piloting them through warehouses, abandoned factories, and alleyways. A familiar rush of exhilaration flowed through him as the drone took flight. In all probability, it would be the last time he would ever fly one. But despite the many months since his exile, it felt just as natural as if he had done it yesterday. All eyes were upon him.

Then he remembered the drone was loaded to maximum payload rating with stolen explosives, enough for one man in particular.

Carlos looked over Tom's shoulder intently as the drone rapidly flew through the village. Tom used the streets and buildings as cover. The transponder had been disabled, but any higher than the building tops, and the drone would surely be detected. Tom tilted his tablet, the built-in gyroscope controlling the flight path, dodging a pair of unwary townspeople. The microphone picked up barely audible curses in Spanish as the two dropped whatever they had been carrying and scrambled out of the way.

He increased his altitude by a hair and buzzed by the corner of a small hut so close that pieces of straw flew up in the corner of his display. The makeshift gate was in view, and he pushed the throttle up to maximum speed for the final dash across the open field. The drone's battery was rapidly draining, so it was fortunate that a return trip wasn't necessary. He needed to get across the open terrain before anybody caught on to the fact this drone wasn't supposed to be there and shot it down.

"Cranston is over the gate, just to the right of the main building," Carlos reminded him, translating some of the responses from his radio. "Martina will have seen to it that he has not left yet." Tom tried not to think about that. Martina had *volunteered* to ensure Cranston didn't leave his post until the drone was ready. That took a positively heroic character, given what Cranston had done, both to Carlos's daughter, and to the battered whores in and around Constancia. Then again, in some small sense, this was Martina's revenge, too.

Carlos's men had the small UN base under surveillance and Enrique had supplied the layout and the target's position. The base was a small affair, mostly using local buildings, created mainly to serve as a transfer point for the drugs ferried over to the captain's men and for temporary housing for the sailors enjoying shore leave and gravity acclimation rotation. It wouldn't be long now.

The drone buzzed over the top of the gate at high speed, and Tom briefly noticed the confused expressions of the tower guards in the video display. Someone must have realized there was a problem, as the staccato sound of automatic weapons fire registered on the mic. The drone was nimble and fast, however, and Tom rapidly turned toward his target, evading the fire. That wouldn't last long, he knew.

The drone flew toward the commanding officer's villa. Cranston tried to reach the door, jumping in and grabbing the door at the last minute. *Not,* Tom thought, *that a thin wooden door offered much protection.*

Behind him, David hit the detonator. For a moment, the tablet stuck on the final frame, a confused face slamming the door shut, just starting to come around to what the drone *really* meant for him, before "connection interrupted" partially covered the screen.

"What the devil?" Cranston wondered, aloud.

He stood, but his *huánuco*-addled mind was having difficulty processing what was going on. A drone flew over the gate and gunfire suddenly broke out. Something was wrong. The drone, he realized in a sudden moment of clarity, was headed straight for him. He opened the door and practically threw himself in, reaching around to shut it behind him.

All Hell broke loose. All was black.

Carlos's men cheered while Tom fought the urge to throw up. He hadn't pulled the trigger, but in effect, he had probably just killed a man. Enrique had assured him the explosives they used were powerful, despite being so light, stolen from the smurfs themselves.

A radio transmission came in from one of the spotters, since there still was no indication the smurfs had caught on to the blocked radio frequencies. According to Carlos, that had bought many victories for guerilla fighters all over Cienfuegos. The ability to coordinate strikes and plans over long distances had made many things possible, including getting enough men together for this attack.

"The villa is on fire, the front porch was destroyed by the blast, we are attacking the gate now," the unknown fighter said in Spanish. Tom noted that his own understanding of Spanish was becoming at least somewhat tolerable. Sounds of battle came over the radio before it shut off, but the fight was apparently brief, if rather fierce. The compound had only a skeleton crew, just enough to ensure sailors taking advantage of Constancia's pleasures stayed under some level of control . . . and to load the *huánuco* far away from prying eyes. More would probably have risked too many people knowing about *that* particular detail.

The radio squawked again. "The officer is severely wounded, but alive. Most of the guards are dead. We have wounded, and Juan is dead. We got them all before they could get to the shuttle. I don't know if they got a message out to their ship, but there is no activity in the air yet."

It would take the orbiting ship time to prepare a landing craft, Tom knew, even if the enemy managed to get off a communication before the ambush. That much he had been able to locate in the manuals he'd downloaded.

Carlos's voice was cold. "Enrique, have them bring me Cranston. Luis, go cut us a stake. Maybe fifteen feet long. Jose . . . we're going to need a hole dug. A few feet deep, no more. And narrow." His eyes were red, a mixture of sadness and rage in them, and he blinked back the water. They were fixed upon the officer's shocked face, still frozen on the tablet's display. A murderous grin wormed its way across his conflicted features.

"And Jose, get some shorter stakes too, to fill in the space between the pole and the edges," Carlos added, walking out behind his men. Elena was there, a look of wicked satisfaction crossing her youthful features. She smiled cruelly and knowingly at David, her expression appreciative, almost *promising*, before following her father out the door. David tried to smile in turn, probably to impress her, but it was a hollow thing. Even Tom could tell that much.

Cranston could hear before he could see. When he opened his eyes, he found himself staring into the face of a smiling Carlos. Terrible fear overcame him, and he heard a sickening moan a moment before realizing it was his own. Wetness stained his crotch and an ammonia stink filled his nostrils.

"*Ah! Que tal?*" Carlos said happily, patting the lieutenant on the shoulder. That brought the pain of his injuries to the forefront. His legs were bent wrong. There was shock from dozens of small cuts all over. His uniform was tattered. Adrenaline surged through his system and fought with the omnipresent pain for his attention. The *huánuco* high hadn't yet fully receded, and his heartbeat raced faster and faster. A grinning fighter was holding a large hammer. Behind him, another man was humming cheerfully as he sharpened the stake . . .

Enrique and the rest of the men seemed almost disappointed to wait on the duo, like they wanted to be a part of what was going to happen outside.

Half an hour later, enough to retrieve the man and bring him to Carlos's villa, it began. Screams and terrifying pleas could be heard. There was a pounding sound, and then more screams, each higher and more terrible than the last. More pounding. More screams and pleas.

Enrique offered Tom the rum bottle that was making the celebratory rounds, and he cheerfully took a pull from it. He found he was even starting to like it, in a weird sort of way.

The screams gave way to very peculiar moans. Tom found they no longer bothered him. If the officer had done even one-tenth of what Elena claimed, or even the village prostitutes had claimed, it was a dose of drone-guided karma.

Once social media was abuzz with news of the Cienfuegos Drone Bombing, he uploaded the Papa Smurf meme he'd been working on. In it, the high admiral was too busy fucking Smurfette from behind to notice a little drone making a "shhhhh" gesture as it snuck behind the pair to blow up a bunch of drunken, drug-addled, half-naked smurfs.

That ought to piss someone off, he thought. The view count went through the roof. There were even a handful of shares. The comments, of course, were even more interesting. One stood out in particular:

"Maybe they should stop fucking once in a while and start doing their duty. That way we wouldn't have to die for their deviant shit." It had been posted anonymously, and the share count was small, for nobody wanted to be *identified* agreeing with that sentiment. But the view count was extremely high for that, too.

Their memes were producing sympathetic posts, finally. They were getting somewhere.

★★★

If High Admiral Hortzmann had been angry before, he was clearly furious now. Pamela felt the anger more literally, as the high admiral flogged her. She was cuffed to the bed, her naked body presented for his pleasure. For hours, he took her, abused her, and angrily finished upon her. Her screams were very real, this time, and not merely for effect. He was *pissed*.

Finally, the blows stopped, and the high admiral was fully spent. This time, he had actually drawn a fair amount of blood. It dripped down her battered buttocks.

"A terrorist steals one of our drones and blows up your man, shoots the rest, and you have nothing for me? Too busy doing that fucking alien cocaine shit?" He demanded, sitting down beside her. Usually, there would be a tender moment after such a scene, a moment of after care, where if he didn't whisper any soft words to her, he at least stroked her body gently, let her come down from her masochistic high. There was none of that now. This wasn't punishment for pleasure, it was punishment for its own sake.

"Sir," she straightened up, trying to ignore the pain flaring up from her destroyed posterior, "that's not true. I told you, I do have something. Maybe not much, but something."

She took his silence as an invitation to continue. "I checked the incoming manifests, and I did find something interesting, two American developers picked up in Mexico several months ago. They were delivered to Cienfuegos, in fact to the very village where the attack occurred. Furthermore, we have discovered that one of our IT personnel may have had his user account hacked somehow. Obviously, he has been suspended from duty pending investigation."

"So, you still have no idea where they are, or how they are doing this?" The high admiral stroked his flogger briefly for effect.

"That's not necessarily true. I have a suspicion. No proof, but a suspicion . . . Sir, I will handle it. I'll get this contained. Please give me a chance." She begged and pleaded with him.

The high admiral stood up and began to dress himself. Pamela knew better than to dress herself in his presence, she would have to wait until he was gone. He turned to her.

"Do what you need to do, Captain. I expect this to be wrapped up when I see you again. Next time it will go much worse for you." The last part was unnecessary. Pamela knew there would be no next time. She would be shipped back to Earth in disgrace, or worse. Especially if the high admiral found out *why* her men had been bombed. Pamela was pretty sure he at least vaguely suspected her drug habit wasn't the only thing she did with the stuff. And while officially it was highly illegal, it was also unofficially a common practice. Some, she knew, had even smuggled weapons to the guerillas operating on the planet. Those *were* severely disciplined when discovered. But drugs? Sexual deviancy? A little slavery on the side? These were minor trifles. Mere nothings.

At least, they were trifles until they caused official notice. Then they became an embarrassment, and *that* could not be tolerated.

The entire operation was going to have to go away, she realized. Her whole scheme to escape from under the thumb of the high admiral, from having to serve her supposed betters, was up in smoke. The drug money that would have freed her from her duty was forever out of reach, now. But there might still be time to salvage what she still had, to at least prevent being shipped back to Earth in disgrace. Or worse, killed by disappointed dealers back on Earth.

Maybe. She didn't like her odds. She didn't even have the men to do the job right, and she couldn't lean on the high admiral for the right sort of men. The risks were too great.

A smile wormed its way across Tom's features. "Time for one last prank, I think, before we go off the grid." Carlos had demanded their tablets be shut off when they evacuated. There was a certain genre savviness to that. Even though it was trivial for David to cut connection and disable the network adapters on both tablets, Carlos was taking no chances they might be tracked. Tom supposed they should both be grateful that Carlos's gratitude extended to taking them with him when he fled the village.

Still, time enough remained for one last gag. David nodded knowingly.

"It'll be a gas, man. They'll never get rid of it."

Tom tried not to laugh, but it *was* funny, given the joke. "Seriously, man? That's what you came up with?" He tapped the upload command, and the worm Tom had written found its way into the *Angela Merkel*'s ship-to-ship comm system, where it would lay dormant for a while, waiting to do its work. It was their parting gift to the smurfs in the sky. If they ever rid themselves of it without a complete reformatting of every solid-state drive on the whole ship, he'd be very surprised. It was, in many ways, their masterwork.

They would probably never create its like again.

Both programmers were pleased to see that the entire social media feed of the occupation force had been effectively shut down, for it was evidence that their campaign had worked. Before that, he had posted long screeds about how the high admiral and the captain of the *Angela Merkel* were in cahoots with a drug smuggling operation full of murder, rape, and intrigue, and the common sailors were the ones paying the tab when the terrorist bombs exploded.

It wasn't entirely accurate. Most of those who died in the bombing and the subsequent attack had thoroughly deserved it. But the resulting shitstorm on social media had been worthwhile. The mood of the occupiers was souring greatly. Some were irritated at being caught, and a few of the better (and more naïve) ones were angry at being used this way. Tom had no idea how he could objectively measure demoralization, but it *was* working.

That the high admiral had ordered all nonessential network usage shut down entirely had driven home just how bad this was starting to look for him. And that, too, would have a cascade effect. The entertainment network (along with its more unsavory varieties of entertainment) had been shut down along with the rest. That too was likely to cause demoralization and outrage, as much for the elimination of porn on the network as for anything else.

Even with the UN restrictions on "sexist objectification," porn continued to be the primary bandwidth sink on Terra Novan occupation networks. Or at least it had been. Topping off a campaign of memetic warfare with a bombing that ended with a corrupt lieutenant getting executed Vlad the Impaler style had really changed things.

"Time to go." Carlos was polite but firm, looking down at the tablets. Tom and David shut them off and dropped them into their bags.

Tom took a last look around the villa. He'd miss the cool fountain waters, piped in via a small wooden aqueduct, he'd learned. Quite ingenious. Carlos, of course, had shrugged it off. "My own ancestors," he had explained, "had done much more with much less two thousand years ago." But the coolness of it, the fresh, clean mountain water, that would be missed. He felt he was leaving civilization for a second time.

And still no choice in the matter, he mused. *But at least it all meant something. At least my work wasn't flushed down a bureaucratic toilet or wasted on idiots.* He was pretty sure most of the code he'd written for the UN back on Earth was wasted. Written because some bureaucrat wanted something and thrown away when he was replaced with another. How many half-completed projects had been cancelled? How many useless applications had he written that nobody would ever use? But not here. For good or ill, his worked had accomplished something.

"I'd almost felt like we were back in civilization." Tom said, looking wistfully at David.

David nodded. But soon his attention wandered to Elena. After the bombing, even Carlos didn't appear to mind David doting on his daughter. He even seemed to encourage it. *I suppose a woman could do much worse than a geek-turned-guerrilla on Terra Nova,* Tom thought. The rotting, impaled corpse of Lieutenant Cranston still stuck plainly in the front yard attested to that well enough. It was still very dangerous, but he supposed if David was serious enough, and didn't do anything *particularly* stupid, it might be a good match.

And so, Enrique was the one who answered him instead. "We are civilized, *señor*. This is why we didn't cut you up for bait. That is why your friend is still alive even though he makes eyes at the boss's daughter. Very civilized." The enforcer gave him a friendly pat on the back and laughed. It nearly pushed him to the ground. Enrique had a bad habit of forgetting his own relative strength. Even now, Tom wasn't sure he was joking. "Here, in case we meet those who are not civilized." The enforcer handed over a small belt with a nine millimeter holstered in it.

"I don't know how to use one. They banned them in America when I was a kid and . . ." Tom protested

"You will learn. This world is a good teacher. I will help, too." Enrique replied, waving it off as if it was nothing. His English was much improved, much as Tom's own Spanish had gotten better. He nodded and trudged off into the jungle.

★★★

Captain Pamela Andego stood to her full five foot, eleven inch height and looked down on the lowly petty officer. "Let me get this straight, you took an order via *e-mail*? How fucking retarded are you?" Her anger was such that she didn't even self-censor the breach in political protocol. One *never* uttered unapproved words. Or at least, so the political manuals said. In practice, Petty Officer Samuel Ellis was hardly in a position to complain.

Ellis gulped and tried not to make eye contact with his superior.

"Get out of my office. Consider yourself relieved of duty and confined to quarters." Pamela dismissed the idiot.

At least, she reflected, they had an idea of what was going on now, and why resistance guerrillas had been so maddeningly effective on Cienfuegos lately. They had been able to coordinate via radio without any chance of interception or triangulation for months. The disappearance of Carlos, his associates, and any trace of the two programmers on the manifest further confirmed it *had* to be them behind both the bombing and the network security breaches. It all made sense, finally.

She glared at the picture her men had sent of the villa. It was burning. Her people had seen to that quickly. There would be no happy homecomings for Carlos. But the image of Cranston's fly-covered body staked out in front of the burning structure, the arms and legs dangling in unnatural ways, was seared into her mind forever.

In truth, I can't blame Carlos for hating us, she admitted to herself. *What we did was wrong, and there's no getting around that.*

Just as the high admiral had certain tastes, so did many underneath her. A former drug lord had his uses even in a primitive, barbaric place like Cienfuegos. But he had to be broken to his role as she had been to hers. Cranston had been useful for that much, at least.

I just didn't expect Slade to go so far, she thought. *He was supposed to have a little fun, maybe even . . .* but even as she thought it, it felt wrong. No, she had known who Cranston was, what he might do, even back then. That was all part of breaking Carlos.

There's something to that, she thought, we're all trying to escape somebody else's control. No, she couldn't quite bring herself to hate Carlos. She would have done the same in his place. Indeed, she had been tempted many times on general principle.

But the idiots back home had seen fit to drop two thoroughly unvetted, well-equipped nerds into Carlos's lap, and everything had gone straight to shit. It was like the whole universe was trying to screw her, not just the high admiral. The exotic drug money she'd never get, the pissed off dealers back home when she didn't deliver . . . She wasn't sure if she could even return to Earth now, if she didn't deliver on her promises. Duty in Terra Novan orbit was probably the safest place to be at the moment, if she could keep it.

On social media, the damage was enough that the high admiral himself had locked down all nonessential network services and blocked the noncritical outgoing data packets to Earth. Even private letters had been completely stopped and that wasn't doing morale any favors. Memes had been going viral, and even her own men looked at her with barely restrained contempt now. Some, of course, looked rather more lustily. It was maddening to know that *everyone in the whole fleet* knew what you looked like naked.

At least now they could track the radio transmissions again. That was something. There would be payment in full for the embarrassment she had suffered. Her dreams of promotion and an idle vacation life were gone, but she could at least get even. Carlos may have reason to hate her, but if he had possessed the wisdom to do as he was told, none of this would have happened in the first place.

Pamela got up and headed for the bridge, knowing what had to be done, but dreading the terrible risk.

She turned to her XO as she entered. "I need two shuttles prepped for immediate launch. Get me twenty of our best men, most experienced on the ground. Open up the arms locker and have Security outfit them."

"Ma'am?"

"Just do it. Coordinates are in your station. Sweep the area, engage from the air before landing. Orders are to secure the area and eliminate any local resistance. Shuttle One is to provide close air support while Shuttle Two lands. Then both shuttles are to remain on station after the away team has landed." This was a bad idea, she knew, but she had to throw the dice anyway.

"We don't have any Marines, ma'am," the XO protested, his voice strained. "We're not even well equipped with small arms and . . . "

"Carlos and his terrorists are down there. We need to resolve the situation *now*," she ordered, cutting him off. Not all of her crew were in on the smuggling, but her XO was. He could be trusted within limits. "We're going to need to carefully select the away team. Only the best."

He gulped visibly and nodded, understanding the implications. His career was as dead as hers if this wasn't cleaned up. And on her ship, very few officers were selected from the diversity rosters, something which had earned her more than a little concern from home office. It served her well now. Her people weren't stupid, at least, and that had to count for something.

Maybe she had a chance to salvage this ratfuck after all.

They had trudged through the jungle for days until they came to the mouth of a small cave, where Carlos and his men had evidently hidden a cache of supplies and weapons. Shuttles and drones had been spotted all over the area. There were even sailors trudging through the jungle. Some of those had regretted the assignment. Carlos's men were quick in their grisly work.

Enrique was instructing them on how to make use of their weapons, and how to stay silent enough in the jungle. There were few enough rounds, and far too little time, so little that Enrique could not give them even a remote fraction of the training they really needed, especially given the need for relative quiet. But he gave them what he could. It was better than nothing. Probably.

"Be careful of the slide, *señores*," he said, pulling it back. "If you grip it too high the slide could cut your hand when you fire, like this." The top of his hand touched the slide as he drew it back. "Two hands, if you can, like this." He aimed the weapon toward the bright cave entrance.

David emulated the stance confidently. Elena laughed, watching David trying to impress her. He looked ridiculous, like he was pretending to be a secret agent from some B-rate flick. "Don't close your eyes when you shoot," she teased.

He holstered the weapon and turned to her, grinning from ear to ear. "Trust me, I won't."

Tom rolled his eyes at the innuendo. He checked the safety and holstered his own weapon, the lesson over. It hadn't become second nature, but it was something he could do with some thought, now. Watching Carlos, worry crossed his features. The smurf captain was clearly on the hunt for them, and everybody knew it.

"It was never like this." Carlos mused. There were nods and murmurs of agreement from his men. "I knew killing Cranston would get her attention, but not this way. I don't understand why she is using sailors to hunt us on the ground. They are the wrong men to send. It's all wrong."

"It's the *huánuco*," Tom explained. "With all that we've done, she's gotta be feeling the heat from her boss. So, she needs to make it all go away on her own. Keep her nose clean with the high admiral. She can't use anybody else. Only her own crew, loyal to her."

Carlos shook his head. "The *pitufos* don't care about the smuggling. They all do it."

"True," Tom replied. "But in her case, it's a political embarrassment. It's one thing to do it. It's another thing to get caught and embarrass your bosses. If there is one thing Earth politicians hate more than anything, it's that. They'll come down on the high admiral, and he'll come down hard on the captain if she's caught. This could shake up the whole command structure up there."

"Come down on her . . . probably literally." David agreed, laughing.

"Probably not even that, Dave." Taking a puff from his last cigar, Tom continued. "Things are fucked up on Earth. I mean, in the old days they'd never have sent us here for a mere overstayed visa. They are consolidating power. Getting rid of people they don't want around. Anybody that gets in the way of that . . . well if the captain is caught and sent back home, she'll seriously regret it. If they even let her live. And that *huánuco* has gotta go through someone's hands. Those folks won't be happy either."

Carlos drew his finger in a throat-slitting motion. "*Si*. They will not be happy. May even be some people I used to know." He smiled at that. "If we can get her sent home, maybe she dies."

"Mind if I ask a personal question, sir?" Tom asked. Carlos merely nodded his assent.

"Why did they exile you? Why did you try to get out of the drug trade?"

Carlos's expression fell. "It was brutal. Uncivilized. Rivals killing whole families to send a message. I lost my wife to them. It nearly broke us. Then the *pitufos* came and stole most of my land. No, I was done with all that. Coming here was the only way I could get away from all that. Otherwise walking away from the business would have been fatal."

Tom was incredulous. "You *volunteered* to come here?"

"*Si,*" Carlos began. "and for a while it was good. Our ancestors were Romans, once upon a time, you know. We could build great things, given the time, if they left us alone. That little aqueduct back in my house? That was my idea. Something I read in a history book once. But then the captain found out who I was, figured I could be useful to her, growing product for her to sell to buy her own freedom from her smurf commanders. And then, just like the other petty drug lords back on Earth, her man went after my family. I realized I had no choice but to fight this time."

Silence reigned in the cave for a while. Nobody had a good reply to that. The last cigars were extinguished. The rum remained, for Enrique had seen to it that the cave was well stocked. "Every man has priorities," he said in Spanish as he broke open the first bottle. Evidently those priorities included liquor but didn't include much in the way of decent food. While he might have been fine with the stale, over-baked bread, Tom certainly wasn't.

The sun began to set, the cave growing dark. A tiny fire was lit, far inside the cave and out of sight from the jungle itself. Tom watched the guerrillas tear into their meager rations and realized for the first time that he probably looked a lot like them now. He was armed and dressed in their same haphazard homespun camouflage. Oh, he didn't have the scars and their rough looks, but he was likewise a killer, now.

He put the finishing touches on the remote detonator he had constructed with his tablet. They could trigger the device from David's tablet, synced over a wireless band not used by the occupation force. It would allow them to get a video feed from the bomb itself and detonate it at exactly the right moment.

"Done," Tom pronounced, running his last test. "When we turn it on, it will attempt to connect to the UN network again. They'll be able to triangulate it easy. If the smurfs are dumb enough, they might take the bait."

Tom tried not to think of his only lifeline to technology finally being severed. David had agreed to share his own tablet after they expended Tom's, but . . . it wasn't going to be the same.

Cut the cord, he thought, *that's what they used to say, back when everything was wired. I guess it's time. Not like any of us have a choice. It's about the only way to get even odds of survival in this shitstorm.*

A hushed conversation in Spanish took place in the corner, and Enrique's voice could be heard above the others. "*Si,*" Enrique said, poking another one of Carlos's men and pointing to the two programmers. "They are getting better. I don't think we have to slit their throats in their sleep." He smiled genially at them. This time, Tom was confident they were joking.

Pretty sure, anyway.

"Tomorrow," Carlos announced, "we will split up. They will find us here eventually." He looked toward his daughter, who was laughing at some joke David had told. There was worry for her there, not for her increasing closeness to David, for Carlos seemed to approve of the budding relationship on some level, but for her survival. Save for revenge against the captain, little else seemed to exist anymore. He'd won and lost two fortunes, been powerful and been at the mercy of others. Carlos was a man who had seen it all, and it showed in the tired, worried expression he wore. "We have to end this. Draw the captain's men out and kill them. Be done with it."

He nodded to himself, looked at David and smiled, some decision apparently made. He turned to face Thomas. "You will come with us. In case we need . . ." He laughed. ". . . technical support with the bomb."

Great, Tom thought, *now suddenly David is more valuable because Elena likes him. I get to be shot at instead.*

He cast a death glare David's way. David, of course, was hardly paying attention.

Tom ducked lower behind the thick tree trunk, his belly hugging the ground. David's tablet was in his hand. He gave silent thanks to the Lord that it hadn't been damaged.

There were shouts. The sailors, probably, he thought. The shouts weren't in Spanish. The guerillas, on the other hand, were silent. Stealthy. And apparently not as stupid as the *pitufos* were. He tried not to think about what would happen if Carlos and his men lost this fight. Video played out on the tablet's screen. A curious and somewhat dull-looking face loomed into view, inspecting the tablet. The detonator and the bomb itself had been carefully buried underneath. Still, whoever this sailor was, he was none too bright. Tom considered that killing him was probably doing the gene pool a favor. He zoomed in to the nametag. Ellis, the tag read. Tom laughed silently at the irony, knowing exactly how the flunky had drawn this duty that was about to get him killed.

Tom chuckled to himself. *Carlos's crazy-ass plan is actually going to work,* he thought. Another pair of men walked into view of the video feed as the curious sailor picked it up. There were exclamations from the others, warnings to drop it and run. Tom thumbed the remote detonator.

The explosion was deafening, even from far away. Carlos had used far more explosives than the drone bomb had possessed, since there were no weight limits this time. Pieces of jungle, men, and equipment blew out everywhere. Wetness impacted the back of his skull, and for a moment he was taken with the irrational fear that it was blood. *His* blood. The fact that he was still capable of thought dispelled that notion. But blood it still was. Probably.

Muffled gunfire was everywhere, suddenly. He tried to make himself smaller, hoping that the Lord, and a fair amount of luck, would protect him. The rest was up to Carlos. It was his ambush and there was little else he could do. But he reassured himself that the nine millimeter was still on his hip, and he slid it out gently, holding it out in his right hand. He reached to secure the tablet in his bag.

If the Lord didn't see fit to protect him, he'd just have to do it himself. He shuffled slowly forward, still hugging the ground.

David's tablet, and their last link to the world he knew, shattered in a shower of plastic, glass, and metal that cut his hand deeply. Gunfire was all around him. He had a momentary vision of one of Carlos's men twisting to the ground, the top portion of his head erased in a shower of gore.

Tom couldn't see the man's killer but fired in the direction he assumed the shot had come from. For a moment the gunfire slackened. Intense concentration filled his awareness, and he prayed that the camouflage Carlos had given him was doing its job. He rolled into the bushes and waited.

Soon, he saw them. Sailors cautiously advancing on his position. He took careful aim and squeezed the trigger. A miss. And another miss. The third round winged one of them. The rifles were pointing toward him.

Shit, shit.

Then one of the sailors was torn to shreds in front of him, gunfire coming from everywhere. The man spun around, rounds impacting him everywhere. The other hit the ground quickly.

Carlos was behind him. "I told you to keep down and be quiet!" He whispered.

"I was quiet . . ." Tom whispered back, protesting.

"I am surprised they couldn't hear you from orbit, the way you move." Carlos answered. But his tone was not angry. To the contrary, it was genial. The sailors were retreating, finally. "You fought well, though. For a noisy *gringo.*"

"Sir," the XO interrupted Pamela's thoughts. "Got something here. Backtracking the area around the ambush and look at this." He transferred the image to her screen.

Angela Merkel's visual tracking covered far too much ground for even the computers to be all that useful in tracking ground movements in real-time throughout an entire jungle. But once narrowed down to a specific area, it was possible to backtrack movements in the video history. She caught the hints of movement beneath the trees butting up against the mountain, identified by the computer as anomalous now that the zone had been sufficiently narrowed.

She might have lost most of her men in the ambush, she knew. But there was still a chance. She stared at the cave, and the brief flicker of movement that came out of it hours before the ambush.

She'd lost at least ten already, in addition to those murdered the day before, and she had no idea how many men Carlos had left. Explaining this to the high admiral was already going to be extraordinarily difficult, if not impossible. The sailors had fallen back to the shuttle, and once the shuttle's weapons could be trained, the guerillas had backed off. Desperate requests for orders came in.

"Get our people out of there," she ordered. "Redirect here. Attack the cave."

She was reminded of the fact that these men were *not* marines.

"Shuttle Two isn't responding anymore, ma'am. I think they've turned off their coms." Yet it was still raising from the ground, heading out of the atmosphere back toward the *Angela Merkel*.

Yeah, that figures, she thought, *they want to get out of there while the getting is good. So, someone probably put a round through the radio. And the wireless network, too. Sorry, ma'am, a lot of bullets were flying around. Must've hit 'em. Not our fault, ma'am. No, we didn't hear the order to attack, no ma'am.*

Guilt gnawed at her awareness. People were dying everywhere, and for what? So that she could keep her post and continue to be a servant? A plaything? It had all gone too far. And now they were deliberately ignoring her. The situation was spiraling out of her control, and she slammed her fist down on the command chair. There was one last die to cast. Maybe if she could present the terrorist's head to the high admiral, she could save something of her career. If he'd left his family in the cave, perhaps an exchange could be arranged. One soon-to-be-dead Carlos for one daughter.

"Get shuttle One over there, then. I want prisoners." It was her last chance.

Fucking hell, she thought. *I'm so screwed. I'm so fucking screwed. There's no fucking way this is going to work, but what else can I do?*

She watched the icons on her display as the anxiety ate at her. Her console pinged. The high admiral was calling, but there was no time. Nothing she could say. It was do or die, now. She found herself going through the same excuses her men had probably played out. *No sir, the comms were damaged by the hackers. It took a few hours to fix, sir. No, sorry sir, I didn't get your call . . .*

Elena and David both shared a common misery. Neither was out there, killing smurfs. If Elena was resigned to it, for her father was stern in his desire to keep her safe, David was adamant that he should have gone. His friend was out there, he knew, and though Tom had always been the troublemaker and rabble rouser, it wasn't right that he was here, safe and sound, while Tom was risking his life with the bomb.

Enrique looked quite satisfied with the way things had gone. "Better in here than dead," he said simply. He was never a man for futile heroics.

An explosion sounded off in the distance, followed by echoing gunfire. The ambush had begun. The fighting was sporadic, and none of the three left in the cave had any idea who was winning until one of the shuttles blasted for the sky at high speed.

"I think our people just won, if I had to guess." David said.

Elena smiled, and David somehow managed the courage to put his arm around her. She was like much of Terra Nova, he reflected, beautiful and dangerous in equal measure. Behind him, Enrique chuckled.

"Took you long enough, *gringo*." He said pleasantly. "She's been leading you on for months."

Elena leaned her head on his shoulder and glared briefly at the burly enforcer. It was a glare that could have cut steel. Enrique clamped shut. But then she smiled happily again. David was struck by two notions in that moment. First, that this was a woman with a temper that could melt iron and was probably exceedingly dangerous to court. And second, that he didn't give a shit. He was going to do it anyway.

For perhaps the very first time, he was grateful to be here.

The whoosh of a turbine engine blasted above them, suddenly, with loose dirt shifting down from the cave's ceiling.

"*Coño!*" Enrique cursed. "Down, down!"

He practically pushed them deeper in the cave and ducked behind a bend in the cave himself, shouldering his rifle. "How the fuck did they find us?"

David spared a glance upward. He had his suspicions, but there was no time. He flicked the safety and pulled the slide back, putting a round in the chamber. Elena was protesting behind him, saying that she had more experience shooting than he did. But he didn't give a shit about that, either. He was going to fight anyway. The iron glare returned, and he turned to Enrique, still feeling the heat of that stare upon him. Carlos's enforcer nodded, a newfound respect in his eyes.

Enrique gestured him to one side of the cave and David followed.

The sailors were quick. *Probably,* some part of David's brain realized, *they aren't the same ones who just got their asses kicked. Those would surely possess more sense.*

Everything slowed, and yet it was over so quickly. David had only the briefest sense of it all, even though it felt like forever as it happened.

He was hunched down, most the way behind an edge in the cave that he knew was dark, Enrique's backup should anything go wrong. The shuttle landed in front of the cave mouth, its weapons trained inward. They had fallen back out of reach. Hopefully the sailors weren't just going to casually blast the mountain out from under them.

There were only three of them, but they wore body armor, and came on doggedly and competently, using the bend in the cave as cover. Enrique's rifle rang out, and one of the sailors fell to the ground in a heap of pain, disabled, perhaps. The groans indicated that he wasn't dead, though. Another sailor likewise fell, a round burning a hole straight through his helmet. Enrique dropped the magazine and reached for another.

Rock shattered by Enrique's position, and the burly enforcer fell, blood slowly soaking his chest from a trio of wounds. David could see the life leaving his eyes. There was one sailor left, and the man advanced cautiously, apparently thinking that the final obstacle had been broken as there had been no other signs of resistance. David waited, all his focus on this one task. He clutched the weapon and took his stance, exactly as Enrique had shown him. Behind the rock face, in the dark of the cave, he was near to invisible, but he was under no illusions. If he failed, he would die.

And then Elena would suffer her sister's fate.

He took carefully aim and squeezed. And again. And again. The first was wide, but by the second shot, he had adjusted. The sailor was diving down to the ground for better cover, but David was quicker. He kept firing, not even remembering clearly how many rounds he possessed.

A round caught the sailor in the chest. Then another. Though the armor prevented his immediate death, he cried out in pain, the ribs behind the armor snapping. Through it all, the sailor kept focus on his enemy, the rifle closing on his enemy.

David's final round caught the sailor in the forehead, and the struggles ceased. The weapon clicked empty.

Elena wasted no time, for David had almost forgotten about the disabled first sailor. Her knife was out, and she quickly slit the throat of the wounded sailor, flashing just a hint of a cruel, vengeful expression as she dropped the man's head back into the dirt. Blood spurt in gushing arterial bursts.

David only just then realized he was shaking like a leaf from the adrenaline surge, and sat down, a ball of nerves. He couldn't look at Enrique's ruined body. Not yet. The old enforcer's training, as little as he had time to give, was all that saved his life. And hers.

When she saw Enrique's sightless eyes, belonging to the man who had long been her father's right hand, the tears began to flow. He held her silently, controlling his own shock and sadness. Enrique had been the first to respect him as a man, not some lumpy nerd. And yet in the battle-high, it was all so distant, somehow. He'd pay for that later, he realized. For now, he had to remain strong for Elena's sake.

Anger vied with fear within her as the communicator continued to ping. There would be no escaping the consequences this time, Pamela knew. She tapped the accept button. High Admiral Hortzmann's face filled the screen, and she blinked back the tears.

"It's over, Pam. Recall your men." His voice was solemn and cold. No desire remained in it, only profound resignation and disappointment. The pain of it ate at her more than the floggers had ever managed.

Her fragile grip on composure failed utterly. It wasn't merely the end of her career, or the foiling of her plans for wealth and freedom that broke her. She was shocked to discover that, in the end, her lover's profound disappointment in her meant more than anything else ever could.

Long Pier, Constancia, Cienfuegos, Terra Nova

Sunlight glittered over the clear waters of Cienfuegos. Fall had come to the island, and a pleasant breeze was blowing in from the east, keeping the heat at bay for the moment. Thomas leaned idly against the dock piling. His linen shirt, a rare gift from a grateful Carlos, fluttered slightly in the wind. He could almost imagine being on old Earth again, just for a moment, living in some tropical paradise.

But a paradise Terra Nova was not. The rickety contraption barely worth of the term "boat" floating alongside the makeshift dock was evidence enough of that. A few haphazard sailors were removing the ropes. It was time to go, he realized. Long months of memes, war, and death had passed, and a measure of peace had taken hold on the island, though probably only for a little while. All around Terra Nova, things were going bad, but in the Latin sectors, it was worse. *Best to get out while the getting is good*, he thought. Certainly best to leave before Carlos started another brush war with a starship captain, and the whole island got locked down again.

"Sure you won't stay?" David asked, his arm wrapped protectively around his blushing bride. Carlos had taken enough of a liking to the man to allow it. Though heaven help David if he ever mistreated Elena. The whole island knew of Cranston's fate on the stake. *David is certainly a brave man*, Tom thought admiringly.

"Nah. You got reason enough to stick around. Me? I'd just be staying for your lame ass." He laughed and David smiled. "And anyway, I want to get my hands on another machine, get another crack at the smurfs, man. Shitpost the world again. Better chance of that in the American sector than around here." Tom smiled. For the first time since all of this began, it was *his* choice. He'd probably never see David again, and that weighed on his mind. But who could say? His life was finally his own. Perhaps he'd come back one day.

David nodded. "Yeah, I figured you'd say that. You think you'll find another computer up there?"

"Maybe. If anyone saved some scraps of technology, it'd be the Americans." Thomas pondered that for a moment. He had plenty of what passed for money around here, for Carlos had not been stingy. And the sailors were Carlos's men. More importantly, he was armed, experienced, and no longer appeared like some helpless geek stranded in a world he didn't understand. He'd get his chance. If it took him decades, he'd get his chance.

"Yeah, you're probably right." Extending his hand, David smiled. Thomas took it and embraced him. They'd been roommates, coworkers, and friends for many years, in several countries and two whole planets. Everything would be different, now. For a moment, he felt maudlin.

"I'll see you around," David said, a trace of regret in his voice.

"No, you won't." Tom smiled.

David laughed. "Come on, asshole, you know better than to use a cliché like that around me."

One of the sailors tossed the last line to the boat and hopped in. Tom's guards fidgeted nervously. It was time to go.

"Yeah, I suppose I do. You take care of that wife of yours, man." It was still strange to think of David as a married man, now.

"Oh yeah." A full grin spread across David's face, before he turned around and walked off. His new bride smiled knowingly and shrugged, waving before she disappeared after him.

Captain Kemal Aydin sent his first message from his new command. The *Angela Merkel* had seen most of her crew replaced in a massive smuggling scandal in the weeks before, the likes of which he didn't fully understand. Those that remained were still morose and demoralized, and thought of the vessel as somewhat cursed. But Kemal appreciated the opportunity for advancement, at least. And he certainly didn't follow the odd superstitions of the leftover crew. The New Ottoman government had seen fit to select him to fill their diversity quota slot for the Terra Novan fleet, and that was a high honor.

The previous captain had been a nervous, utterly disheveled wreck when she'd transferred command of the *Angela Merkel*. She appeared like a woman expecting death around every corner. And then there were the rumors of her sexual depravity. Of course, some of *those* stories included High Admiral Hortzmann himself. His nickname *whore's man* was known to all, even a fresh-off-the-crossing captain, and was spoken aloud openly by nobody with even a modicum of common sense.

Either way, Kemal decided he wanted no part of the ship's checkered past. He would give the vessel and its crew a fresh start. His console chimed, and the high admiral appeared on his screen.

"Congratulations on your new command, Captain," the high admiral began, though the man seemed oddly preoccupied.

I wonder if the rumors are true, Kemal thought.

"Thank you, sir," he said diplomatically. "We are assuming station at . . . "

The fart that blasted out of the speakers was loud and disgusting, sounding very much like someone had just shit his pants. Kemal looked around the bridge.

"Captain?" The high admiral was caught between laughter and professional disgust.

Another fart rang out. And another. Kemal looked around. There were shrugs and confused looks all around from the bridge crew. The comm officer was furiously punching at his keyboard, his face turning a particularly deep shade of red.

The last fart sounded very wet and then tapered off into a long, thin squeak.

"A moment, sir, we appear to be having some ah, technical difficulties."

Cursed ship indeed, Kemal thought. He had the first inkling that perhaps his appointment hadn't been much of an honor at all.

INTERLUDE:
From Jimenez's *History of the Wars of Liberation*

At this point in the history of the wars of liberation, it is perhaps questionable even to call them "wars." Instead, what was going on were a series of scattered resistance movements, most not even aware of the others' existence or, at least, not in contact or cooperating, not always violent, and almost always low scale. And, if it seemed like war to our ancestors, the UN certainly didn't officially admit to any such thing yet.

However, what was admitted to officially and what was understood, even if not spoken of in public, were not quite the same things. Thus, as we know from captured records, at the highest levels of Old Earth's United Nations the realization gradually dawned that they had a problem on Terra Nova, which problem was likely to interfere with their program of resettling Earth's most recalcitrant traditionalists and antiaristocrats, and, which must have been maddening, forced them to stop resettling those same antiprogressives until matters of Terra Nova could be sorted out. This, of course, also meant more trouble on Old Earth and a slower than desired implementation of their entire program.

We may imagine, but are not privy to, the negotiations, the screaming sessions, the cajoling, and the bribes that led to General Titus Ford being named Inspector General, though the commander of Earth Forces in all but name. Why the Secretary General chose an officer from the only one of Earth's significant nations not to receive a colonial grant on Terra Nova remains a mystery . . .

12.
THE REDEEMER

Tom Kratman[13]

"And Australia, as everyone knows, is inhabited entirely by criminals."
—Vizzini, The Princess Bride

UNSN *Amerigo Vespucci*

The Inspector General awakened on the floor of his cabin, belly down, with his own vomit trying to force itself back into his mouth and up his nostrils, and with every nerve ending in his body screaming with the memory of the agony of conscious passage through the transitway that linked the solar system and the system containing the colony world of Terra Nova. It was a memory of being torn apart, atom by atom, being reassembled, outside-inward, being torn apart once again, and then falling into infinite nothingness, forever.

---

13 Tom Kratman is a defector from the People's Republic of Massachusetts, having enlisted into the Army in 1974, aged seventeen. He served tours as an enlisted grunt with both the 101st Airborne and the 193rd Infantry Brigade, in Panama. At that point the Army gave Kratman a scholarship and sent him off to Boston College to finish his degree and obtain a commission. Commissioned, he served again in Panama, then with the 24th Infantry Division, and with Recruiting Command.

Saddam Hussein (UHBP) rescued Tom from the last by invading Kuwait.

Tom got out in '92 and went to law school. He became a lawyer in '95 but stayed in the reserves, taking the odd short tour and doing a bit of white collar mercenary work to retain his sanity and avoid practicing law.

In 2003 the Army called him up to participate in the invasion of Iraq. As it turned out he had a 100% blockage in his right coronary artery and wasn't going anywhere fun anytime soon. Instead, he languished here and there, before finally being sent on to be Director, Rule of Law, for the U.S. Army Peacekeeping and Stability Operations Institute. Keep in mind the divine sense of humor.

Retired in 2006, he's returned to Virginia to write. His books published to date include the Countdown series, the Desert Called Peace series, three in John Ringo's Posleen universe, plus *Caliphate* and *A State of Disobedience*. He's also got several books' worth of columns on everyjoe.com, which he'll someday collate and assemble, as well as a number of essays on the art of war up with Baen. Tom's married to a (really beautiful) girl from rural western Panama.

"Ohhh . . . my head," he croaked, pulling his stocky, five foot eight frame up to rest on hands and knees. He shook his grayed head, but only once. The agony of that collapsed him right down again into the pool of his own puke. "Never drink again . . . what am I talking about? I don't drink." He sniffed the air. "And I don't lie around in my own vomit, either. Stand up, old man; stand up."

Shakily, unsteadily, the IG forced himself to his own two feet. He swayed on them, back and forth, left and right. As he did, memories—memories from before his dis- and re-assembly—came flooding back. *I know who I am. I know—more or less—where I am. I know why I am here.*

The "who" of the matter was Titus Ford, a retired Australian officer, currently employed and remilitarized by Earth's United Nations, to be Inspector General for all Earth forces on Terra Nova. The where of the matter was, still more or less, on the Terra Novan side of the transitway, a worm-hole by any other name, aboard UNSN *Amerigo Vespucci*. As for the why . . .

I am going—I have been sent—to Terra Nova to push aside the nincompoops who have completely fucked up the planet and to bring it back to order and subordination to the United Nations.

And my powers are close to absolute. "Forget diversity, Titus," *the SecGen told me.* "Forget all that ever-so-sensitive crap. We can't afford it anymore. If we don't settle the planet down, then exiling troublemakers from here threatens our future here." *Well, that was nice to know.* "You are the ultimate authority for military and civil legal matters," *he said.* "You want someone shot? Shoot him. Or her." *Also happy news. And the press? I foresee some tragic accidents in the near future for any number of them. Bastards; don't they know whose side they're required to be on? The only real problem is that I have to keep my hands off the damned Americans' colonies.*

Of course the happiest news was for my ears alone . . . but if I can succeed . . .

The pain was ebbing fast, now. As it left, stamina and intelligence, both, began to return, the latter more than the former. *Well, hell, I'm closer to seventy than sixty, mid-level rejuvs notwithstanding, so stamina is less of an* is *and more of a* used to be. *But intelligence . . .*

Though much detested in his own country and by his own army, in good part for his extreme faith in and devotion to the United Nations, nobody had ever called Ford "stupid."

And I am not coming alone, either.

In comparison with the haphazard, undisciplined, poorly led and worse trained rabble that made up a good deal, even most, of the existing forces on Terra Nova, Ford had, in the *Vespucci* and the three ships following it over the next several months, over seventy thousand permanent UN troops, all raised, equipped, paid by, and trained for the UN by himself and his hand-picked underlings, plus another ten thousand officers and senior noncoms to replace the worst of the human filth currently in command. The officers and men had been hand-picked from among the most ruthless and mercenary elements of Earth's increasingly bored armies. These were not the kind of rabble that had accompanied Ford's de facto predecessor, the unmissed, unmourned bastard Kotek Annan, to his richly deserved death. These were real soldiers down in *Vespucci's* hold, as well as in the holds of the others.

No, not alone, either. And I've brought the sweepings of any number of prisons for things I may have to order that are really *nasty.*

There came a *wooshing* sound from behind him, followed by a clipped Bantu accent enquiring, "General Ford, are you all right."

He recognized the voice. Without turning, he answered, "I will be, Captain Mzilikazi, as soon as I navigate myself to the shower and wash this filth off of me."

"Very good, sir. I'll have some crewmen sent down to clean up the mess." Sympathetically, the captain added, "And, no need for embarrassment; some of us the transition bothers, some it does not. It's no reflection on character or worth."

"Of *course* it's not a reflection on *my* character, Captain," Ford snarled. "Who would imagine that it could have been?"

Embarrassed now, himself, Mzilikazi coughed in embarrassment before scurrying off.

In an earlier age, Ford would have sat at a large wooden desk, files full of reports piled high around him, as he made his way through the military, political, and literal jungles of the new world. Instead, and now fully sanitized, he read from a large computer screen the reports—*as many as a quarter of which may be reliable*—generated from the headquarters ahead and from its subordinates. On the way to the transitway, Earth-side, he'd sorted those he suspected contained more truth than the others, though most of even those he hadn't read yet, relying instead on subject matter and the censors' opinions.

If the censors wanted the information suppressed, there's a very good chance that it is true. It's even more likely to be true the more they demanded it be suppressed.

"Blame the mess on the failure of the first colonization effort?" Ford mused, reading one of the first reports on his list. "On the fact that we recreated the ethnic nations of Earth here? There may be a very *little* merit there, but it's not as if there were any choice."

He closed that window and opened the next. This he read with concern. Rolling his eyes, he thought, *Did those assholes in the frozen south* really *think they could have gotten a major mining operation going and the fleet not be aware of it. Hmmm* . . . He pulled up orbital patterns and assignments and then wrote a note to himself: HAVE INTERNAL SECURITY CHECK THE FILES FOR THE THREE SHIPS CAPABLE OF OVERSEEING THAT SECTION OF SECORDIA. SOMEBODY WAS—OR SEVERAL SOMEBODIES WERE—ANTICIPATING A PAYOFF.

Ford tended to shout a lot, when dealing with subordinates, hence also tended to write his notes in caps, as well.

He was something of a rarity in UN circles, was Titus Ford, an apparently devout Christian. How genuine that devotion was a matter of considerable speculation in certain circles. It certainly didn't seem to be in evidence when he wrote, WHO, FOR THE LOVE OF GOD, WAS STUPID ENOUGH TO HIRE MOSLEMS TO ATTACK A CHRISTIAN VILLAGE? FIND AND RELIEVE; POSSIBLY TRY AND EXECUTE. DOUBT ANYONE DUMB ENOUGH TO HIRE MOSLEMS FOR A MILITARY ACTION COVERED HIS TRACKS TOO WELL.

And then: SECORDIA AGAIN? ODDS THAT ROGER LAMPREY HAS SURVIVED LONG ENOUGH TO MAKE IT WORTH WHILE PUTTING A BOUNTY ON HIS HEAD? NO MATTER; IF HE'S DEAD I DON'T HAVE TO PAY IT, DO I?

The next report was half technical, and technical in an area in which he had little expertise. *I'm no medico, but I know this, if*

someone in Balboa had the ability to defeat a biological attack, that
someone also knows how to create a biological attack. Worse, they may
well have diseases to use we haven't the first clue about. Still worse, we
have to believe them when they say they can launch and will launch a
biological attack on Earth if we try that again. We need another
method of dealing with the rebels in Balboa Colony.

To be fair, so far they've been playing it straight up, them against us,
trying to make us sick of it. We can keep that up for a good long while
without getting fancy.

About the other problems there he only wrote the colony name,
BALBOA and the words, THINK OVER CAREFULLY.

On the other hand, there's no reason not to interdict the flow of
arms into the colony, is there? A small team introduced into southern
Columbia, too, to seek out and destroy undesirable elements there?

He'd read the next set of reports before, but had never been able
to make up his mind about what to do in Cochin Colony. *Give him*
his due; the frog is making progress there. And he's only a liability where
the press is concerned. Since I will be allowed to control the press, most
of it, there should be no problem. I think . . . yes, Cochin goes on least
priority; let Arcand have his head.

Reading on, Ford came to a short paragraph in the report from
Cochin concerning discipline, morale and . . . *Leave it to the Frogs,*
field brothels. On the other hand, they don't seem to be having nearly
the problem with desertion one would expect.

There had been a lot of desertion from among the national forces
seconded to the UN and sent to Terra Nova. It was bad enough that
they'd typically walked off with their arms and equipment, as well as
whatever ammunition they could scrounge up. Worse were the ones
who took radios, night vision equipment, or the rare crew served
weapon. But the very worst . . .

FIND THAT HELICOPTER. AND COURT-MARTIAL AND
THREATEN TO SHOOT THAT WOMAN'S FORMER CO-PILOT.
THAT SHOULD BRING HER AND THE CHOPPER BACK. HMMM
. . . THE HELICOPTER? WELL, PROBABLY NOT, NOT IN THAT
CLIMATE. BUT IF IT DID STILL WORK, GETTING HER TO
SURRENDER WOULD BE ENOUGH. THE GUERILLAS ARE NOT
TOO BLOODY LIKELY TO HAVE A SPARE PILOT ON HAND.

Though normally a humorless sort—Ford never had quite gotten the joke, "and Australia, as everyone knows, is inhabited entirely by criminals"—he couldn't keep the smile off his face over the pirated porn films from the *Angela Merkel*.

SOMEONE ELSE WITH A DESPERATE NEED TO BE RELIEVED AND SENT HOME IN DISGRACE, THE CURRENT HIGH ADMIRAL. OR SHOULD I JUST SHOOT HIM OR HAVE HIM THROWN OFF A CLIFF. WEIGH CAREFULLY.

Wellington shouldn't be too hard. It's an island; we can interdict arms from space easily enough. And it's not so big that we can't totally saturate it if I put the whole corps into it at once. We can stage out of Atlantis Island; it's halfway there anyway . . .

PRIORITY ONE: TURN ATLANTIS INTO A REAL BASE. PRIORITY TWO: CRUSH THE REBELS IN WELLINGTON.

One report he found particularly troubling. It concerned a bombing that matched very closely the *modus operandi* of a group on old Earth, half political terrorist and half criminal. *Or maybe a little more than half criminal. We'd wondered why they'd toned down operations on Earth. Maybe now I know; they just moved. They're going to be tough to deal with, as tough as they were back home. They're smart, skilled, dedicated, ruthless . . . and why is our intel so goddamned poor here? I shouldn't have to be figuring this out on my own fifty million miles from the new world.*

INTEL. INTEL. INTEL. WHATEVER IT TAKES. ANY MEANS NECESSARY. I MUST HAVE BETTER INTEL.

Hmmm . . . intel . . . and rapes . . . and field brothels; the rabble the worst armies of the Third World, back home, give to the UN have done our cause more harm than . . . well, it's not clear to me they've done any good. But maybe, just maybe, I can set up a system of mobile field brothels to keep the troops happy, stop some, at least, of the rapes, and maybe gather some intel, too. Got to be careful about that, though; the girls—well, boys, too, I suppose, for some tastes—are going to be an intelligence sieve for us, as well.

MOBILE FIELD BROTHELS; THINK OVER CAREFULLY. TIGHT CONTROL OF THE INFORMATION FLOW.

Ford sighed, then leaned back in his leather chair. While fixed to the carpeted deck beneath him, it was of an altogether superior construction to any on the ship, barring only Captain Mzilikazi's, reclining nicely.

We need a base, Ford thought, interlocking his fingers behind his head. *We need an unassailable base, someplace we can defend with only the lightest force—maybe even automated, in whole or in part. We need a place the locals can't bribe our people to loot for them. We've plainly been feeding this insurgency . . . these insurgencies, from the beginning. Those arms coming out of the Americans' colonies were not made there. Erased markings or not, they're our designs, muzzles to butts.*

I also need a place to rest the troops where they're not going to need to watch out for a grenade rolled under their tables while they chat up a joy girl.

Atlantis Island

Instructions from the ship moved considerably faster than the ship itself, in system. Those instructions, from Ford to his new command, had come in daily bursts, without a great deal of give and take on the other end. The first of these had been:

"High Admiral Hortzmann is hereby relieved of duty and placed under arrest. Vice Admiral Qin is likewise. Vice Admiral Beattie will assume Qin's position, *pro tem*, as Deputy Commander for the fleet. His first priority is to see to Hortzmann's and Qin's incarceration, incommunicado. His second is to prepare to build, and then build, a base on Atlantis Island sufficient to billet, rest, train, familiarize, and support a full corps of infantry together with their supporting arms. Further details will follow, especially as regards the intelligence collection and interrogation center. If Beattie does not wish to join Qin and Hortzmann . . . "

None of this, of course, is really an IG's job. But then I'm not really an IG, either.

Damn, but it's good to be off that miserable ship.

"Do a spin around the island," Ford told the pilot of his shuttle from the *Vespucci*. "Take your time; I want to see what Beattie's accomplished."

"Yes, sir. Sir, there *are* troops standing by for your arrival parade."

Ford scowled. "They won't break or wilt for waiting in ranks an extra hour. Moreover, I don't need your advice on ceremonies; do as you're told."

"Yes, sir."

Ford pulled up a map on his tablet, matching what we could see to what he had demanded. From half a mile up, it looked fairly good. There was a large area between two peaks for an artillery impact area, with what appeared to be a series of ranges along two sides of that. He saw a mix of tent cities and more solid barracks to greet the troops as they were thawed and debarked. A ring road around the island wasn't complete yet, but Beattie had explained that well enough to satisfy the IG. Though the shuttles weren't nearly complete with bringing down the makings of the two disassembled airships he'd brought from Earth, the massive sheds in which they would be put back together were going up.

On the whole . . . "Well . . . I suppose the weasel can keep his job for now. Take us to the landing zone by headquarters."

"Yes, sir."

The shuttle didn't need much of a landing strip, though some fuel and wear and tear could be saved if there was one.

"I don't care about that," Ford explained to the pilot. "Just take me down to the area by the port."

"Aye, aye, sir. Sir, but what about . . ." The shuttle banked, accelerated, then pulled up, nose first, and began a gentle descent. From the pilot's compartment Ford could see what were at least hundreds, maybe thousands, of laborers, probably barely clad and working under the hot sun. He was too far away to see that they were under the lash, as well, but he knew that Beattie had put the prisoners of war to use.

"The troops? The band, sir? They're . . . "

"Give a call down below and have them dismissed. I'm not in the mood for a parade or a speech, anyway."

"Aye, sir," said the pilot, while thinking, *Asshole.*

As the shuttle descended, more of the work became visible and in detail. This included the—*Might as well be honest and call them what they are*—slave laborers.

"I wonder," Ford mused aloud, "what the interrogation procedures are for captives?"

★★★

"Talk to me about intel, Beattie," Ford commanded, in the air-conditioned comfort of the first building finished on the island, the Headquarters. Next to it, naturally, was the not quite finished officers' club. The admiral looked soft and fat compared to Ford's lean frame.

"I can get the intel . . ." Beattie stammered.

"I didn't *ask* for the intel officer, dummie; I told *you* to tell me about it."

Oh, dear, thought the vice-admiral. "This is not really my . . ."

"Talk, Beattie, now, or go join Hortzmann in the stockade and then the prisoners on construction detail." Ford gave Beattie a grin replete with menace.

Beattie's face paled. He gulped with dread. Being a senior UN officer, set among the prisoners, amounted to a death sentence. *And a very bad death at that*, he thought, near enough to panic. He forced himself to remain calm. *This one is not known for excessive sympathy but, on the other hand, even less for understanding when you try to pull the wool over his eyes. Honesty? In United Nations service? Well, it will at least have the virtue of novelty.*

"We know hardly anything about them, sir!" Beattie blurted out. "They hardly use any radio, so our signals intel is nonexistent. We have informers among them but our consensus is that most of the informers are informing on *us*. Patrols bring back nothing useful; we either own the areas we patrol in or the enemy does. The end result is exactly the same, nothing.

"For long range communication they use what the locals call 'trixies,' archaeopteryxes, and alleged to be very bright birds, carrying written messages. Those, and human messengers. And we're not allowed to engage the trixies because the UN Commission on Preserving Indigenous Fauna got them declared endangered."

Quite despite the air conditioning, Beattie felt sweat drip down his back as he continued, "General . . . sir, you cannot tell the difference between a perfectly secure area to us and a perfectly secure area for the enemy, because in neither case are there any indicators to judge from.

"We're blind as bats, flailing about without point of aim."

Ford sat silently, for a long moment, letting the vice-admiral sweat. Finally, when he judged Beattie to be done almost to a turn, he asked, "What about the prisoners?"

"They just spit at us."

"Do they, indeed?" Ford smiled, still more grimly. "*Now* you can go get me the chief of intelligence. I have a little book for him to read."

"A book, sir?"

"Yes, a book. I brought it from Earth. Some hack science fiction author—of all unlikely things—penned it, oh, it must have been over a hundred years ago, I think. It tells you how to get information from a rock, provided you have at least two rocks with the same information. We're starting to use the techniques on Earth to deal with some of the more . . . mmmm . . . troublesome . . . *citizens.*"

The UN didn't have much on the prisoners, but at least it could identify where they'd been captured, and why. Since Ford had picked Wellington for his first pacification effort, the forty-nine prisoners taken there were his first targets.

Listening to a young woman screaming and begging was harder than I expected, Ford thought, said screams echoing from the concrete and coral walls of the new interrogation building. *One might be forgiven for believing this one was innocent. But she was caught, red-handed, with explosive residue on her hands and clothes, She's not innocent at all.*

Besides, the two others being put to the question were caught with the exact same residue on their hands and clothing, and fingered her out of a pictorial lineup, separately. She's guilty as sin.

Though Ford forced himself not to think about it, the Maori girl was also tough as nails. She'd withstood the electricity, the driving of long pins under her nails, the brutal removal of a couple of those, and a good deal of time in Skevington's Daughter, a sort of compressed racklike device, giving up nothing in the process but screams, not even conversation. Now they had both her feet in wooden contraptions—"boots," they were called—being slowly crushed.

"I wonder," he asked himself, "what's worse for her, the pain or the knowledge that, in the future, she'll be a permanent cripple if she doesn't cooperate?"

The screams suddenly stopped, replaced by mere racking sobs, then what sounded like broken sentences, framed by weeping. The interrogator came out, a few minutes later, looking grim. "She'll talk now. She's already corroborated one piece of intel from the other two Wellingtonians. I think she'll spill her guts pretty easily from now on."

"And if not?" Ford asked.

"The dentist is standing by," the interrogator replied.

"Funny," said the interrogator, "the *Pravda* was always that you can't trust torture because people will say anything to stop the pain. What they missed was that anything includes the truth and if that is the only way to stop the pain, once they become convinced that that is the only way . . . "

"Then they sing like birds," Ford finished.

Little by little, an intelligence estimate built up on the island of Wellington, out in the *Mar Furioso*. A lot of the intelligence was too dated to be useful, but there were gems within it, lasting, durable gems, nonetheless. Terrain, for example, did not change, and corroborated eyewitness reports of the terrain of a place gave strong indicators of where the limited numbers of guerillas might be hiding. There were places no food could be grown or gathered, or where just about everything was poisonous. Unless those spots were close to farms or towns of fishing villages, there would be no guerillas there because they simply couldn't survive there.

Moreover, though seven of the Wellingtonians, unfortunate wretches, had died under torture, several dozen safe houses had been identified from the remainder. Ford and his chief of intelligence also thought they knew where the enemy's explosives were coming from, and those three locales were very high on the list for eradication.

"We even have the rudimentary sketches of the enemy chain of command there," Ford said, patting his intel chief on the shoulder in appreciation. "Well, such as it is."

If it wasn't a stormy night, it was at least a dark one, with none of Terra Nova's three moons in position to shine a light on Wellington. And as for the storm? That impended from the roughly thirty-six hundred paras from Ford's Parachute Brigade, standing by, indeed, some of them standing up, rigged for a drop onto the western island of the Wellington Archipelago. On a lower deck, heavy equipment was rigged for a drop, resting on wheeled conveyors and awaiting the push.

The pathfinders had come in earlier, aboard normal UN resupply missions.

While it some sense this was to be a mass drop, the largest unit dropped on any place would, in fact, be a company or a battery, and the company, actually, to secure the Drop Zone for the battery. For the most part, the troops would be going down as squads or platoons, to stake out ambush positions to bring a complete halt to all movement on the island. The pathfinders' job had actually for the most part been to set up radio beacons for the benefit of the airships. Only the three drop zones for the batteries had been actually staked and secured.

Up on the bridge, still wearing his usual wicked grin, Ford mused, *Anybody trying to escape our sweep over the next couple of days is going to find himself, or herself, waltzing into one kill zone after another, subject to observation at all times, and hence to artillery.*

Not that it will be over all that quickly; I'm giving it five terrestrial months to completely break the resistance here. But this will give us the upper hand right away. The enemy below is going to be thinking survival and little but. As we take more prisoners . . . well . . . we get more intel, especially since I've now got a thoroughly practiced group of interrogators.

"Captain?" Ford asked the skipper of the airship he rode.

"Sir?"

"Their motto down there is *kia mate toa*, I understand. It means something like 'fight to the death.' Do you think they will?"

The airship captain just answered with his own wicked smile, a silent echo of Ford's. Then his finger reached out to push the button that would turn red blinking lights to solid green, launching the first of the paras out into the moonless sky.

"Everyone but the rump of my headquarters is on the ground, sir," announced the parachute brigade commander, Colonel Langlais, skinny, square-jawed, and exuding an air of utter ferocity. "I'll join them below now, with your permission."

"Do it, and good hunting, Langlais. I'll be back in six days with two brigades of regular infantry to begin the sweep. I am confident you can hang on until then."

"We may die of boredom," the colonel answered, before sketching out an informal salute and turning on his heels.

Nine days later, New Wairakei, Wellington

After a bit over five dozen ambushes disastrous to the resistance, word began to spread rather quickly: Do not leave wherever you happen to be. In the nature of things, that meant there were resistance members, leaders especially, in one place who had come from someplace completely different.

"And that's how we catch them," murmured Ford, watching the entire population of a village marched through a DNA testing station under the guns of one of his four Military Police battalions. "Well, some of them, anyway, enough to be worth the effort."

The interrogation tent, like the other fourteen tents set up nearby, had MPs at both the front and rear entrances. It was a smallish tent, maybe a dozen feet across, with a field desk and a chair set up. Another chair sat on the ground next to the field desk.

"Why are you here, Mr. Singh?" asked the interrogator, a plain-faced woman with a stocky build.

The local, a man light enough in complexion, as well as blond and blue-eyed enough, to give the lie to the name, "Singh," resisted the urge to answer with his actual thought and the truth, *I'm here because your armed goon squad dragged me here.* No, this wasn't the time for honesty.

Unlike most UN troops, the interrogator's uniform bore no nametag, though she went by the name of Loretta Castro. She asked the same basic question again with a little more implied to it. "Why are you here when your people are all over in Whirinaki?"

Whirinaki had been subject to the same routine a few days prior that New Wairakei was experiencing today. Eventually, the entire island, and possibly the entire world, would be DNA registered, the better to allow UN forces to know who belonged where and, more importantly, who did not.

"I married one of the local girls," answered Singh. He was not—not quite—a prisoner yet and would have been just as happy to remain that way. His cell would have preferred it, too.

"Indeed?" Castro typed a few words into her keyboard, then turned around a computer monitor that sat on her field desk, though off to one side. The monitor had pictures of several score of the local females. and said, "Point her out to me, please."

"Ah, well, she died, you see?"

"Indeed? And so point out your mother-in-law, please?"

"Her, too. Dead. *Pouakai* attack." The Pouakai were a very large brand of eagle, extinct on Old Earth for more than half a millennium, but still flourishing on Wellington, on Terra Nova.

"Indeed? And they're both in the cemetery? How are their graves marked?"

"Ummm . . ."

"And why is there no record of an attack here by one of those birds?"

"Ummm . . ."

"And no record of a marriage?"

"Ummm . . ."

Castro stuck one hand in the air, extended a finger, whirled it around twice and then pointed at Singh. "Take him away," she told the MPs, while thinking, *Thank whatever powers there be that I failed that course.* "Mark him down for a class one interrogation."

Uh, oh; that doesn't sound good.

Two months later

Daily, Ford checked the map in headquarters as slowly, inexorably, it changed from red to UN blue, even as the prison camps filled with the detained, the dispossessed, the desperate, and the doomed.

As a general rule, Inspector General Ford didn't shoot even the worst prisoners. Instead, he put them to work. The most recalcitrant he moved out of Wellington, and put to work growing food to support his army. These, with their families, were fed a portion of their production, just enough to keep body and soul together.

And that frees up hull space—a lot of hull space—to bring munitions, fuel, and other supplies in system.

Still others could be seen on any given day on Atlantis, cutting and hauling lumber, smashing coral into aggregate, building, clearing. These couldn't have their rations matched to what they grew of course, so norms were set, beneath which rations were sharply curtailed.

Mortality is, of course, high with these. No matter; their lives are not worth much to them and to me they're worth nothing at all.

On Wellington, on both East Island and West Island, some, along with civilian corvées temporarily impressed, spent their days clearing and building roads to facilitate logistics to support his troops as they hunting for the enemy. A few he permitted to be recruited into his own forces, as scouts.

And none of those who don't have families we can hold as hostages.

He'd had to have two entire families shot, in fact, which tended to reduce the numbers of Wellingtonians trying to join his force but made those who did want and were allowed in *much* more reliable.

They've got to be getting desperate now, I think. And desperate men . . .

Wellington Community College, Canterbury, Wellington

There were plans somewhere to turn the colony's sole institute of higher learning, WC3, into a four-year degree granting institution. Those plans remained on indefinite hold due to both a shortage of professors and a perceived lack of need. For those colonies fortunate enough to have them as yet, high schools actually, and unlike on Old Earth, produced children who could read.

Still, such as it was, WC3 was also, as with colleges and universities of earlier days, a hotbed of antiestablishmentarianism.

"We've just got to *do* something," said Professor Graham Kelsey, Ph.D., Anthropology. "The movement is collapsing!"

"It was always silly to try to resist the UN with arms," answered Professor Jane Ngati Whakama Smith, LLM (Law). "Nonviolent civil disobedience is the thing. It *always* works. Always."

"The students?" Kelsey asked.

"The students!" Smith replied. "And I know *just* where to lead them!"

Jacinda Hobbs, in pink, and Marion Ardern, in a rather dowdy gray, stood at either end of the hastily painted banner demanding

FREEDOM for Wellington from the UN. Behind them walked Smith and Kelsey, while behind the two professors marched some twelve hundred students of the WC3. All of them chanted what the banner proclaimed: "Freedom!"

Hobbs and Ardern made an interesting pair, the former being lanky, horse-faced, and toothy, while the latter was a close approximation of the Pillsbury Doughboy, in a mildly feminine idiom. The column turned left on Ohinehou Road, marching slowly toward the little port that served both Canterbury and a good deal of Ford's seaborne logistic effort.

The port was actually key; Thomas had that much right. With more than seventy thousand UN troops between both islands, including those previously there, and with one of the airships down for maintenance at any given time, plus the time required to load cargo at Atlantis Base that couldn't load itself, Ford had come to depend on contracted merchant bottoms to keep the campaign going. Any delay or disruption in that could have required him to reduce both the size of the force and the strenuousness of the effort in the colony.

And the shuttles are more trouble than they're worth, thought Ford, circling overhead in his command boat. *Even if I could spare the fuel, for routine logistics, which I cannot. But I'm going to have to use some fuel now.*

"Get me *Oberst* Schmidhuber on the line," he told his aide de camp, seated behind him. "And notify Beattie that I'm going to need more than thirty shuttles to transport the Special Action Battalion from Atlantis Base to here."

Thanas Schmidhuber, Ford thought. *I don't think I've ever met such a non-introspective, bigoted, willfully blind piece of shit in my life. He thinks of himself as a progressive, a stalwart supporter of the United Nations, peace, and global governance. He hates even the idea of Nazism, as he'll tell you at the drop of a hat. But he displays in full measure all that stereotypically German pigheadedness, inability to see any point of view but his own, strategically imbecilic short view, and toadying to superior authority that makes him nothing but another Nazi in the larval stage. And his idiot refugee from the customs police, Loehr, is even worse. And neither has absolutely the slightest clue, none whatsoever, that this is so. There were reasons, a century and a half ago, that, while fascism sprang up in many places, Nazism could only arise in Germany. And Germany, at core, has still never changed.*

And, as a larval stage Nazi, he's perfect for the position in which I have placed him, command of what, were I being frank, I would call "My Prison Sweepings for Special Purposes."

"And tell Beattie I'll want the thirty shuttles standing by at the nearest pickup zone to Schmidhuber's battalion within two hours."

"Oh, and get me some surveillance drones on that mob; I want clear faces and for us to be able to identify who's in charge."

Atlantis Base

Oberst Thanas Schmidhuber was a half-Albanian, half-German, raised in German culture. He greeted the news that a use had been found for his somewhat troublesome command with something approaching joy unstinted. Now, at last, he could show his devotion to the United Nations and its cause, while, at the same time, giving his troublesome rank and file a chance to take out their aggressions.

They frightened him, those reprieved criminals, under his nominal command. Dressed in full riot gear, with batons, it was only the firearms of his non-coms and officers that kept the swine in line. But then, nearly everything frightened him. Only with the power of the state fully behind him—and the bigger and more powerful the state, the better—did Thanas feel safe.

After a timid glance at the long, staggered trail of shuttles being boarded by his men, he turned and bounded up the ramp to his own boat, a standard model with the logo, "Stardestroyer," emblazoned along its side.

Ohinehou, Wellington

This is the way to do it, Jane Thomas self-congratulated. *Faced with non-violent resisters the powers that be cannot use vio . . . Hmmm . . . those are an awful lot of aircraft coming in to join that one that's been circling for the last half day. Ah, but they're not coming to attack, they're landing. Whew, that's a relief.*

"What do you suppose those are up to?" asked Kelsey, handing Smith a cup of tea catered in by the WC3 cafeteria, in support of the student protest. He pointed with a fat, rummy nose at the area the shuttles had gone to land.

"Can't be much," Jane answered. Then they heard the singing, distant, at first but growing louder.

The hills to either side of the road leading down echoed with the sounds of two big drums and the voices of men, singing, "*Das Lieben bringt gross Freud, es wissen's alle Leut . . .* "

Did they sing this song on the way to Lidice? Ford wondered. *It would not surprise me in the slightest.*

"*Weiss mir ein schoenes Schaetzelein . . .* "

I wonder if those innocents blocking the port . . .

"*mit zwei schwarzbraunes Aeugelein . . .* "

. . . have even the slightest idea of what they're in for.

"I'd feel a little better about this," said Thomas, "if the media had shown up to cover it."

"Relax," answered Kelsey, "they're setting up now." He pointed a finger to where a white-painted, horse-drawn wagon had stopped, and where a team was setting up a tripod for a camera along with some solar panels.

"Finally! They wouldn't dare get violent with the press watching." Thomas relaxed visibly, then sipped at her tea.

"Just in time, too." Kelsey again pointed with a broad, fat, veinous nose to where the point of the oppressor's column was emerging from a cut in the slope overlooking the town. The singing, they both noticed, had stopped, though the pounding of the big bass drums continued.

The column seemed endless, though in fact it was, including gaps between companies, only about half a mile long. The groups peeled off, first one going left, then the next to the right, then left, then right, and so on until the final group stopped in the center.

Then came commands over a loud speaker. Kelsey thought they were in some language other than English, but this was just mistaking a sergeant major's bellow for a foreign tongue. In some ways, of course, it *was* very foreign to a cultured academic.

The predatory growl that came from the line of men as they fanned out into a long double line didn't need any translation.

"They mean to harm us," Smith said, disbelievingly.

"The press will protect us; never fear," answered Kelsey. "Besides, even if they move forward it's only going to be to push us away from the port and the road to it."

"Then why," asked Kelsey, "are their end groups—'flankers,' I believe they're called—racing to form a line all the way down to the sea?"

"I don't . . . "

They heard a bugle call, nineteen notes, four, four, two, two, four, and three.

"What does that . . . ?"

Kelsey just shook his head. The call was repeated. On the last of the last three notes, a sound around from the head-to-foot armored troops. It was a sound of sack and plunder, of pillage and rape, of the wolf pack clustering to pull down the old elk or the baby moose. It was a sound that none of the mob around the port, students, professors, dock workers, or just the idly curious had ever heard before.

And then, still howling like madmen, which, indeed, a good third of them were, the troops raised their batons and charged.

For a long moment, Jane Smith stood, open-mouthed, at the sight of UN troops charging her with obvious intent to do harm. She might have stayed that way until they reached her, except that the students, perhaps a bit wiser, reacted immediately with flight toward the sea. That moving sea of humanity carried her along with it, away from the troops.

Where Kelsey was, she didn't know. (In fact, fat in body as fat in nose, Kelsey tried to flee with the rest. Thanas Schmidhuber's maniacs quickly caught up with him and cracked his skull in the course of bludgeoning him to the ground.) She knew there was danger and she knew there was screaming from every quarter. Most was fear but some sounded like pain, as well.

In a slight eddy in the human tide Jane stopped to risk looking behind her. She saw a boy from one of her classes, lying on the ground while two armored thugs kicked him in the ribs and head.

Between her and the student dozens more ran, male and female, clutching broken ribs or with blood seeping through fingers pressed to open scalps.

Jane took the further risk of remaining to see what was happening to the news team with the tripoded camera. Inexplicably, they, their white wagon, and the dray horse stood in place, filming unmolested. *That makes no sense*, she thought. *None of this makes any sense.*

In didn't occur to her as even a remote possibility that, if something really did make sense, it was most likely the evidence of her own senses.

The troops line slowed now. Jane saw she didn't have to run anymore; she could walk and keep ahead of them. Why that was, though . . .

It's the sheer mass of us, they can only push with their shields now to move us because we can't move much further, no matter how much they threaten with their batons.

This turned out to be not entirely true. A boy and a girl, both aged eighteen or nineteen years, at the edge of the frightened mob couldn't move any further. The UN troops simply smashed the boy over the head, then pulled him out and threw him to the ground. At a whistle's signal team of two from the second line of troops then taped his hands behind him and his feet together.

The girl was in for an altogether different treatment. Instead of clubbing her, she was dragged out of the mass. A foot was stuck out and she dragged over it, causing her to fall to the ground, skinning her knees. A rough hand slapped her once, hard across the face, knocking her to the pavement completely. Then, at another whistle blast, the two who had previously taped the boy were joined by two more. Those four took all four of her limbs in their control, holding her spread-eagled on the pavement. A fifth, apparently the one who had blown the whistle, knelt down between her splayed legs. Hands reached out, ripping her warm weather blouse apart. She screamed at the indignity. No matter, she was cuffed to silence again. At a hand signal she was lifted by her legs so that her skirt could be raised over her arse to her waist . . .

None of this, NONE of this, makes any sense!

Thanas Schmidhuber had never been much of a ladies' man. No, he'd lacked both the confidence and the looks for that. Nor did he smell like much of a man to any woman who had ever gotten close enough for that. Back on Earth, he'd paid whores. On the ship, he'd been frozen. Here, on Terra Nova, there hadn't been enough women for him to hope to snag one of his own.

Now, however, standing uniformed by the airship's ramp, he could have his pick of the girls. "Take two, if you like;" Ford had told him. "Your men did a fine job here and you deserve the reward. Take them, use them, sell them; whatever you like. Just don't forget that this won't be the last job for you and your psychopaths, Thanas."

Reaching one arm out, Thanas pointed at a very young thing, weeping and clutching the remnants of her clothing around her. He dropped his arm thinking, *No, she's just used goods. Aha; there's one.*

"Take the slut in pink to my stateroom," he ordered. "Chain her to the bed."

Jane and Graham, along with a dozen other professors and student leaders, were soundly taped and segregated from the rest. Before their eyes, a huge airship hovered a few feet off the ground with its cargo ramp lowered. Up it marched a horde of bloody, weeping, disheveled students and what were probably some innocent bystanders. More than the few of the girls clutched the ragged remnants of their clothing to cover as much of themselves as they could.

Gradually, Jane became aware of someone very calm, also very uniformed, looking at the segregated group from one side. She recognized him from a couple of places, the odd appearance on local television and the wanted posters put up by the resistance.

"What are you doing with those children?" she demanded of Titus Ford.

"Exactly what you were doing," Ford replied, "using them for my own purposes without much regard for their welfare." He gave a deep laugh at the nonplussed expression on Jane's face. "Oh, you want to know in detail? Sure, why not; the knowledge won't cost me anything.

"The boys are going to become agricultural slaves on Atlantis Base. It's a hard life and mortality is high, so I can use the replacements, thank you. As for the girls . . . they'll be staffing field brothels for my troops. Some of them may get redeemed if their families prove sufficiently helpful."

"That's—"

"Perfectly sensible use of what would otherwise be liabilities," he finished for her. "As for you people"—his gaze took in all the segregated group—"you may know some things of use to me, so you'll be going to a different part of Atlantis Base for some special attention. If you're all smart and lucky, it won't be too hard on you."

"And afterwards, if we cooperate?" she asked.

"You, what's left of you, will join the others."

"None of this makes sense," Jane insisted. "Why, *why*, do you do these things?"

"That's very easy," Titus Ford answered. "And your knowing it won't harm me or my cause any, either, not where you're going.

"Soldiers, and the more senior, the more this is true, are covetous of power, privileges, perks, and prestige. If I can show good progress in suppressing the rebels here, the Secretary General has promised me that I shall be viceroy for this planet. Think of it; for the first time in history a soldier shall rule an entire planet . . . and that soldier shall be me.

"And I shall be remembered forever for my part in civilizing this place for mankind. What more can a soldier ask than that?"

POSTSCRIPT:
From Jimenez's *History of the Wars of Liberation*

With the final subjugation of Wellington, the pattern was set. For the next seven years, the state of the resistance on Terra Nova went from bad to worse. One movement after another was crushed. First went the island colonies of Cienfuegos and Asturias. After those, Secordia felt the hard hand of Titus Ford's pacification. Then came the turn of Northern Castille, then Southern Castille. Of course, some elements of the resistance went deep underground, hoping to emerge and resume the fight later. But for all practical purposes, once Ford and the much-improved UN Marines settled on pacifying a colony, and then did so, few were bold and brave enough to raise their heads again once they moved on. And the informers and collaborators left behind when Ford moved on were many.

On the whole, things looked bleak for our ancestors in those years.

Ford, however, for all his capabilities, made several key mistakes. He forgot, as many generals are wont to do, that, in war, nothing fails like success, that, rather than following normal linear logic, war was the environment where nonlinear logic held sway, where victory contained the seeds of and led to defeat, where success led to failure.

In other words, with the example of Wellington, Asturias, and Castille in hand, the resistance learned to simply let him occupy their area and wait him out. He, after all, had an entire planet to pacify on a presumptively noninfinite allocation of time. We had only our own little colonies, and all the time in the universe.

Secondly, he forgot that enemies in war tend to come to resemble each other, often quite closely. If he could massacre a village where a bomb destroyed one of his platoons, so could—and did—we learn to exact frightful reprisals on cities, towns, villages, families, and individuals who collaborated with our occupiers. Did the UN torture for intelligence? God pity the man or woman from their forces who fell into our hands except as a reliable deserter to us.

Then, too, the more he used modern weapons, inevitably the more modern weapons fell into our hands. We had a claim on the produce of the armories of all of Old Earth, and that claim grew with time.

Thirdly, Ford presented our scattered resistance movements with what amounted to a global war. This, too, drove us to greater cooperation between movements for so long as the UN occupation lasted. It was not so very long before Sachsen guerillas were to be found fighting in Gaul, Tuscan in Illyria, Dacia, and Attica. We never did achieve a global command structure, of course, barring only the parties assembled for negotiating the final peace treaty, but the UN threat directly drove us into regional and continental cooperation and coordination.

Fourthly, he forgot that his people had someplace to go home to, Old Earth. We were stuck here, with no place else to go, and the choice of continuing resistance or accepting our status as slaves. Too many, of course, embraced that status. Most, ultimately, would not.

Finally, Ford's biggest miscalculation was to forget that he was, longevity treatments notwithstanding, only mortal.

But that is a tale for the second volume of our history.

AFTERWORD:

I joke rather frequently that the reason I wrote three books in John Ringo's Posleen universe is that I don't play well with others. It's sort of true, too. You see, originally, I was supposed to do a new series with John, one to be called *The Drift Road Wars* and for which he'd written up an extensive outline. As it turned out, I couldn't, just couldn't. In a year of trying I'd written maybe fourteen thousand words, each one of which I hated separately but equally. Note, too, I've written more than a million words, some years; a mere fourteen thousand represents a psychic shutdown of no mean order.

Yes, if you're curious, I was pretty damned difficult in the Army, too.

So why this? There were a number of reasons.

The big one was that I wanted to read some stories in my own universe that I didn't write. Why? Because I tend to write in a spiral—in one case I took particular note of I went through that spiral twenty-seven different times. Yes, that's right; I rewrote the SOB twenty-seven times. When you do that, you know what? You would rather be duct-taped to a chair, face down, in a prison, than read your own work again.

Get someone else to write the stories and you don't have this problem. Clever, no?

Then, too, while various states show up, more or less incidentally, in the Carreraverse, there are a whole bunch more that there was never room or time to explore. So why not get someone else to do the explorations? Fresh point of view? New personal writing style? If there's a downside here, I am not seeing it.

And then there were the writers. Go on, go look at their qualifications. Try not to be envious; if I could do it, you can. We got Academy grads, SEALs, Nuclear Brain Scientists (sorry, Rob, I just couldn't resist), Harvard Law, Oxford grads, and I don't mean Oxford, Mississippi . . . smart fuckers all around. Some are newer to writing and some are old hands. All of them have talent.

I told Libertycon, assembled, a few years back that I'd, myself, assembled an elite team for this and, by God, I did.

There were a few who dropped out due to work commitments just overtaking them. I understand and, though I replaced them, it was without rancor. They're welcome back to continue the story of the Wars of Liberation if they can fence the time. So are the ones I recruited to replace them.

No, I'm probably not going to have an open call for stories. I've seen how those tend to work out and it isn't pretty from anyone's perspective.

So what's next for the Carreraverse and me? Besides death, eventually? Well, sales depending, probably two more of these. As of this writing I am about half done with the final part of Patricio Carrera's war against the Tauran Union, Ming Zhong Guo, and the United Earth Peace Fleet. I'll finish that and then put the reconquest of Earth on hold for a couple or three years. It's its own story, and deserves a somewhat fresh start. After that who knows, but I am inclining toward about six alternate histories, none of them serialized.

We'll see.